when James fell

Phil Coleman

WHEN JAMES FELL
Copyright © 2022 by Phil Coleman

Cover design by Cherie Chapman

ISBN: 979-8-9851273-0-0

Edition: 2024.05.01p v30

10 9 8 7 6 5 4 3 2 1

For Ellen

Last night I opened eyes to drift,
Among the worlds within my mind.
But when I opened eyes to see,
The worlds I saw were dreaming me.

PART ONE

1. Free Fall

Five pairs of sneakers thumped across the overgrown field. James felt the damp from the weeds soak through his shoes with each footfall, but he didn't dare slow his pace. He would need to be the first to scale the batting cages if he hoped to win this race.

James kept his eyes forward as Seth—the new kid—pulled farther away. From the corner of his vision, he could see his friends Greg, Duncan, and Marc fanned out beside him. The race always started close, and why not? Whether in the classroom or on the playing field, the four friends were as well-matched as they were inseparable. Only Seth had been an unknown. And while James had mocked the new kid's request to join their race, he and his friends knew they had competition. Seth had a clear lead, but James—three-time reigning obstacle-course champion—had no intention of letting an outsider win. After all, today was his thirteenth birthday. Today was *his* day.

Seth reached the batting cages first, a cymbal crash of chain-link answered moments later by the others. Adrenaline surged in his veins. This was where he set himself apart.

"Get him, James! *Go!*"

Releasing a whoop, James sprang upward. While the other boys fumbled with hand-over-hand ascents, he bounded like a squirrel. His wild mess of curly hair bounced with each extended lunge. Reaching the top in a few short seconds, he moved to secure his lead. Crouching low, arms outstretched, he loped in a half-crawl, half-jog across the chain-link roof.

He had crossed two of the batting cages when he heard the other boys catching up to him. He didn't dare pause to look. After all, Duncan was the best swimmer when it came to crossing the pond, Marc was the best at the ditch crawl, and Greg hurdled azalea bushes like a suburban Olympian. He needed to stay focused to keep his lead, to keep his friends from overtaking him.

And Seth? No way, no how, was the *new* kid going to win.

With renewed determination, James picked up speed. He moved as fast as he could, paying no attention to either the clang of the cage or the cruel heat of the North Carolina sun. But just as he was nearing the edge of the fence, his vision blurred, then sharpened, and then—

James fell.

* * *

Panic seized him. James yelped as he tumbled, but the wind tore the sounds away. He spun once, twice, a third time. He cringed, bracing for impact—but it didn't come. He snapped his eyes open. Though he spiraled and flailed, he saw no batting cages, no grass, no schoolyard, no soccer fields, and no sign of his friends.

He plummeted through auburn skies, clouds whipping across his brow in rapid succession. Dropping through a cloudbank, he saw the ground miles beneath him. A city sprawled below, so immense it seemed to extend forever. But this city looked wholly unnatural. It pulsed not with the yellow and red of lampposts and taillights but a flickering blue light.

Clouds streaked past him in staccato bursts. Each one covered him in cool mist as they whipped by. As he dropped, the city became etched in greater detail. Now he understood. The glow was not from lamplight, but from turquoise-colored flames radiating from the building tops. The city wasn't pulsing, it was burning.

His panic returned. His mind howled in protest. He shrieked as his fingers clawed against the wind, searching desperately for purchase. And still, he fell. The dying city raced closer and closer, until—

* * *

White light filled James's vision. He tried to squint, but his eyes were held open by a steady hand. The beam from the penlight swung from James's left eye to his right, then flipped off as he was released. A man in blue hospital scrubs returned the penlight to his breast pocket. The lettering on his uniform told James the rest: "North Carolina Regional Medical Center." The paramedic grunted as he buttoned the pocket shut.

"Looks like yer buddy's comin' around," the medic called over his shoulder. "You took quite the tumble there, boy. Least from what your friends said. Now, how about you tell me yer name?"

"James Winters," he croaked.

His body reverberated with pain. Ribs, arms, back, knees. His jaw throbbed along its right side, pulsing with each heartbeat. His right leg burned with an ache that stabbed him when he tried to move. He sucked in his breath and cursed.

The paramedic smiled. "Take it easy, now, hoss. Just relax. Breathe deep. Now, you know what day it is?"

"It's my birthday." His head pounded; the ache made concentration difficult. "I'm, I'm thirteen."

The paramedic chuckled. "All right, all right, but what day of the week you reckon it is?"

"Saturday?"

"Good. Now, I want you to slowly count up by threes 'til I tell you to stop. You can start at three. You ready?"

The paramedic's next words were lost in the yells behind him. James looked up to see Greg, Marc, and Duncan brush past the paramedic. Their eyes were fierce with curiosity. Seth hung behind them, elbowed out of the way by the three cajoling friends.

"He's awake!" Greg called. He grinned over at Duncan standing beside him. "Man, I told you that fall ain't gonna take James down easy." His smile dropped. "We were worried, though. Worried bad. You wouldn't wake up when we shook you, so Seth ran out to get his brother. We didn't want to move you or nothin' if that would make things worse. My daddy taught me that. And we were just hoping you'd come around and..." Greg's face flushed; his eyes squinted. "Man. Just glad you're alright."

James cracked a weak smile. "So, who won?"

Greg's brow wrinkled in puzzlement. "You mean the race? We didn't finish. So, I guess that means you're still the champ. Though if you ask me..."

James clutched his friend's shirt and pulled him close. "Greg, I was *falling*." He spoke rapidly, his voice an excited whisper. "I must have fallen for miles. I was over this city. It was on fire and..."

Greg recoiled from him, jerking his shirt free. His eyes shone with suspicion and disbelief. "We watched you, man. We all saw you go down." He shook his head. "You hit your head on the sidewalk. Caught your foot an' tripped or something, and..."

"You're wrong. I *didn't* trip. I wasn't even here. I thought I was at first, and then I was above this city, and there were clouds and..."

The paramedic cut him off by the judicious placement of a tongue depressor in James's spouting mouth. "That's enough. Ya'll run along now. Give him some space. He's a little crosswise, I reckon. You say 'ah,' now, James. We need to get you to the hospital. Last thing we want is for you to trip and fall again."

James spat the tongue depressor away. "Listen. I didn't trip. I didn't fall. I was *falling* but I didn't fall. I was just falling, and…"

The paramedic reached over to place an oxygen mask over James's face but was stopped by a man in a tweed coat with small round spectacles.

"I'll take that, thank you very much. Go on, shoo. I'm a doctor." The spectacled man frowned, then smiled. "I said: I'm a *doctor*. So, move along." The man slapped the oxygen mask over James's mouth. He grinned around at the onlookers. "Don't you folks listen to a thing this poor boy says, he's clearly a bit scrambled. Falling? Hah! Ridiculous, preposterous, and ridiculous even. Pay him no mind, he'll be right as rain in due time."

The strange man motioned once more for everyone to step back, then he leaned close to him. He dropped his voice to a whisper. "Breathe deep, brother. You need to take it easy. Be careful. Lay low. I'll be back to help, but you'll have to be patient. Until then, I just need you to keep things together. And remember, don't talk to anyone about what just happened. That's Rule One. And that's enough for now."

2. Dr. Huckabee

Five months later.

James waited and searched, but he no longer hoped. From his nest in the over-stuffed armchair, he scanned the waiting room for a sign of hidden character, something to indicate today would be different. But all he saw, amongst the rows of journals, the collection of pamphlets, and the stacks of perfectly fanned magazines, was dreadful familiarity. He sunk lower into the chair, his descent heralded by the furtive groan of stretching leather. Nothing here was any different. Doctors, though adept at giving theories, prescribing pills, and jotting notes, couldn't help him. Five months had proven it.

Driving rain and rolls of thunder outside were metered by the tick of the grandfather clock. He ran a hand across his scalp. His once-thick mop of loose curls had been reduced to stubble. Apparently, his hair had gotten in the way of some experiment or other, or x-ray or other, or test or other. He hadn't gotten used to his shorn hair: not the way the wind hit his scalp, the way the ocean lapped over it, and not the feeling of the squeaky leather chair on the back of his head. But his hair was the least of his problems. What he missed were his friends.

The muted buzz from the next room grew louder, and James knew his wait was over. Jerking upright, he snatched a *Sports Illustrated* from the side table just in time for the door to open. His mother, her face creased with worry, walked through first, followed by a bespectacled man with a trimmed beard. No lab coat, only a worn tweed one. That could be either a good sign or a bad one. Doctors in lab coats liked to poke him with needles. Doctors without them usually just talked. He hesitated. He would have sworn he'd seen this man before. But then again, he'd seen enough doctors to last a lifetime.

"James," his mother said, "this here's Dr. Huckabee. He's going to see if he can help us."

The doctor cracked his lips to reveal perfectly symmetrical, perfectly white teeth. "Good day, Master James. Would you please follow me to the adjacent room?" The doctor's voice oozed cordiality, each word delicately pronounced and tinged with a slight British accent. "Mrs. Winters, we'll just be a short moment."

With a sigh and a shuffle, James followed Dr. Huckabee into his office. The room, a reflection of its antechamber, substituted the magazines and pamphlets of the former with diplomas and academic trophies. Twin leather armchairs faced one another across a table so highly polished that the rain outside seemed to run across its sides. James paused to admire the storm then sat.

The doctor peered at him. "So, James, you know why you're here, don't you? Used to this sort of thing by now, I imagine."

He gave the now-tired response. "You're going to figure out what's wrong with me."

"Something like that. Something indeed most exactly like that. But to do so, I need you to tell me the complete truth. Can you do that?"

He shrugged.

"Splendid." The doctor smiled. "Let's start at the beginning. When was the first time you had your little spell? The first time you 'fell.' You may approximate if the circumstance dictates, but specifics are preferable for my purposes."

James wrinkled his nose. No doubt this doctor, like all the other doctors, had studied his file. Fainting to others, falling to him. Every day for the past five months he would feel a sudden rush. And then he'd fall.

He would find himself twisting and plummeting through the air, always rushing to the ground, never hitting. Never landing. The sensation of the fall was as real and sharp and tangible as if he had jumped from a building. But the 'falling' rarely lasted more than a few seconds. And then he would be back—though more often than not face-down, bruised and battered. To the people who watched, he would just collapse. Faint. Sometimes he'd mumble, sometimes his body would jerk and convulse, sometimes he'd simply freeze. But in the end, he always went down.

"Last September was the first." James sighed. "On my birthday."

"Very well. And how many times since then?"

"I don't know. Too many to count. It happened every few days after that first time, and almost every day now. But never more than once a day."

"And can you describe the particularities of what happens? Not when you are 'falling,' as you insist on calling it. I've got more than enough on that. Tell me about what happens right before you fall. Are there any circumstances, events, or activities that incite these episodes?"

James had done this part before, too. He'd tell the doctors of the clarity of vision, the pricks on his skin, the electric sensation running throughout his body. He would talk of how colors became brighter, smells more pungent, and sounds crisper than ever before. He would tell of how before he fell the world became at once loud, alive, and real. That was how doctors liked to hear of his "symptoms." They liked the gritty, physical sensations. But they didn't like to hear what he thought of it. Doctors liked to speculate for themselves. So, he no longer tried to explain. He kept it simple.

"It ripples," James mumbled.

"Beg pardon?"

"The world. The whole world ripples."

Dr. Huckabee tapped his pen against his chin. James gathered this was an acquired—and highly contagious—mannerism from medical school. "When you say that the world ripples, do you mean it looks like it ripples, or that it feels like it ripples?"

"Well, what it looks like is…"

The doctor snapped his fingers, cutting him short. "Never mind what it looks like. Tell me what it *is*. Is it the air rippling? The ground? The walls? What exactly is the rippling element, per se, etc., and so forth?"

"Well, it all does. It's everything. The world, the whole *world* ripples. It's like I suddenly see everything sharp and real and clear, and then it ripples. Like it wasn't real after all, but I just now noticed. Like I could reach out and peel back one layer only to find something behind it. But when I try…"

"You fall."

James shut his eyes tight. He didn't want to land in one of the doctor's traps. That only brought on pills and too-long speeches about hallucinations, seizures, proper diet, exercise, and the trials of a growing boy. He had had quite enough of that. "I faint," he corrected. "And I can't stop it."

When James reopened his eyes, Dr. Huckabee had set his pen on the table. No more notes. he knew what that meant, too. The doctor had made his decision. And no matter what else James said, no matter how his story twisted and turned, the man's opinion would remain unaltered. He braced himself for another in a series of fruitless verdicts.

"James"—the doctor leveled his gaze—"I want you to make me a promise."

He didn't reply.

"I want you to never, *ever* repeat what you just told me. Not to anyone. Not even to your parents. I can't stress the indubitable importance of this."

A chill crept across James's skin. This wasn't how psychiatrists were supposed to talk—and he had visited enough to know. Not psychiatrists, not internists, not neurologists, not even priests. This was different.

Dr. Huckabee continued, "What's happening to you—if I may be so bold as to generalize but not trivialize your case—is not *completely* unique. But nearly so. And if the wrong people knew about it—and with you not being equipped and ready—well, you could be in a terrible paradigm of the utmost calamity. Because these little excursions of yours aren't dangerous as they currently stand. My advice, my sound professional and personal advice, is to *never speak of this to anyone.* Just lay low; pretend nothing is wrong. We'll discuss this again, in say, fifty years, or so? I'll come back then. But not now. Heavens no. You just aren't ready yet."

James shifted in his chair. "But I… What do you mean that I…?" He closed his eyes and ground his teeth. He tried to stay calm. James usually thought it was easier to be resigned than to get mad at what he couldn't control. But five months of acceptance was too much for him to bear. The blood surged in his ears; frustration exploded around him. "What do you mean *fifty years?* What kind of answer is that? I can't go a single day without falling and you say fifty? If you know what's wrong with me, then why won't you tell me? I mean, my friends'll be taking driver's ed next year, or be riding bikes, or lots of things I'm not allowed to do. So, if you won't help me, my parents'll find a doctor who can."

The doctor sprang from his seat. The sudden movement caused James to lurch backward. In an instant, Dr. Huckabee was on his feet and pacing furiously. He muttered as he walked. "Stupid psychiatrists and their stupid notes and their stupid computers and stupid reports. It all makes finding people altogether too easy—and hiding them too precarious." He turned to face him. "You're right, James, this 'fainting' is a quandary. It makes you stick out and makes people ask questions. And I can't have that, because we don't want you discovered. Now I can help you learn how to stop fainting, but first I need your understanding. I can't have you making things worse."

James opened his mouth to protest, then paused in disbelief. With the same speed with which the doctor had leaped from his chair, he now crouched on top of his desk. Dr. Huckabee perched with bare feet overhanging like a domestic gargoyle. The doctor pulled a crayon from the pocket of his three-piece tweed suit, unwrapped the paper, and nibbled the end.

James stared in horror. "Are you *eating* that? And why are you up on the desk? And where are your shoes?"

The doctor took the comment with a mixture of disdain and surprise. "Ugh. Shoes, dreadful things, like prisons for the toes. I can barely think with them on." Dr. Huckabee rolled forward off the desk, executing a flip before landing neatly on his feet. He smoothed his suit and settled again in his chair. "Now where were we?"

"You're crazy." James scowled. "*And* you won't help unless I say I understand you—which I don't. And you're nuts."

"You're only half right, my brother." The doctor smiled, then thrust his bare foot forward to pluck a jellybean from the dish on the table. With the dexterity of a chimp, he flicked the candy into the air and caught it in his mouth. Dr. Huckabee swished the jellybean from cheek to cheek before spitting it across the hardwood floor. "But perchance may we return to the matter at hand? I *can* help with your problem. As I mentioned, you're entirely too noticeable at present. We need to get you back under the radar, under wraps, low profile, and whatnot. And while what I can teach you isn't foolproof, it is conditional. You have to promise not to tell anyone, not to ask any more questions, and for the love of your good name and my own, try and stay out of sight."

James grumbled, "Fine. I promise."

The doctor grinned, crooked teeth bristling from his lips like a mouthful of corn. James furrowed his brow, recalling the smile as perfect minutes earlier. But it was more than the smile or the erratic behavior that tickled his brain. There was a reason behind it. He turned back to the peculiar man. His anger was replaced with wariness.

"I'm glad to hear it. Maybe you'll be all right after all." Dr. Huckabee grabbed another jellybean with his toes, popped it in his mouth, then sent the candy skittering across the floor to join its compatriot. "Ok. This is simple enough but should help you all the same. By *seeing* the differences, your mind will quit *searching* for the differences, as it seems so clearly to be doing. This should keep it—and you—from wandering. And if all goes well, and fortune is with us, I suppose it will keep you from fainting. We just need something… that's… I've got it." The doctor fished a polished brass coin from his pocket. The coin was twice as wide as a quarter, thick in the center and tapering at the outer rim. The object had a hole punched through its middle, reminding James of a subway token. Dr. Huckabee flipped the coin into the air with his thumb then snatched it with the toes of his left foot. He smacked the piece flat on the table between them.

James stared at the coin, then the doctor's talented foot, and then back at the coin.

"I don't get it," he murmured.

"Aha! But you do. It's a gift. But I wouldn't recommend spending it. Not if you're going to learn anything."

"What does it do?"

The doctor chuckled. He placed his arms on either side of the chair and effortlessly lifted himself into a handstand. The doctor pivoted to face him; then plopped again in the chair. His legs were folded Indian-style above him, and his hands rested on the ground where his feet had been. The doctor winked from his now-inverted position. "Well, my inquisitive student, it doesn't *do* anything. What's important for this exercise is what it is and where it's from. Pick it up and tell me what you see."

James plucked the coin from the table. The metal felt smooth and solid, still warm from the doctor's pocket. But something was wrong with the edges. They were there, but not—quite—there. The edges struck a note of discord against James's hand, like a cartoon character in a live-action movie. The coin had the same *otherness* as the cartoon. The coin was false, somehow, and true to itself at the same time.

"What's wrong with it? Why is it so…?" He fished for the right words. "It's slippery." He returned the coin to the table.

The doctor winked. "Now look again. Look around you."

James raised his eyes. The office was still unremarkable, generic, and scholarly. But the furniture, books, diplomas, windows, even the trees outside were somehow clearer, more familiar. He looked back at the coin, and at once—completely and absolutely—he *saw*. He *understood*. Everything was one thing, but the coin was something different. The world was *This*, the coin was *That*. The coin was different, so *completely* different, that the rest of the world was uniform by comparison. And James noticed something else.

The doctor was different too.

James ventured, "You're just like the coin. You're a *That*. Not a *This*."

Dr. Huckabee smiled his crooked smile before rolling around to sit upright. "And how about now?"

James frowned. The otherness of the doctor was gone. His teeth had straightened, his posture normal, his lack of shoes almost unnoticeable. The doctor was still not a *This*, but he wasn't so clearly a *That*. James said, "Um, well, not so much now. Not anymore. A little bit, but not a whole lot."

The doctor clapped his hands in delight. "Then I'd say we're done for now. Hold on to that trinket. There's a good chap. And if you feel lightheaded, take a look and remind yourself of where you are—here, that is—and that that's the only place you need to be."

James picked the coin from the table. His head buzzed with the object's unfamiliarity.

The doctor continued, "And remember, you need to pretend to be an ordinary, run-of-the-mill, snakes, snails, and puppy-dog tails boy." The man drummed his toes on the wooden floor. "As I promised, I'll come to see you once it's time and once you're ready. But not a moment sooner. And don't tell *anyone*. Especially not…"

Dr. Huckabee clamped his mouth. He leaped to his feet once more. He aimed a smile at the opening door.

"Mrs. Winters, come in, come in, come in three times. We were just finishing up. And ahead of schedule, I might add." The doctor tapped a wrist devoid of a watch. "And I think you'll be quite pleased with what I have to say." The doctor motioned for James's mother to take a seat on the windowsill and then sat back in his chair. He crossed his legs and casually wiggled his bare toes.

James's mother pursed her lips in the practiced bracing-for-disbelief he had seen so many times before. But if she noticed the doctor's shoeless nature or the horror on her son's face, she gave no indication.

"And?" she asked. He could hear the strain in her voice.

"He's hale, hearty, healthy, and fit. His fainting spells are nothing but a little lapse in concentration. A type of sensory overload, if you will and I will. I've taught your son a few concentration exercises, and as long as he stays away from television and things with too many colors, he should be fine. No flashing lights or video games for you, my boy. I imagine his brain will be patched in a few short weeks. And I'll be surprised if you have any problems again."

James stood aghast. What in the world was wrong with his mother? Did she believe this psychotic, shoeless, monkey-man? Did she think that any of this was true? Why didn't she jump up and shout and storm away? It was like she was hypnotized.

"No television?" His mother asked. Her words crept slowly from her mouth. "And no flashing lights? Is it—is it epilepsy? We had him tested for that."

Dr. Huckabee paused—and the world paused with him, even the tick of the clock, and the rain outside. James looked back and forth in disbelief from the doctor, who struggled to come up with a response, and to his mother, who had not blinked in the last thirty seconds. Then, with James's mother still entranced, the doctor skipped to his bookshelf, removed a worn copy of *Encyclopedia Britannica*, and flipped the book open. He took a few moments to read the text before returning to his seat. Dr. Huckabee peaked his fingers, his face a shroud of scholarly concern. As James's mom jerked back to reality, the clock to ticking, and the rain to falling, the doctor spoke.

"Well, Mrs. Winters, your son's condition is not the product of excessive neuronal activity, such as with epilepsy. But rather a matter of innate cognitive diffidence between multiplurilous perceptions on tri-plicit levels. But I won't get technical. As I said before, the exercises I showed him should do the trick." The doctor stood as if to say that the conversation was well, done, good, and concluded.

James's mother arose as well, her face puzzled. If she was recovering from her trance, she was doing so slowly. "Should he be on medication of any kind? Or, um, should we come back to see you if anything happens? The fainting *has* been going on for months now. And the other doctors all said…"

"Oh! Oh, yes. Please do. Please schedule a follow-up appointment with my receptionist. But I assure you, no medication will be necessary. In fact, I forbid it. We want his wits about him." The doctor smiled and waved, pausing only to give James a wink.

Dumbfounded, James pulled himself from the chair and trudged along behind his mother. Just as he neared the exit, he glanced back at the doctor.

Dr. Huckabee looked up, his legs folded in a lotus position. "Remember, James. Don't tell *anyone* about *anything*. That's Rule One."

James hesitated, but his mother did not slow her pace. She stoically put one foot in front of the other. James watched in disbelief, then hurried to catch up with her as she stomped from the office, through the waiting room, past the empty receptionist's desk without stopping, and out of the building.

3. 221 West Oleander Place

By the time James had gotten home from Dr. Huckabee's office, he had shifted from confusion, to anger, to disbelief, and finally to extreme nervousness. Whatever trance his mom had entered at the doctor's office still stuck with her. She didn't respond to James's questions about the doctor; she didn't seem to think it was weird that James was suddenly 'cured,' or have any other reactions to the bizarre man. In fact, she was so resistant to any type of questions, that he started to worry that the doctor had done something permanent. The thought made the strange coin feel heavy in his pocket.

James's mother pulled the car to a stop in front of their house at 221 West Oleander Place. She turned to say something to James, but he didn't wait to listen. He flung open the door and took off across the yard and into the wooded area separating his house from the drainage ditch running through the neighborhood.

Perched on that border between suburban and wild was James's tree. This was the one place where he sought refuge when the world was unfair, unjust, or otherwise undecided. The oak was sprawling and gnarled, with hooked branches and twisting roots which crept the ground like a tarantula's legs. He ducked beneath the outer limbs and dropped to his hands and knees, crawling beneath the outer canopy to the shelter within.

Stretched out on a branch, the forked limb forming an arboreal hammock, was his friend Seth. The lanky boy was working to pick apart pine cones in search of the pine nuts within. James felt a wave of relief at seeing his friend—one of few he had left. Ever since he had started to have his falling problems, his other friends had drifted away. James didn't blame them for most of it. He could no longer play sports with them, or run, or go biking, or any of the things that used to hold them together. But outside of the games, they still steered clear. James knew that the kids at school talked about him behind his back. He hadn't been careful enough at the beginning. He told too many people about the things he saw—the things he *thought* he saw—and was labeled as being just plain weird. Even after he learned to keep his mouth shut, his former friends steered clear. And for that, James *did* blame them.

"Hiya, Jim. How'd the analyzing go?" Seth asked. His eyes did not lift from the pine cone in his hands.

James crawled to the base of the tree and settled into the nook of roots. "Oh, I'll tell you how it went. It went ridiculous. That's how it went."

James tried to give Seth the "edited" version of events. He left out the parts about *Thisness* and *Thatness*, but he had no reservations talking about the doctor's antics. Through it all, Seth offered no comments, only interrupting when James started to tell of his mom's apparent hypnosis.

"Hold on for a second, Jim. So, you're saying the doctor was crazy, or something? But your mom was, too? They were *both* crazy, or just the one? Or are you just jealous 'cause you're not the only crazy one anymore?"

James ignored the last question. "My mom may have acted a little weird, but the doctor was an absolute nut-job. Between the handstands, the bare feet, and not even counting what he said—he was wacko."

"Hmmm, and why do you think that is?"

"Since when do you need a reason to be crazy?"

Seth raised an eyebrow, an expression he often used in school. He had an uncanny—and infuriating—ability to dissect problems. The talent got him labeled as a weirdo, not so much for the answers he gave, but for the way he paused at peculiar times. Nevertheless, if anyone could figure out this situation, it was Seth.

"Come on. You're missing my point. You said he's a psychiatrist. Right?"

"Exactly. He's a doctor, Seth. Doctors are supposed to be professional."

"Not so fast, Jim. He's not the shots and tongue depressors kind, he's a *mind* doctor. Catch my drift? A psychiatrist doesn't just look at you and say what's wrong. They try to get inside your head, learn what makes you tick. Maybe he was just testing you. Maybe the shoes and things were to see how you'd react. Or to make you faint, or something." Seth squinted one eye. "I'm just saying maybe it's like a game."

"He wouldn't be the first," James said, a wave of relief washing over him. "There was this other doctor who had me doing all kinds of exercises—stretches and balancing and stuff. He thought if I stayed distracted, I wouldn't fall, faint, whatever. Didn't work, though. Just made me feel stupid."

"And," Seth continued, "if it *was* a trick, it would explain your mom, too."

"How so?"

"Well, maybe she was in on it. Maybe that's why she pretended not to notice his feet, or him calling after you. Of course, if you want to take it further, there is an even *simpler* explanation." Seth allowed the moment to stretch, his face remaining grave until finally breaking into a grin. "You've finally gone over the edge, Jimbo. Flipped your lid, lost your marbles, or whatever—and *nothing* you said *really* happened. It's not like you haven't been seeing things before."

James flicked a pinecone at Seth, who plucked it from the air and threw it back.

"I'm not crazy."

"Never said you were. At least not full-crazy. Just that it's a possibility. And we have to look at all of 'em."

James leaned back against the trunk. "There's one other thing he said." He paused. "And I'm only telling you since you already know all about the other stuff. He told me that I should never, and I mean never-ever, tell anyone about what it's like when I fall. He said someone *bad* might come looking for me." James held his breath.

"Then you shouldn't. Not even with me."

"Huh? What do you mean? I thought you said this whole thing's a test?"

"I said there's a *chance* it's a test. Just like there's a chance it's all true. And you have to play it safe there, too. You have to be careful."

James felt the pit return to his stomach. He wished it would just go away. "More likely I am crazy, Seth. Like you said, even if I'm not full-crazy."

"That's still my best guess. But if the doctor *was* right…" Seth trailed off without finishing. "Um, Jim, *have* you talked to anyone else?"

"A few people, right after it first happened. But not recently. And I guess I won't anymore," James said. "You're right. Again. But here's a better question. How do I even know what the truth is? How do I know if the doctor was just playing me, or if my mom was in on the whole thing, or if he was being honest, or…?"

"Or if you're crazy?"

"Bingo."

Seth wrapped his legs around the tree limb to steady himself. He dusted the shards of pine cone from his chest. "Well, for starters, you said he taught you a trick to stay awake. So does it work? If it *does* work, that'll go a long way to seeing if he's full of it."

James frowned deeply. Though he had told Seth everything about the doctor's behavior, he hadn't mentioned the details of the strange coin, or the revelation of *Thisness* and *Thatness*. James wanted to tell his friend the rest of the story, to show Seth the bizarre token, to throw himself at his friend's mercy. But he hesitated. On the one hand, maybe Seth was right, and he shouldn't be talking about it. But really, he just didn't want to scare off his last friend. Not now. And he could always tell him later. There'd be time enough. "I won't know for sure until the next time I fall. I'm supposed to just concentrate on something and that'll keep me awake."

"Sounds too simple."

James cast his eyes down. "Simple is good, I guess. And you're right, I'll know soon enough. If I can keep from falling—even once— then I'll know it can be done."

For five minutes, they remained silent. The only sound was the chirp of cicadas as daylight melted away. The evening damp rose to fill the void. James glanced at Seth, then he closed his eyes. They had become good friends over the past several months, but it was still strange to talk about their *real* problems. James hadn't talked this much about his falls since when they first started happening. In a way, their friendship was built on that silence. Whether James's falls or Seth's trouble with the bullies at school, an unrepairable topic was an unmentioned one. James hoped he hadn't crossed an invisible line.

"Well, I guess we better get inside," he offered with false cheerfulness. "My mom made spaghetti if you're interested."

"I could *dominate* some spaghetti. Better than fish sticks at my house."

The friends stood and shook loose the bark and leaves sticking to them. As James brushed off his pants, he grazed the bump formed by the strange coin in his left pocket. The coin felt strangely heavy, as though refusing to allow him to forget it. He winced.

Seth looked back over his shoulder. "What's the matter? You ok?"

"It's nothing. My head's just a little scrambled, that's all. Nothing to worry about."

"Then let's go do some serious *eating*. Race you."

Seth took off at a sprint toward the house with James close on his heels. James tried to keep up, though the taller boy pulled further ahead as they ran. Seth was fast. Even before James had gotten to know him, he'd known he was fast. James used to be fast, too, even if not as fast as Seth. But now he took things easy. There was nothing like fainting at full speed to teach patience.

The two boys sped forward, stopping only after slapping the large painted column on the right side of the front porch, which was their traditional finish line. The house was a two-story building sided with wooden slats covered in moss-colored paint. Like most of the neighborhood houses, the small porch in the front was mirrored by a larger screened-in one behind the house, where James assumed his parents waited to start dinner. Lights shone from each corner of the front porch, in contrast to the rest of the house which was completely dark. His parents were strong advocates for conservation, though more due to their social conscience than the electric bill. They liked eating on the porch for just that reason, eager for the chance to be outside and away from phone and television alike.

Seth cursed under his breath. His eyes darted back and forth between James's mom's wood-paneled station wagon and James's dad's Jeep. Seth started to fidget. "Listen, Jim. Actually, um…"

James knew exactly what Seth was going to say, some excuse of why he couldn't eat the same dinner he'd been excited about moments before.

"Look, I, uh, I forgot that my mom's got company tonight. My aunt's in town and I said I'd be there for it, and… well you know it's not the food. Your mom can cook and mine can only…"

"No. It's alright. It's cool. I'll see you tomorrow, ok?"

Seth nodded vigorously. He turned and took off back toward his own house. In a few seconds he had disappeared from sight. James turned to look at his front door, sighed, and walked inside.

After passing through the darkened hallway, James reemerged onto the back porch where his parents were settling around the table. His mom filled water glasses, while his dad distributed pasta with wooden tongs. James's mom looked up and smiled.

"Is Seth not joining us?" she asked. "He's always invited."

"No, um, his aunt's in town. I guess."

James's dad looked up across the table at James's mom. "Honey, I swear that boy's afraid of you. He always seems to run off when you're here."

"When *I'm* here?" James's mom protested. "I was going to say the same thing to you. He seems to get scarce when you're around."

James picked up his fork and twiddled his spaghetti. His parents were both wrong—at least by half. Seth wasn't afraid of either one of them, but when they were together, he stayed away. Sometimes Seth sat through the inevitable fights, but on a day when James had been to the doctor, it was too much to ask.

"You going to tell dad about the doctor?" he mumbled. It was better to get it over with.

"Oh, yes," his mom whistled. "Apparently, our son is cured."

"Really?" His dad set down his fork. "Cured how?"

"Mmm-hm," James's mom continued with mock-sincerity. "It seems he just wasn't concentrating hard enough. The doctor taught him some exercises and there should be no more problems."

His dad coughed into his napkin. "He didn't *really* say that, did he? That's ridiculous. If it was just a matter of concentrating, then I think that James would have found that out on his own. These shrinks are a waste of time and money."

"Oh, and the hospital's any better?" His mother's voice was beginning to rise. Whatever trance she'd suffered from Dr. Huckabee was markedly absent. Her voice grew more strained. "He's been stuck with a thousand needles already. And the tests. Lord have mercy, how many more tests do they need?"

James's dad folded his arms across his chest. "At least tests can *have* results. Not just some suggestion to 'concentrate harder.' Seriously. You should've—"

The world rippled.

James jerked his head to glimpse the impending curtain. The wave began beyond the corner of his eye, brushing the hairs of his neck, tickling his nostrils, whispering into his ears. Sound dropped first to nothing, then was replaced by a high-pitched whine, like a thousand televisions blaring static. The noise barreled forward until it was so great that James felt his skull crushing from its might. Next came the needles: pinpricks assailing his skin in controlled-chaotic spirals of pain, pleasure, cold, and burning. His skin became fluid, sliding around itself in electric throes.

Like the sun rising over a desert highway, James's vision wavered as pooled light and smoothed texture became one; the real and the imagined blurred. The ripple began in the corner of his sight and swept across, arcing down and across before disappearing to leave behind an intense clarity. Accompanying the acuity was the certainty—complete and absolute—that something lurked behind that curtain. And that knowledge toppled his mind.

James braced himself for the inevitable fall. Only then, as his brain started to shut down, did he remember the coin. He did not reach for the strange token, as his limbs were unresponsive. He could not see it, as the object was stowed in his pocket. But somehow the coin's presence shone clear. The coin's aura was so different from the surrounding world, that James was jerked back to reality. He could still see the *Thisness* of the world in all its blinding detail, yet it was no longer painful. Instead, James felt that it—and he—belonged.

"—slapped that doctor right in the face. It's criminal the way they take advantage of you. I'm going to head down there tomorrow, and…" He paused. James's dad turned to look at him, his anger faded into concern. "James? Son? James, are you ok? You're white as a sheet. Are you ok?"

James's confusion gave way to euphoria. He'd done it! He'd actually done it! He hadn't fallen! He hadn't lost sight of the things around him. And best of all, he hadn't awoken face-down in his spaghetti. But could he do it again? Did he dare tell his parents? No. Absolutely not. If the doctor had been right about the coin, he *must* have been right about the rest. And that meant that… his stomach knotted. He *was* in danger. It wasn't all some mad psychological game. His cramping stomach turned to nausea. "I, I don't feel so good."

"Scratch that," his dad murmured. "You're not white—you're green."

"May, I… may I be excused?"

"Of course," his mom said. She shot a worried look at her husband. "Of course, James. It's been a long day, and I know how much you hate going to the doctor." Her eyes narrowed as she shot an angry look at his dad. "Well, he does. He told me that yesterday. Don't look at me like I don't listen…"

James interrupted, "Ok, thanks. Don't worry. I'll be fine."

* * *

The pale light of the half-moon streamed through James's bedroom window, casting an image of four lit panes on the carpeted floor. James shivered in the late spring breeze. The soft whip of the wind sounded unnaturally loud in his ears; goosebumps raised along his bare arms. His parents' arguments had picked up as soon as he'd left the room. They shouted for a while, then quit speaking altogether. The only sound since had been the clink of dishes as they cleared the table and went back inside. Despite the quiet, James couldn't will himself to sleep. The peculiar coin, the source of his earlier success, no longer offered solace. It answered no questions. What the coin did do was to remain in shadow, *despite* being in the path of the moonlight.

At first, James thought it a trick of reflection. But as he swung his hand from shadow to moonlight and back to shadow again, the coin's appearance did not waver. *Thatness.* James could think of the quality in no other way. Real—but not *completely* real.

The moon dipped behind the trees. The coin, which once seemed so dark, now shone with an inner light. Real. Unreal. Real. The line blurred. James began to wonder first if the coin existed, or if it was all a trick by Dr. Huckabee. Then he wondered if the coin was the *only* real thing. Perhaps everything was an illusion.

James's mind was beyond exhaustion. He clenched his fist and closed his eyes, but he could not relax. The surrounding air seemed to burst with potential. But James wanted no part of it. He wanted only to rest. Squinting behind closed eyes, James willed himself invisible, to be unnoticed. Not here. Not now. Not here. And then—

James fell.

4. Water Fall

James awoke with the strange coin clenched in his fist. But as he opened his eyes, his stomach dropped. He flailed his arms but found no hint of his bed's stability. No bed, no room, no walls, and no fan. He was falling from a height of fifty feet, seconds from impact into a turquoise sea. He had only time enough to utter a curse before splashing into the waves.

Downward he plunged, sinking fifteen feet before buoyancy slowed and reversed his path. James fought to the surface. He exploded upward in a sputter of water and gasping. His head screamed in panic. He darted his eyes left and right; he flailed his arms and legs. He took quick rapid breaths, inhaling more water and sending himself into a coughing fit. Then he paused, breathed, and listened. Nothing answered him but the slosh of waves.

His first thought was not of where he was. He marveled instead that he'd landed. For five months, he'd had visions of falling. But not one of those had been longer than a few seconds. But this time he had actually *landed*. But where? Apart from the dripping crimson of the setting sun, there was nothing else. No trees, no shoreline, not even a seagull skimming the ocean. But for that matter, how was he even in the ocean at all? Let alone at sunset? And why was the water so much warmer than the North Carolina shore? And how did he get here? And…

"What Is Going On!?"

James drew an exasperated breath, when a faint reflection of his voice interrupted him, "*going…on…*"

"An echo?" he said aloud. "There's no echo in the ocean." He raised his voice. "You hear that? There's No Echo In The Ocean!"

"*the…ocean…*" his voice returned.

He closed his eyes. Heartbeats reverberated in his temples. *This will soon be over. It's just a dream. It's just another stupid dream, another stupid fall, and another stupid hallucination.* James reopened his eyes, but still he bobbed in the nameless waters. And for the first time, he had another thought, if this wasn't just a dream, then he was in serious trouble. There was no land in sight. Maybe he should try to deal with the—

"No," he muttered. "I *don't* have to deal with this. It's a dream. Just like always. It's the same thing, and it'll be over in a matter of seconds. It's just going on longer because of that insane doctor and his stupid coin."

James gritted his teeth. He dragged his eyes to his tightened fist. One by one, he loosened his fingers. The coin with the smooth bore rested lightly on his palm. Once cold and heavy, the token now seemed as light as a feather. He held the coin up between thumb and forefinger. "This is all your fault. And I'm through with it." Without further thought, James hurled the coin as far as he could. The object made a satisfying plunk as it disappeared beneath the surface.

He grinned wickedly—until distracted by a tickle on his palm. He looked in his open hand. There, resting smugly, was Dr. Huckabee's coin. Just as if it had never left. He snapped his fingers shut again.

James closed his eyes and took a deep breath. The feeling of the water soothed him, and for a moment he imagined that he was simply back home in the ocean just a few miles from his home. The salt tickled against his nostrils. The sensation was so real and tangible, that he expected to open his eyes to see the North Carolina shore. But when his eyes did open, the only vision was the featureless sea.

James held the coin up once more. He studied the smooth bore punch and the reflective surface. And then he decided to look at the coin once more, but not as he did now. He would concentrate as Dr. Huckabee had taught him. James focused his eyes, and as he did so, the infuriating *Thatness* became clear once more. And just as before, his surroundings also sharpened, though with a *Thatness* all their own, and quite different from that of the coin. A chill tingled his spine. The clarity was too much, too *real* to be dismissed. And just as the world felt real, it also felt different.

What is this place?

James looked down at his hand and saw that Huckabee's coin had begun to rise from his palm. It hovered, slowly spinning several feet above the water. The object rose higher and higher, and then it dropped.

The sudden descent took James by surprise. Though he lunged for the coin, he missed, and it plunked into the water. But the water didn't slow the coin's descent. James watched as the spinning token disappeared below. And this time, it did not reform on his palm.

"No!" he protested. "Now what do I do?"

Nothing answered him, and yet James was tickled with a strange idea. Maybe the coin wasn't really important. Maybe the coin was just a way to concentrate, and that's what was important. Huckabee said the coin was a way to see the "differences", but there was enough difference here already. *He* was different.

James held his hand in front of him, palm down. And though his hand still trembled, he understood what he had to do. He concentrated first on his hand, and how its *Thisness* was so different from the *Thatness* of the surrounding waters. Then he concentrated harder and harder, the contrast between the two presences becoming clear, evident, and terrifying. James felt his *Thisness* begin to separate from the surrounding *Thatness*. His skin tingled as though pricked by one thousand electric needles. His vision became first intensely detailed and then wavered as it flooded with a kaleidoscope of light. And then—

James fell.

5. School

James opened his eyes to the slow turn of the ceiling fan, his alarm squawking in time with the blades' rotations: Swoop, buzz, swoop, buzz.

He bolted upright. The reality of being back in his bedroom, still dressed in clothes from the night before, stung like an unexpected slap. That James had awoken in his room wasn't peculiar. Indeed, he had done so countless times before. What *was* different was the dream. Its memory did not fade as normal dreams should. The nameless sea remained as clear in his mind as the walls around him.

James reached over to silence his alarm. He plopped back on his bed. He wasn't tired—not from the abrupt awakening, and not from a real/imagined swim through a foreign ocean. His muscles felt rested, his mind as well. But the act of sleeping seemed never to have happened. He felt he'd simply blinked: an ocean one moment, his bed the next.

He craned his neck to look at his nightstand, topped with the now-dormant alarm clock, a paperback copy of "Hatchet", an empty water glass, and nothing else.

No coin.

James threw his covers aside, scrambling to search for Huckabee's coin. Whether or not the coin had been the source of his too-real dream, it had prevented him from fainting the night before. In an instant, all other thoughts became unimportant. That coin could save him—could allow him to be normal. And now it was gone. James dropped to all fours, he scanned beneath the bed. A hot nervousness spread across his body. The coin wasn't on the floor, the bedside table, his pockets, his dresser, or even in the folds of his sheets.

"It *can't* be gone. It has to be…"

A knock at the door. "James? Are you all right in there? Did you faint, sweetie?"

"No. No, I'm fine, Mom. Just looking for some stuff."

"All right. Come downstairs when you're ready."

James grunted in acknowledgment. He resumed his search, though at less frantic levels. Five minutes later, when his mom had called again—and with still no sign of the coin—he paused to think.

"Either it's here and I can't find it, I did drop it in some ocean, or…" James held his head with his hands, "or it never was real to begin with." He glanced at the clock. "Ugh. The bus." He jumped up, switched out his T-shirt, gathered his things, and crashed downstairs. Without paying attention to the cereal boxes on the counter, or the milk beside it, he flipped open the cupboard to extract a Pop-Tart. As he rotated to leave, he came face to face with his mother.

"James, I…"

He hated this. If his parents' dinnertime arguments weren't bad enough, they could at least be forgotten by morning. Not anymore. His mother now started every day with an apology, leaving a bad taste in his mouth for hours to come. Oddly, James mused, it was usually a fall that distracted him.

"James, I just wanted to say I'm sorry you had to hear your dad and me fighting last night. We only want the best for you. And when the doctors can't—"

"It's ok," James mumbled. He eyed the door.

"I just want you to know that we love you very much, and—"

"Oops. Bus is here. Gotta go, and—" James darted toward the door, his eyes focused outside.

"Wait. James, wait!"

He spun back to face her. "What?"

"Brush your teeth."

In an act more ritual than hygienic, he gave a perfunctory scrub and then crashed out the screen door. He leaped from the steps and took off at a lope, running as much to the bus as he was away from home.

* * *

"Dreams. What do they mean? Where do they come from?"

James snapped his eyes to the front of the classroom. His teacher's drawl caught his attention. Concentration on schoolwork had been difficult that morning. Thoughts of the strange dream (James decided it was a dream), and his mother's apology churned his thoughts. But both were annoyances versus the loss of Dr. Huckabee's coin. How could he pay attention when his weapon against his fainting/falling spells was gone?

His teacher droned on, "Modern psychologists see dreams as the window into the subconscious. Note that word, ya'll. Sub-Conscious. It's *below* the conscious mind. Now a psychologist says that by taking a close watch of dreams, we can know a person's hopes and fears. Another advantage—at least if you follow the mainstream thought on such things—is that sometimes people are more willing to talk about their dreams than their actual feelings. But it's the same thing, ya'll. The dreams *are* their feelings." The teacher placed his fists on his hips. "Historically speaking, these are very new ideas."

James stole a look at Seth beside him. His friend mimed a yawn.

"Now ancient cultures, even up through very recent times, have seen dreams as windows to another world. A *spiritual* world, and one greater than our own. Asian, African, and European cultures have all echoed this same belief. That's why Freud and Jung were revolutionary. They saw dreams not as some window to the beyond, but instead a glimpse into the hidden self. But were they right? Are our minds truly divided? Is our subconscious the—dare I say—the dominant part?"

A strange feeling crept over James, and he began to feel his teacher's eyes roaming the classroom. Was he looking for guilt on the students' faces? Did he know about James's dream last night? Why would his teacher care? Or anyone? Dr. Huckabee warned that someone might be looking for James, but he never said why. Did his dreams have anything to do with that? What did the doctor know that he wouldn't tell?

The ringing of the school bell jolted James from his thoughts.

"Alright, class, now don't forget to read chapter six of your textbook by Friday. And there will be a quiz. Ya'll understand what that means? Don't just look at the words, pay attention. Ok, see ya'll tomorrow."

James crammed his book into his grey canvas backpack and slung one strap over his shoulder. He waited as Seth finished the last of his notes and put his books away.

Seth said, "I hope you found that entertaining enough."

"What do you mean?"

"You spent the whole class scowling. Probably hurt Mr. Pendergrass's feelings, too."

James shrugged. "Got a lot on my mind."

"Like what? You faint this morning?"

"Not yet."

A belch of forced laughter clamored behind them. James's muscles tensed, and Seth's eyes narrowed. The first deep laugh was joined by two others, hyenas echoing the grunts of a warthog. James flinched as a strong hand slapped down on his shoulder. "Hey, Greg," he mumbled without turning.

A thickset boy shouldered Seth out of the way and swung around in front of James. Marc and Duncan, the first lanky, the other short, moved around so that James was boxed in on three sides. All three boys wore a combination of cargo shorts and camouflage T-shirts. James wasn't surprised to see them dressed alike. When Greg, Duncan, and Marc had been *his* best friends, they occasionally came to school in similar attire. That was something friends did.

Greg grinned at James, his eyes darting from left to right. "Why didn't you speak up, James? Why didn't you jump up and tell Mr. Pendergrass where to stick it? You know more about dreams and stuff than anybody. That reminds me"—the grin widened—"when's the last time you fell asleep, James?"

"Last night."

"Not that, good buddy, old friend, old buddy. What I mean to say is: when was the last time you—FELL?"

Greg lunged forward, his palms striking James square in the chest. James hopped backward to absorb the blow, but Duncan and Marc hooked their feet behind his legs. James flailed as he crashed down, clattering over a desk and banging his head on the speckled-grey tile.

Seth tried to push past Greg. "James, are you…?"

"Shut up," Greg spat. "Shut the hell up, pansy-boy, or you might catch some of what he's got. Or maybe you already—HAVE!" Greg lunged at Seth, but he sprang out of the way. The dodge incited fevered laughing from Marc and Duncan. "Whatever." Greg snorted. "See you around, James. Be careful."

Greg, Duncan, and Marc snickered as they tromped away. The chuckles faded as they passed out of the classroom into the hall. Seth walked back to where James lay and offered him a hand. He pulled his friend to his feet.

Seth shook his head. "I can't believe you used to be friends with those guys."

"They didn't use to be like that."

"Maybe from where you're sitting, Jimbo. That's about how they always were to me, even if you didn't notice."

James watched the door until Greg, Marc, and Duncan disappeared. His voice dropped to just above a whisper. "Well," he sighed, "we did use to have a good time together." James brightened. "Do you remember that time we all raced together? That was fun, wasn't it?"

"They didn't ask me to race, James. *You* did. I never forgot that."

The memory of that day and his first fall reminded James of Huckabee's coin. Frustration rushed to his temples.

James muttered, "I've *got* to get it back."

"Get what back?"

"I… well…" He darted his eyes around. Seeing that no one was left in the classroom, he continued. "Ok, remember what I told you yesterday about the doctor? He told me not to talk to people about my falls and—"

"I remember."

"Well, you were right, Seth. I didn't give him enough of a chance. I should have seen if he was right. He gave me this coin, but it wasn't like a normal coin. The doctor told me to focus on it if I started to fall. And it *worked*, Seth. It really worked. I started to fall at dinner, and then I thought about the coin, and it just stopped it. Like nothing ever happened!" James dropped his voice low. "But I lost it, Seth. It's gone."

"Why didn't you tell me earlier?"

James snapped his head up. "I didn't tell 'cause you *told* me not to. You said if the trick worked, I should listen to what the doctor said and not talk about it anymore. Including you."

"But you *are* talking about it."

"Come on, Seth. Be serious. What should I do?"

Seth yawned. "I don't know. Use a different coin, I guess."

"I just told you, it wasn't a normal coin. It was special."

"Then just go back to the doctor's office. I'm sure he'll give you another. He'll get to charge you twice and everyone's happy." Seth squinted one eye. "Now if you really needed me to come up with that, Jimbo, then I don't know how you manage to get up and out of bed in the morning, much less read and write and walk upright and stuff."

James's jaw dropped. He hadn't even considered getting another coin from Dr. Huckabee, not once.

"But that's the whole way downtown," James replied weakly. "It'll take an hour to get there."

"Leave now. Nothin' keeping you here."

"Leave? Seth, you're a genius. Not that you don't know that. Can you cover me?"

Seth finally smiled. "If there was ever someone who could fake being sick, Jimbo, you're him. I'll just tell everyone you went to the doctor. That happens more than enough. And it's technically true."

With a renewed smile, James left the classroom and headed for the exit. He was going back to Dr. Huckabee's. And this time, he expected some answers.

6. Downtown

James had never skipped school before. Not that he was afraid to skip school, or that he didn't ever think about it, but he'd never felt the need. Especially not halfway through the day. So, he thought about how best to go about it. And the best way to commit a crime, James decided, was to pretend nothing was out of the ordinary. Only the guilty ran from the scene of the crime. At least that's what a diet of cop movies had taught him. So, he did the simplest thing that came to his mind. He gathered his things, exited the school, and stood patiently by the curb as if waiting to be picked up. After two minutes of standing, and no teachers or principals rushing to catch him, James strolled down the street. In another five minutes he was on the city bus and headed downtown.

As a middle-class kid, James rarely found himself downtown. If he was to make a trip anywhere, he usually went to the beach. And because of the way the school district had been redrawn, none of his classmates lived downtown anymore. Instead, he visited the business district only when going to the endless streams of doctors and psychiatrists about his condition, or an occasional visit to the public library.

James gritted his teeth. He hadn't fallen yet today—assuming the dream last night didn't count. And without Huckabee's coin, it was simply a matter of time. James hoped that when it did happen, he wouldn't be crossing the street or anything dangerous. He'd bruised himself pretty well from his "little spells" and imagined he'd suffer a few more to come. After the first falls, James's mom quit letting him do anything too dangerous, like climbing trees or riding a bike. The only real exception had been her willingness to let him be around water. James didn't know if that was because she didn't consider it dangerous, or if being a water person herself, she couldn't bear to make it off-limits.

The cross-town bus deposited James on the corner of Third and Jackson. On his visit to Dr. Huckabee's the day before, he had made note of the Eastern Orthodox Church standing across the street. The observation had been lucky as James wasn't familiar enough with the downtown area to remember the exact location of the clinic, and the church made an easy landmark.

The somber red brick of the office building appeared industrial versus the spires of the opposing church. Stepping into the lobby, James studied the building's directory for the room number. He scanned the tarnished bronze plaque slotted with plastic white-on-black name strips.

James paused. No "Dr. Huckabee" was listed. On the third floor, where he thought the doctor's office had been, was the single word "vacant." He walked past the directory and into the first door he saw, a yellow-wallpapered shop filled with boxes of prints from old nature books, some framed, others loose. James stepped to the counter where an elderly black man with wispy white hair and half-moon reading glasses leafed through the pages of a book.

"Excuse me, sir?"

The man folded his book and set it on the counter. His voice was soft and deliberate. "Yes, can I help you, son?"

"I'm looking for Dr. Huckabee's office. But I don't see it on the sign, and I'm sure it's here."

"Well, that would be up on the third floor, now wouldn't it be? Way down at the end of the hall."

James started to turn.

"Of course, you won't find him thereabouts. He was only here for a day. Strange, that one was. Moving truck pulls in yesterday mornin', fills up the office, and then the good doctor was moved out again by the time I was a-closing up. I guess he didn't like the place. Though it seems to me to be an awful waste of effort, if ya hear me. He didn't give this ol' building half a chance. Didn't even speak to his neighbors—not that I'm judging or such a thing. Then again, mayhaps he was in trouble."

James turned back to the counter. "Trouble?"

"Well, son, when I got here this a-morning someone was waitin' at the door. Just bustin' a fit, full of fire and pacin' she was. Now I'm usually the first person here, and this lady had nothing but questions, and all about the good Dr. Huckabee. She wanted to know *where* he was and *if* he had seen anyone while he'd been here." The man peered over his glasses. "They asked if the doctor had any visitors. Wanted to know iffin' he'd had any at all."

The old man left his words hanging. When the silence stretched on, James finally said. "Are they… are those people still here?"

"I think so. But I wouldn't rush to go lookin' for them. I've been around a long time, and I know when people *are* and when people *are not* up to no good." The old man's serious expression melted back into a smile. He reached under the counter and pulled out a pen and ink etching of a skylark. He placed the print in a brown paper bag and slid it across the counter to James. "But that's not why you're here, now is it? You came to get a little somethin' for your mother. A birthday or holiday or some ol' thing, I can hardly keep my customers straight, much less the rest of the building. Old man like me can barely put my pants on the right legs." He winked. "And lookee here, you found something you liked after all."

James numbly took the paper bag from the shopkeeper and turned to leave the store. As he walked, he brushed past a woman in a dark-grey suit and mirror-tinted glasses. She was tall, thin, and had a face so cold and so angular that it looked to have been chiseled from ice. The woman turned her head slightly in James's direction. She scanned him from head to foot and then turned away once more. She crept up the staircase, her wooden heels making no sound on the red brick steps. James's pulse quickened as he ambled from the store. He tried hard not to break into a run. Only the guilty would run from the scene.

* * *

James clutched the print the entire bus ride home, his grip putting a deep fold along the edge of the drawing. James couldn't shake the feeling that the ice-faced woman hadn't been looking for Dr. Huckabee at all. She had been looking for *him*. Huckabee had warned James not to say anything to anyone, that it was dangerous. But James hadn't listened. He thought the doctor was playing a game with him. Even if last night had been nothing but a dream, it didn't change the fact that he had probably been Dr. Huckabee's only client—*ever*. The doctor had only been in the office for one day. That meant he had done everything to talk to James. He'd done it all just to warn him to stay quiet.

A tingle began at the base of James's spine. He could feel the air turn electric as a bright white light in the upper right-hand corner of his vision grew and swept across to block his view. James felt his skin prickling as if stung by a thousand needles, the beat of his heart resounding like a gong in his ears. And then—

* * *

James shrieked across a star-filled sky. He exploded through a luminous cloud that left him coated in cool, phosphorus mist. The rest of the fragmented cloud trailed behind him like the tail of a comet, diminishing then being replenished as he hit cloud after cloud after cloud. Still, James fell, dropping further and further down. But wherever the ground was, if there indeed was a ground, James couldn't see it through the banks of glowing strata.

Falling again, James thought. *For a moment there, I wondered if the Doctor really had...*

* * *

James awakened to see the bus driver crouched over him in the aisle. He felt no motion in the bus, and the only sounds were murmurs from curious faces pointed in his direction. James pulled himself upright. He absently rubbed the knot forming on his head from where he hit… the seat? The floor? Or was that from his fight that morning?

"I'm ok," James mumbled. He composed himself. "I faint sometimes."

The bus driver looked skeptical but helped him back into his seat. He stood there watching him as if he'd fall again at any second. "Where are you getting off, boy?"

"Magnolia Street."

"After that? Where ya headed?"

A wave of panic hit him, then quickly subsided. The bus driver wasn't trying to discover where he lived. He wasn't trying to track him down. He was just concerned about a kid that took a hard fall on his bus.

"I, I live right across from the bus stop," James stammered. The lie flowed easily across his teeth. *Very* easily.

"Ok then. Sit tight, boy, and don't work yourself up. Keep lookin' out the window. Eyes ahead. We'll be there in just a few minutes. Then you go straight home, you hear?"

James nodded and returned to watching the trees and buildings pass by. If nothing else, he knew that he wasn't cured of his falls. As if there'd been any doubt.

After getting off the bus, James enjoyed the small sense of relief he always felt after falling. Usually, he wouldn't fall a second time in the same day. He welcomed that relief, even though he was bitter about how much he looked forward to it. James cut through the patch of woods near the bus stop and past the forested area that backed up to his neighborhood. A trace of honeysuckle, in its last bloom before autumn set in, brushed his cheeks as he made his way through the foot-beaten path. James exhaled gently; he was almost home.

* * *

Despite the encounter with the ice-faced woman, the failure to locate Dr. Huckabee, and the fall on the bus, James believed his escape from school had gone off perfectly. His parents didn't mention a thing, and if there had been trouble from his teachers, Seth would have warned him. James spent the rest of the afternoon playing with the dogs, enjoyed a nice re-heated spaghetti supper, and used his impending test on dreams as an excuse to stay in his room.

For two hours he sought distraction in his schoolbooks, trying to catch up on what he assumed he'd missed. When the moon was again streaming through his window, just as it had the night before, his thoughts returned to his dream of the strange ocean. Would he have another *real* dream like last night? Or with the coin gone would things go back to just a normal daily fall. Well, as normal as his life had ever been.

"Whump!"

The sound of something heavy banged in his closet, sending a shock of surprise through him. James walked to the door, trying to decide if a basketball or some other item had dropped. He paused to see water trickling from underneath the closet door. What could be leaking? A water bottle? Those certainly made a lot of noise when they fell.

He swung open the door, a yelp slipping past his lips as he jumped back. Standing in his closet, dressed in a three-piece tweed suit, barefoot, and soaking wet from head to toe, was Dr. Huckabee. The doctor held the peculiar coin between thumb and forefinger, a scowl on his face.

"Do you have *any* idea how deep that confounded ocean was?"

James staggered back until his legs hit the bed. He sat down hard. Dr. Huckabee sloshed out of the closet and then shook his entire body in the same manner as James's dog, sending droplets of water flying in all directions. When the doctor finished shaking, he was completely dry. The doctor cart-wheeled to the side, vaulting off one hand before assuming a gargoyle-like perch on the dresser.

Dr. Huckabee tossed the coin to James. "My brother, you just *can't* go leaving things scattered all over. It creates a clear and definable trail. And if they find the trail, and they track the signature, it will lead them back to *you*. And more importantly and more consequently, back to *me*. To *us!* It's a terrible risk, and one which you swore in your excessively and unproductively mendacious ways *not* to take."

James's mouth opened and shut several times before words came out. "My parents…"

The doctor dismissed James with a wave of his hand. "Pish-posh and osh-kosh-bagosh. They can't hear us, so don't worry about that. And I won't tarry. I'm only staying long enough to keep you from getting yourself killed. And to keep us *all* safe. The Styx could be moments away!"

"Who are the Styx? Are they the ones after me? And why? Who was that lady at your office today? Is she one of the Styx?"

The doctor's eyes bulged outward. "What? Did you go *back* there? To where we met and discussed the things we agreed to not speak of ever again? Today? And there were people there? Stupid, stupid, foolishly stupid. I explicitly told you…"

Somewhere in James, the line between fear, confusion, and apprehension crossed over to defensiveness. "Now, wait a minute. You didn't tell me anything at all. You said not to tell anyone anything. But you didn't say what not to tell them. And you didn't say that I couldn't leave that coin anywhere. And you didn't say *not* to go back to your office. You didn't tell me anything except how to look at the coin. Which I *didn't* mean to lose. Now I want some answers." He folded his arms across his chest.

"Certainly not," Huckabee said.

"What do you mean? You just told me you were going to tell me what was going on."

"No, I said I'd tell you how to keep yourself from getting killed. And though they may hesitate to make sure they aren't trapped, they won't wait indefinitely. They know that you're here, even if they don't know who you are. Don't forget that."

"They don't know where I live. I don't even know who you're talking about."

"Not *here* here. The *world* here. There's not just one, as you must certainly know. This is your home. Your native place. And here, you are just like everyone else."

James's hands shook in near-rage. "What are you *talking about?*"

Dr. Huckabee rolled from his gargoyle perch to land in a lotus position on the floor. He folded his arms across his chest. "Too dangerous to talk here. I'll send someone to meet you later. The best I can do for now is to tell you the Rules."

"The what?"

"The Rules. But only on one condition."

James glared at Huckabee. "That I swear to never tell anyone as long as I live?"

"Precisely. But I must be quick." The doctor pulled a pocket watch from his coat and glanced at the time. "So here we go. What happened to you last night is called 'Traveling,' the spiritual transportation from one world to another. Your little falls were just a taste, but last night was the real thing. And while Traveling has a higher purpose, there are many dangers. The Rules are to keep you safe. Understand so far?"

James nodded, too dumbfounded to speak.

"Rule Number One: Don't tell anyone who you are or what you're doing. Blending in is the most important thing. More important than anything else you do. Never tell anyone your name or anything that could trace you back to your life here.

"Rule Number Two: Don't stay out too long. Unless you get things under control, the clock is always ticking, and you must never forget that your life *here* is just as important as what you do out *there*. And if you *do* stay out too long, you may run the risk of never coming back at all."

James interrupted, "Too long? What do you mean too long? How long is too long when I can't control going, and…?"

"Rule Number Three: whatever you do out there, don't harm anything you don't need to, and never, ever kill anything."

"I'm *not* going to kill anyone."

"And Rule Number Four, and the last of the Big Rules, never, ever…"

A klaxon alarm sounded from the doctor's pocket watch. And in the space between the first and second blare, the doctor—*folded*. Dr. Huckabee twisted and contorted, his body crumpling like an origami puppet, over and over until nothing was left but the thin puddle of water where he had sat. James watched in disbelief as the water pooled and disappeared as well.

A furious barking sounded from downstairs, the vicious snarls of a canine that likely wagged his tail with as much vigor as he growled. The sound caused James to lurch in fear. He crouched low, as though about to be struck by an unseen hand. With the barking still filling his ears, he crept to the window. He peered one eye over the sill.

Standing on the lawn in front of his house, stood a tall, thin woman in a business suit, with harsh angular features, and an icy expression. She studied James's house, though her eyes did not drift to the second-story window. After a long moment passed, the ice-faced woman turned and set her hands deep in her pockets. She stilted away, turning sharply once more at the sidewalk, and continued down the street.

A burning seized James's lungs and he realized he had been holding his breath. Slowly, deliberately, he allowed himself to exhale and then breathe in again. The moment of relief became fear as he dropped to sit on the cool, moonlit floor.

"Did that just happen?" James questioned his room. He looked over at the closet door and saw no water, no remnants of Dr. Huckabee's visit. But he couldn't deny one simple fact: Huckabee's coin rested in his palm.

James pulled himself to his feet and paced the room, kicking aside dropped clothes as he went. The doctor's words, the warnings, the rules—everything came back to one thing. This wasn't just a sickness. And it wasn't going away. There *was* no cure. And what's more, he was being followed. But why?

He lay back on his bed, kicking the covers aside as he did so. He held Huckabee's coin in front of him, the face shining clear though the moonbeam was almost six feet away. Huckabee wasn't much for answers, so maybe James just needed to get them by himself.

"Alright. So, all I do is concentrate." He focused on the coin. And then—

James fell.

7. Snow Fall

James opened his eyes to nothingness, an absence of color like static from a busted television. Even despite his vision having no form or texture, the falling sensation was all too familiar. He was dropping, twisting, plummeting, and the colorless ground was fast approaching.

James plunged face-first into the snow bank, feeling much like a bird colliding with a glass window. Just as unaware, just as surprised, and just as clobbered. His body burrowed into the soft snow. The disorientation sent him into a panicked flounder until, flailing his arms, he twisted upright. James's head and shoulders erupted from the snow, punctuated by a long satisfying gasp.

If the last time James had landed (actually *landed*) had been into the Caribbean Sea at sunset, or somewhere close enough, James was certain that this time he dropped into the middle of the Alaskan wilderness at midnight. And if Dr. Huckabee was right, this wasn't just another dream. James had Traveled here, to another *world!* And what a world it was. Angular mountains, snow-covered except for faces of sheer granite, dominated the horizon. The peaks were so sharp and so jutting that James thought they looked either like a collection of titanic razor blades or the bristling teeth of a deep-sea creature.

The snow bank which had so kindly served as James's parachute was nestled on a mountain slope, several hundred yards above a narrow valley snaking between James's mountain and the next. Despite the initial disorientation, he considered himself fortunate. If he had fallen twenty feet to his left or right, he would have been sent into a slide halfway down the mountain.

James paused. Why wasn't he cold? He was wearing his pajamas, chest-deep in a snowbank, and he didn't feel the slightest twinge of cold. Was that all part of 'Traveling' as Dr. Huckabee called it? Or was the coin in his fist responsible? The absurdity of it all made him laugh.

"So, I'm in my P.J.'s on a mountainside with nothing but a subway token. All hail the 'Walker of Worlds.'" James chuckled. "This is not what I would have imagined."

He cast his eyes to the sky. Stars glittered overhead behind faint wisps of sapphire-streaked clouds. The clouds shone with incandescent fury, though night must have fallen hours earlier. Then he saw why. Though the sky was moonless, there was a star on the horizon so intense that it rivaled the moon. The light was bright blue, pulsing, and intense as a cold flame. The sight of the star chilled something within him, and he had to wrench his eyes away.

In the valley below, another light shone, though far warmer and softer. A vehicle chugged noisily across the valley floor, a lantern swinging from its front and smoke belching from its rear. The contraption seemed an amalgam of wood paneling atop an iron frame propelled by heavy treads. James saw someone sitting atop the contraption, while another person kept pace a few yards behind. *It's a snowcat,* he thought. *Maybe I am in Alaska after all, not some other world. If only I could just see a little better.*

On a whim, James decided to use the trick of focus that he'd tried in the Ocean World. By concentrating, he had not only been able to see the *Thatness* of the world, but he had been able to see in greater detail than normal. He clenched the coin in his fist and concentrated.

James cried in pain as anguish streaked across his temple to his right eye. He winced, closing his eye tightly until the discomfort faded. When James reopened his eyes, the intense detail of the *Thatness* shone around him. But unlike the *Thatness* of the Ocean World, there was something wrong here. Something, very, *very* wrong. The world—the entire *world*—wailed in pain. And though James did not understand the words, the meaning was so clear and so unequivocal, it couldn't be denied.

(Help me, Save me, Help me, Rescue me, Save me, Help me, I'm dying, I'm dying, Help me, Save me, Help me, It's killing me, It's killing me, Help me, Save me, Rescue me, Help me, Save me.)

James released his concentration. The intensity of *Thatness* faded along with the screams of the world. *This world is dying,* James thought.

No. James knew.

A sharp crack echoed around him and an outcropping of ice exploded beside to his side. James ducked low, the thunder of the gunshot echoing from peak to peak around him. *They're shooting at me? But I didn't do anything. I didn't even…*

Another gunshot boomed, and the snow behind him exploded once more. And with the second report, the mountain shifted. Then broke.

The snow covering the mountainside shifted in a single slab that cascaded around him. James tried to claw to escape, but it was like wrestling a tidal wave. The churning froth of ice and powder bore him along, gaining more and more momentum as he was carried on its crest. James fought hard to keep from slipping below the slough. For a few seconds he succeeded, and then was overwhelmed.

The avalanche engulfed James. He was flung and cartwheeled, caught in the slide like the breakwater of a stormy sea. He curled into a tight ball to try and keep his arms and legs from being further thrown. He gritted his teeth to endure the tumbling. And in a few short seconds, it was over.

When James came to a stop, he found himself unable to move. His arms and legs were cemented in place. His vision was black with the lightlessness of the buried. His heart beat in panicked bursts, his ears ringing. He had to figure a way out of this, to break free and dig. But which way was even up?

James felt something wrap tight around his ankles and he was jerked backward as he was plucked from the snow. As he flailed to brush the snow from his eyes, he found himself staring at the upside-down face of a man—nearly a giant—covered from head to toe in a patchwork of black and grey furs. His chest was crossed by a bandolier of high-caliber ammunition, and he held a still-smoking shotgun loosely in one hand.

Oh my god, James thought. *I've been captured by an Abominable Bandito Snowman.*

"Oy? What have you there, Brine?" a voice sounded from behind him. The accent reminded James of the cockney Englishmen he'd seen on late-night television.

The giant grunted and dropped James onto the ground. He exclaimed in a deep baritone, harsher, and more musical than the other man, but still with a British tinge. "It's a kid. It's a wee, bloody, squirmin' kid. And he's not even wearing a coat."

The angular face of a second man peered at James lying helpless in the snow. The man's skin seemed composed entirely of scar tissue. He was dressed in furs, though he seemed to have preferred slick otter pelts to the lupine patchwork of the giant. "A kid? Way out in the middle of nowheres? You ask me, it's a mite suspicious. Runic, I'll wager. You think he's a spy, or just some kind of tricksy trap? See any runes? Something's keeping him warm."

"No. No he ain't all marked up at all. Nothing that I can see leastways. But I'll be deviled if I know what he's doin' out here."

James opened his mouth then clamped it tight again. Whoever these people were—if they decided not to kill him—maybe they could help. And if they couldn't get him back home, maybe they could at least let him know what was going on. Of course, they'd probably want answers, not just take it for granted he was a kid that didn't get seem to get cold.

At the thought of the word "cold," it hit him. James was seized by a shock of overwhelming frigidity. The cold sucked his breath from his lungs and made every bone in his body convulse in large aching spasms. His head pounded, his fingers, toes, legs, and arms numb. James couldn't even make a fist, his appendages half curled in icy rigor. He tried to speak but only muffled sounds and the chattering of teeth emerged from his mouth.

The scar-faced man frowned down at him. "Reckon we kill it, Brine?"

"Well, he'll be dead if we leave 'im here," the giant said, shaking his head. "But I'd rather get some answers, aye? Let's take 'im with."

"Who…wh-who are you?" James managed to break in.

The Bandito Snowman swore in surprise. He glanced over his shoulder and shouted to the snowcat. "Cap'n! Oy, Cap'n Sylph! I'll be flamin' by buggling hull-broaching winds of damnation! Cap'n, get out here. Need your take on this."

James pulled himself from the snow to half-crouch, his shoulders hunched, and his arms clutched to his body to try and fight the oppressive cold. He cast his eyes in the direction of where the large man had called. The snowcat was no longer billowing smoke into the air, only puttering. The wood housing atop the iron frame seemed comical to James, and yet it was the otherness of the device that struck him most. The snowcat was like something from a fairytale or fevered dream. And why shouldn't it? The large man looked like a gun-toting Viking, and the scar-faced man could have been the villain in a "B" movie.

The top hatch of the snowcat opened, and a slender woman slid out and hopped to the ground. Like the others, she was wrapped in thick fur, though all of one piece. The fur fit no more tightly than a bear rug would have, cinched at the waist by a wide leather belt lined with two rows of grommets. The woman had five pistols circling her belt, each of a different length and style. She was as dark-skinned as the giant, though with pale eyes the color of the surrounding snow. She rested one hand easily on the butt of one of the pistols and walked to where the giant and the scar-faced man stood.

"Brine, darling, this better be important enough to nearly bring the mountain down." The woman's accent was far softer than her companions, nearly Irish. "And what did I be telling you about firing shots out here? The whole place could give way and…" She paused. "What have you there? What in the eight winds is that?"

"You can see for yourself, it's a wee laddie," the giant, Brine, chuckled. "But you can ask 'im yourself. Speaks the island tongue like a native."

"Does he now? Isn't that a mite peculiar?" The woman's voice remained even, the surprise faded to mild irony. The scar-faced man remained silent.

James looked up, his body convulsing. "Please, ma'am. I'm so cold. I'm s…so c…cold…"

The woman frowned. "For the winds and tides and all the…" She stopped short, scowled, and tapped the butt of one of her guns. "All right, crew. Check for runes. Everything: feet and tongue, palms and ears. Get him some blankets and put him in the wagon. Brine, you keep an eye on him there. Teak, you drive. I'll take a shift outside."

The giant and the scar-faced man rudely grabbed James and turned him in all directions. Inspecting him, James imagined. They were looking for something, but James had no idea what. He was too busy chattering from the cold.

"Don't see a mark on him, Cap'n," the large man said. "We could give 'im over to Slagish and the Scrim once we reach the shore. Just to be sure."

The woman shook her head. "No, that's not how I want to start with them. We can't be giving him an edge. And even if we did, Slagish would probably take him for his own. And then we wouldn't learn anything. I'm curious, aren't you, lads?"

The scar-faced man frowned. "Uneasy maybe, not curious, if you will. He's an unknown. And these aren't our waters. Not waters at all, if you hear me. I say we leave him, but if you two think otherwise…" The scar-faced man gave a flippant nod to his far-larger partner, then turned back to the wagon. James winced as Brine grabbed him by the waist and casually slung him over his shoulder. James was too astonished to resist, and so remained limp and speechless as he was hauled to the wagon door and placed inside.

The inside of the carriage contained a loose collection of opened food tins and flattened water flasks packed around what appeared to be a rectangular box wrapped in canvas and banded in leather. The giant crawled in after James, occupying nearly half of the open space, and shoved a pile of furs over to him. James wrapped the blankets around himself, his fingers having difficulty grasping the thick musty folds. He pulled the blankets tight until only his face remained exposed. James looked over at Brine eyeing him carefully.

"Oy. Lad? You understand me?" the man grunted.

James nodded. "Do *you* understand *me?*"

The bandito's lips trembled, then parted to reveal a wide smile of gleaming ivory. "Hah! Knew I wasn't hearing things. Where you from, laddie? You look a wee pale for an island boy? How is it now you speak our tongue? And what are you doing out here in the gods forsaken middle of nowheres, anyhows?"

James opened his mouth to reply and was doubled over by a pain streaking across his scalp and down his spine. The words of Dr. Huckabee rang in his ears. *Rule Number One: don't let anyone know who you are.* He looked up feebly. "I'm not sure, sir. I…"

"Sir? Hah… *Hah!*" Brine banged on the small hatch door dividing the cargo hold from the driver's compartment. "He called me 'sir!' Do I look like a sir to you, laddie? Do I look like I've a knightin' coming my way?"

James shook his head, paused for a moment, then replied. "Um… what should I call you?"

The giant puffed out his chest and offered his hand. "They call me Brine. Most of which because it's my name, though I do say I've enough of the sea in my blood to have earned it my own self. So, if you prefer, you may call me Highest Brine, Lord of the Oceans, and Czar of the Million Islands and that which lies between. In short, I'm a West Islander, bred, born, and weaned."

James raised an eyebrow. "Islander? Ocean? But we're in the mountains…"

"Temporally displaced, laddie."

"Temporarily?"

"That too." Brine winked as he shook James's hand. "But where are you coming from? Out in the elements with not nearly enough to stay warm on this godforsaken, godawful ice?"

James didn't have a good answer and certainly didn't want to break one of the only rules he knew. He shrugged. "I'm a little *displaced* myself. Though I'm having a hard time—remembering. Anything really. I'm kind of completely lost."

The snowcat lurched forward, the great engine resuming its chug once more. What James *really* wanted to know, was *where* he was, *when* he was, and just *who* in god's name these people were.

Brine smiled. "So, I'm guessing you've some bits on your mind, then. Like whereabouts you are and whomsoever *we* are? That right?"

"Yeah, pretty much exactly that."

"As I said, I'm Brine. I'm boatswain on the *Killdevil III*. The ol' scarfaced sourpuss out there is Teak, our navigator for the trip, and you met Cap'n Sylph. And don't you drop that 'Captain', either, lad. She's earned it if ever a missy has."

"But where are we?"

"We're in a snow-crawler, now aren't we? The locals call 'em sleds but I'm stuck for the difference. Where did you think we were?"

"No. I mean—*everything*. Not just the sled. The snow, the trail, the—I mean what year is it even? I know I'm somewhere else, but I don't know where. Do you understand anything I'm saying? And…" James clamped his mouth shut.

"Listen, laddie," Brine began. His voice was soft, and his brow wrinkled in puzzlement. "I need you to calm yourself down and start overs like. Do you really not know where you are? You don't know how you got out there in the snow? You must have some idea where you came from."

James hung his head in defeat. "No. I mean I have an idea. It wasn't the first time."

Brine released his grip. "You mean you forgot who you were before? Or did you mean this isn't the first idea in your wee life?"

"No, I mean I…" James shook his head. "I don't know what I mean."

"All right, all right, calm down for a second. Let's start at the beginning. I'm Brine. Pleased to meet ya. And your name is?"

"It's Ja—" Pain ripped across James's forehead, doubling him over. The pain coursed down his spine and throughout his legs. James found himself panting in disbelief.

Brine's brow wrinkled with concern. "Don't strain yourself, laddie. We can go easy. Jay is it? That's enough for now. No questions for a bit. How's that?"

James nodded, afraid to respond.

"Alright, Jay. Now I know you're cold and tired. So lay yourself down and fetch a bit of sleep. We'll worry about the rest later. Your pal Brine will keep an eye out? Ya ken?"

James nodded again. He leaned back onto the mass of furs and closed his eyes.

* * *

But James didn't sleep. He *couldn't* sleep. The condition wasn't normal restlessness. It wasn't that he was tired and sleep eluded him. James didn't *feel* tired. He didn't *feel* he needed to sleep. The cold, once paralyzing, had been replaced by ambient nothingness. Unnoticeable as either warm or cold: the temperature simply didn't matter.

For a long time, he remained still. Though his back was to Brine, James felt the giant's eyes studying him. The feeling was tangible.

Just go away, James thought. *Just leave me alone. Just ignore me. I need to think. I need some time alone. I just want you to go away. Even if only—*

James heard Brine's fist rapping on the front panel of the wagon, and the vehicle chugged to a stop. The door creaked open, then shut again, leaving James alone. For two minutes, he remained still. When his anticipation lessened, he sat up.

"Brine?" a voice rang loudly in James's ears. "Why are we stopped and why are we out here? Shouldn't you be guarding the kid?" James whipped his head around to look behind him, searching for the voice that cut through cleanly through the air. There was nothing but the pile of discarded furs.

Brine replied, "The lad's out of it. More than a bit addled. I think we let him rest."

Teak said, "I still say this is a trap. If not a trap, he's a spy. He could be rigged to blow."

"I be thinking not," a female voice said. "A rune like that can't be hidden easily. More likely he's a runaway. Maybe a project gone wrong, or something. Or could be just a local driven over by the exposure. These aren't the West Isles, and that boy's no Islander… no matter what language he speaks."

James crept forward to peer out the window. He gasped. Outside the window, at the end of a trail of footprints nearly a hundred feet away, Brine, Teak, and Captain Sylph stood in a tight ring. Yet their voices rang in James's ears as though he stood next to them.

Teak said, "I've said it before, the kid's a freakin' liability. But you're the boss, and…"

Sylph interrupted, "And we have more serious things to worry about. Brine, how far are we from the pass?"

"We'll be there by daybreak, Cap'n," Brine replied. "Even with our stops, we may still beat Slagish and his men there. Listen, and I don't mean to be out of line or nothing, but are you sure this is a good idea? We got no business running transport this far away, even if we didn't have to cross the Alpinsea. Slagish's lads are crazy and the Kai'ja even crazier if we make it that far. You can't just take two groups of crazies and throw them together and expect us not to get caught in the fray. You're putting too much trust in this one. And…" Brine snapped his jaw shut. James wondered if the big man had crossed an inadvertent line.

Sylph glanced from Brine to the scarred man. "What about you, Teak? What's your take? Everyone on my crew gets a say."

Teak said, "Money's too good to pass up… long as you trust the runics, that is. Well, long as you trust 'em and don't take chances. Like that kid. That's a chance we shouldn't take."

Brine jerked his head at Teak. "Fergit the laddie, Teak. It's Slagish and the Scrim we need to worry about. He's got our ship and…"

"And we have no choice." Sylph's words came down with finality. "We're committed, lads. And until our cargo is delivered, we've our ship on the line as well as our lives. I'm not going to take chances, but I'm not going to leave bodies behind, either. The boy stays. Does anyone disagree?"

James heard noncommittal grunts from Teak and Brine, then footsteps—loud as the crushing of stones—as they made their way back to the wagon. James returned to the pile of furs and curled again into a ball. He tried not to flinch as the door to the wagon opened and Brine climbed inside.

It's just too weird. What's happening? It's like I walked into the middle of something. It's not really real, but it's not a dream. But what am I doing here? And how do I get back home?

James flinched. He knew how to get back. He could return just like he did when he landed in the ocean. Huckabee's coin would show him the way out. James opened his hand to look at it. The coin remained smooth, nothing upon its face but the smooth bore punch. He tightened his fist around the coin, concentrating with the hope that he'd get a sign of some sort. But when James reopened his fist, a single word etched on the face, then dissolved into nothingness: "Patience."

8. The Scrim

As the snowcat ascended the mountain pass, fields of snow gave way to an erratic collection of shards of ice bristling from the ground like inverted icicles. The ice fragments were varied in color, clarity, and shape. Some were perfectly cylindrical and opaque, while others were thin as paper, hooked like talons, and so clear they distorted the surreal landscape beyond. The higher the snowcat climbed, the more bizarre the shapes became. When finally James, Brine, Teak, and Sylph reached the summit, James shivered with anticipation of what must lie beyond.

James gasped in surprise as he leaned from the window of the snowcat. There, stretched out for miles before him, was an inland sea. The waters were pale grey from a fog that effused from its surface. The mist concealed the waves beneath, only parting when an errant wind sent the fog spiraling away. The layer of mist contrasted mightily with the frozen spikes and spires which encircled the sea alongside titanic frozen pillars. The barriers were solid sentinels to the liquid waters within.

"The Alpinsea is quite a sight, eh Jay?"

James pulled his head from the window to look at the enormous man across from him. Brine grinned back.

"That ice ya saw on our way up the pass, that's from the winds. When the gales start their blowin', the Alpinsea overflows the mountain's rim and freezes. You can't even come up here in the springtime when the winds are at their strongest. You'd be frozen in an instant." Brine traced his finger from the ridgeline down to the shore. "That's also why the shore looks like that. If a wave gets too big, and crashes too far out, it's frozen before it draws back."

"Why doesn't the whole ocean freeze?" James fished for an answer. "Is the water too salty or something?"

"Not at all. Too warm. You could go swimmin' in it if you wanted. Something under the sea keeps the whole thing bubbling and steaming. It's that fog that makes the water so hard to read, and navigating the ship is no easy piece itself. That's why Slagish hired us to carry him. He wouldn't trust any but the best."

James swayed as the snowcat rumbled from side to side. He took another long look at Brine. James wasn't sure what to make of the enormous man, or any of the crew for that matter. For as intimidating as he was, Brine had been friendly. Captain Sylph had also treated him with reluctant hospitality. Only Teak, the navigator, had been particularly hostile. He didn't seem as willing as the others to accept James's inexplicit arrival.

On the other hand, why should James even care? While it *seemed* like all this was real—and Dr. Huckabee said it would be real—he couldn't shake the thought that he was curled up in bed back home. And if that was the case, did it really matter what he said or what he did? Aside from not giving himself away, that is. Was there even a *reason* he was here?

To test a theory, James opened his focus to the *Thatness* of the world. The terrifying detail consumed him with a sharpness of vision and precision of sound that made his senses seem blurry only moments ago. But as the clarity set in, so did the world's screams. The world cried out to him in a voice injured and panicked.

(Help me, Save me, Help me, Rescue me, Save me, Help me, I'm dying, I'm dying, Help me, Save me, Help me, It's killing me, Help me, Save me—)

James shuddered and released his focus. His previous sense of wonder fell, sickened, and died. Panic crept across his skin, telling him to get away, go home, escape. But James wondered if he had gotten his answer. Maybe there was some purpose to being here. Maybe he was supposed to help. But how?

The reverberations of the snowcat sputtered and died, leaving the world around him silent except the slap of waves. James looked over at Brine who flashed a grin before kicking open the cabin door and sliding out. James crawled out behind him. The ice crunched as he landed.

The snowcat had stopped at the dividing line between the crushed white of the icy road and the obsidian sands of the Alpinsea shore. Where the road ended, a wooden boardwalk began. The pier extended across the sands and then several dozen yards into the still-shifting waters of the Alpinsea. But there were no boats at the dock, and indeed, none as far as the eye could see.

James heard the crunch of footsteps behind him and turned to see Teak, the scar-covered navigator, adjusting his otter pelt clothing.

"We should toss the kid overboard before Slagish and the Scrim get here," Teak muttered.

Captain Sylph sprang from the snowcat to land beside Teak. "Now then, lads, we've more to worry about now. They'll be here any second. Brine, Teak, let's get unloaded. And as for you, Jay, hold out your hands."

James held out his open palms and was surprised when she clapped him with a pair of handcuffs. Scratch that, not handcuffs, nothing so advanced. Manacles.

"Don't think nothin' of it, lad, just a precaution." Sylph winked. "It'll put our friends at ease, maybe they'll even let you aboard."

Just then, James heard a faint rumbling behind him. He turned to see that six snowcats, much like the one he had ridden in, had crested the mountainside and were descending to the Alpinsea shore. The tanks lumbered to within fifty feet of the dock. One by one, the engines cut to silence.

"Alright," Brine muttered to James. "Stay close and keep mum, ya' ken? Don't answer any questions, don't look at anyone too close in the eyes, and don't do anything to get us all murdered and whatnot. Got it?"

Teak snorted in disgust. "Has *he* got it? Have *you* got it, Brine? Do you even understand what's at stake out here? You've never dealt with these men before. These are the Scrim. Every bleedin' one of 'em's a runic. And that Slagish, he's the worst of all, most dangerous runic I've ever met. If you try and change the deal on these people, they'll just as soon change the deal on you. You'd best remember that."

Captain Sylph silenced her crew with a stern look. "Focus, lads. Here they come. I wager it's best if I do the talking."

"Did you call them the Scrim?" James asked.

Brine gritted his teeth. "It means 'the written'. Like 'scrimshaw'. It's what Slagish calls his crew. They take a certain pride in all being runics. Though it just goes to show they're crazy."

"Runics?"

"Another time, lad. Just keep your mouth shut."

One by one, the hatches of the snowcats opened and the passengers trickled out. The first thing James noticed was how fundamentally different the Scrim were from his captors/companions. First of all, whereas Sylph, Teak, and Brine were as tanned as Pacific Islanders, the members of the second caravan looked Slavic. Their complexion was as fair as the surrounding ice; their hair and beards, dark and sleek. Not only was their skin pale, but James was amazed by how much of it he saw considering the winter weather. Of the four-dozen people who exited the wagon, easily half the men were bare-chested.

Only three women stood amongst them. The first wore a dark-black bikini top which complemented the thick fur legging of her pants, and the second was wrapped in fabric no thicker than silk. The third woman—James assumed she was a woman—wore a thick mess of black robes that were feathered and patched. This woman stood close by the only person who seemed as distinctly out of place as James himself felt. The outsider was a grim-faced man with a robe as pale as the winter sky.

Each person carried a hodgepodge of weaponry ranging from curved swords to assault rifles. But aside from their clothing and weapons, what drew James's attention were the tattoos. Each person was decorated with tattoos inked so darkly that they appeared to have been painted with motor oil. The symbols looked like a combination of Japanese, Islamic, and Roman characters. He now understood why they called themselves the Scrim. They were lettered from head to foot.

Even more intriguing, was that as James looked at each tattoo, he received a flash of inspiration. The meaning of the characters shone through. "Fire, Water, Ice, Strength, Vision, Fog, Poison, Earth, Wind, Light, Shadow, Crushing, Sound, Hate." The symbols spoke to him in a way James did not fully understand. Did that mean they were important?

When the tattooed individuals finished filing out, the hatch to the fifth tank opened and the last man emerged. While he wore the fur-and-leather garb of the others, his clothes had a sleek, refined look. The man's jet-black hair was cut short and slicked back, complementing his long tapered mustache. The man leaned forward against an ebony cane topped with a silver-worked knob shaped as a fist.

The mustached man marched past his subjects to approach Sylph. He scanned his eyes from Brine, to Teak, lingered on James, and then back to Sylph again. "Captain, so good to see you made it safely. I assume my rune is safe as well?"

Sylph nodded. "Of course, Lord Slagish. But first, let's see my ship."

"Certainly." The mustached man took a step back. He eyed each of them in turn once more. "These are your crew, I take it? What's left of them."

Sylph gestured to the large man beside her. "This is Brine. He's my boatswain and first mate. He's in charge of maintenance on the ship, rigging, sails, and stormwatch. He's the one who'll turn your soldiers into sailors—at least for the journey." Sylph gestured to her right. "And this is Teak. He's our navigator and ice master. This is his fourth trip across the Alpinsea, first time on my crew. But I take it you've met."

Slagish shook his head. "I know him only by reputation. But he was highly regarded, nonetheless."

"That may be," Sylph said, "but he's my crew for the trip, and under my employ. You're not to command either of my men."

"Fair enough, Captain Sylph. And what of this one?" Slagish pointed a pale finger at James. "Our bargain was simple. You were to have two fighting men only. The rest are mine."

Sylph tossed a flippant nod at James. "A fighting man? Hardly. Slave and deckhand, no more. I can't trust your men to keep my ship in order, and I can't flog them if they don't. And don't start counting your coin, either. He won't get a cut of haul."

Slagish steadied his eyes at James.

Just leave me be, James thought, the words urgent in his mind. *Just forget about me, don't worry about me. I'm nothing… can't you see that I'm…*

The thought was barely formed in James's mind when something peculiar happened. Lord Slagish's focus seemed to waver, to slide back and forth as though the man was having trouble concentrating. Slagish shook his head, and when he looked over to James once more, he seemed not to see him at all. The man's gaze passed right through him.

Slagish squinted. "Yes… yes, I see. Nothing to worry about." He leaned forward on his cane. "Then it is settled. How soon can we sail? And how long until we reach our destination?"

Sylph crossed her arms beneath her breasts. "Depends on my ship's condition. If everything is in order, and the winds hold steady, we'll have two days of sailing, and another overland. You wanted to reach Kai'nau by the full moon, aye? Even if the winds are poor and the weather holds us back, we should make it in time." Sylph squinted one eye. "But there is still the matter of niceties, and I've done my part. Now, aren't you going to introduce me to your crew?"

"Certainly not." Slagish snorted. "Neither you nor your men are to speak to one of the Scrim unless to give an order. Other than that, contact is forbidden. This was part of our agreement, as you may recall."

"Aye, I remember it. Remember it well." Sylph gritted her teeth. "Now as for my ship…"

The mustached man cast one last unfocused glance at James, shook his head, then turned back to his troop. He called in his guttural Russian accent, "Bring forth the vessel."

Two of Slagish's men walked to the back of the last snowcat, this one oversized, and released the clasp on a wide double door. The door folded down into a set of wide steps. James suppressed a gasp as he saw for whom those steps were intended, an enormously obese man, perhaps four hundred pounds. The man appeared nothing but a mass of fat and skin and folds. The only distinguishing feature, apart from his enormous girth, was the tattoo spreading across his bulbous head. The flash of inspiration told James it meant "Burden."

The obese man was led down to the pier by the two helpers, one on each arm. His face was a combination of pain coupled with relief. Step by deliberate step, the fat man and his escorts moved along the snow and onto the pier. The man waddled the length of the ice-crusted wood to the very end, stopping in front of the foggy waters. The man turned, closed his eyes, clasped his hands, then fell backward.

James couldn't see the splash. The mist hovering above the water swallowed the man before he impacted. James didn't hear the splash either. Instead, there was a dull roll, as loud and long as the thunder from a summer storm. The crack was accompanied by effusing black smoke, which bellowed from the Alpinsea, both mixing with and overwhelming the mist of the sea's surface. The smoke did not ascend, but rather compounded on itself, growing thicker and thicker until it solidified. Shapes formed. First a tall spire at the top of the cloud, which broadened to a wide berth at the bottom. Clouds became ropes; mists became sails; smoke became planks. When the boiling stopped and the smoke cleared, what remained was a sleek ship, nearly seventy feet long and a third as wide.

James gawked in amazement. What had just happened? This was magic. *Magic.* Never mind how he had gotten here in the first place. What had just happened wasn't just a trick of falling asleep one place and awaking in another. There was *real magic* in this world. Once more, James realized how terribly out of place he felt. The ship in front of him had to be Captain Sylph's vessel, the Killdevil III. But no one except him seemed surprised it hadn't been there two short minutes ago. James felt like he was going to throw up. He tried to push his unease aside, and instead make sense of what he could see and understand.

The ship possessed two masts with runners for two main sails, as well as a smaller jib which fastened from the foremast to a spar eight feet from the end of the bow. The deck was a combination of stained teak and a darker wood that James didn't recognize. Though accustomed to being on the water, and having spent quite a bit of time on sailboats himself, James was impressed by the high quality of the ship's condition. Every rail was spit-polished, and unbroken in line. The gunwales were riveted and capped with inlay, and even the pilot's wheel had been fashioned with pine and ivory striping. Without a doubt, this was the most beautiful ship James had ever seen. Even if it had come from nowhere.

Brine and Teak hurried to the ship's side, tossing ropes over the rails to secure the vessel to the pier. Sylph swung onto the deck. She inspected her craft, muttering to herself as she did, correcting the odd misplaced line and open hatch. With her survey complete, she returned to the pier and walked back to where the others stood.

Lord Slagish crossed his arms as he surveyed Sylph and the crew. "Is everything to your liking, Captain?" James noticed that the man managed to twist an untoward amount of contempt into the word "captain" as if something about Sylph struck him as disagreeable.

"At first glance, leastaways." Sylph ran a quick finger across her eyebrows, then pointed to the ground, a single motion James interpreted as being for luck. "And unless you've changed your mind about your uncommon urgency, I suppose that the Alpinsea herself will be our judge. As she always is. *But*, every hour I'm given will increase our confidence. These aren't friendly waters. Nor our own."

"No need for delay. Our runes are strong, the bearer worthy. Your services are expensive, Captain Sylph." The man shrugged. "So show me you are worth your price."

"And for our return? I'm not leaving the ship while we cross overland, and I'm not splitting my crew to escort the cargo."

Lord Slagish feigned surprise. "You Islanders worry too much, Captain. Is unladylike. We have another bearer for the approach to the mountain of Kai'nau. And then… Well, comrade, once we are there, runes are not so scarce."

James watched with amazement as Sylph and her crew scurried to prepare the ship, and with equal amazement at the way Slagish's men jumped to Sylph's every command.

"I feel like I should be helping," James muttered to himself. He stared down at the manacles around his wrists and the long, loose chain, once held by Brine, which had been abandoned as soon as the Killdevil had appeared. *That's odd*, James thought. *It's like they completely forgot about me. Slagish's men hardly noticed me. And Sylph, Brine, and Teak forgot I even existed.* Brine had mentioned that James would be such a novelty that he could endanger their mission—whatever that was. But they didn't care at all.

James reached to scratch his head, then crossed his arms across his chest. His jaw dropped in astonishment. The manacles, which had held his wrists so firmly just seconds ago, were lying neatly on the snowy ground. *It's not just the people that forgot me. It's not just Brine, or Slagish's men, or anything like that.* Everything *seems to have forgotten me. It's like I'm not even here. Like I don't need to be here. And if they're forgetting me, maybe it means I'm almost done with this place.*

James closed his eyes, wondering if he was really standing on the shore of a strange frozen sea, in a strange frozen world, strangely unfrozen. And at that moment—

James fell.

9. Daze

The portal loomed in front of James, open and expecting, a bright-yellow edge fading into shadows within. A faint form shone within the darkened interior. The buzz in James's ears, a dull drone punctuated by a sporadic hiss of air, was interrupted by the snap of fingers in front of his face.

"James? Hey, Jimbo! Snap out of it? You gonna faint?"

James lazily turned his head to see his friend Seth's face transform from irritation to concern.

The bus driver called from her seat just inside the door. "Come on, honey. I ain't gonna bite ya."

James lurched into an awareness of his surroundings in much the same way a person awakes when traveling across the country, only to find that day has broken and they are hundreds of miles from when last they opened their eyes. He felt the weight of the books on his back, the acrid smell of the bus's exhaust in his nostrils, and the already too-warm heat of the morning sun. Without responding to either Seth or the driver, he climbed into the school bus and settled into a seat.

Seth plopped beside him and proceeded to fish through the paper bag containing his lunch. "I'll tell you what, Jimbo. You've always been a spacey one, but you stared at that bus for so long, I'd wondered if you really had snapped for good. I mean, I joke about you going off the deep end all the time, but I never really took it too seriously. Hey, you listenin' to me?"

"Yeah… I'm listening." James shook his head to clear the fog. "How long did I space out for."

"'Bout a minute, I guess. We were all waiting for you to hit the dirt, but you just swayed. Not like usual where you fold and… 'Biff!'" Seth illustrated by smacking the palm of his hand against his head

The bus's door swung shut with a pneumatic hiss. The bus pulled away from the curb and rolled up to speed. "What about before that?" James asked. "Was I weird all morning?"

"No weirder than normal, you're always a bit sleepy first thing, so I don't take you too seriously 'til after homeroom." Seth cocked an eyebrow at his friend. "Why do you ask?"

"I don't know. It's just that I don't remember even getting up. I remember going to my room last night. I remember my freaky-freaky dreams, but I don't remember breakfast or anything."

"Maybe you never woke up 'till now. My brother's like that. I swear he can be up and moving around for ten minutes before he *really* wakes up. It's kind of funny. If you know he's sleepwalking, you can ask him all kinds of questions and he won't remember later."

"Why don't you just shake him awake?"

Seth shrugged. "It's his own fault."

James turned to the window and watched the live oaks stream by in evenly spaced blurs. He may not remember eating breakfast, but he certainly remembered sitting on the shore of the Alpinsea. James would have sworn he was there only moments ago. But not as a dream. The memory of that Frozen World wasn't fading like a dream was supposed to fade. It hadn't felt like a dream, it hadn't seemed like a dream… so maybe it wasn't. Had Huckabee really told the truth? Was he *actually* moving between worlds? He had, hadn't he? The Frozen World had been real, which meant the Ocean World had been so as well. In fact, the most surreal part had been not his otherworld excursions, but instead the encounter with Huckabee the night before.

The ice-faced woman…

James shuddered. In the excitement and wonder of the Frozen World, he had forgotten about the strange woman with chiseled features and frigid, corpse-like eyes. She had been looking for Huckabee, both downtown and then again at James's house. Was she looking for James as well? Huckabee had warned against her, called her one of "the Styx." In fact, Huckabee seemed as scared of her as he had been of anything else. Was she really looking for James? Had she found him? And if so, what would she do?

Seth poked him in the ribs. "So, is that it? Is that the wonderful coin? See, I told you the doctor would just give you a new one."

James glanced down. He realized that he was flipping Huckabee's coin idly in his fingers. He snapped his hand shut. "I… uh. I guess I found it."

"Can I check it out?"

With great reluctance, James handed the coin to Seth. To James, the object's strange unreality shone forth like a noonday sun, paling all else in comparison. But Seth didn't seem to notice. "It doesn't look all that special to me," Seth said. "Looks like a subway token. Haven't been on a subway in a while, now that I think about it." Seth flicked the coin back at James who cupped it against his chest before shoving it into his pocket. He turned to look out the window when Seth poked him once more. "Better idea, Jim. Let's analyze you."

"Huh?

"You keep saying you're having freaky dreams. Well, we're studying dreams in class, aren't we?" Seth pulled out his textbook and flipped to the current chapter. "So, what did you dream about?"

"I don't want to talk about it," James grumbled, partially from not wanting to talk about it, and partially because of Dr. Huckabee's warnings of secrecy.

Seth snickered, "Ah! It was a *good* dream, wasn't it? A health class dream? Involve anyone I know?"

"No… *No*. Nothing like that." James sighed, he knew Seth wouldn't drop it. "Fine, I'll tell you. I dreamed I fell into a snow bank in Alaska or somewhere. Only it wasn't Alaska, it was somewhere else. The mountains were almost pure ice, and there was a big lake up in the mountains, and snow and…"

"Did you go to bed hungry?"

"What?"

"Sometimes cold and snow means that you were hungry or missing out on something. That or just frustrated. Of course, Freud seems to think that everything means you're frustrated one way or another. You feeling frustrated?"

"No. Just… just listen to me for a minute, Seth. I was rescued—or maybe taken prisoner, it's hard to say—by these… I guess I'd call them pirates. They had the accents for it at least. Then we met up with these Russian guys covered in tattoos. I think they were following us or something."

"Who was it that was following you? They say if you're being chased it means that something's on your mind. Did you see who it was?"

"I just told you. They were these tattooed Russian guys. But they weren't really following us, more like they met up with us. And there was something about a boat… And… Look, this wasn't like a normal dream, so I don't think it means anything, like for psychology or anything. What I'm saying is, it was real. And it wasn't about me. It wasn't *my* dream. I was just there. So, it doesn't really matter if they sounded English or Russian, or…"

"Russian," Seth interrupted. "That is weird. Russian, Russian, Russian… I think Freud was around before people started being afraid of the Russians. You're not a communist, are you?"

James rolled his eyes. "That's it. Put the book away. I'm not talking about this anymore."

"Relax, Jimbo. I'm just trying to help. You're the one who said you were having weird dreams. I'm just trying to help you understand them. If you didn't want to talk about it, you shouldn't have told me."

James's frustration bubbled over, not just from Seth's apparent unconcern, but out of the general confusion of the day. Where had his morning gone? If he'd really Traveled to another world, then how had it happened, and more importantly, why? Was it as real as it all seemed?

Were Sylph, Teak, and Brine real? Were the Scrim? Was he supposed to just go on as if nothing had happened? Dr. Huckabee said he should. But should Dr. Huckabee even be trusted? And then there was the ice-faced woman…

"Listen, Seth," James snapped. "I shouldn't have said anything, ok? I've just had a weird couple of days, and I don't know what to make of it. So back off."

"Fine." Seth thrust his lunch back into his book bag, followed by the textbook which promptly squished his lunch. "But if you're gonna be like this all day, I'm not covering you next time you want to ditch school."

* * *

Friday afternoons always dragged on too long. The promise of the weekend made concentration difficult, and James was too preoccupied with thoughts of fainting, falling, the Frozen World, and Dr. Huckabee to pay attention to his schoolwork. The only class he even halfway listened to was the one continuing the discussion of dreams. But James saw no symbolism in the things he'd done, no whispers of the subconscious in the people he'd met. The things he'd seen had been very strange, but very real. Just as Dr. Huckabee was strange but real, and Huckabee's coin was strange but real.

James wrote diligently in his notebook, pausing to look up at his teacher at all the appropriate times, though absorbing none of the words. But he didn't write notes from his class, he put down everything he remembered from the night before.

"Rule One:" he wrote, "Try to blend in. Never tell anyone who you are. Because that would be bad. Rule Two: Don't stay out too long. Time passes back home as well. I get that now. Rule Three: don't hurt anything and don't kill anything. And Rule Four: Dr. Huckabee is a worthless ass."

James chewed on the eraser of his pencil. He'd spent all day trying to conjure the exact words of the rules, and though he thought he had their essence, he was sure that he wasn't remembering them exactly. Only Rule Four—the important but unspoken rule—had James kept consistent throughout his day.

Assuming he *was* waking up in other worlds, then the rules made sense. First off, he was supposed to keep his mouth shut. James thought that meant both in real life and in one of the capital "D" dreams. And except for talking to Seth, he was doing a pretty good job. If James's recollection of the Frozen World was at all accurate, he would get one of those blinding, ear-splitting headaches if he even came close to giving away who he was. And two reminders had been enough.

Rule Two said that time kept passing. And that one had already been proven. He'd stayed a whole lot longer in the Frozen World than he had in the Ocean World (assuming they were kind of the same thing), and in a way maybe he stayed too long. Maybe that was why he didn't wake up until he was already at the bus stop. Maybe Seth had been right. Maybe James *had* been sleepwalking. But he thought it odd he could have made it so far without anyone noticing. Best not to take the risk anymore.

Rule Three, about not hurting or killing stuff, seemed more moral than anything. James thought it a kickback from "Thou shalt not kill," or something else Sunday School-related. Either way, James didn't think he was much of a threat of breaking the Rule. In the Frozen World, at least, everyone had been twice his size and heavily armed. But what would the *next* world look like? Would every night be a different world? And what would happen to the Frozen World, Brine, Sylph, Teak, and everyone? James remembered the intensity of the world's screams for help, but he hadn't seen anything wrong with it. And he certainly wasn't sure what he could have done differently. What was he missing?

All in all, it wasn't much to go on, but James thought the rules were still answers of a sort. Because having rules to follow leaned weight to the "realness" of the dreams. And if the other answers had fallen into his lap, then James didn't see any reason why he couldn't figure out what he was supposed to be doing in his dreams when he had one. Or maybe it was just waiting for Dr. Huckabee to show up and finish off the rest of the Rules. Or maybe it wouldn't be Huckabee. When last they parted, he said he was going to send someone to find James. But when, and more importantly, where?

The class bell rang, and the students began to file into the hall. As he normally did, James held on for a few moments to finish his notes, even though today's notes weren't school-related. James heard a chuckling behind him and the hairs on the back of his neck rose. *I am not in the mood for this today.*

James's notebook was jerked off his desk, his pencil streaking across the surface as it was yanked away. He looked up at the smirking face of Greg, with Duncan and Marc standing dutifully to either side of their ringleader.

"Well, well, well, what have we here." Greg began to read in a high-pitched voice he told James was 'just like he sounded.' "'Rule One Try to blend in. Never tell anyone who you are 'cause that would be bad. Rule Two…'" Greg paused. "What is this crap, James? You starting some kind of secret club for pansies? Don't you and your butt-buddy Seth do enough of that?" Greg wadded up the sheet and threw it at James. The paper bounced off his forehead and onto the floor. Though he knew it would only attract attention, James reached down to grab the wad and slipped it into his pocket.

"Oh, jeez. How lame can you get?" Greg chuckled.

James gritted his teeth. "Go away, Greg. Not now. Find someone else to bother."

"Woo-ooo-ooo! Better watch out, Greg," Duncan said with mock-seriousness. "I think you're making him angry."

Greg snickered. "Yeah, what gives, James? Not now? You not in the mood? Tell me, are you in the mood for *THIS?*" Acting in unison,

Greg and Marc gripped James's chair and tipped it backward. James was sent sprawling to the floor, his books and pencil falling beside him. As James untangled himself from the chair, Greg, Duncan, and Marc walked away, laughing as they went.

James dusted himself off and gathered his fallen items, thrusting them one by one back into his book bag. He didn't deserve this. He had enough problems to not have to worry about his old turncoat friends who couldn't bear to be near someone different. *They should have stuck by me*, James thought. *They didn't have to put me down. They could have seen this through.* He sighed, shouldered his backpack, and headed for the door. He wondered if he would have done the same if it had been Marc or Duncan who started to fall. Would he have stepped in and helped? Or would he have jumped at the chance to rise one notch higher in the middle-school social ladder?

James thought he knew that answer, but he wasn't sure. The only thing he knew for sure was that he wanted to get home, go to sleep, and leave this behind… at least for a little while.

* * *

James had a plan.

Distractions seemed to be his biggest problem. School, bullies, fighting parents, and fickle friends. They all got in the way of him thinking clearly. And he knew that the best way to get some thinking done was to spend some time alone. He'd go camping. Camping and fishing. And he knew just the place. There was a collection of spoil islands between the mainland and the beach that could be reached by a short paddle in a canoe. They should also be warm enough that he wouldn't need much more gear than a sleeping bag and his fishing pole.

Seth would have to come, of course. James knew his mom wouldn't let him have it any other way in case he did fall at the wrong time. But James knew that Seth could tell when he wanted some peace. Sometimes, no words needed to be spoken between them. And if Dr.

Huckabee decided to pay another unannounced visit, all the better to have a witness.

By the time the school bus reached James's neighborhood, his and Seth's argument from the morning had been forgotten. Unfortunately, Seth wasn't going to be able to go camping as he was supposed to head to Columbia to spend the weekend with his cousins. But, James thought, his mom didn't have to know that.

James strode into his parents' kitchen. His mother was sitting at the kitchen table, peeling shrimp for dinner. The salt from the shrimp tickled his nose like the miasma of the marsh. He rifled through the cupboard to extract a granola bar, then sat down at the table opposite his mom.

"Hey, Mom, can I camp out on Greeson's Island tonight?"

James's mother set her shrimp aside and then gave him the look he knew was reserved for ridiculous suggestions. "Not tonight. It'll be dark in an hour and a half, and it'll take almost that long for you to get your things together. I'm closing you down on this one, kiddo. Just you and Seth? Or was anyone else planning on going?"

"Just us." James fumbled with the wrapper of his granola bar. He knew fighting his mother's snap judgment was rarely if ever successful, so he shifted to his secondary plan. "What about tomorrow? Can I go camp out tomorrow? I'll leave in the morning, so I'll have plenty of time to do everything I need to do. I'll even get it all set tonight. Can I? Please?"

"Well"—his mother dragged the thought out, though James knew he had already won—"I suppose so. But you have to wait until after your little spell."

James cursed to himself. His mother had pulled that maneuver more than once, not that the catch wasn't reasonable. If he had fainted once in a day, the chance of it happening again was slim to none. *After* James had fainted, his mom treated him almost like an everyday, ordinary boy. But until then, he was watched, and watched, and watched. James pondered the dilemma, wondering if he could fake passing out when it finally hit him. He *hadn't* had a fall today. The head rush, the blurred vision, the hallucinations, none of it. On the other hand, he may have fallen that morning in the lost time between waking up and the bus. Or maybe last night's fall had been big enough for two days' worth.

His mother interrupted his musings. "It's settled then. Oh! I almost forgot. One of your teachers came by earlier today asking about you. She wanted to know where you went yesterday." James felt his cheeks flush. "She wanted to know if you'd left school early, but I told her that had been the day before—for your dental exam." His mother gave him a conspirator's wink. They had long used the "dentist excuse" for people they didn't know overly well. No one *ever* asked about a trip to the dentist. Psychiatrists were different.

"Who was it, Mom?"

His mother furrowed her brow. "You know, I can't remember. I'm sure she told me, but I can't for the life of me place her name. Striking appearance though. Looked European." His mother laughed. "I'm certain I've never met her before, which was why I thought it odd she'd come here. Especially during the school day. Really didn't seem friendly enough to be a teacher to me."

A chill ran James's spine. "Don't you think that's weird?" he asked.

"Never thought about it."

As his mother returned to humming and peeling shrimp, James tried to reverse his sinking mood. His mother *must* have been talking about the ice-faced woman. If only his mom had remembered the name, then James could have been sure. And that was even more peculiar. His mom knew the names of every teacher, coach, church leader, and friend that James had ever had. Her memory was frustratingly accurate. Had the ice-faced woman done something to her? Like Dr. Huckabee did? Is that why she couldn't remember?

Be cool, James, he thought. *I can't overreact. I have to blend in. Look normal. Rule Number One.*

"Alright, Mom. I'm going to finish up my homework now so I don't have to worry about it on Sunday."

"Aren't you going to call Seth?"

"Oh, right," James tried to correct his mistake. "I'll let him know we're off until tomorrow."

* * *

That night, James did his homework, packed his camping gear, played with the dog, ate a dinner of shrimp and rice, watched TV, talked to Seth, played basketball in the driveway, cleaned his room, and read his book.

What James did *not* do was fall. The urge never came, and the problem never occurred. But with his mind so full of anticipation for the dreams ahead, he didn't dwell on the issue. Later that night, when the moon had risen and the cicadas began their chirp, James fished Huckabee's coin out of his pants pocket. He gripped the coin hard within his palm and concentrated.

10. Land Fall

James flew across the surface of the water like a low arcing cannonball. He could clearly see his startled face in the mirrored face of the pond. For several seconds he whizzed across the surface, not slowing—and not dropping any closer—until gravity finally prevailed. As James hit the water, he skipped like a stone: Pish-pish, splish… splish… sploosh… sploosh… splash! James sunk to a stop. He floated for just a moment, his body reeling from the shock, and then straightened to find he could just touch bottom. He regarded his new surroundings, not with fear, but with wide anticipation.

Fluffy clouds drifted across a bluebird sky, the image perfectly reflected in the water below. The only disturbance on the face of the pond was the broadening ripples where James stood. He thought that the water was the most reflective he had ever seen until he took a closer look. This wasn't water at all, but a silvery liquid like mercury. Once the ripples settled, it was nothing short of a perfect mirror.

The pond was long and skinny, and James counted himself lucky that he stopped where he did, as the shore was only a dozen yards away. Circling the lake in haphazard piles was a collection of toppled monoliths. Each block of sandstone was perfectly rectangular, a hundred feet long, ten feet wide, and just as deep. The blocks were bunched in piles like firewood.

"Jesus. Where am I this time?"

A dark, liquid voice called from behind him, "You shouldn't do that, my friend."

James turned to see a man wearing a loose-fitting serape sitting cross-legged at the base of one of the monoliths.

"Swearing can be a dead give-away. It's very bad. Not so bad as saying your name or anything. But put the two together, and you may be found out."

More curious than scared, James waded over to the shore and studied the man. The observer was tanned and dusty, grime covering every inch of visible skin. His skin was reddened by the sun, and his face deeply wrinkled at the corners of his eyes and mouth. The man's deep brown eyes regarded James through shoulder-length black hair that hung in windblown locks.

"Who are you?" James asked. "And what shouldn't I do?"

The man tilted his head back and laughed. The sound echoed around him. "Look, friend, there are quite a lot of things you shouldn't be doing. But what I'm saying, is that you shouldn't swear."

James huffed, "What's it to you?"

"Not me. I don't care myself, but it should matter to you. Swearing can give you away. You said 'Jesus.' And the way you said it made me think you weren't talking to someone named Jesus, but that you were swearing." The man rose to his feet and started to amble toward him. "Of course, I've never heard of any Jesus, so I'm guessing he's a god or something, but not from around here. So maybe I do a little digging, I'm likely to find a world where there is a Jesus. Then maybe I watch you a little closer. Next time you mention where you grew up, or something you used to like to do, or a food you like to eat. Every time you tell me something about yourself, I get a little closer to figuring out who you are and where you're from. And then one day, I might just find you."

He gulped. "And if you do find me?"

The man chuckled again, but this time, James didn't hear the same humor in his voice. "I already found you, friend. That's how I followed you here. But you can sit easy for now, I'm the only one who did, and I'm here to help. Or at least give a warning. From a friend."

James's fear changed to understanding. A grin stretched his face. "Dr. Huckabee sent you, didn't he? You can Travel to other worlds, too?"

The face of the man dropped into a scowl. "And *definitely* don't do that. Name him, that is. You need to quit using names entirely. And never come right out and talk about Traveling, not unless you're absolutely, positively sure no one can hear. What if someone had been watching us? Now they know exactly who we are and who we know. You need to keep a low profile. *Low.*"

James replied sarcastically, "Because someone might be looking for me. Someone bad. I heard that part already."

"Good that you did. That'll save us time. They're called the Styx. And they don't very much care for what we do."

"Why would they care? It's just like a dream, isn't it? I'm not totally sure they aren't dreams. Or that this isn't a dream."

The dusky man squinted one eye at James. "These aren't dreams, friend. You can quit pretending they are and snap out of your warm and fuzzy little reality. And we're not just visiting, this isn't for our amusement. We're not sightseers and we're not tourists. Though many Travelers are, of course, far more than I'd like. But I hope you're different." The dusty man paused, he folded his arms across his chest. "Our friend the doctor said he saw something in you. So, I'm here to give you a choice."

James swallowed hard. "What kind of choice?"

"Walk with me. And here, dress local."

The dusky man tossed a checkered serape at him. James crawled from the pool and draped the garment around his shoulders. He stepped quickly to the man's side.

"You can decide to be a tourist if you want. I won't stop you. But before you make that decision, tell me. Have you heard the screams of these worlds? Do you hear them now?"

James recalled the howls of agony that he'd heard in the Frozen World. The land had pleaded for him to help. To test the waters, James concentrated on the *Thatness* surrounding him. As he did, a new wailing began. This world was also in pain, though the cries were less urgent, less overwhelming. James released his concentration, and the ultra-fine clarity of the *Thatness* drifted away. "Yes. Yes, I can. I hear them."

The tanned man nodded. He folded his thick arms across his chest. "The reason we can do what we do is that these worlds need help. They call to people like us that can hear them, people who can look beyond their own fragile reality. Now you can answer that call, or you can watch the worlds die."

"Is that what the Styx do?"

The dusky man shook his head. "No. The Styx don't just watch. They are out to destroy worlds. And to stop those who'd do otherwise. That's why you have to keep your head low. And no matter what you do, don't let anyone know you're doing it."

"But… why? Why do the Styx want to destroy worlds? How is that even possible? Seriously, destroying an entire *world?*"

"I'm not here to give you a history lesson. There are books for that. And saying the S-word is about as bad as saying your name. Just suggesting they exist is enough to send one after you. I think we are safe to speak here, at least for a minute or two. But it's a habit you should practice. And that's all I'm going to say about that."

For a minute, the dusky man remained silent. James followed behind as he walked up a short trail to the top of a rock outcropping. The man sat down and gestured for him to do the same. James looked out over the reflective lake at where mountains and sky were a perfect copy of the real ones overhead. Finally, he spoke.

"So, how do you save a world? I don't know where to even begin."

"Keep your eyes, ears, and mind open. That's really all we have time for now. As I said, I'm not here to give you a history lesson, and I'm not here to give you a Traveling lesson either. Our friend wanted me to warn you, and so I am. But I'll take it one step further. So, here's some advice. You need to choose and choose now if you're going to pick a side in this fight, or just be a tourist. There's no switching sides later on, much as you might like to." The man looked at James with a discerning eye. "But for now, it's time for you to go back."

"But I just got here."

"Not back home, not yet. I think you should take one more look around you. And this time, think about what I said."

"Um, ok." James felt the man's fingers tighten on his shoulder. "But I have more questions."

"Humph. I'll bet you do. Another time, perhaps."

"No! Wait, I—"

11. Spout

James's vision blurred. He felt himself falling through the dark, and then the light slowly came back. He wasn't falling, he was sitting in a small, dank room enveloped in the musk of numerous piles of furs. Just beyond the walls, he heard the sloshing of waves. A boat. He was belowdecks in a boat, and the heavy salt air filled and surrounded him. As his senses adjusted, James noticed a kaleidoscope of other scents. The oiled teak of the cabin walls layered against cinnamon, saffron, peppers, clove, and other spices. James inhaled deeply; then exhaled with contentment.

A deep voice interrupted him. "Ah, lad. Welcome back to the land of the living. Enjoy your lie down?" James looked straight above him to see the grinning face of Brine looking down through the hatch above him. The large man lowered himself through the hatch and took a seat across from James. "I hope you don't mind having to bunk in the storeroom. I thought it would be better to keep you away from Slagish and those bloody runics." Brine dropped his voice to a whisper. "I mean, from those bloody traders. The last thing I want is for them to start sizing you up and try to pass you off as a Blank. That said, I recommend you getting a tattoo. Fake'un of course, though once we get there, you can get the real thing if you want. Me, the captain, and Teak all got fitted before we left."

Realization clicked into place. James's heart leaped in his chest. *I'm back! I'm back in the Frozen World and I didn't even realize it. But how did I get back? Did Huckabee's friend put me here? And for that matter, why didn't I fall out of the sky? It's like I never even left. And I don't think that Brine or anyone else noticed I was gone either. But I'm back... I'm really back!*

The momentary elation washed away, replaced by the memory of Huckabee's friend. Put here or not, James was back for a reason. This world was dying. As such, it needed saving—whatever that meant—and James had to decide if he was here to help. *Alright*, James thought. *I'll keep my eyes open. I'll see what there is to see, and what I can do. I'll give it a go.*

"Oy, Jay? You listenin', laddie?"

James, still deep in thought, took a moment to react to his borrowed name. "Yeah, sorry. Just had my mind on something else. What were you saying?"

"I said you should get yourself a tattoo."

"Are you kidding? My mom would throw a fit."

Brine looked him over, one eye squinted in disbelief. "You're a long way from your mother, laddie. Right now, you need to be worried about the runics. We don't want Slagish and his men after you, and having a tattoo can help guard that." Brine paused. He placed his hand on his knees and cocked his head to the side. "You don't know what I'm talking about, do you? You really are confused, not just fakin' it."

"Sorry, sorry, I'm just… a little foggy. But you're right. This is all new to me. I don't know where we are, what we're doing, where we're going, anything." James fished for the brief collection of facts he'd gathered from his last visit to the Frozen World. "The only thing I do know is that you and your friends were hired by this guy Slagish to sail him and his friends somewhere. And that's *all* I know." James paused. "Except that we're way off in the middle of nowhere."

"Hah… hah!" Brine broke into a grin. "The 'middle of nowhere', I love it. Hadn't heard that one before, but that's the best way I've ever heard this place described."

"So, where *are* we going? I mean I heard that guy Slagish say we were going to some mountain. Aha! Now I remember. We're going to Kano, or Kai'nau I think he called it. Kai'nau, that's it. That's definitely what he said."

Brine looked back at James in horror.

"What? What did I say?"

"Great wind-crashin' typhoons of a red-runnin' albatross! You understood 'im? You understood what Slagish said? You mean to say, you *understood* 'im?"

James's ears burned in embarrassment. "Yeah. So?"

Brine threw up his hands in disbelief. "So? So, Cap'n Sylph spent three years trying to learn that demon-blasted language, and she can still only poke by. You're telling me, sitting right there—not two days gone since ye were yanked from the snowbank—that you speak Slagish's language *and* ours? Here, stick out your tongue." Brine held him by the chin. James obliged him with a prolonged "Ahhh" which the large man used to inspect all sides of his tongue, the insides of his cheeks, and the roof of his mouth. Brine let go of James's chin, apparently unsatisfied.

"What were you looking for?"

"A mark. A rune. Wee one, I suppose, otherwise I'd a seen it earlier. That's one I wouldn't mind having myself, sometimes. Especially around here. But I'll tell you, laddie, if you do understand their language, then I think we'll find you a job alright." Brine broke into a grin. "You'll be scrubbin' decks, of course, everyone gets to do that. But I've got another job for ya, too. While you're workin', you can be listenin'. The cap'n says we can't talk to Slagish's men, but it doesn't mean you can't overhear what they have to say." Brine snorted with mirth. "Deck hand and translator, all the best men wear two hats. So, do we have an accord?" Brine extended his hand to the somewhat confused James, who paused before grasping.

"So, now will you tell me what's going on?" James asked.

"Why would I hide something from one of me mates? But first, I need to clear it with Cap'n Sylph. So, what do ya think?"

James returned Brine's infectious smile, then shook heartily.

At Brine's suggestion, James shed about half of his furs. The steam rising from the Alpinsea warmed the otherwise-frozen wasteland. Slagish and the tattoo-covered men, however, did not seem to notice the warmth any more than they had noticed the cold when at the port.

He followed Brine up through the hatch and onto the deck of the Killdevil III. A fifteen-knot wind blew steadily across the port rail, heeling the boat slightly as it cut though the waves on a reach. The sloop's sails were rigged at full-haul and James saw no hint of damage across the pristine canvas. Even the tattooed entourage seemed relaxed by the journey. Only Slagish kept a perpetual scowl, alternating his glare between Sylph at the helm, a locked hatch at his feet, and the distance where the Alpinsea's fog obscured the path.

Captain Sylph seemed unaffected by the emotional state of her passengers. The easy smirk on her face changed into a genuine smile as Brine approached with James in tow. She nodded for Brine to take the wheel as she moved aside and began a series of stretches that James would have attributed to a yoga master.

"How tacks the wind, Cap'n?" Brine asked, his eyes fixed on the horizon.

"A five-degree north, not ten minutes ago. She'll keep moving, but the heading's true for a ways now." Sylph nodded to James, between stretches. "So, our wee sleeper's up again?"

"Yep," Brine replied. "And I've a spot of good news for you. Guess who speaks Scrim?" He jerked his head at James.

"Rune, then. Did you find it?" Sylph asked.

"Ain't a rune."

Sylph ceased her stretching to regard James. "Not a rune? So, where'd you learn it? You don't look like one of Slagish's countrymen. Not pale enough. And it's not usual to do things the old way. I was proud of myself in that regard."

James shrugged. "I'm still having a hard time remembering. But… wait. What's the old way?"

Brine interrupted before Sylph could answer. "Guess what else he can do, eh? Scrub decks. Said he's spent a wee bit of time on ships himself. World traveler, ya ken?" A grin spread across his face. "So, can we keep him? I've always wanted a pet."

Sylph sighed. "Ok, Brine. But remember, he's your responsibility. And you have to speak for him if Slagish or any of the rest of the Scrim start asking questions. Do *you* ken? Though I think we're past all that. Ok then, Jay, if you're on our side, I need to know where you're a-coming from. Do you know any other languages? Hunni or Foltrick? Those could come in mighty handy once we head home."

"Uh, I speak a little Spanish. Un pocito." James held his fingers up in the universal symbol for "little bit." He wondered if Spanish even existed in this world. And if it did, did they call it Spanish?

"Not familiar with that one." Sylph mused. "Next question. How about weapons. Can you fight a bit? Daggers, swords, guns, bows, load a cannon? Don't be mistaken, I'm not arming you 'til I trust you. But I need to know if we get in a pinch."

James thought for a second. On the one hand, he didn't know a thing about fighting. On the other hand, if Rule Three was to be followed, he wasn't supposed to hurt anything even if he could. He opted instead for a little mistruth. "Um, I'm kind of not allowed to fight. I'm a, uh, pacifist."

"A what? What's a pacifist? Is that some kind of monk?"

"I guess. I, uh, I swore that I wouldn't hurt anything. Sacred oath." James bit his lip, awaiting Sylph and Brine's response to the obvious lie. Jesus, could he stutter a little more? Couldn't he come up with something better? But when seconds passed, and neither Sylph nor Brine reacted, James realized they had believed him. Completely.

Sylph said, "I guess we can't win 'em all. And like I said, I wasn't going to give you anything pointy or loud."

Brine jumped in, "What about shipboard, then? What have you sailed?" His face wrinkled in distaste. "Tell me you're not a steamer."

James shook his head. "I've crewed on J-24s, Tartan 37's, and a couple of single-handed's. Lazers and Sunfish—no Cats or anything like that." James paused. "Never a three-masted boat. Nothing this big."

"Can't say I've heard of half those boats. Any for that matter. But at least they're boats, aye? At least you know wind and water. Can you swim?"

"Of course." James smiled back.

Time passed with only the whip of the breeze and the flap of the rigging playing harmony to the steady rush of the waves. James wondered if he had been found worthy. In a way, he didn't think it *mattered* what he had said. If they didn't know what Spanish was, they certainly wouldn't understand a Sunfish, or pacifism. But they did know the water. James hoped that was enough to tie them together. He relished the feeling for only a moment. He may have Rule Three covered with the pacifism bit, but he still didn't know where he was. The time had come to get the answers Brine had promised.

"So where are we going? And what's that Slagish guy have hidden in the hatch? He's been staring at it ever since I've been watching."

Sylph and Brine exchanged worried looks. Finally, Sylph answered. "We're headed to the mountain of Kai'nau. After we've crossed the Alpinsea, we've another day's journey on foot to get there."

James didn't have to work hard to look confused. "What's at Kai'nau?"

Sylph smiled, the kind of smile reserved for a child or the naïve. "He really doesn't know anything, does he, Brine? How can someone be so smart and so ignorant at the same time?" Sylph motioned for Brine to move over and she regained her place at the helm. "Ok, Brine, if Jay is your pet, then you win the honor of bringin' him up to speed. If he's going to be any use to us at all, he needs to know the basics. Got that?"

Brine nodded. "Right, we'll just hang out on the fishwell then."

"Aye. Just check the lines before you go."

Brine ordered James to wait for him at the boat's stern. Though confused, James was certainly excited to have someone explain things. Maybe he could finally start doing whatever it was that he was supposed to be doing, maybe even figure out what Huckabee's friend wanted. He crawled to the stern of the boat and rested one hand on the base of the thick traveler running from either side and acting as the connecting leg between the mainsheet and the Killdevil's boom. He had only a second to inspect the craftsmanship of the boat before Brine had returned.

"Alright, follow me, laddie, and don't fall in." Brine swung over the stern of the boat and climbed down to a small platform hanging off the rear. The prevalent smell of fish implied that this was where anything caught by the vessel was gutted and cleaned. The platform, framed from weathered teak, dipped occasionally into the water, though Brine and James received no more than the occasional splash of water from the incongruously tepid sea.

Brine settled down cross-legged on the fishwell and leaned back against the stern. "For sailors like me, Sylph, and Teak, there are things you want to do, and things you don't want to do, and things you just stay as far away from as possible. An Alpinsea crossing is one of those things you just don't do when you've got any sense whatsoever. Look around you, Jay. The fog makes it impossible to see, you've got ice chunks floating around, the depth is unpredictable, and if you ever went overboard, you'd be dead in a matter of seconds. What's more, there's no way to make repairs even if you needed to. There's only one reason to cross the Alpinsea."

"To get to Kai'nau?"

"That's the destination, not the reason."

"What's the reason?"

"Money, laddie. Great big stinkin' gobs of money. And that's what Slagish and his boys are paying us. The Cap'n and I talked it over before we took the job. And we decided that it's something worth doing once, and only once. Any more than that and yer pushing yer luck. That's why I think Teak is a bit crazy. I think this is his fourth or fifth run across the Alpinsea, but I'm not judging."

James nodded. "Ok, so you have to cross the Alpinsea to get to Kai'nau. So why are we going there?"

"Money. I just said that."

James sighed. "Then why does Slagish want to go there?"

"Now we get to the meat of the matter. The only reason anyone *ever* goes to Kai'nau is to get a rune drawn. Slagish and his boys buy and sell runes, take orders for them, and carry 'em. They are pretty good at designing runes, too. They're supposed to be the best in the world when it comes down to coming up with designs for one. But when it comes to drawing them, actually etching them, you need a master artist. And there is only one of those in the world."

"At Kai'nau?"

"Exactly."

Realization swept over James. "The tattoos? You're talking about the tattoos! That's what runes are, aren't they? Wait a minute… how do you trade a tattoo?"

Brine closed his eyes. "So, you don't know what a rune is either, huh. Ok, I'll give you the short version. Runes are how normal people can do magic. You see, it all started…"

Brine was interrupted by Teak shouting from over the transom. "Spouts! Brine, we need you topside. Six spouts coming in fast. We need to take a reef. Now."

Brine was on his feet and over the rear lifeline before James could react. After the large man disappeared over the top, he reached down to help James follow. "We'll talk later. We've work to do now, laddie. Ready to earn yer keep?"

James nodded dully; then grasped Brine's hand and clambered back over the rail.

The deck of the Killdevil III swarmed with activity. The Scrim scurried under the steady bark of orders from Sylph and Teak. Brine soon joined the fray, shouting commands at the Scrim as they furiously worked to lower the jib to one-third mast, gathering the excess and wrapping it tightly so that the sail could still function. James had seen the same activity during his own excursions on boats. The crew wanted to reduce the power of the sails. And now he saw why.

On the horizon, eight funneled shapes were winding toward the Killdevil III. Waterspouts, the sea's version of the tornado, and enough to destroy the most durable of even modern craft. And though James was impressed by the construction of the Killdevil III, the ship was still primitive by his standards. If a waterspout hit, they were done for.

James looked at Sylph, his eyes pleading for instruction.

"Hatches. Now," the captain barked. "Close and fasten, miss nary a one. Then into my cabin. There's a black trunk with silver buckles. Check it's latched and secure. Go."

James took off at a run, his sea-legs adjusting to the side-sway of the lilting deck. He scurried from hatch to hatch, closing and securing the bronze clasps surrounding the unhinged sides of the portholes. Two in the stern, four surrounding the mast, two on the foredeck, and one in the bow. He secured all the hatches except for the one leading into the captain's cabin. That one he climbed through, twisting his body as he entered to land crouched in the center of the room.

He had only a moment to appreciate the luxury of Captain Sylph's cabin. The wooden surfaces were highly polished. The bronze buckles on the cabinets lining the walls did not even rattle with the heel of the ship. Everything was in its place, secured with the utmost care, and precisely ordered. The same could be said for a chest in the corner of the room. The black surface of the chest was smooth and reflective like obsidian. If the cabinets, lanterns, bed, and cupboards were secure, the chest was impenetrable. It was fastened to the floor with seven hex-headed bolts—seven per side that is. Held shut by nine latches, locked by two padlocks as well as a key in the center, James thought a bank vault would be in more danger of flying open. Then why did Sylph want him to check on it? What did it contain that was so important?

The cabin door slammed open. Two bare-chested Scrim speckled with dark tattoos—runes—grinned at him. James received the same flash of inspiration he'd had when at the port, as though the tattoos spoke to him. *Pain. Nightshade.* The words echoed through his mind to where James could no longer divorce the unbidden names with the people approaching. But whatever their intentions, he had no intention of standing his ground. Even if he stood a chance against the muscled, tattooed men—which he didn't—he had Rule Three to consider. Without hesitation, James leaped for the portal above his head. He twisted his body and had landed on the deck with an ease that took him entirely by surprise. He thought that such an ascent would be painfully difficult. But whether adrenaline or simply another oddity of the Frozen World, the act had been effortless.

"Captain Sylph! Captain Sylph!" James darted across the reeling deck. The winds had risen to a terrible force, both unbalancing him and snatching away his words. He closed the gap quickly. "Captain Sylph, two of the Scrim were in your cabin. And…"

"The chest? Was it closed?"

"Yes, but…"

"Good enough. Go help Brine. Move!"

James darted his eyes around. The large man was on the windward side, the mainsheet clutched in his hands and his leg hooked through one of the deck lines.

A wave crashed over the boat, tumbling James across the deck. If not for grabbing a loose halyard, he would have been swept over the rail. The screams from behind him indicated that not all the Scrim had been as fortunate. He whipped his head to see the fallen men, then turned back to watch the oncoming storm. The ship was in the center of the tempest now. The eight waterspouts danced around them, snaking in all directions. The chaos, completely without reason to James, seemed the source of Sylph, Brine, and Teak's concentration. For every tilt of the vessel, Sylph would adjust the helm, Brine the mainsail, and Teak would dance around the foredeck, cinching, loosening, and pulling the ropes spidering from the mast.

James watched in awe. Sylph's orders to aid Brine had been washed from his mind as cleanly as the wave had washed across the deck. The three Islanders were amazing. They conducted a ballet of nautical skill that James had never seen in his whole life being around boats. Their extreme prowess was contrasted by the floundering Scrim, as they desperately clung to ropes and stays. And most astounding, the Killdevil III seemed to be winning. Of the eight waterspouts, six had either passed or disappeared into the swirling fog. And of the two, only one appeared a threat. The conical monstrosity twisted and danced across the water, leaping hundreds of feet in the air before touching down again. Without reason. Without purpose.

"Ready about!" Sylph roared as she swung the ship to starboard, turning the nose through the headwind. The sails snapped to the opposite tack, the deck heeling in the opposite direction. Sylph glanced first at the heading, then scanned the ship and the placement of her crew. Her eyes mirrored the determination and chaos of the churning sea.

Another wave swept across the deck. James nearly lost his grip on his lifeline, the rope burning across his palms. After the wave had passed, he released his grip and scrambled to the opposite rail, securing himself again on the high side. A cry leaped from James's throat. The waterspout had shifted as well. The course was unmistakable. Unless it changed its path, it would plow through the Killdevil III. The time for maneuvering had ceased. Only time now to hold on.

James became suddenly aware of Huckabee's coin growing cold and heavy in his coat pocket. *Time to go*, James thought. *If there was ever a time to go home, that time is now. I can do this. I've just got to concentrate.* James opened his mind to the world, he looked for the inherent *Thisness* of himself and contrasted it against the *Thatness* of the Frozen World: deck, crew, storm, sea—all of it. James increased his focus and—

A roar. Not the roll of thunder, but the single deafening echo of a cannon. The sound was like the crack of a whip swung by the hand of god. James's concentration slipped through his fingers, dropping him back into the horrible reality of the Frozen World. His senses blinked again to the feelings of cold and wind, the duality of *Thisness* and *Thatness* forgotten.

The sea glowed with a color like the purple afterimage following a lightning strike. The glow focused into a singularity, a pinpoint of darkness so intense it seemed to have poked through the sky itself. The point raced toward the waterspout, and upon reaching its destination, exploded, becoming a column of darkness, twice as thick as the waterspout and reaching from the unseen depths of the Alpinsea to the storm clouds overhead. Then the column of night collapsed, the thunderclap sounded again. And in its place—nothing. The waterspout was gone, as though it had never existed. The ocean where the spout had stood had been erased from the surface to the depths. Even the clouds overhead had been sucked to nothingness. The world paused, as if nature had been caught off guard, and then the waters collapsed again on themselves, a splash rocketing upward as the water filled the unexpected gap.

James darted his eyes to Sylph. The unflappable captain was not staring at the clean bored hole of reality. Her eyes, as well as the rest of the remaining crew, were fixed upon Slagish. The Scrim leader's arms were outstretched, his fur-lined coat long since whipped overboard. Across the man's back was a tattoo. The rune shone with brilliant white light, fading quickly to return to its dark form. And from the stroke and loop of the character, a word appeared, then vanished in James's mind.

The Nothing.

12. Cargo

The storm was now only a darkening of the sky to the south. Sylph, Brine, Teak, and Slagish's men toiled with stoic reluctance. Three of the Scrim had been swept overboard, never to be seen again. Five others were recovering from their drenching—two scalded by the Alpinsea's heat, and three chilled from the winterland's cold.

James looked over the ship's rail, his feet dangling over the edge. Until now, he'd never seen death. But the firsthand experience with mortality, and his own near demise, seemed insignificant versus what Slagish had done.

Magic. Power.

James still considered his falls and waking up in different worlds to be something like dreaming. Terrifying in their newness, but relatively benign. Even Dr. Huckabee's vanishing act seemed harmless. But what Slagish had done disturbed James in a way that he did not anticipate. The Scrim leader had erased a force of nature. *And no one cared!* Everyone but him went along with their business, as though nothing strange had happened. Until now, he had not grasped the alien nature of this world.

"Maybe I am just a tourist," James muttered, remembering the words of Dr. Huckabee's friend. "Maybe I don't belong." But James thought he did belong, at least a little. Or at least, people seemed to *think* he belonged. Sylph and Brine both had taken him in, and he'd become an instant confidant. They were telling him things they shouldn't tell a stranger, but why? Why would they trust him when they so clearly mistrusted Slagish and the Scrim?

The answer crept forward slowly, tickling the corner of James's mind and then creeping toward the center. These people trusted him because… because the Frozen World wanted them to. The world wanted James to help it, and so *it* in turn was helping *him*. That's why he could understand their languages. That's why people told him things without thinking. That's why he was sitting in a boat, crossing a sea, on top of a mountain. This wasn't some bizarre coincidence. This was deliberate. Some greater power *did not want* him to be *just* a tourist. A pad of footsteps caused James to glance over his shoulder. Brine, sweat glistening on his brow, settled beside him. The large man stuck his trunk-sized legs over the railing, his feet dangling almost a foot below James's.

"You ever see a thing such as that before, laddie?" Brine muttered. The normal spitfire was markedly absent from his tone.

James shook his head.

"Aye. Was a first for me, too. Sure I've seen the little stuff, but nothing quite like that. It was actually a lot harder for me—emotional-wise—to watch the 'Devil get shrunk to nothing than to see Slagish suck up a waterspout. Personal attachment or some such."

James glanced over at Brine. He paused for a second to register that for him it had been just the opposite. James's mind had somehow ferreted away the memory of the Killdevil III materializing from nowhere—perhaps because he had fallen from the Frozen World so quickly afterward. But the obliteration of the waterspout was unshakable. That had been magic. Not a trick. Not a mirage.

"It's those tattoos, isn't it?" James whispered. "Those are the runes. Is that how it works? You never answered me last time."

Brine didn't reply immediately. Instead, he regarded James with a querulous eye. "Of course it's the runes, laddie. You can't be telling me you've never heard of a runic before? Never once in your wee bitty life? How can you speak Scrim language and not know of runes?"

James groaned in frustration. "I've been *trying* to tell you from the beginning. But every time I do, we get hit by tornados or storms, or someone pulls us in one direction or another. So please tell me what's going on."

Brine shrugged. "Fine. I suppose you can't stay stuck in yer ignorance forever—though you've been doing a fine job so far, I reckon. I mean, if I had gotten to your age without knowing what a…"

"Brine. Come on."

The large man grinned. "Got ya. Ok, here's the rough version, leastaways. There's magic in the world. You know it, I know it, everyone's known it since the beginning of when people were knowing things at all. But what we also know is that magic isn't in wands or jewels, or magic lamps, or any such stuff of stories. Magic is only in people, ya ken? For all the guns and steamships, only people have souls. Only people have magic."

James remained silent.

Brine continued, "Now the problem is that it takes years and years and years of training to do the tiniest wee little bit when it comes to magic. And some people may never even have the ability in the first place. So why bother your bleedin' head about the thing? Why spend your whole life looking for something you might not ever be able to do? Then—or leastaways I hear it—someone discovered the runes."

Brine scratched his head. "A rune is a mark, imprinted not just on the skin but on the soul itself. The rune is a shortcut to the magic that used to take a lifetime of training. You get an etcher—that's someone who can draw the runes—to Inscribe you. 'Inscribe' is a fancy word for doin' you up with a rune. And if all goes well, the power's in you. You rune-up someone and they can do just about anything. Get stronger, breathe water…"

"Make tornados disappear?"

"Aye. That too. Like I said, just about anything. But there's a price, ya ken."

"A price?"

"Ya-bugger there's a price. And I'm not just talking about the fees the etchers charge—though that's enough to make a crashing wave pause and take notice. Nope, the price is in life. Your own personal-like life. Putting a rune on you is as good as cutting your life right in half, maybe three-quarters, maybe more." Brine shrugged. "Or maybe just a wee bit. Or maybe not at all. Some people can have a hundred runes before they've had too many. Some will die from just one."

James asked, "And there is no way to tell how many is too many?"

"Not that I know of, but there are people that do. Just like some people can judge a good horse or a fast ship just by lookin' at it. Slagish, now he's one of those that can tell. That's why he's made a name for himself as a runic trader. He can tell what kind of person can take what kind of rune. It's the how that's lost on me. You ken what I'm sayin'?"

James shrugged. "Sure. Runes are magic, but they're risky, too. You go too big, and it could kill you. It's kind of like Russian Roulette.

"Russian Roulette?"

James opted against explaining the game to Brine. "It's a game of chance. Like poker, or cards, or dice, or anything. But if you lose, you die."

Brine leaned back against the deck. He put his hands behind his head and closed his eyes. "You're a quick one, Jay. Aye, a right lightnin' devil of wit and learnin' you are. I suppose you have to be to speak all those tongues, but you're still quick."

For a moment, James wondered about how neatly and easily the idea of the runes and runics felt in his mind. This wasn't something to be questioned, it was simply the truth. If runes and runics were the way of this world, then James wouldn't argue. To do so would be arguing the rules of any game. But you can't play a game without knowing the rules. And if he was going to help this world—or see what it took to help it—then that's exactly what he needed to know.

James leaned back on the deck in imitation of Brine. "So, what's in the hold?"

Brine sat up straight. "Beg pardon?"

"What's in the hold? What are we carrying that's so valuable? If Slagish can change the weather with a flash of purple light, then what's so worth protecting?"

Brine sighed deeply. "I won't hide it from you, laddie. But if you look at the facts, you'll know the answer to that too. You asked earlier how you can trade runes."

"Yeah, that still doesn't make sense to me. I understand buying a tattoo for yourself, but how do you turn around and sell that to someone else? You can't move a tattoo, can you?"

"No, laddie, you can't."

The blood drained from James's face. He realized what had been unspoken. "There are people down there, aren't there? Slagish sells *people*. That's what this is all about. Slaves. You're slave traders."

"Not us. Slagish and his boys are the traders. And these aren't just normal people, either. They're runics, or at least they will be. Once they get their runes, there's no telling what they can do."

"But you're still helping Slagish sell *people*. I don't see what the difference…"

Brine poked him square in the chest. "Listen, laddie. I don't like what we're a-doing any more than you do. Do you think it's the Alpinsea that makes me hate being up here? Nonsense. This here sea don't scare me, I've crossed ten times worse. I hate it here 'cause I know what we're helping to do. But Captain Sylph, she lets on she knows something I don't. So, I take my orders, and I keep my nose down. And I trust you should do the same."

James heard a shuffle of footsteps behind him and looked up to see Sylph. Her legs were spread at shoulder width, and her arms were folded across her chest. Sylph's eyes carried a look caught somewhere between scorn and criticism. "So, Jay, you learn what you be needing to know?"

James frowned deeply. "I think I learned too much. I kind of liked it better when I didn't."

"Well, lads"—Sylph's face was stern—"we all do the jobs we're given. So now that you know what we're on about, are you willing to help?"

"Do I have a choice?"

Sylph shrugged. "Not really. If you don't be holding to us, then you can get off at Kai'nau. But remember, we're the only thing between you and Slagish taking one more for his quarry. You hear me?"

James stood from the railing and took a long look at Sylph and Brine. For the first time, he wondered if he wasn't put in this world to help the Islanders after all. Maybe it wasn't as easy as Sylph, Teak, and Brine were *good,* and Slagish and the Scrim slavers were *bad.* Maybe they were all bad. Maybe what James needed to do was to stop all of them from reaching Kai'nau. Was that his purpose?

"I'll help," James stated, his voice hollow. "What do you want me to do?"

Brine grinned. "For now, nothing. We wait until we hear from Teak and see about making landfall. I can't see a thing in this fog, so we're taking him on his word. There'll be plenty to do when we reach shore. For now, we all sit tight."

James followed Sylph and Brine back to the helm of the Killdevil III. Brine hadn't been kidding. The fog was still too thick to see more than a hundred yards off the bow. James raised his hand to his eyes and squinted, trying to see the far shore through the mist. Then, with a strange snap, his vision cut through the fog, seeing the edge of the sea as cleanly and easily as though there wasn't a cloud in the sky. He gasped in surprise, staggering backward as his sight returned to normal. He stumbled, nearly tripping on the ship's rail.

"You alright, laddie?" Brine snorted.

James nodded fervently. "I got disoriented."

"The fog'll do that. Don't let her bother you."

James looked back out into the nothingness, but the fog remained as thick as ever. But if what he had seen was true, they should be on shore in a matter of moments.

"Land ho!" Teak shouted from somewhere above. James looked up to see him straddled halfway up the height of the mast. "Fifty yards and closing!" After the scarred man issued his warning, he swung down the ship's rigging to the deck below and assumed his place at Sylph's side

Sylph called, "All hands to deck. Drop the main'sl and loosen the jib. I want four to port and anchor ready." As she shouted orders, Slagish's men scrambled across the deck. Though the tattooed helpers didn't show the same comfort on the ship as Sylph and her crew, they responded quickly to her commands. For those that didn't, or who acted out of line, Brine was on them in seconds. Only Teak, poised in silent vigil, did not aid the ship's landing. James noted that the man's steady hand on the hilt of his sword showed his function all too well.

"I smell an ambush, I do," Teak muttered to Sylph, though she did not so much as shift her eyes in his direction.

"Of course," she replied. "It's just a matter of when."

"Wait a minute." James poked his head between the two. "Who would be ambushing us up here? I thought the people at Kai'nau wanted to trade? Why would they ambush us?"

"Cause it ain't them," Teak replied. "But they aren't the only ones crawlin' through them hills. Sometimes traders don't get as quite the pickins they think they should of. It's just a skip, jump, and a tumble for traders to turn pirate. Until we reach Kai'nau, we've got other things…"

Teak's words dropped to nothing as a thunderclap shook the boat, causing James' heart to skip a beat. An instant later, lightning, peculiarly following rather than preceding the thunder, struck the Killdevil's mast. The solid pine pillar exploded in a hail of sparks, flame, and splinters. Teak and Sylph dove under the shelter of the helmshade dragging James with them. By the time James had recovered from his surprise, Sylph had drawn two of her pistols. Teak also stood ready, sword gripped in both hands.

"Brine!" Sylph yelled. The big man was at her side within seconds. Brine's cheek bore a long thin slice where he had been scored by a splinter. His right arm was darkened with blood. "Brine, you ok?"

"Fine. What's the call, Cap'n?"

"Hold our own. We have to protect the 'Devil or we'll be stuck here forever."

"And the cargo?"

"That's for Slagish to worry. But don't let them touch the 'Devil! Now, let's go!" Sylph shot her two shipmates a vicious look and then darted a glance at James. "You, lad, stay here where I can see you."

James was too stunned to move. But something tickled at the back of his mind. The *last* thing he wanted to do was stay in one place. If another of those thunderbolts came, he'd be a sitting duck. And if his instincts were right then one was coming at any…

"Boom!"

He darted his eyes upward, his eyes flinching as the arc of lightning rushed to meet him at his perch behind the helm. He was barely able to shut his eyes when—

James fell.

13. Grand Central

James's ears rang from the thunderclap. The boom diminished in his mind, fading to the ambient buzz of the overhead fluorescent light. The adrenaline pumping through his veins was second only to the joy of remaining alive. Both emotions gave way to dim confusion as to why he was lying flat on a stainless-steel examination table.

Puzzlement became alarm; James snapped upright. He was in a hospital, no doubt. James's falling spells had wound him in enough of them to know what a clinic felt like. The pale walls, generic drawers, and fluorescent lights were all *too* familiar. What was *un*familiar was the lack of sheets or any of the comforting elements of hospital rooms. There were no pillows, no posters, no flowers, no cute stickers, and no get-well-soon balloons. Not a patient's room, then. An examination room.

James slid from the stainless steel table. As his feet touched the tile, he noticed how healthy and whole he felt. While he still throbbed with wariness, he didn't feel any physical pain. He didn't even feel the confusion normally following his falling spells. And surprisingly, he was dressed in the same clothes as in the Frozen World, and not from home.

Did I stay out too long? he thought. *That's Rule Two, right?* James glanced around him. Time must certainly have passed back home. But where was he now? He didn't remember having a doctor's appointment, but then again, he rarely kept track of them anymore. Was his checkup about to start, or had it just ended? And what would the doctor say to the suburban kid wearing animal furs better suited to a Viking?

James hopped back on the examination table and waited patiently. But as the seconds changed to minutes, and the minutes strung together, he began to nurture an entirely different feeling. That he had either been forgotten, or he was wrong about where he was.

Dismounting once more, James rifled through the surgical cabinets. What he found was similarly perplexing. Instead of the ordinary collection of latex gloves, syringes, and cotton balls, the cabinets contained boxes filled with empty boxes, which were in turn filled with even smaller boxes. The ensemble reminded James of the Russian dolls Seth's sister had received for Christmas. In the last cabinet, however, James found a pale bathrobe with the texture of moleskin. That at least seemed less incriminating than his current garb. James threw the robe across his shoulders and headed for the door. He pushed it open and stepped into the hall and into a sea of voices.

At school, James's science teacher was fond of saying that confusion was the natural result of man's expectations at odds with his reality. Only by receiving an entirely different result than what was expected, did a person ever learn the true nature of the world. When James left the exam room, he expected the brightly lit hall of a hospital. Now, *this* was confusion.

The first thing he noticed was the immensity of it all. The corridor—if it could be called a corridor—was over two hundred feet wide and covered with a repeated pattern of hexagonal tiles which fit precisely together, and yet curved and flowed with the slender grace of an ocean wave. On either side of the corridor, doors next to doors next to doors stretched in a repeated pattern as far as the eye could see. And considering that the hall stretched to the horizon, James saw no break in the landscape. The overwhelming regularity was so overpowering that James looked for the seam of a mirror. In fact, the only time he had experienced such a sight was in the endless mirror-halls of the Ripley's Believe-it-or-Not museum.

Filling the space were people moving with purposeful bustle. If all the streets of New York had been laid end-to-end, perhaps they would have fit here. The variety of people, however, was something else. The pedestrians were dressed in clothing from every era, every city, and every style he could imagine. James felt he was on the site of a Hollywood movie studio where businessmen, armored knights, body-paint models, men wearing dresses, children on stilts, samurai, Tibetan monks, bikers, showgirls, cavemen, astronauts, and geishas walked side by side. *Halloween,* James thought, *it's just like walking through a Halloween party. And I fit right in.*

James remained fixed in his place. His desire to explore was stymied by the utter sameness of the corridor, and the extreme variety of its inhabitants. Should he start walking further down the hall, or should he try one of the millions of doors?

"Excuse me," James waved at a passerby coming his way, dressed in a fluorescent-orange skintight suit. "Excuse me, but could you tell me where I am?"

The man paused for only a brief moment before gesturing to the door behind James's head. "You're here, of course. We all are." The man brushed past him without explaining further and disappeared into the crowd.

"But where is here?" James muttered.

He paused. He wasn't in the Frozen World anymore (of course), but this certainly wasn't home, either. But why *hadn't* he just gone home? Why was he here now? Is this what happens if you stay out too long?

James held his hand in front of him, palm-up. Not surprisingly, Huckabee's coin rested there, though he didn't recall waking up with it. *Not important,* James thought. What he needed now was to get home. He'd had enough of strange worlds for one day. James focused on the coin to see its *Thatness* and see if concentrating on the coin would send him home. But the *Thatness* of the coin, the *Thatness* of the Hallway World, and his own *Thisness* were identical.

"No black, no white," he mumbled. "This place is nothing but grays."

James slipped the coin into the pocket of his acquired robe and glanced around. If everything was so much the same, then where was everybody going? On a whim, he opened the nearest door and stepped through, only to emerge in another hall just the same as the one before. James thought that he'd stepped right through and back into the same hall again. He opened another door and walked through, then another, then another. But each passageway just returned him to where he started.

"What *is* this place?" James spoke aloud.

A familiar voice answered, "Why, it's nothing at all. And everything. It's a passageway and a joining and a splitting. We call it Grand Central. 'Grand,' because it certainly is grand—being infinite. And 'Central' because it's the middle of all things and all ways, all places, all times. This, my brother, is the axis of worlds!"

James spun to face Dr. Huckabee. Though unlike the doctor James had seen in his own world, this Dr. Huckabee stood no more than three feet tall. Furthermore, the doctor's feet, always absent shoes, were no longer feet at all. They were oversized hands—matching the hands on his arms.

"You!"

"Of course, it's me." Dr. Huckabee chuckled. "Or were you expecting someone else? But before you say another word, I have a present for you." Dr. Huckabee reached into his waistcoat and removed a small white business card. He handed it to James. Embossed in black ink were three lines.

Say nothing of the Styx;
Say nothing of our Mission;
Rule One.

Dr. Huckabee waited for a few moments then plucked the card from James's hand, returning it to his pocket.

"You're not very helpful," James grumbled. "And your friend, he wasn't too helpful either. I deserve some answers."

"And you shall have them. But first, tell me what you see."

James looked down the endless corridor in first one direction, and then the other. The peculiar people thronged from one end to the other, some walking along, while others entered and left the multitudes of doors. Nothing was organized. Not like in a city where people gravitated to either side in a neat flow of traffic. This was more like a swarm of ants.

"I see lots and lots of doors, lots of weird people, and it all goes on forever. Is this your world? Weird enough to be."

"Not my world, and you are quite incorrect to think it even could be. This is Grand Central, and it's not *really* a world at all. It's more of a way station between worlds—and unique in that respect. Grand Central has no destiny, motivation, Probability, or Possibility. That's just the way it is, and just the way it will be. And because Grand Central lacks that purpose, we can relax our guard about one thing in particular. Because there is one thing everyone here has in common. They're all just like you."

James had strong reservations that he was the same as the hula-hooping mime that skipped past him or the man plodding step after inexorable step in a 30's deep-sea diving suit. "Like me how?"

"Well, they can all do what you can do. I hesitate to give it a name as there are so very, very many names. 'Traveling' is most common, but others call it, Walking, Gliding, Shifting, Slipping, Sliding, Hopping, you name it. You, my brother, would probably call it Falling. Everyone here is a Traveler such as you. We're the boundaryless masses. Everyone here can cross between worlds."

"I guess that explains the weirdness…" James shook his head in disbelief. "But how can there be so many of them? How come I've never heard of this before? Is anyone else I know a… a Traveler?"

"Oh no-no, no, no, no. Only one person in a billion might ever be a Traveler. And only one of those in fifty ever actually Travel. The chance of two Travelers coming from the same world is negligible in an infinitesimal in an impossible chance. So don't expect to see your schoolmates."

"But *why* can we do it?"

Dr. Huckabee's jovial expression flipped to one of the utmost gravity. "That is something you should already know. Perhaps you've had this conversation in another world as well?" Dr. Huckabee let his words trail off. "My friend *told* that me he found you."

James thought about the words of the dusky man in the world with the metallic pond. The vagrant told James that the reason they could Travel was that the worlds needed help. The worlds were dying. And because they needed help, they called to Travelers from other worlds to help them. But what the man had also said, was that not everyone was there to help. Some were just tourists. Still others sought to destroy worlds. The Styx.

"Yeah, he found me. Told me to think about what side I was on."

"And where did all your thinking leave you?"

The frustration bubbled inside James. "You're asking me what I think? I think it's an impossible task. Even if I wanted to…" James stopped himself short, remembering the small index card Dr. Huckabee had shown him moments before: *Say Nothing of the Styx, Say Nothing of our Mission, Rule One.* "What I mean is, even if I wanted to do what we're out there to do I don't have any idea where to begin. And since you won't talk to me about it, then how can I ever even know?"

Huckabee's frown deepened. "You think I'm being foolish, my brother, but I'm being careful. People have been watching you back home. I've seen them myself though I hope they haven't seen me. Our enemies suspect that you are a Traveler, and one sympathetic to our cause. You saw them yourself at my office, and again on your street."

James nodded. "The ice-faced woman."

"Indeed." Huckabee frowned deep. "So, don't think my secrecy is without merit. But if you want answers, I can tell you where to find them." Huckabee swung his arms beside him and began to stomp a circle around James. "I've left you a package. Back home, that is. It can help you understand how to do what you need to do—if, of course, you decide to do it. But I caution you to be careful."

"Rule One, yeah, yeah."

"More than just that. You likely have found that in other worlds you have *abilities*. But at home you are a native. You are just one of the gang, or so you must appear. I've been watching them, and I'm convinced that our enemies do *not* know who you are, not yet. I think they suspect that it's someone at your school, maybe even in your class, but they don't know for a fact it's *you*. And as long as they aren't sure, they won't try to make a move to stop your Traveling. Rule Three—not killing things, that is—applies to the enemy as well as to us. But once they know for certain, you can guarantee they will act. They'll kill you, my brother. Indirectly if they can, directly if they must."

James snorted in laughter. "If they're so ruthless. Why do they care about making sure it's me? What's it to them if they kill the wrong kid?

Why don't they just take out the whole school? Or the town for that matter."

The doctor's frown turned once more into a comically wide grin. "Well, because they don't want to get stuck in your world. But you can't expect me to explain all the intricacies of inter-reality dynamics, the specifics of Probability/Possibility constants, and the dimensional flux inside of five minutes. I've been studying for over a thousand years, and I only barely understand. For now, just stick to the Rules. And you're forgetting Number Two."

James paused, then remembered. "Don't stay away too long?"

"Exactly. And it's been quite some time since you went home, hasn't it? I can tell."

"Don't change the subject. You said you had something for me."

"Oh yes. I forget that you are so easily distracted. Now, I need you to remember a name for me. When you get home, I want you to look it up. The name is 'Doctor Thomas Huckabee.'"

"But that's your…"

"No questions! No comments! Rule One! Understand?"

James scowled back.

"Ok, so now all you have to do is go home. Surely you can do that."

James shrugged. "I don't know. The coin you gave me doesn't seem to work here. Of course, you probably can't help me with that either."

"Of course, I can help you. And you shouldn't need the coin anymore anyway. You've seen more worlds than just your own, and you know how they feel in your mind. Just think of your home world, but not the way that it is. Think of the way that it feels. Think of its essential nature."

"Its Thisness?"

The doctor's face brightened. "*Thisness*! I love it, that's perfect. Most Travelers call it *Essence*—but it's all the same. Now I want you to imagine the *Essence* of your spirit sliding into the *Essence* of your home world. And if you do it just right…"

But James did not hear the rest of Huckabee's words. He was too busy focusing on the *Essence* around him, the strange grayness so unlike the *Essence* of home. But once he knew what to look for, he felt it solidify in his grasp. He felt his consciousness become unstuck from the world around him. And then—

James fell.

14. Greeson's Island

James snapped to attention as the surf-rod lurched in his hand. The whine of the CasterPro reel squealed with the strike of the fish. James tightened his grip and jerked once to set the hook. But he had moved too slowly. Whatever fish had hit his lure—probably a Bluefish this time of the year—had come loose and was on its way. And with the immediacy of his task passed by, James was able to absorb his surroundings. After all, he had stood on this very spot, just beyond the lap of the ocean waves, on countless occasions.

Grand Central was gone. Dr. Huckabee was gone. The endless corridor and the countless hordes of people were gone as well. James had returned to his own world and his own time. He was on Greeson's Island, just as he told his mom. But with the sun dipping low in the west behind him, a chill ran his spine. If today was Saturday, almost a full day had passed, and he remembered nothing of it. He didn't remember paddling his canoe across the channel or packing his rod, or even the day he assumed had been spent fishing. The only memories were of the Frozen Land, the peculiar Grand Central, and his encounter with Dr. Huckabee.

"Dang. I forgot to find out about Rule Four," James groaned. The newness of Grand Central had been too distracting for him to remember to ask Dr. Huckabee about the last and as-of-yet unstated fourth rule. And who knew when he would see the doctor again?

"At least I'm making progress," James said. "He left me directions. Of course, why wouldn't he? I just need to look him up, 'Dr. Thomas Huckabee.' Then maybe I can get some more answers. Time to go back to the mainland."

James wound in his line in slow spins, hoping he might attract a fish in the process, but to no avail. He checked the cooler beside him and was surprised to find three good-sized Spanish Mackerel and a small Bluefish within. James thought that the idea of being a better fisherman when he couldn't remember a thing had a peculiar amusement to it. The ice in the cooler gave him a different feeling entirely. He was normally very careful to pack enough ice so that no matter how hot the day his fish wouldn't spoil. But the ice cubes inside had almost completely melted. Had more time passed than he thought? James shrugged. He replaced the lid and headed back to the other side of the dunes where his canoe should be waiting.

The sight of his canoe returned the smile to his face. The aluminum Grumman was tied to the same lump of driftwood that he typically used as a mooring. A glance inside told him that Seth must not have come fishing after all. Seth never traveled anywhere without his own set of fishing and crabbing gear, all of which was absent. Humming to himself, he repacked his canoe with the cooler, rod, and small overnight bag housing both tent and sleeping bag. He had almost finished packing when he heard the angry whine of an approaching motorboat.

The approaching craft was one of the orange, inflatable boats of the Coast Guard. James waved as the stern-faced men approached, clad as always in personal flotation devices covering standard-issue flak jackets. James didn't feel the slightest hint of concern as he had his required PFD stored in the stern of his canoe. Canoes, after all, had very few requirements as to what they did and did not need to carry.

"You there, boy, are you James Winters?" The boat coasted to a stop, the bow nosing onto the sand near where James stood.

"That's me," James replied.

One of the coastguardsmen sprang from the side of the boat and walked up to him as two others disembarked to hold their craft steady. "You're in a whole heap of trouble, boy. Your parents expected you home hours ago."

"They knew I was camping out," James replied, somewhat confused.

"Not on a school night, I reckon."

James's stomach knotted as the realization hit him. He'd been gone for two days. And though his mind reeled with anxiety, he managed a baffled smile. "Oh, right. I guess I just lost track of time. I'm really sorry. You wouldn't mind getting them on the radio, would you?"

The thickset guardsmen nodded. "Sure, we will. Get right to it. Here, we'll give you a tow." James nodded. He shuffled to the bow of his canoe and tossed the painter to the Coast Guard boat. He kneeled on the floor of his canoe and grabbed a paddle to help steer the vessel to be ready for the tow. And though he kept his face calm—at least as calm as any boy who knew he was in trouble, his mind screamed in protest.

Oh god, oh god, oh god, oh god. TWO days? I can't believe I lost two days. Gone, nothing left. And I don't remember a second of it. And, oh my god, my mom's going to kill me. She'll never let me go anywhere by myself again. And she must know Seth's not here. I screwed up. I really screwed up this time.

James forced a smile and waved at the Coast Guard boat as they gradually picked up speed. James had four short minutes of calm as he kept his canoe stable behind the towing boat, but even as he landed, he could see his mom's car in the lot of the public dock. She paced furiously as James's dad stood with arms folded in stoic silence.

Though worried about the impending storm, James managed to stay calm as the Coast Guard released his bowline, leaving him just a few yards from the dock. The guardsmen waved goodbye and sped away. Though his arms felt heavy, James guided his canoe to shore, where he was assaulted by his parents.

"James! Good god, James, you have no idea how worried we've been. You can't do this to us. Not with your condition. You just can't take a boat out by yourself with no one to watch out for you. What if you'd fainted? What if the boat tipped in the middle of the channel? You could've drowned before you'd woken up. And for what? So you could *fish* for a few more hours? Is that all that happened? Is that why you're so late?"

James's eyes had opened wide. He looked from his frantic mother to his father, who studied him in disapproval. Unsure of which—if any—of his mother's questions to answer, he decided to defend himself.

"What's the big deal? I just lost track of time. The fishing was really good, and… You know, I was on my way back when they found me. I was just having a good time and…"

"Just. Having. A. Good. Time." His mother glared. "And what part of lying to me saying that Seth was coming along with you did you find particularly enjoyable? I'm not mad, James. I'm just disappointed. Your father and I care for you. And when you go off on your own like this, especially with your condition, you are taking a terrible risk."

"But *nothing happened,*" he pleaded. "I'm fine. I'm just late, that's all."

His mother's face turned bright red. "That is *not* all and you know it. You were dishonest, reckless, disrespectful, and could very nearly have gotten yourself killed. Now get in the car. This Instant."

Knowing that further combating his mother's wrath would worsen the situation, James slunk into the back of the car. He sat silently as his father and mother strapped the canoe to the roof and then loaded the rest of James's equipment in the back. The whole time both of his parents worked in stony-faced silence. The mood lightened briefly when James's father tapped on the window, pointed to the cooler loaded with fish, and flashed a grin.

The ride home was a dizzying change from the berating by James's mother to her version of the silent treatment. James spoke in his defense once but received only a harsh glare in return. Resigned, he crossed his arms and stared absently out the car window. He watched as the thin salt-twisted trees of the beach gave way to the live oak trees and magnolias of town. He allowed his mind to wander, a task that had become easy as of late. James had been given a lot to think about. But one thing he no longer considered, one item which had been concluded as fact, was that he wasn't just dreaming. He was traveling across worlds. And that was the truth.

But even if his conviction was madness, he was frightened by the whole unconsciousness of the endeavor. When James would have his visions of falling, his body would collapse, shut off entirely. Sometimes he fell to the ground, and aside from knowing that he would probably never get to drive a car as long as he lived, at least he knew that he had fallen. But now, when James traveled from this world to the next, his body went about its daily business. His body kept going to school; kept holding conversations. And if the cooler in the back of his dad's car was any indication, his unconscious self was one heck of a fisherman.

The best that he could come up with was that the whole operation was like talking in your sleep. Seth did that sometimes. His friend would go to sleep, and yet James had been able to have full conversations with him, conversations Seth would never remember. What if his body did the same thing when the rest of him was drifting from world to world? Maybe the body left behind performed his daily routines. And—to take it a step further—maybe it was acting *exactly* the same way that James would if he was in it himself.

"It's all too complicated," he whispered.

His mother darted her head around. "*What* is too complicated?"

James's cheeks flushed. "Nothing. I just lost track of time. It's too complicated to keep track of everything."

"I said it before. It's not about losing track of time. It's about you doing things you shouldn't do with your condition. And when you lie to me and *then* put yourself in danger? Well, that makes me sad. Just plain sad. What if you fainted in the boat? What if you slipped and fell into the water? What if you…?"

"Mom!" James's emotions had reached a breaking point. "I haven't fainted in a week. Didn't you notice? Dr. Huckabee cured me, I think. I just didn't want to say anything in case it came back. I'm cured, Mom. Don't you get it? I'm cured."

James expected his mom to be shocked, overjoyed, perhaps even ecstatic. But she was none of those things. Her eyes filled with the same longing sadness he had seen whenever the doctors disappointed her. She dropped her voice to a whisper. "James, honey, you fainted yesterday morning before breakfast. You slipped and hit your lip on the breakfast table. Tell me you didn't forget that, James. Tell me you didn't forget."

James raised his fingers to his lips, only to recoil as he touched the bruise. He sat in shocked silence. Why couldn't he remember? Weren't his falls his mind's way of wanting to travel to other worlds? Wasn't that what Dr. Huckabee said? Then why would he fall when he was already *in* another world? It didn't make any sense at all.

"Mom?" James's voice diminished to nothing. "Mom, I don't feel so good."

"I understand, honey. Don't you worry. Everything is going to be ok. We'll just get you home and get you some rest. You've had a long day in the sun." His mom broke into a warm smile, her concern for him overshadowing her disappointment. "How would you like it if I cooked up a couple of those fish you caught? What do you think?"

James smiled weakly. "I'd like that."

* * *

When they returned home, his mother grilled his fish just as she'd promised with a side of brown rice and a sour lemon glaze. After eating, James made the excuse of being tired and slunk to his room. But he was *not* tired. His mind raced from the prospects of the knowledge gained from Grand Central, and from the stinging revelations of the time he was beginning to miss.

His first order of business would usually be to contact Seth and see what his friend would say. But James was getting too nervous about Dr. Huckabee's "Rule Number One" to bring even his closest confidante into the circle. Not yet. There were a few things to check first.

Turning on his dad's computer, James opened the browser. Dr. Huckabee wanted him to look up a person by the name of "Doctor Thomas Huckabee" and James could think of no easier way. The first attempt brought up the same type of information he typically encountered whenever trying to search for someone (such as himself) who was decidedly not famous. There were several pages about genealogy, a few promising to locate old schoolmates, and even a link that the Adult Content filter prevented him from accessing.

Only one site piqued his interest. It was a library catalog citing a book by a "Dr. Thomas Huckabee." But far more interesting was that the Dewey decimal number for the book was the same as the digits of James's birthday. And if coincidences were not enough, the page was not from some distant city in some distant town. The library was the downtown library, and only a half-block from where he had first met the doctor. The title of the book gave James pause: *An Alternative History of Universal Dynamics*. He nearly dismissed the book until he read the subtitle: "The governing principles of Probability and Possibility". How many times had Dr. Huckabee talked about those very things? This had to be it.

James pulled out one of his school notebooks and scrawled the name and reference number of the book. According to the computer, the book was indeed checked in and available. He folded the piece of paper up and tucked it into the outside of his book bag. He switched off the computer and flopped down onto his bed. The library would be open until nine tomorrow night, but James was fairly sure that his mother would be keeping a tight leash on him for a few days. He could expect to be—not grounded, per se—but certainly not released from his mother's sight. There was another way, of course. With a smirk, he sprang out of bed and dashed downstairs to ask his mother for permission to work in the after-hours study hall.

Ten minutes later, with both his alibi and a bowl of vanilla ice cream secured, James knew that all he needed to do tomorrow was to wait until the end of the day. Dr. Huckabee's book would be in his hands, and he'd finally know what was going on.

Sleeping, however, could no longer be trusted.

15. Check Out

James stayed awake for the entire night. Ever since meeting Dr. Huckabee, whenever he had gone to sleep in his own world, he had awoken in another. And the gaps in time between leaving and coming back were getting longer. And while James thought that maybe moving from the Silver Pond World to the Frozen World to Grand Central may have explained the long delay, he couldn't risk waking up only to find that he had already been to the library and back. James didn't trust his unconscious self to anything so important.

As anyone who has ever tried to stay up late can attest, remaining awake is not always the simplest of tasks. James, however, found the endeavor simple. While his body still had a gnawing desire to sleep, he pushed the urge away with ease. But the need for sleep never left entirely. And when the sun rose, filling his bedroom with morning light, he felt a flood of relief.

James stumbled downstairs to meet his family for breakfast in the stoic—somewhat dazed—manner of the chronically weary. But after a helping of pancakes and a glass of orange juice, he felt revitalized. And where rest had been denied, the excitement crept in after.

He arrived at the bus stop only to notice that Seth was conspicuously absent. This wasn't unusual, though was a bit of a relief as he didn't feel like having to explain himself. To take his mind off the exhaustion itching at his skull, James played with his awareness of the world. Even without concentrating first on Huckabee's coin, James found that he could easily attune his mind to the complete clarity that came when he not only looked at the world's *appearance* but looked at the world's *Essence*. The effect was not unlike the lens of a projector being tuned to fineness. James became aware of detail—millions upon millions of details. He noticed the chaotic arrangement of the almost-invisible hairs upon Susie Newman's arm. He could smell the wafting soup of twenty sack lunches: bologna, peanut butter, apples, cheese, and crackers. He could feel the waves of cold air swell from the outside to roll down the bus's corridor, only to settle on the floor. And he could hear the individual strikes of the bus's pistons as they droned up and down. James was not just aware, he was completely aware.

"Eight inches," James murmured.

"What's that?"

James was snapped from his meditations by the voice of the person in the next seat. He flinched. He had been concentrating so hard on the entirety of the bus that he had been unaware of the person beside him. Patrick Nelms had always resided in the quasi-realm between mere acquaintance and actual friend of many schoolmates. James had sat next to Patrick as it had been a nearby open seat, and for no other reason.

"You just said 'eight inches.' What did you mean by that?"

James hesitated for a moment. "I didn't sleep last night," he blurted.

"So?"

"Well, you know how when you're tired you feel like everything is at a little bit of a distance? That's how I feel now. It's like everything is where it should be, but I'm looking at it as if I'm eight inches away from it all. I'm here, but not *quite* here. You ever get that feeling?"

"You mean like things are happening, but you're just watching? Like on TV. Yeah, I guess so. Like if you yelled out, no one would even hear." Patrick hung his head somewhat. "I feel that way a lot at home. I've got six brothers."

"Six? Holy cow." James's jaw dropped. "I'll bet you have to fight to get your dinner, don't you? You the youngest?"

"Second to last. Even worse. I'm not quite the baby so I don't get special treatment, but I've still got five brothers who are bigger than me. How about you? You got any brothers or sisters?"

James opened his mouth to reply that he was an only child—but the words caught in his throat. He tried twice to speak the truth but was only successful with a rolling lie. "I've got two younger sisters. I'm older by six and eight years, so they're too little to bother me much."

As Patrick nodded in agreement, James was hit by a wave of astonishment. He hadn't told the truth. He had *tried* to tell the truth, but the lie came easier. James realized that his silence must have signaled to Patrick that the conversation had ended and the boy had returned to gaze out the window. Patrick had thought nothing of James's words; he had no idea that he had lied.

But why would I lie? James thought.

The answer came as easily as the lie had. Rule Number One. Of course. He knew that his subconscious was trying to obey the rules. Somehow, the Rules now seemed both serious and important—where before they were only a guideline. But it didn't make any sense. He was back in his home world now. If anything, lying too much would only draw attention to him. Hadn't Huckabee told him to act natural?

James leaned back against the hard aluminum seat and allowed himself to stare with the same aimless gaze of so many of the other kids and watched the pines and oak trees pass by the side of the road. The trees slowly gave way to the brown brick shops, and then those, in turn, rose to form the urban jungle surrounding his school. As the bus driver pulled to a stop, the air brakes exhaled in a short exasperated screech. James hoisted his backpack and began counting down the hours until he would be released from school. Then he would journey to the library and find Dr. Huckabee's book.

* * *

Math and P.E. passed with painful slowness. James found that while he was still able to hold his weariness at arm's length, he was less successful at paying attention. He let the words wash over him without actually absorbing the material. And every time he nearly succumbed to sleep, he opened his mind to the world, to drink deep of the *Essence*. And whenever James did so, he became more and more convinced that the rough watercolor of the world that he had always thought of as real was only a shadow. The detail brought by the *Essence* was intoxicating, and yet James found that he could only keep his awareness open for so long before the effort was too great and his concentration would lapse, his view of the world returning to normal.

By the time Spanish class began, James had turned the awareness of *Essence* into a game. He would open his mind to the world's *Essence*, and keep track of how long he could maintain his focus. At the beginning of Spanish class, he could maintain concentration for fifteen seconds. By the end of class, he was holding it for forty seconds. By the end of Chemistry, he held it for over two minutes, and when lunch had ended, he had held it for almost ten minutes. When the bell rang to signal the end of the school day, James couldn't have told you a single thing any of his teachers had said. In fact, he hadn't said more than a handful of words the entire day. Nevertheless, during his entire English class, the final class of the day, James had not once let his perception of the *Essence* falter. So enthralling was the exercise that he had packed his books and made it halfway to the bus stop before he realized that he wouldn't be taking the bus home. He was headed to the library.

The downtown library possessed a solemn architecture similar to many of the downtown buildings. The structure was a combination of faceless industrial adorned with the federal elements of a capital building. James had been to the library quite a bit in the past two years as part of one of the school's summer reading programs. However, the introduction of a program where the library would deliver books directly to school had lessened his visits over the past year. James hadn't set foot in the library in four months. He still checked out books, of course, but seldom made trips downtown.

This excursion was to be a bit more private. James was too conscious of Dr. Huckabee's warnings of secrecy. And the fear of the ice-faced woman burned into his head a little too fiercely to put such a strange book as *An Alternative History of Universal Dynamics* onto the school library list. Who knew what the ice-faced woman was keeping track of?

James knew that he needed an appropriate excuse as to why he would be in the library in the first place. And while he found that lies about who he was and what he was doing were coming ever more readily, he found this one more difficult. Then James remembered the last time he had gone to the library, he hadn't gone to get books. He instead had accompanied his cousin who needed to look through old newspaper clippings. That was a decent alibi, and he didn't need to check anything out to do it.

James pushed through the large glass doors and into the cool, overly quiet interior. He walked through the upright scanners designed to make sure that no un-checked out books walked away, and through a second set of glass doors into the atrium. He approached the desk and waited patiently until one of the librarians emerged. The girl who greeted him looked to be of college-age. He was glad as she didn't seem to have the look of many older librarians who wanted to know not only *what* you wanted, but *why*.

"How can I help you?" she asked, her voice tinged with an accent appropriate to magnolias and antebellum dresses.

"I'm looking for old newspapers. And… do you have one of those things that say where everything is located? I have the book number." James slid a rumpled piece of paper across the counter with the Dewey Decimal number scrawled on it.

The librarian glanced at the number then pushed it back to James. "Why, this is on the eighth floor. You'll find it in the back stacks. Newspapers are in the basement, sweet pea." The librarian paused, an eyebrow raised in puzzlement. "This sounds kind of weird, but that number is the same as my birthday. Isn't that just enough to make you fit and giggle?"

James shrugged, though a surge of emotion made his ears ring. He dragged the piece of paper back across the counter and shoved it into his pocket. Muttering a quick "thanks," he headed for the stairs.

Eight flights up and James began to wonder why he had avoided the elevator. *Might be unsafe*, a voice inside him whispered back. *Can't take any chances of being caught. We're too close.* James trudged up the last flight and then scanned the shelves. After a few misdirections, he found what he thought should be the correct aisle, but something seemed a little off. The sign at the end declared this to be the "sports history" section. There were books on ballet; the history of baseball faded into the history of basketball, then further down information on card games, diving, golf, and equestrianism. James looked at the section of the shelf where the book should have been and was astonished to find that sandwiched between *A Pictorial Review of the 15th Olympics* and *A Pictorial Review of the 16th Olympics*, was his book. The tome, almost two inches thick, was as worn as the paperbacks in a used bookstore. The title *An Alternative History of Universal Dynamics* was not printed but hand-written in faded blue across the binding.

James pulled the book from the shelf. The front cover was missing, as were the first several pages where James would have anticipated copyright information to appear. He turned the book over and was surprised to see a picture of an elderly man with pronounced Asian features and a wispy beard. This was not the Dr. Huckabee James knew. The caption gave a birth date and death date. James found that he was unsurprised to find that the author, who appeared to be approaching ninety, had the same birthday (including the year) as James. The date of the man's death was also familiar to James. He glanced at his wristwatch just to make sure. Today's date.

A chill ran through him. If he was supposed to be keeping his presence a secret, then why were all of these clues indicating this book was intended for him and only him? Furtively, James shoved the book low into his knapsack and headed back to the stairs. The need to escape the library with his book was almost overwhelming, and yet he couldn't wait to read the information in his hands.

"Rule Number One," James muttered. First, he needed to cover his tracks. He had told the librarian, and he would soon tell his parents, that he went to the library to look at newspapers. To do anything less would be to open himself up to more questioning. He needed to keep a low profile. Then, he could reap his reward.

As he walked down the stairs, swinging down the banister to take several steps at a time, James felt a tickle of wariness. He paused mid-stride. The people circulating the stacks seemed to be paying him no mind, and yet he couldn't shake the feeling. James descended further and further until he dropped back to the first floor, and then into the basement.

The library basement betrayed the building's attempt at modernization. Aluminum vents crisscrossed the ceiling, and the hum of the central air-conditioning was so pervasive that James felt he was in a terrestrial submarine. The shelves, not the polished wood of the other stacks, were unpainted industrial grey.

James wandered to the closest archive and found a series of back-issues of the London Times. He pulled the most recent from the shelf, then grabbed the most recent Wall Street Journal, and finally that day's local paper. If anyone asked, he'd be comparing the news in all three and start talking about "regional priorities in the news". The idea sounded so plausible that he thought he might do his current affairs report on that very topic. Worst-case scenario, he'd just have to keep coming back.

With newspapers in one hand and the backpack with the strange book nestled inside, James made his way to one of the cubbies lining the wall. He first spread out the papers, then removed the book. A curse escaped his lips.

The pages were blank.

16. Universal Dynamics

An Alternative History of Universal Dynamics lay on the desk before James. For this book, he leaped from world to world and back once more. All that for a collection of empty pages.

His *first* thought was that it had been a trap set by the ice-faced woman—or maybe Huckabee. Who was to say the doctor was completely on the level? Maybe the book had been planted to draw James out, to make him reveal his presence. And he had fallen in nicely. But if it was a trap, then why weren't people rushing to get him? Should he run? Should he leave the book and see who came looking for it?

But James's *second* thought was that this book was perhaps much like Huckabee's coin. Maybe this book was something that made sense in the same way that only James could tell that the coin was special. After all, when he had shown Seth Huckabee's coin, he had thought it no more remarkable than a quarter—even less. A mischievous grin spread his face. He'd been practicing all day, and now it was time to put it to the test. James opened himself to the *Essence* of the world. As soon as he did, he knew he was correct. The book in his hands, *An Alternative History of Universal Dynamics* was not of this world at all. It too was from another world, a *That*. And as James looked at the book with his mind open to the *Essence*, the book filled with words, the first of them, the subtitle. James began to read.

"*An Alternative History of Universal Dynamics: The Mechanics of Worlds, World Traveling, and an Advocacy for their Preservation.*" James smiled. Jackpot.

"First off," the book began, "a word of congratulations for not being dead. You are one of very few who has made it this far, and such a feat should not be understated. Travelers are rare—incredibly rare. And the rarity of a Traveler is exceeded only by the peril of *being* a Traveler. So again, congratulations, congratulations, and congratulations again. But no doubt you didn't come seeking praise, but answers. And while perhaps you've been Traveling for a thousand years, and perhaps only a few days (as you count them,) the information within should be able to help you understand a little more of why you *can* do what you *can do*.

"Most people go through their lives thinking that their world is the only world. This is not true. At the time of this writing, there were approximately six trillion, two hundred eighty-six thousand, four hundred and nineteen worlds. And while new worlds are occasionally brought into existence (see chapter nine) the overall number of worlds is steadily decreasing. Worlds, you must understand, are much like living organisms. They grow, they thrive, they progress, and when in peril, they call for help. If you are reading this book, you can hear those cries. The question, my friend, is will you answer them?"

James looked down to see every hair on his arm standing on end. He remembered the overwhelming wrongness in the air when he first landed on the Frozen World, a sense that everything around him was perched dangerously on a cliff, soon to topple if someone didn't do something. Not someone. Him.

"While you ponder whether you will be an Advocate, seeking to help worlds, or whether you follow the way of the Styx, seeking to destroy them, you are still bound by the Rules. Of the four Rules, the first two are optional, and the second two are not. Rule One, to keep your identity a secret, is primarily concerned with lessening the chance of someone following you back to your home world and seeking to eliminate you there. Remember, this is a battle, and there are sides. Rule Two, not staying out too long, is far more of a guideline and a recommendation to keep your life at home and abroad in balance. Bodies sans spirit can maintain themselves for a while, but the longer the spirit is missing, the quicker the body will 'forget' how to act on its own. Keeping a balance is necessary to sustained health and happy Traveling.

"Rules Three and Four are one and the same. Both are a reminder that if a Traveler becomes *too* attached to a world, that he or she will become incapable of ever leaving as they are too spiritually entwined. Rule Three, stating that you should never, ever kill anyone or anything, is crucial in this regard. If a Traveler ends a life, his or her spirit will become entangled in the departed spirit, and he or she will never be able to Travel again. The Traveler can never return home.

"Rule Four is far more subtle, and far more difficult to measure. Rule Four is to never fall in love. Becoming too emotionally attached, whether romantically or by the ties of friendship can bind you to a world as surely as ending someone's life. The recommendation is to be as businesslike as possible. The worlds you visit are for rescuing, your home world is for enjoying. And while it may seem odd to both seek to save a world but not care overly about doing so, remember that by remaining detached, you can save another world, and another, and another. It is up to you to position yourself to do the greatest amount of good possible."

Fine, James thought. If those are the rules, those are the Rules, even if Rule Four was kind of a letdown after all the secrecy surrounding it. But what James really wanted to know was how to figure out what was wrong with a world. After all, knowing what was broken could go a long way to determining whether or not trying to rescue a world was something he was even capable of. James flipped past the introduction, which continued for several pages, until he found the remnants of an index. James ran his finger down the page.

Chapter 1: The Constants of Probability and Possibility

Chapter 2: The Cosmos and the Countless Worlds

Chapter 3: The Art of Relative Non-existence…

He scanned the chapters, few of them making any sense until halfway down the page where he found what he was looking for. He flipped to the open page, arriving at:

Chapter 17: Diagnosing the Illness of the World

James's heart quickened.

"Sometimes worlds simply die. They wink out of existence because their time has come. Far more common, especially since the rise of the Styx, is that a world will be destroyed in a single cataclysmic event. If we think of worlds as living organisms, then what we must consider is that the worlds *know* how they are going to die, but can't do anything about it themselves. When a world calls a Traveler for aid, the world, though not doing so consciously in the strictest sense of the word, will place the Traveler in the very position where he or she can hope to avert the world's fate.

"The world cannot speak to a Traveler directly, but messages are still given. The people you meet freely give information, they are quick to trust you. Their speech is easily understood, and though they may not realize it, they are accepting of a Traveler in a way that they would never be of one of their own. The world desires cooperation so that it may be saved. And its inhabitants listen to that demand. Because even if a world's natives may not hear the screams of their world as a Traveler can, they still hear it unconsciously.

"So to determine how a world needs help, to determine what calamity will wink the world from existence, a Traveler need only remember this: when Traveling, there is no coincidence. Acts of chance are bent to the will of the world, the things people tell you are bent to the will of the world, randomness is gone, mistakes are gone, there is no longer serendipity. So when a Traveler sees a sign, they should remember that it *is* indeed a sign."

James reached to turn the page, conscious that his fingers were trembling. Dr. Huckabee's friend had told him to "Keep his ears open" but James hadn't understood what he meant. The whole time he had been looking for the answer to be told to him when he should have been looking around him. He turned the page, surprised to see a small index card tucked in the pages. James recognized it instantly, it was the same card that Dr. Huckabee had shown him in Grand Central. Printed on the front in neat lettering was the doctor's message:

> *Say nothing of the Styx;*
> *Say nothing of our Mission;*
> *Rule One.*

But on the back of the card, hand-written in frantic script, was another message:

> *You're not still in the library, are you? Get out of there now!*
> *-your brother, Dr. H.*
> *P.S. I told you to be careful. Weren't you listening?*

A chill ripped up James's spine. He snapped the book shut with one hand. His mind still opened to the *Essence* of the world, James's ultra-sharpened senses reached out around him. He could hear approaching footsteps, two sets descending in eerie synchronism from the two staircases leading to the basement. Two unwelcome someones were coming his way. If Huckabee was to be believed, it was the Styx. He had to escape.

James darted his eyes around. If the stairs were off-limits he had few options available to him. He could try one of the elevators, but such a prospect seemed even more terrifying. If these someones were seeking to stamp out his life, he didn't want to be trapped in a box. Then his eyes saw it. Never in his life had four letters seemed so welcome or so wildly appropriate. The glowing green "EXIT" sign hung beyond the last of the stacks above a heavy metal door.

Wasting no time to return the newspapers to their proper places, James leaped from his chair and darted to the door on the back wall. He could hear the people descending the stairs hastening their pace, their footfalls still perfectly in sync. In seconds he was at the door, large and looming, with a single push bar and a sign proclaiming, "Fire Exit, alarm will sound if opened."

"Good," James muttered. "Maybe that will slow them down." James threw his weight against the push bar. He panicked for a moment before the opening gave way, opening a mere nine inches before stopping. The klaxon blare of the alarm echoed throughout the basement. James could hear the footsteps of what he knew in his heart were his pursuers running his way. Within seconds they would round the stacks. At that point, they would know his face, and it would be too late.

James whipped off his book bag and lunged at the narrow opening. The impact on his forehead felt like he'd been cracked with a baseball, and yet he was able to slide through to the other side. Pulling his book bag through with his trailing arm, his eyes darted around. He was in a stone stairwell leading up into daylight. He was out, but he had to run.

He darted for the stairs, ignoring his throbbing head or the blood now trickling along his temples. Twelve more steps, eight, four—and he was out into the daylight. He didn't slow down, he ran as fast as he could, darting across the street, drawing the yells and horns of the slow-moving traffic and into the strip mall adjacent to the library. On he ran, dashing through the afternoon crowds and around the cheap displays of sunglasses and trendy sandals. He ran until the sense of being followed, the sense of malign presence, was finally gone. James plopped onto a bench outside of a Gap and panted heavily. He held his head in his hands and tried to slow his breathing.

"Easy there, son," a deep voice called from beside him. James's heart redoubled its pace as he felt a stern hand on his shoulder. "What're you doing tearing around through here?"

James looked up, expecting to see the ice-faced woman sporting a voice with deep-South tones. Instead, he saw a perplexed mall security guard. James paused for only a second before he panted a reply. "Big kids… tried… to beat me up." Again, the lie flowed easily, but he knew his expression of terror was genuine.

"Maybe, maybe not. But I best see inside that backpack just in case. Shoplifters run too, you know."

James handed over his backpack. If this guard was one of the people out to get him, he was already caught. The guard unzipped the bag and rifled through the contents. His eyebrow raised as he pulled the coverless *History* out.

"Why do you have a blank book in here, boy?"

"It's a journal," James replied. "I haven't started yet."

The guard grunted and returned the backpack. "Probably should just toss it, looks like it's been through hell and back." The guard shook his head. "Alright then, you run along. And keep out of trouble. And be careful to wash up before heading home. Those boys must have done a number on you."

James wiped his brow and looked numbly at the trickling blood on his hand. "I will," he mumbled. He stood and searched for a bathroom. But what he hoped was that whoever was chasing him—*if* someone was chasing him—hadn't gotten his description from the librarian. His second thought was far more chilling. The index card from Dr. Huckabee was still sitting on the library desk.

* * *

The streetlight outside of James's room buzzed with flickering apathy. His brain whirled with not only the information in the book, the fevered chase, and the questions in his mind, but also the intense weariness, now seeming to sink into his very soul, that came with having been awake for over thirty hours. Only one thing was resolute in his mind, and that was that he had to get the *History* to a safe place, far away from where it could be traced back to him. He needed to get it not just out of his house, but out of his world. Until that happened, James was too terrified to even pull it from his bookbag. But could he take it with him? He was fairly certain he could. If it worked with Huckabee's coin, then it should work with the *History*.

James needed time to think, to understand what all this was about. But how much time would he lose here, in his own world, if he slept and Traveled once more? A day? A week? What if it was longer? What if a year slipped by? What little he'd been able to read had been very clear: Traveling was dangerous. It *was* a miracle he'd survived as long as he had. But that wasn't the only miracle. Being able to Travel was a miracle. Seeing the *Essence* of the world was a miracle. Going a whole day without a fall was a miracle. Maybe all these miracles were working together. Maybe fate—or whatever—really wanted him to succeed. Maybe it wasn't just in strange worlds where coincidence no longer applied. Or maybe he just needed to fall asleep.

And so—

James fell.

17. Caged

James opened his eyes to the frigid air of the Frozen World. Night had set in, clear and cold. Through the bone latticework of the cage, he could see the pristine curtain of the night sky. In the center of his vision was the brightest star that he had ever seen or imagined. The star burned with intense blue light that sent a chill down his spine, far more so than the cold in the air. For a moment, James couldn't tear his eyes away, only marvel at whether the brightness of the star, so intense it washed out all others around it, was even a star at all, or was he simply looking at one of the Frozen World's moons. Who was to say that this strange place only had one?

The enthralling brightness of the star held James's attention for only so long when he realized that he saw it through the bars of a cage. He'd noticed the cage when he'd woken as well, but at the time it hadn't seemed important. But now, the veil of unreality pushed aside, he realized he was trapped.

James bolted upright. He darted his eyes around to take stock of his situation. He wasn't alone. Three children, each roughly his age, leaned against the bone slats of the cage. The children were clothed in a mass of furs like him, each bearing a distinct ethnic origin. Of the two girls, one had olive skin and Asian features with silky black hair which poked from beneath her hood and ran nearly to her waist. The second girl had skin so black that she reminded James of the Haitian exchange student at school. As for the boy, he had platinum-blonde hair and pale skin. But Sylph, Brine, and Teak were nowhere to be seen.

James leaned forward against the bars to look around. The cage was set in a semicircle with three others, all empty, around a smoldering fire. James thought that the fire was less of a luxury than a necessity to keep the captives from freezing. Beyond the fire on three sides were sheer ice walls. The fourth side opened onto a beaten path leading to an area forested with tents.

He knew he was a captive, but he didn't understand why. Then the memories trickled back in. He remembered being aboard the Killdevil III when the waterspouts came. He remembered how Lord Slagish had erased one of the waterspouts from existence. He remembered learning from Brine that the ship carried slaves. And he remembered the ambush. There had been an ambush, hadn't there? Right before he had left this world and journeyed to Grand Central, the ship had been attacked. And from the look of things, the ambushers had emerged victorious over both the Islanders and the Scrim.

"Captain Sylph? Brine? Are you there?" James called into the night. "Teak? Anyone?"

A low, heavily accented voice called from his side. The voice sounded just as Haitian as the girl's appearance. "You must needs be quiet now, boy. Yellin' will only make de boss-men angry."

James turned to face the Haitian girl. "What happened? Where are we?"

"Well, boy," she replied, "not so sure what you do be rememberin', and what you don't be. You were out to the world when dey brought you in. Dey done attack us when we hit de shore. And dat's da truth. Many were killed, many ran off, many were captured. Dey saved us 'cause of our age, and dat's da truth."

"Our age?"

The girl laughed and one of the other children, the blonde boy, replied in a clear, if not somewhat sophisticated, English accent. "They were looking for Blanks, mate, and they found a few. But you weren't with us on the ship. Where'd you come from?"

James cleared his throat. "I'm with Sylph, Teak, and Brine… the Islanders. That was our ship you were on."

The English boy chuckled. "Oh, so then this here slavin' bit must be new for you. As far as I'm concerned, it doesn't matter if we're held by Scrim, Islanders, or whoever these new chaps are. They look almost local by the dress, but it's all the same to me. We'll all wind up at Kai'nau in good measure."

"You don't care that you're in a cage?" James asked. "Aren't you afraid of what they'll do to you?"

"Look, mate, we were in a cage on the ship, and in a cage on the wagon before that. And I can only speak for myself, but I was in a cage back at the port before that too. I've been in cages for two years running. Such is the life of a slave, mate."

The concept of slavery ricocheted through James's mind as much as seeing magic, or any of the other fantastic things of the past few days. And yet, Brine had admitted to as much. These kids must have been the precious cargo that the Scrim had gone through so much trouble to transport across the Alpinsea.

The dark-skinned girl spoke, "And what of you dere, boy? What be your reason for being here? Quite young for a fightin' man, and a bit surprising you be speaking the language of the Scrim."

"I'm a, uh, a translator. And a deckhand. As I said, I'm with the Islanders." James slumped against the bone bars of his cage. The lies had begun again, just as easily as before. And just as unbidden as the lies he had told to Patrick on the school bus. But at least now he knew that the lies had a purpose. Rule Number One—it could keep him safe. It would keep him and his *world* safe. The thought of Rule Number One reminded James of the book he had taken from the library. That book had said that the key to finding out what was wrong with a world was to throw away the concept of coincidence. Wherever he landed, whatever he saw, and whoever he talked to, all were there to give him clues.

James rubbed his temples. If there was no coincidence, then Teak, Sylph, and Brine were part of the issues, so too were the tattooed men, and—the thought struck him—*so were these kids!* Maybe the only reason that bandits had attacked and taken him hostage was so that he'd wind up exactly where he was now. *These kids* were the tattooed men's cargo.

These kids were the reason they were traveling. So if coincidence was a thing of the past, then *these kids* were some part of the world's impending doom.

But it was all too tenuous. James wanted confirmation. He needed to read more… but where was the *History*?

"Where did it go?" James said aloud.

"And what be dat?" the Haitian girl asked.

"I, uh, I had this book, and now I can't find it. Have you seen anything like that?"

The Haitian laughed. "Don't be surprisin' me you can't find a ting. Whoever ambushed us, dey took just 'bout everyting but da clothes on our backs. It's all piled over dat way." The girl pointed through the bars to a collection of loot nearly twenty yards away.

James strained his eyes to see if *An Alternative History of Universal Dynamics* was in that pile, but he couldn't make anything out in the darkness. *Wait a minute*, James thought. *I forgot all about the* Essence. He opened his eyes to the wider world, to sense the world's *Essence*. As before, he was shocked by the clarity of vision. But even beyond the *Essence*, James felt what he had sensed when he first arrived in the Frozen World—the screams of a world that was sick, dying. That was why he was here, to help make it well.

Pressing his face to the bars, James peered at the collection of junk scavenged from the captives. Poking from the rubbish, no more than a corner visible, he could see the *History*. He was certain that it was his book, not by sight, but by the *Essence*—quite different from the *Essence* of the Frozen World—but still familiar.

"Thank god. At least it's not gone," James whispered.

"You can *see* it?" the boy with the English accent exclaimed. "You must have the eyes of a hawk, mate. Or else a rune on your lids. So which is it?"

James turned to respond, but as he did his eyes, still sharpened and aware of the world's *Essence* fell on the last and most silent member of the cage. The girl with olive skin and Asian features had at first only stood out to him because of the length and silkiness of the hair curtaining her solemn face. But with his eyes opened to the world's *Essence* James saw something entirely different. The girl's body pulsed with an *Essence* all its own. The *Essence* was the same as that of the Frozen World, and yet something about her stood apart. Did that mean that *she* was the key to all this madness? Was she the one at the center of it all?

"Who is that?" James asked, his voice a mixture of terror and awe. And with the words spoken, he could no longer maintain his hold of the *Essence* of the world. He let his perception return to the mundane.

The English boy laughed. "Sound a bit smitten there, mate. Just a fellow slave is all. Just like all of…"

James cut the boy off, scooting over to the far side of the cage and offering his hand. "Hi, I'm… Jay. What's your name?"

The girl looked up with eyes as deep and brown as rich soil. Her eyes glistened with apprehension, though she did not respond.

The Haitian girl answered, "Now listen good, boy. I know you be new to dis whole slavin' bit. But you need to know da rules. If you be a slave, you ain't got no name, now don't cha? You best be learnin' your place, or we'll all be a-sufferin' for it."

James felt hurt. "Well, I just can't call you kid one, kid two, and kid three. How do you keep each other apart? That's stupid."

"Dassum be stupid," the girl replied. "But dat be da rules, and if…"

"Criminy." The English boy grinned. "Ain't no one around. I'm Charles, at least I was once. And our pouty friend is Bellacroix."

"And what's your name?" James directed the question again to the Asian girl.

"My name is Ling." She tilted her head in a slight bow. "And while I do not recall making your acquaintance, you seem familiar to me."

James grinned, pleased to have broken the ice. "I get that a lot. You wouldn't believe how often I get that. My name's Jay. I know I told you once. So let's start over again." He glanced around the cage. "Where are all of your runes? I thought the Scrim traded in runics, but I don't see a tattoo among you."

Ling replied, her voice soft and deliberate with a tinge of a Chinese accent. Not really a Chinese accent, James reminded himself. But he didn't know the nationality it would belong to in the Frozen World. "We do not yet have our runes. Not yet. That is why the Scrim take us to Kai'nau. Only once there will we be given runes. The Scrim are adept at designing runes, but they are not as skilled at etching them. But soon we will reach Kai'nau. Soon we will learn which of us are to receive runes."

James thought of the black trunk in Sylph's cabin and the way the captain had protected it so assiduously. Was it possible that the trunk didn't hold any treasures at all? Did the trunk merely hold the plans for the runes? The idea felt right in James's mind, but questions remained unanswered.

"What do you mean, you *might* get runes?"

Ling snorted with disdain and turned away. Bellacroix, the dark-skinned girl, answered instead. "We all be Blanks, boy. But not all Blanks can have dem any runes in de world. One of us must have potential, but that don't mean we all do. There's always a chance that some of us are decoys."

"I get it." James nodded. "A Blank is just someone without those magic runes. That makes sense, I guess. So what now? Where will they take us?"

Bellacroix cursed and turned her back. This time Charles chuckled. He patted James on the shoulder. "Don't mind old Bella, mate. She gets a bit of a temper. And Ling is a sulker if I ever met one. I, on the other hand, am happy to oblige. You seem like a smart enough chap, but you're a mite out of touch with things. Where did you say you were from again?"

"I didn't," James muttered.

"Easy, mate. Easy. We're in this together. You had questions, so I'll answer them. We'll still be taken to Kai'nau. Don't matter if we're in this cage or another. That's where all Blanks wind up in this part of the world. They'll sell us again, and life goes on. The Kai'ja—those are the people who live at Kai'nau—from what I hear, they don't care much about how they get their hands on Blanks, just so long as they do."

James nodded. Things were beginning to click into place. And if the *History* was right, and there was no coincidence anymore, then this conversation was a message. The rune, the magic that was going to be drawn on one of these three kids, was the key. Either to save the world, or maybe to destroy it. And if luck was really on his side, then James knew which one: Ling. That's why her *Essence* looked special, because she was special. And so James knew he needed to stay close.

"Did I lose you there, mate?" Charles asked, snapping him back to attention.

"Oh. Oh yeah. That makes sense. We're going to Kai'nau. Sorry, I just got kind of mixed up on some of the words." James went out on a limb for an explanation. "This isn't my first language, you know. I sometimes get confused."

"Well, you speak it well enough. Better than me, I daresay. Now, what else can I tell you?" Charles leaned his head back against the cage and closed his eyes. "We've got nothing but time, eh mate?"

James turned back to the bars of the cage. "How do we get out?"

Bellacroix scowled over her shoulder. "You can't done get out, boy. And dat's da truth. It's a cage. You stay in de cage. And even if you could be getting' out, where would you go? You'd die on your own out dere. Be'sum glad for dis here cage. Dey will take us to da Kai'nau. Dat's where all de Blanks are gonna go. We will be sold, and dat is dat. Now leave me peace."

"But what about my friends? What about them? They could be hurt or dead. You can stay here, but I'm looking for a way out. Even if it's just to get my book." James looked again at the plunder his captives had piled. Even if Bellacroix was right, he could use this time to read his book. And maybe, just maybe, learn a little more about what he should do.

James's thoughts were interrupted by a high-pitched howl followed by guttural laughing. The laughs of men and a woman's curses got closer until the group finally became visible. Sylph, her clothes in tatters and bruises and cuts covering her body, was being dragged by three oafish men clad from head to toe in jet-black fur. Their faces were covered behind white cloths, all but their eyes which shone with intense blue. The eyes seemed locked in an expression of utmost cruelty, squinting with mirth as they laughed at Sylph's protests.

"I'll kill you all, you buggers," Sylph spat. "Let me loose or I'll bleed you right! Your deaths will be slow and painful, that I swear. I will cut your hammy's and leave you freeze. Let me loose. Let me back to my ship. Let me back to my ship!"

One of the black-furred men gave a sharp kick to Sylph's side. Beside him was the ebony chest James has seen on the Killdevil. The man patted the box affectionately. "You help us out, and we'll help you out. What's in the box? Open it, and maybe we'll go easy on you. Such a pretty little girl would do well in our service."

Sylph lurched forward, her teeth gnashing mere inches from the man's face. He jerked back in shock, then laughed again. "Put her in the cage." The men opened the bone cage next to James's and tossed Sylph inside. They wrapped a chain around the gate and locked it. "You wait here, my pretty. We're going to look for your friends. Maybe their pain will encourage you, since you seem to care nothing for yourself. There are other ways to make you talk. Other ways to see inside that head of yours." The man kicked the cage, inciting another convulsion from Sylph, then walked away with his friends.

James remained silent. Rule One aside, he wanted to stay inconspicuous. If those men knew that he and Sylph traveled together, they might try to use him against her. He didn't want that to happen, for both of their sakes. Sylph remained silent as well, panting heavily, her breaths becoming shallower and shallower until they had resumed a normal pace. Only then did James speak up.

"Sylph? Captain Sylph, are you all right?"

Sylph rolled her head in James's direction, then looked straight forward again. "So you *are* alive, Jay. A charmed life you lead."

Apparently, James thought. "Where are Brine and Teak? Did they escape all right? I don't remember much from the attack."

Sylph grunted. "Doesn't surprise me, lad. I thought you'd been fried by one of those thunderbolts. Lost track of you for the whole of the fight. But by the time they'd boarded us, 'twas too late. We just assumed you were dead, captured, or run away. Teak and Brine escaped, at least. Though without a ship and without supplies they're as good as dead. All of us."

James could feel the pain radiating from Sylph. Pain from loss of friends. And the loss of her ship. She was down, but she didn't look defeated. He smiled in spite of himself. "I saw your guns. They're over there with my book. If I can get out of here, we can still escape."

"Well, you're the escape artist. Show me how it's done," Sylph replied.

James felt a nudge at his shoulders as Charles and Bellacroix edged beside him, clearly far more interested in Sylph than they had been in him. "What's she mean by that?" Charles asked. "That you're an escape artist. What's an escape artist, mate?"

James shook his head. "I don't…"

"You do understand," Sylph grunted. "You got out of those manacles we put on you in less than a minute. You did it so fast I had Teak recheck you for runes. *Then* I had one of the Scrim do it. Teak didn't find any and neither did they. But you still got out. And that's talent."

I did, didn't I? I don't know how, but I did.

"You listening to me, lad?"

"Yeah, I'm listening. I just slipped out, I guess. I don't think those cuffs were on too tight."

Sylph snorted again. "Well, think you can just 'slip out' of that cage? Maybe bring me my guns while you're at it?"

James glanced around the cage, searching it for weaknesses. The bones making up the bars were a hand-width apart, too close for him to squeeze. The joints of the bones were hard as well, fastened by cartilage and melded together without seams. The cage seemed inescapable, but then, what if there was something he missed?

"Look, mate…" Charles began.

"Shhh. I'm thinking." James opened his mind to the world's *Essence*. He probed every aspect of the cage and found it to be even more solid than it first appeared. He allowed his perception to return to normal. He knew he could get out, just as he knew something was wrong with this world, just as he knew that Sylph and Ling, especially Ling, were part of the way he could help save it. How *had* he gotten out of the manacles? He was in them one second and out the next. The manacles had ignored him in the same way a lot of the people in the Frozen World had ignored him. The manacles had ignored him, and he was free.

"All of you. Look the other way," James spoke calmly and clearly. "Try to forget about me. Just ignore me." But even as he spoke the words, he realized that Sylph and the three kids had done just that. They occasionally looked in his direction, but they didn't *see* him. Just like you can look in a crowd of thousands and not pick out the one person you know. He was there, and yet not there. He had slipped into obscurity.

Then James realized something else. He no longer kneeled on the bony bars of the cage, but the cool soft of the snow. He was out of the cage—just as if he had never been there in the first place.

James stood up and began to walk around the campsite. He glanced back at the cages, yet saw no recognition from Sylph, Ling, Charles, or Bellacroix. It was like he was invisible. *First things first,* James thought. He walked over to the pile of plunder and removed *An Alternative History of Universal Dynamics.* The pages were again blank, though James knew that he had but to become aware of the world's *Essence* and they would return. Next, he took Sylph's gun belt, all five guns of varying designs still holstered in their respective sheaths. Lastly, he grabbed a short dagger. He thought maybe he could use it to pick the lock. Not that James had any idea how to pick a lock, but that should be easy enough for the luckiest boy in the world.

He walked up to Sylph's cage and tapped on the bars. "Captain Sylph, I've come to get you out."

Sylph jerked in surprise. She looked warily at him. "Jay? You startled me, lad. Where did you come from? I thought…" She paused in confusion. "Where did you come from?"

"I slipped away. Hurry, we don't have much time. Look here. I brought your guns." James slid the gun belt through the bars, and Sylph buckled them around her waist. She quickly drew one of the guns from her right side, this one long and slender with an overly fat barrel. James thought it looked like a silencer, but he knew there was no way that in a land of ships and swords that a silencer—

The gun emitted a champagne-cork pop and the lock blew open. Sylph kicked the remnants aside and then dropped from the cage. She scurried over to the plunder and sifted until she found a small pack among the belongings. She paced back to James and spoke in a whisper.

"Nice work, lad. Now we need to move fast. Stay close and follow me." She pulled a small pistol, no larger than a Derringer, from the back of her gun belt. "Here take this, but only use it if you have to."

Rule Number Three! The words rang through his head. Don't harm anything. Never kill anything. You'll get stuck in the world and never be able to leave. "I can't take a weapon. I… I swore never to touch one."

Sylph replied dryly, "You just brought them to me."

"I know, but I could never use one. I swore an oath to never—"

"Oh right, your oath. I understand. Understand you're not a fighter, at least. Now let's move."

"What about them?" James pointed to the cage where Charles, Ling, and Bellacroix watched with interest. "We can't just leave them." He paused. "They're important."

Sylph regarded James with a querulous eye, as if trying to determine just how much he did and didn't know. "Aye. They *are* important. But we can't all get out together. I saw a path out of here. But with five of us, we haven't a chance. I swear we'll come back for them, lad. As you said, they're important."

"But…"

"Jay. Without those three, I've got no way to rescue my ship. Believe me when I say we'll come back for them. Do you believe me?"

He nodded.

"Then let's go. Try to stay unnoticed."

A smile cracked the corner of James's lips. That was something he was learning to do. If he could go so unnoticed that he could drop through the bars of a cage, sneaking out of camp should be child's play. "I'm ready."

Sylph took off at a quick pace, her shoulders hunched low and the silenced pistol held tight in both hands. James raced behind, trying to will himself into obscurity. After the first fifty feet, he thought he was succeeding. Sylph hadn't turned around to check on him once. When she did glance backward, her eyes seemed to skate over him, not registering his presence. She moved with the grace of a stalking feline, pausing only once when one of the men in the black fur coats turned in her direction. Sylph's pistol coughed, and the man dropped to the ground. She wasted no time in stealing the man's coat and the white scarf on his face. In moments, she appeared to be a bandit herself.

Then, her demeanor changed. Her shoulders, once hunched in a lithe stance, moving fluidly with the rest of her body, she thrust upright. Her gait seemed large and brutish. The feline demeanor was gone. If not for the soft brown boots on Sylph's feet, James would have wondered if he had lost her entirely. Now unhurried, they strolled through camp. No one noticed Sylph as anything but another bandit. No one noticed James at all. After they had crossed beyond the perimeter and had trudged up a snowy slope into a stand of evergreens, he quit trying to make himself inconspicuous. In that very instant, Sylph turned to him. She pulled the white scarf from her face and smiled.

"And that, Jay, is what you call a clean getaway. I don't think they even noticed us. Well, they'll notice their fallen friend soon enough, but not us." A puzzled look spread her face. "You know, *I* barely noticed you. I think I even forgot about you for a while."

James feigned being hurt. "Well, that's not very nice."

"No, no. I mean I knew you were there, but…" Sylph looked confused again, then shook it off, the thought sliding easily away. "Never mind. Now we just have to find the others."

A deep voice boomed from the trees. Brine stepped out, a grin on his face. He looked relieved, though James could tell that he had suffered some heavy wounds in the skirmish. "Consider yourself found, lassie. And consider me the winner of a bet. Teak thought it wouldn't be until morning when you got away. Though we did agree that you would. My hat's off to ya."

Sylph seemed to shake off the presence of Brine without surprise. "Jay brought my guns. The rest was simple." She tugged her black fur coat. "I had to kill one on the way out. They'll be missing us soon enough."

Brine snorted. "Good riddance. Now let's get you two back to the others before the dogs come. And they will come, no doubt in the eight winds of that. Unless, that is, they managed to get into that chest of yours."

Sylph shook her head. "Not yet, at least. Though if they make it to Kai'nau before us, it won't matter. I'm sure the Kai'ja won't check a deed of ownership."

"That's loyalty for you. Then again, that's never been those bloody runics' strong suit. Let's get back to the others."

18. Shadow

Despite the fire blazing in the confines of the ice cave, the cold of the winter night cut through to James's bones. While he found that he could ignore the cold to the point where he felt no temperature whatsoever, doing so seemed to make *him* just as ignorable. He would ask questions, and no one would answer, or people would walk right into him, only then acting surprised that they hadn't noticed him before. James wondered if his "ignorability" would in some way be explained by *An Alternative History of Universal Dynamics*, but he hadn't had an opportunity to open the book since he and Sylph had arrived at the camp.

Huddled around the campfire were Sylph, Brine, Teak, Lord Slagish, and the remnants of the Scrim. James was surprised to see that almost three-quarters of the tattooed warriors were present. Then Brine explained that once the Blanks had been captured, the bandits had fled into the woods. The children and Sylph's black chest were the Scrim's valuable cargo, and the reason the Scrim had gone to so much trouble to enlist the services of Sylph and her crew. The amount that the Scrim had paid Sylph for safe passage was the topic of most of the campfire arguments. They were angry at her for allowing the attack to happen, and she was angry that the runic fighters hadn't been able to repel it.

When the arguments had diminished, the group settled on the one thing they could all agree on: the Blanks had to be recovered. Lord Slagish made it clear that without the Blanks and Sylph's chest, they would lack the funds to even return home. But what James didn't understand was how the group of thirty-odd Scrim intended to take on a force five times that amount.

Slagish rose from his seat and turned to face the rest of the group. As he had been aboard the Killdevil III, the man was bare-chested, allowing the massive tattoo stretching across his chest and shoulders to glow eerily in the firelight. James winced at the thought that the man standing before him had erased a waterspout from existence. He inadvertently pulled himself back to appear less noticeable. Within moments, he could feel that it had worked. The cold did not seem bitter, and the people sitting to his left and right became less careful about the placement of their elbows.

"My crew. My comrades. My blood-kin." The Scrim leader's accent still sounded Russian in James's ears. "We have been surprised by our enemy. We have been weak. We have dropped our guard and paid in blood. What's worse, our attackers have taken what belongs to us. We will reclaim it. We will take it back. And in this, we will not fail. Or are we not the Scrim?"

A murmur issued from the crowd. One of the other Scrim, perhaps only a few years older than James, found the courage to reply. "We may have power, Lord Slagish, but why did we not use it when we had the chance? Now we risk destroying the Blanks. We risk everything." The young man shifted uneasily. "We can't risk harming the Blanks… What if the bandits kill them when we attack? They'd rather destroy them than let them be recaptured."

The mustached Scrim leader pursed his lips in a thin smile. "You doubt yourself, friend Ivanovic." The smile dropped into a scowl. "And now you doubt me. That, I will not abide. But I have no intention of risking what is mine. There are other ways to strike a blow. And if you doubt that our current powers are not sufficient, perhaps you desire… *more*. Comrade Tabitha, step forward."

A Scrim woman rose to join Slagish. She was squat, shorter than James, though three times as stout. Unlike all of the other Scrim, she was decorated not with the mysterious runes, but with piercings of every size and shape. Bracelets and studs riddled every bit of exposed skin. Jewelry ran from her shoulder, along her neck, and spiraled around her face until centering on a single jade-colored eye. Tabitha reached into the folds of her cloak and removed an ivory carving of several snakes entwined, but whose tails all formed a single point. Nervous murmurs reverberated through the group.

James tugged on Brine's coat. "What's that thing?" he whispered. But Brine, like everyone else, seemed not to notice him.

"Tabitha is not my servant, as you have been told." The mustached man continued, "She is an etcher, as you have instead suspected. Her skills lie in the Necrotic Arts. She can waylay death itself. Ivanovic, you doubted our sister's skill. Perhaps you would be best suited to ensure our victory."

Like a sea of grass, the crowd parted from the young man who had dared to doubt their leader. At first Ivanovic's face was stern, then it melted as the restrained tears made their way to the surface.

"Come, Ivanovic. Step forward, comrade. The time has come for you to receive your final rune."

Step by fragile step, the young man walked forward. He collapsed on his knees before Lord Slagish. The mustached man placed his boot on the back of Ivanovic's neck and pinned him to the icy ground.

Tabitha the etcher tightened her hand around the ivory quill. She hobbled over to the young man and kneeled astride his body. The ivory quill exploded in pale light, and the witch brought it down onto the man's back.

When the quill touched his skin, James heard a sizzle, and the air filled with the smell of burning flesh. Stroke after stroke, the witch etched the rune onto Ivanovic's back. With every sweep, the man's body writhed in pain. James also saw that the man was savagely biting his arm to keep from crying out. For ten minutes, the witch worked to create the rune. During that time, not one person spoke. Whenever James tried to ask a question of Brine, he was either immediately silenced, or completely ignored. James gave up trying and simply watched.

When the cruel ritual ended, the Scrim leader lifted his foot from the boy's body, while the etcher rose and faded back into the crowd. For almost a minute, Ivanovic lay weeping. Then, the lines on Ivanovic's back darkened, achieving an almost midnight black. The man tensed, and his low sobs halted. Ivanovic shakily rose to his feet, a grim expression on his face. A cheer went up from the crowd, startling James so much he cried out in surprise.

Lord Slagish smiled his grim smile once more. "Young Ivanovic?"

"Yes, Master." The young man's voice echoed distant and solemn.

"Take your sword and go to the bandits' camp. Take back what is ours. No blade or bullet can undo what has been done."

Another surge of cheering from the crowd. Ivanovic turned toward the direction of the bandits' camp. He pulled his sword from its sheath and began to march.

James pulled hard on Brine's coat. "Brine, what happened? What's going on?"

The big man looked lazily down at James. He seemed surprised to see him standing there. Brine replied, "Bloody winds and bloody tides… the Scrim etched him with a rune—right with us watchin'. They said it was to make him so he couldn't die—but I've never heard of such a thing. And I think I *would* have heard of such a thing. Whispered if nothing else, ye ken?" Brine rubbed his temples. "It must be something else. It must be."

"But where is he going?"

"Back to the bandits' camp, aye. Though I don't envy the lads who run into him." Brine's voice wavered. "Bloody hell. What do you think'll happen?"

James dropped his voice low. "I'll follow him."

"No, laddie," Brine nearly yelled. "You *don't* want to see this. Whatever they did to him was dangerous. And it'll be dangerous for you too, you ken? We don't need to be knowing. We just need to wait."

A strange resolution surged inside of James. And for the first time, he felt that he needed to take a role in this mysterious play of which he possessed only an observer's part. James knew, suddenly and terribly, that if he was to make a difference, he needed to know what he was dealing with. He had to see what the Scrim woman had done, what she was capable of. Could she perhaps, as James suspected, draw a rune that could destroy the world?

James gave a reassuring smile. "Don't worry, Brine. You'll never even know I'm gone."

Once more, James pulled himself away from the world. He concentrated on being small, on being forgettable. As he did so, the cold dropped away and the sounds of the crowd became muted. To test his ignorability, he tapped on the shoulder of a Scrim, but the man flicked his hand as if brushing away a fly.

Time to go.

James took off at a run. As he expected, not a single Scrim or member of Sylph's crew gave him a second glance. He dashed in the direction that Ivanovic had walked. It was easy to follow the man's footsteps in the falling snow, and within minutes, the young Scrim was in sight. James slowed to a creep. For a moment he considered that he had run for several minutes and wasn't tired, but this too seemed oddly appropriate. With James close behind, Ivanovic lumbered toward the bandit's camp. The man's expression didn't seem to change, his footfalls heavy and regular.

When Ivanovic came near to the furthest outpost of guards, the bandits took notice immediately. They shouted jeers and insults, but Ivanovic kept marching forward. The insults quickly turned to warnings and one of the bandits aimed a rifle at the Scrim, but Ivanovic kept walking. When the Scrim had come within a few short yards of the bandit, the guard's gun boomed, and Ivanovic dropped.

James winced in surprise from his hiding spot. He had expected Ivanovic to shrug off the gunshots like the zombies on late-night "B" movies. Instead, the once-stoic Scrim had fallen at the first shot. James waited, careful not to move on the outside chance that his talent for inconspicuousness might wear off.

The two guards waited patiently; their rifles fixed on the fallen body. James saw no hint of reduced wariness. But after several minutes and no movement of the fallen man, one of the guards began to inch forward, rifle never veering from the body. The other guard dropped to one knee, the barrel of his gun remaining steady. He could sense by the guards' caution that they were not completely convinced of the Scrim's death. The approaching guard stopped short a few feet of the body and then aimed his rifle at Ivanovic's head. James watched as the man pulled back the hammer.

Two gunshots rang in perfect simultaneity as the guards discharged their weapons. But instead of the body falling still, it seemed to crumple. The rune on Ivanovic's back grew, enveloping the body in a black shadow so dark that it etched against the night in sharp relief. James heard a horrible crunching sound, as the bones of Ivanovic cracked under the force of the living rune.

The rune jumped.

The apparition shot forward, its shape indefinable, and engulfed the closest guard. James winced as the guard's muted scream died in his throat, and the shadow leaped again—now doubled in size—to the guard behind the barricade. The guard fired over and over, but the bullets caused only a twitch in the ravenous shadow. The gunshots and the screams roused more of the bandits. The rest was a disaster.

James was only able to watch for a moment more before the carnage forced him to look away. His stomach knotted in fear. The gunshots, screams, and the horrible crunching sound continued. Over and over again, James heard the bandits' lives being wrenched from their bodies. James was able to hold himself together until the smell hit. He collapsed on his knees, retching again and again. He felt his mind was trying to purge itself as quickly as his body. His head throbbed, his joints sang with pain. James was seized by a panic so intense that rational thought shrank to nothing.

I have to escape! I have to escape! I have to get out now before it's too late. Let me out, let me out, let me out, let me out!

James spat once to try to purge the taste of vomit from his mouth. He held out his palm to concentrate on the *Essence*, the only way he knew to escape. All thoughts of remaining inconspicuous had evaporated, replaced only by terror. The frantic fumbling was useless. he realized that if he didn't remain calm and concentrate, that *Thing* would know he was here. He darted his eyes to the camp. The shadow-beast had finished its feast of bandits and was rolling his way. The indefinable form spiraled and unfolded as it simultaneously collapsed.

James forced his mind to a tentative calm. He opened himself to the world's *Essence* and closed his eyes, not sliding from the world, but ripping himself away. As the shadow-beast leaped—

James fell.

* * *

And yet, he did not *quite* fall.

James tumbled through a lightless void. He could feel the motion of his body; he could smell the ever-so-cool whip of damp air. Sounds drifted across the void, tickling his ears. He could hear a thousand whispers in a thousand languages as he turned and drifted. Cries of pain, laughter, screams, and accusations. Each sound seemed to ride the emotion it conveyed. The sounds became higher and more shrill until so highly pitched that James wasn't sure if he still heard them at all. Then the pitch plummeted, becoming audible for only a moment before disappearing again from his range of hearing. Then, incredibly, the sounds coalesced until solid. James could first sense the sounds as tangible objects, and then the sensing became seeing as they brightened into pinpricks of light.

Though his body remained without form, James's eyes opened wide in astonishment. He was free-falling through a galaxy of a billion stars, a billion points of light. But each star was not *simply* light. The glows contained voices, sounds, smells, and a myriad of feelings. James knew that he was not in a galaxy of stars, but a galaxy of worlds. He had but to reach out his mind and he would be drawn into any one of the billion realities streaming around him

Contentment washed over James's body, only to be replaced by disquiet. For as he fell through the void, he could tell that some of the worlds, *many* of the worlds, did not glow with strong healthy light. Some of the worlds were pale, their lights waning. When James looked at these worlds, he was physically pained by their suffering. He felt the sick worlds plead to him for help, and yet he drifted on.

Further and further he fell. Not down, but rather to center. James drifted until a soft pillar of light appeared below him. The light was not a pinprick of intensity like the worlds, but instead a current of energy stretching into infinity. He slowly descended until the soft light engulfed him. His field of vision became awash with light. His vision became as formless and white as it had been formless and black just a short time ago. A hum filled his ears, soft and singular until diffusing to the sound of voices in a crowd, becoming tangible and present.

And then he blinked.

19. Coaching

"Back again, my brother? Don't you have better things to do?"

James blinked in surprise. He was standing in a long corridor that seemed to stretch without horizon in front of him. Lining the corridor were doors upon doors, each identical to the last in both size and shape. James looked down to find himself wearing a pale white robe with a consistency not unlike moleskin. He knew exactly where he was.

Grand Central.

He had returned, somehow. And yet he wasn't surprised. James had drifted through the galaxy of worlds to the center. And according to Dr. Huckabee, Grand Central was the axis of all worlds.

James darted his head around to see that the doctor was waiting anxiously for his reply. Just like the last time he had encountered Dr. Huckabee, the man looked quite different from when James had met him at the psychiatrist's office. Dr. Huckabee now stood only three feet tall. Poking from his trousers where his feet should have been, were a pair of hands which matched those on the ends of his arms. For a moment James remained silent, trying to adjust to his new environs.

"I found your book," James finally said.

"Capital! And what did you think?"

"I didn't get much of a chance to read much of it. Some people chased me down at the library. I barely escaped. They were looking for me. Waiting for me."

Dr. Huckabee looked momentarily troubled; then he smiled. "But you're standing here, so you must have been smart enough not to linger. That, or you found my note in time. Kudos to you. If they'd found you, we most likely would not be speaking today. But pish-posh, water under the bridge, I suppose. But let me ask, are you finding it easier to Travel? Move about, Slip or Fall or whatnot?"

James shrugged. "I guess. I still have trouble aiming. Which is why I'm here. Wasn't really on purpose."

The doctor nodded. "It all gets easier with practice."

James glanced around the corridor, pausing to watch a man in a basketball uniform holding hands with a seven-foot Amazon wearing a Fred Flintstone-style leopard print outfit.

"Wait a minute!"

Dr. Huckabee looked surprised. "What's that?"

"The last time I was here, you were shouting at me so quickly my head was spinning. You wouldn't tell me anything and were trying to push me on my way. What's the difference this time? Why are you talking to me? Why are you being so friendly? Are you up to something?"

Dr. Huckabee somersaulted, landing in a handstand and then placing his feet-hands firmly on his hips. "The difference isn't me, brother. It's you. The last time you were here, you could barely hold yourself together. But now you seem quite aware of both yourself as well as your surroundings. This brings me to another question, are you seeing the Cosmos yet?"

"The Cosmos? Like stars?" James shrugged. "I think so. It was like I was floating through these lights that kind of looked like stars until I saw this beam of light—"

Dr. Huckabee interrupted, "That was stretching forth in all directions like the beam of light of countless worlds? Yes, I know. As they say, 'This isn't my first rodeo, cowboy.' As you probably guessed, each of those lights is a world, a particular slice of reality. Usually, it takes a while to see the Cosmos, because the transition from one world to another is so abrupt, and so forceful, that the entire event seems to happen instantaneously. But now that you are seeing them, it means

that you are gaining a degree of mastery of your ability to Travel."
Huckabee gave James an exaggerated wink. "So now that you're here
and we're talking, what do you want? The battle is out there, not here."

James was shocked. "Well, I... I wouldn't mind asking a few
questions. But I thought we weren't allowed to talk here."

"Not here-here. Follow me." Dr. Huckabee dropped to all fours
and padded along the corridor until coming to a door that, unlike every
other door on the floor, was exactly the height of the crouched Dr.
Huckabee. The doctor turned the handle and disappeared inside.

James hesitated for only a minute before dropping to his belly and
wriggling through after the doctor. When he had wormed the whole
way through, the door slammed shut behind him, and the room
brightened. To James's surprise (though he thought he was becoming
harder and harder to surprise) he was in a small field covered in daisies
swaying in a slight breeze. Overhead the sun shone down pleasantly,
with a just-so-appropriate amount of puffy clouds floating overhead.

"Where are we?" James pushed himself to his feet. "What world is
this?"

"It's not a world at all. This is just a room in Grand Central.
Because Grand Central is a pivot point for all worlds, it can adjust to
your expectations. For example, the first time you entered Grand
Central, you didn't land in the hallway, did you?"

"No. It was more like a hospital room. I used to go to lots of
hospitals because of my…"

"Rule One!" the doctor shouted. "Even here. Even when you
think you're alone. Always Rule One."

James hopped in excitement. "Rule Four!"

"No, Rule One."

"No. I mean I finally learned what Rule Four is from the book.
'Don't fall in love,' but I don't think I quite understand it."

"You don't understand love? But you're so old and wise?" Dr.
Huckabee grinned, and James realized the little man was making fun of

him. The doctor continued. "Well Rule Four is quite important, and at the same time the hardest to avoid. When we try to help worlds, we necessarily become attached to them. But you can't get too attached—emotionally speaking—or you'll be unable to leave."

"So you can't fall in love or you'll get stuck."

"Precisely. Your spirit becomes entwined in the world, and simply won't let go."

"But how 'in love' is 'in love'?"

Dr. Huckabee sat down amongst the dandelions. He crossed his legs, then motioned for James to sit as well. "First, don't get confused and assume I'm talking about romantic love. The best way to think about it is whether you are keeping your focus. When you quit doing things just to save a world, and start doing things just for the people you've met, you're starting to get in trouble. Best just not to get too attached, stay at a distance."

The doctor lay back. He picked a dandelion with one of his feet-hands and begun plucking the petals. "There have been some real fine Travelers that lost sight of their mission, or maybe just got tired of fighting. Quite a few fall in love and are never seen again. And that's ok, I guess. But it wasn't their world. And it wasn't where they belonged."

James shrugged. "I'm not concerned. I'm only fourteen."

Dr. Huckabee laughed. "Age hasn't got anything to do with it. When you get involved with trying to heal a sick world, you start getting involved with people's lives. You *will* start to care about them, there's no way to help it. Just don't let it go too far."

James chewed on the doctor's words carefully. There was some truth in what he said. He found a friendship growing between him and Brine, even Sylph. But it wasn't love. Ling on the other hand. James felt his cheeks flush at the thought of the pretty, dark-haired Blank. His embarrassment became fear with the thought that the shadow-beast may have gotten her. But somehow, he knew that it hadn't. Lord

Slagish wouldn't have risked his prize unless he was certain it would be safe. The man was cold, but he was also smart.

"Lost in thought, my brother?"

"I… I was just thinking." James felt color rush to his cheeks again. "Different question. The *History* said that there's no coincidence for Travelers. How far does that go? I mean, I think I'm starting to get on the right track with the problem of the world I'm in. You see, there are these people called runi—"

"No! Rule One!"

"But I'm not talking about myself."

"Rule One goes further. You can't talk about the places you've been to either. What would happen if I were to be captured by the Styx? I'd be forced to tell them everything I knew, and that means about your worlds too. They could track you."

"But you already know my home world, what's the difference?"

"The difference is that they may find you, but maybe not the worlds you visit. It's the dying worlds they are most concerned about. So remember, limit your secrets, so that you can't be followed." The doctor hopped to his feet. "But it sounds to me like you are getting up and running and doing just fine without me. Good luck and…"

"Wait—I still have questions!"

"I'm certain you do, my brother. But the work isn't here, it's out there. And…" The smile fell from Dr. Huckabee's face.

"What? What is it?"

"Listen, my brother. I need to be quite careful. I don't quite know how to say this, but I'm afraid I've been a little careless."

"I don't understand."

"I, well I." Huckabee wrinkled his brow in concentration. "The last time I was in your world, I think I may have been seen. I'm usually quite careful about such things, but there is a chance I've been found out. So, I'm afraid I should never return to your world again, and the less I speak to you, and the less I learn about any other worlds you visit is probably for the best. I'm on to something, my brother, but it's quite risky, and I can't get you involved."

"Maybe I can help."

"No-no, you have much too much to do, and much too much to learn. Just one last piece of advice before we part our ways." Huckabee smiled, but his eyes were imploring. "Whatever you do, never forget about your home. Your home life and being a real person there are just as important as the things we do out here. Because when you're home, that's when you really can be a real person. Only when you're home can you truly care, or feel, or even fall in love. And if you don't have those things, then my brother, you are missing the whole reason of the *why* we do what we do. So don't forget to go home once in a while. I'm sure you've seen it already, time moves differently when you're Traveling. Time won't stop and wait for you—unless you ask it to—and neither will your life." Dr. Huckabee walked to the door which hung against nothing in the flowered field.

"But…"

Dr. Huckabee crawled away, glancing once over his shoulder. "This is goodbye, my brother. But don't worry, it's all in the book." And the door shut.

James sat in the dandelion field. He idly picked flowers one by one. He pulled the petals from the stem, then flicked them to the ground. *All in the book, all in the book. But who has time to read the damn book?* James snorted and rose to his feet. At first, he thought about returning to the Frozen World to find the book, sneak off and read it once and for all. But another voice told him that he should be heading back home to his real life, and his real home. James held out his hand. He focused on his own *Essence* and the *Essence* of his home world. And then—

James fell.

20. Lies

James stared at the wood grains on his desk. His eyes focused on the pattern, and then on the cartoon rendition of Mr. Tucholke with his overlarge ears. James took only a moment to register his surroundings, from the industrial brick on the walls, to the periodic table just to the left of the dry-erase board. He must be in science class. Third period.

"But why should we care about ocean currents? James?"

He replied seamlessly, stepping back into the rhythm of school. "Because ocean currents can affect climate change, wind patterns, hurricanes. They don't seem important at first, but they matter."

James didn't bother to pay attention to his teacher's response. It didn't matter anyway; he wouldn't be called on again. He raised his eyes from the desk and looked around the room. Everything appeared just as normal as a school should appear. Mr. Tucholke was drawing furiously on the chalkboard; the students watched with listless gazes; the jocks snickered to one another. The only thing that gave James a start was the calendar on the wall. The large red X's tracking across the month were far too numerous. A chill went down James's spine.

Three days had passed. Three days.

It isn't fair! a voice shouted inside of him. The escape from the bandits, the discussion around the campfire, even the attack of the shadow beast. That had all happened in a space of maybe six hours. And how long had he been in Grand Central? Surely no more than twenty minutes. But *three days* had passed. It wasn't fair.

Being in science class, James's mind provided a curt but unsatisfying answer that the Theory of Relativity would explain his problem very neatly. If James, when he traveled outside of his body, was going fast enough, time would go slowly for him, but at the same speed for the rest of the world. It was *completely* possible that more time would pass than he remembered. But he fought back with another thought, just as irrational as the first had been rational. What was happening to him wasn't about science at all. This was magic. And magic didn't need an explanation.

The bell rang, signaling the end of the second period. James had to look down on his class schedule to make sure he knew where to go next. The concept of lost time was just enough to disturb his sense of order. The crumpled printout indicated that on Friday (today) James should be going to his free period. At least that much was lucky. Maybe he could find out from Seth what had happened in the real world these past three days.

When James arrived in the study hall, Seth was already there, his notebook open and his pen sketching furiously. James was excited by the prospect of not only finding out what had happened in the past three days, but even more excited to finally get to talk to someone who was his friend—and not some otherworldly doctor, mercenary for hire, or part of some outlandish magic-wielding slave caste. James scurried across the room and slung himself into the seat beside Seth.

Seth glowered at James. "And what do *you* want?" His tone was harsh and biting.

"Nothing much. Just seeing what you were up to, that's all."

"Oh, and now you care. Is that how it is, Jim?"

James paused. Seth's mannerisms were always a little off, but the two had been good friends for months. James feared that something must have happened while he was out of body. If they had gotten into a fight of some kind—which did happen from time to time—then James wished he knew what had happened. "What? What did I do?"

"I don't know, *buddy*," Seth's tone dripped with sarcasm. "Why don't you tell me? Or are you not ready for that?"

"Look, I don't know what you're talking about."

Seth snapped back, "Just tell me. I don't know why this is such a big deal to you. And don't tell me any more lies. I've heard enough lies out of you to last a long time. Where did you go on Monday?"

Monday? That's when I went to the library, James thought. *Was I supposed to meet Seth somewhere?*

"Or," Seth continued, "if you don't feel up to that, how about telling me where you went on Tuesday. Or maybe Wednesday. Or yesterday?"

James felt his cheeks flush. "Seth, I can explain."

"Oh, I'll bet you can. I've heard your little explanations. And you're good at 'em, too. You're full of crap, James. Now leave me alone. If you don't want to be my friend, that's fine. Just don't lie to my face and expect me not to notice. Or care. Now, I've got some work to do." Seth gathered his books in a huff and stomped to the far side of the room where he threw them back down again. He deliberately angled his desk away from James and hunched over an open book.

James sat dumbfounded, his mouth parted in disbelief. Seth was his best friend in the world, and yet something he had done in the past three days—the past three *missing* days—had driven a wedge between them. But at the same time, James knew exactly what he had done. He had lied. He had lied to cover up going to the library. And whatever else he'd done, he had lied to cover that up too. James guessed that the lie had come just as easily as the one he had told on the bus about having sisters (when he didn't), and just as easy as the ones he told to Sylph's crew or the Blanks in the Frozen World. Whatever auto-pilot piece of his brain was working when James was in another world was working just a little too hard to protect his identity. And while neither Sylph's crew nor the Scrim knew the real James from the character he was playing, Seth did. Seth could see through James's lies, and he was hurt by them.

James gripped his backpack with one hand. He needed to tell Seth everything. Not only was it the right thing to do as a friend, but Seth was smart. If anyone would know what to do about the lost days and the other worlds, that person was Seth. James cursed himself for putting his faith in Dr. Huckabee and some strange book that only he could see. It was crazy. This whole thing was crazy. And now his only real friend hated him. He had to tell him everything.

Rule One, his mind whispered.

You can take your Rule One and shove it, James shot the thought back. And yet he couldn't will his legs to rise. He gripped the edge of the desk until his knuckles turned white.

What are you waiting for? the voice in his mind asked. *Afraid? Well, you should be. Remember the library? Remember being chased? Do you think that those people in the library are any less dangerous than the Scrim's shadow-beast? If you do, you're wrong. The shadow-beast is only one little thing in one little world. The ice-faced woman and her friends at the library are looking for you, James. Like it or not, you've got no choice.*

James allowed his fingers to relax. The voice in his head—not *the* voice of reason, but certainly a voice—was right. The slightest slip and the ice-faced woman could find him. And if Dr. Huckabee was right, she would kill him. She may already have found the doctor. But that didn't mean that James had to lose all his friends. He rose to his feet and walked over to Seth.

"Seth…"

"Are you still here?" Seth shot back. "Leave, me, alone!" Seth screamed the last words, causing the other students in the study hall to turn and stare. Mrs. Copperfield, the proctor, raised her voice, stern and clear. "James, please take your seat. You are disturbing Seth. And in turn, disturbing us all. This is a *study* hall, and I expect you to study."

James, red-faced and ashamed, did not return to his seat. He stormed to the door and exited the classroom. He heard the voice of his teacher calling behind him, but he didn't slow. The door slammed shut behind him.

Emerging in the hallway, he thrust his hands deep into his pockets and took a quick turn through the emergency exit. A sticker on the glass exclaimed "Exit Only, Alarm will Sound" but James had learned long ago that such threats were idle. Once outside, he trudged along the faceless brick corridor between the school buildings. He walked until finding a niche where a pile of old cinderblocks formed a crude bench. He sat down hard on the bricks and leaned back against the wall. He hadn't come here, to this quiet haven between classes in quite some time, though he used to often with Greg, Duncan, and Marc. The once-good friends used to use it as their private hideout to escape from teachers or upper-classmen.

The thought of his ex-friends made the hairs on the back of James's neck stand up. He remembered his reasons for staying away.

A voice mocked from further down the brick wall, "Well this, this I don't believe."

James narrowed his eyes and glanced to the side. Leaned against the bricks just twenty feet away were Duncan, Greg, and Marc. The three boys had discovered smoking at the beginning of the school year and considered Study Hall an unofficial opportunity to indulge their habit. Greg flicked his cigarette butt on the ground and scratched his temple.

"This ain't your place no more, James."

"Don't test me, Greg. Not today, I'm just chilling out. I won't bother ya'll."

Duncan and Marc snickered to themselves, and James could see from their widening smiles that laying low wouldn't be an option. Greg continued, "I think you already are bothering us. This is our spot. You're not invited." Greg stomped over to where James sat, fists balled.

Fire igniting within his belly, James sprang to his feet. He set his jaw. "What is it, Greg?" he spat. "Can't go ten seconds without having to feel all high and mighty? I'm through with your shit."

Greg lunged forward, both arms outstretched and hitting James hard in the chest. James was knocked back, but unlike their last encounter, his footing was sure. James snapped forward, his arms returning the push, palm striking hard against the center of Greg's chest. The larger boy recoiled as well, a momentary look of confusion that the normally passive James had dared to stand up for himself. Confusion transformed to rage, Greg's face reddened, his lips parted to reveal a single drip of spittle that joined his lips. As Greg's jaw tightened, his teeth bared. He drew back his clenched fist, the individual muscles in his arms tightening as he recoiled, and then he moved to strike.

James saw each action with minute slowness, then realized why. He had snapped himself into awareness of the *Essence*, his heightened senses taking easy stock of every action. As Greg's fist swung forward, James dodged easily to the side. He clenched his fist and jabbed hard into Greg's unguarded belly. As his knuckles connected, a surge of adrenaline tore through his veins, and the awareness of *Essence* snapped away. James found himself back in the stark reality of the moment, just in time for the other two boys to pounce.

Marc and Duncan tackled James, knocking him down and then raining blows across his chest. Occasionally they connected full punches into the side of his head. After the first direct strike, James jerked into a ball, arms desperately shielding his face. He endured several more punches, a single kick and then the assault ended.

"That's enough," Greg called. His fury seemed lessened. "We'll get him later. We're not getting expelled for you, James. But be ready. You'll get yours." Greg connected one more kick, then James heard his ex-friends stomp away.

For several minutes, James lay in pain. His ear throbbed from where the blow had landed, and yet he knew that there would be few lasting signs. For better or for worse, he didn't bruise easily, a fact that Duncan, Greg, and Marc tended to exploit. James pulled himself to his feet and dusted the grass clippings and dirt from his clothes.

"They were supposed to be my friends."

* * *

James sank into obscurity for the rest of the day. A trip to the bathroom had cleaned him up enough so that no one asked questions. Seth seemed to notice the scuffs on James's face, but he, too, said nothing. And so James became nothing more than another blank face in a sea of students. He didn't think he was quite as unnoticeable as he had been in the Frozen World, but he felt he was close. Here, no one cared enough to notice him. In the Frozen World, they had been unable.

He tried to concentrate on school, to tear his mind away from both thoughts of lost friends as well as the strange worlds. Even the school texts had a ghostly feel of seeming remembrance, each word giving a slight deja vu effect as James wondered if his unconscious self had read the same words before. But he didn't care. He simply wanted the day to end.

The bus ride home was uneventful. James had made one or two efforts to speak with Seth, but his friend had made it clear that he was in no mood to talk. In the end, James decided to let Seth cool down, and then he would work on some kind of apology. After all, Seth didn't need to know every little thing that he did, not at all. As for the lies— well, the lies were regrettable. But Seth would come around, he always did.

When the bus dropped him off, Seth slunk back towards his house. James, on the other hand, was in no mood to go straight home. Nevertheless, he wanted to check to see if anything strange had happened there as well, or if his problems were confined to school. So instead of taking the five-minute walk back to his house, James decided to play a game that he, Greg, Duncan, and Marc used to play quite a lot. The idea was to sneak home as furtively as possible. Roads were off-limits, of course, as were sidewalks and anywhere truly visible. The boys would pretend they were spies, or sometimes pretend that they were being chased. All in good fun, of course.

James cinched his backpack tighter. He ambled from the bus stop with the rest of his schoolmates, now dispersing. He paused beside an azalea bush—and then the race was on. He ducked under the bush and snuck under the tunnel formed between the thick leafy brush and the ground. He dropped to his belly and snaked for fifty feet before the line of bushes ended.

Next, there was a short dash to the creek. James waited until he was positive that no one could see him, and then darted across the corner of a yard and then dropped into the small ditch forming the runoff creek. James huddled behind the embankment, waiting to catch his breath before raising his eyes to check for followers.

The creek continued for several hundred yards before James made another dash, this time into a wooded patch that bordered some of the houses in the neighborhood. From there James crossed to another creek, through a drainage pipe, and lastly completed the—although not stealthy—extremely entertaining task of walking along the top of a fence to the edge of the lot to where his house was.

James had perfected the last hundred feet of the route. Under the cover of a magnolia, behind another patch of azaleas, and finally underneath the crawl space below the tool shed. When he finally reached his back door, he was covered from head to toe in mud and dirt. But thankfully, his worries of Seth, of Dr. Huckabee, his ex-friends, and the loss of three days had faded to a passing thought. Then, James saw his father's car.

He paused in confusion. His dad was rarely home this early in the day. On the outside chance he escaped work, he usually went to play golf, tennis, or maybe go fishing—depending on who else was off that day. James knew that for his dad to be home with daylight left to burn, meant that maybe his mom and dad were having a "talk". Usually, such talks were about him.

On several occasions, James had heard his parents arguing about "what to do with him." Usually, these were discussions about what he would and would not be allowed to take part in because of his fainting spells. Sometimes they were worried about his safety, other times that he wasn't making friends. On more than one occasion, his mother had begun to cry when she and his father had these talks. More than once, James had cried just from listening.

He lay on the cool ground below the tool shed. The open window of the kitchen was no more than six feet away, and his parents' voices were easily audible. James gritted his teeth and begun to listen.

"I thought you would be happy," James's father said, his deep easy voice gliding through the window.

The frantic voice of his mother answered. "Happy? What should we be happy about? I don't see anything to be happy about."

"Well, he hasn't fainted in almost a week, not since he got picked up from his camping trip. I called his school just to make sure. So maybe that's all behind him. Maybe one of those doctors you took him to finally got their stuff together."

"Oh, and you think this is better?" his mother replied.

"It was just a little lie. Boys his age tell them all the time."

"A little lie? He hasn't said one true thing in days. It's, it's compulsive. After the first one, I started asking around. None of it is true. I don't know *where* he has been going. Seth doesn't either. James disappears after school and then shows up for dinner. And that's all I know."

"It could be anything. Maybe he has a girlfriend. Maybe he's just embarrassed about something." He paused. "You don't think it's drugs, do you? Or alcohol?"

"No, no I don't think so. It's just that… when I ask him a question, it's like he's… absent. That's the word. It's like he's there, but not there." His mother sighed in frustration. "I don't know exactly, but something's not right."

"Look, now I know things aren't perfect. But James is a growing boy. Soon he won't want to just run and play with his friends. He has to grow up, too."

"But the lies…"

"Never mind the lies. We just need to give him our love. Be patient, Rome was neither built nor burned in a day."

"But I can't *trust* him. Don't you understand?"

James's father's tone became stern. "You can and you will. He's our son."

"Don't 'he's our son' me. Don't try and take the higher ground. Because frankly, it doesn't sit well on you. I've heard what you've said, and I've had it."

"Oh, like you're any better? Are you forgetting when you…"

James winced in pain, both emotional as well as from the welts from the fight earlier. He slunk backward, the sounds of the argument becoming less distinct in his ears until they were nothing more than a frantic murmur. He thought about sneaking back to the bus stop, only to approach the house much more loudly and noticeably.

James slid backward until he was out from behind the shed. Then he reversed his path behind the azalea bushes, over the fence, and into the patch of woods running diagonally behind his block. When he had gotten away from any potentially prying eyes, he slumped against the base of a dogwood tree. He brushed the dirt from his hands and knees.

First his old friends, now Seth, now his parents—there was no one left who trusted him. And if Dr. Huckabee was right, he shouldn't try to trust anyone, anyway. But there had to be a way to keep friends and family happy and still keep his secrets. James held his head in his hands. It was the lies, of course. The people who knew him couldn't stand the lies. James knew he could try and not lie when he was home, but what about when he was away? How could he control his body as it ran on its bizarre autopilot?

The answer was as simple as it was painful. If James wanted to make sure he didn't do anything strange, he couldn't allow himself to go to sleep. If he slept, then he would Travel, and his days would slip away as easily as they had before.

Another thought gnawed at James's mind. Why should he care about what happened here? What value was his life if a world's existence hung in the balance? Dr. Huckabee said his life at home was important, but Dr. Huckabee didn't have to deal with time slipping away. So why fight it? Why bother going home at all?

First, James thought, *I'll figure out Traveling. Then, I'll deal with things at home.*

James gritted his teeth. Time would pass. One way or another, time would pass—and the clock ticked in both his world and the Frozen World. But James didn't plan on spending his time in either. His parents, Sylph, Seth, Teak, Brine, Greg, the ice-faced woman, and even the Scrim—they could all wait their turn. Each of them posed a problem that James would wait to answer. For now, only the *History* could break him from this cycle. The knowledge contained in those pages had to be able to help, it just had to.

He swallowed hard. The *History* was still in the Frozen World, as was the Shadow-beast. Before he'd have his answers, he first had a literal demon to face. And the way time had been sliding around, James had no way of knowing when he'd land.

No time to waste.

James opened himself to the *Essence* of the world. Then he fixed the *Essence* of the Frozen World in his mind. At first, his mind seemed torpid, reluctant to move without first being asleep. But James didn't relent. He felt his mind begin to slide, to become unstuck in its place in this world. And then—

James fell.

21. Aftermath

The Cosmos of one billion worlds rushed past James. The last time James had seen the combined galaxies, he had drifted and fallen, a free fall that was nearly lazy. But now, with the *Essence* of the Frozen World locked in his mind, James moved so quickly that the points of light, each a unique world and universe, sped past with the blur of a poorly developed photograph. With his mind's eye, James could see the light which contained the Frozen World, streaking closer and closer, larger and larger, until he was completely engulfed in the white-hot aura.

The light became form. A galaxy, a single star, then a planet—not singularly white and frozen as he had anticipated, but a swirl of blue, green, and white much like Earth—and entirely different. James plummeted, dropping at an indistinct white patch flecked with green. The shape developed texture, and he could recognize mountains, the Alpinsea, and the towering evergreen forests. James dropped further, the ground rushing to greet him. Then, the descent slowed, each heartbeat pounded like a slow, steady gong. James realized that his awareness was hovering just inches above his own motionless body, frozen in a moment. And a mere foot away, frozen in mid-leap—

The shadow-beast.

As James collided with his own body, the world resumed its normal pace. He had just enough time to dive out of the way of the pouncing creature. He landed, sliding on his side as the shadow-beast missed him by inches. But James had no illusions that he could somehow outrun or fight this monstrosity. And though the panic nearly seized him, James put all his concentration into making himself unnoticeable, untraceable, invisible. He tried to pull himself almost completely from the world, leaving just enough trace of himself that he did not drop back into the Cosmos again.

The growl of the shadow-beast, an inhuman crunching, and guttural utterance came closer. For a brief moment, James allowed his eyes to open, then shut them fast again. The shadow-beast was moving directly over him, not stepping, but a kind of touch-and-glide as tendrils of darkness reached to the earth to move the creature along its way, leaving no trace but the scent of damp and death and dying.

I'm not here. I'm nothing. I don't exist. James repeated the mantra in his mind, his will forming a shell around him. He could feel the shadow-creature moving slowly away. But its mannerism had changed. The beast no longer seemed to be on the hunt. It ambled without direction.

James rolled onto his stomach, being sure not to lose focus on his ignorability. The creature had indeed slowed. Its movements were becoming short and jerky. The steps seemed heavier. And the darkness of the shadow-beast's body was not quite as defined around the edges.

A shot of intuition sparked James's mind. Though he did not know *how* he knew, he knew. The creature was starving. Its short, horrible life could only be sustained by the consumption of life. That was why the Scrim had unleashed the shadow-beast without fear. They knew that this entity, though ravenous, would starve to death before crossing from the bandits' camp to their own.

The beast had stopped now, its dark non-light so pale that it was nothing more than a wisp of fog across the snowy ground. And then, the shadow was gone. The only remnant of the killing entity was the destruction left behind.

James pulled himself to a low crouch. He did not allow his mind to relax in case the shadow-beast still existed in an ephemeral way. And though he had returned to the Frozen World solely to recover the *History*, he first wanted to make sure that the Blanks were safe. Making his footfalls quiet, James crept toward the heart of the bandits' camp, his direction firmly set upon the area where the Blanks had been held. His senses were razor-sharp, and yet the feeling of danger no longer tickled his brain. James crept past the line of tents where Sylph had encountered the one bandit she had shot. He was unsurprised to see that the man's body was the *only* corpse in the entire camp. Everything else had been eradicated by the shadow-beast.

Passing through the last barricade, James saw the first of the holding cages. The first cage was empty. And why not? Nothing else had stopped the shadow-beast. But the second cage, the second cage was occupied. Ling, Bellacroix, and Charles were alive, though terrified. The three held each other close, the pretense of aloofness that Ling had shown James completely gone.

Ling looked in James's direction. She flinched in surprise. "Jay? Jay, is that you?"

James flinched as well. Having not released his unnoticeability, he had not expected the Blanks to see him.

Charles, the English-sounding Blank replied, "Who are you talking to, Ling? What do you see?"

Bellacroix answered, "It's Jay, dassum troublin' boy who was with de Islanders. He's be right over dere."

While James wasn't certain why Ling and Bellacroix could see him but Charles couldn't, he released his unnoticeability. He suddenly felt heavy and a part of the world.

"Criminy, there he is!" Charles shouted. "He snuck right up on us. Jay, what's going on, mate? What's happening out there? This shapeless black thing came and…" Charles's face darkened. "It was *eating* everything. It came to the cage, but… but it couldn't get through the bars. Where is everyone else? What happened to them?"

James crept forward, careful to keep his voice low on the chance the shadow-beast still prowled, though weakened. "Shhh. You need to stay put for a bit longer. It's not safe outside."

Bellacroix, the dark-skinned girl, raised an eyebrow at James. "Was it you, den, boy?"

"Huh?"

"Dat shadow. Was it you? Now be tellin' da truth." Bellacroix fixed him with a chill stare that felt eerily like the presence of the shadow-beast.

"No. It was the Scrim. They did something to one of their…" James stopped himself short. "Look, I don't know if it's safe. But I'll come back. The Scrim will be here soon. We'll get you out."

Bellacroix frowned. "So it wasn't you. Den how be you here? Dat be *very* interesting."

Ling looked at James. Her eyes seemed to bore into his skull and James felt again that flighty sense that he wasn't completely in possession of his actions. "Yes. Pray tell, boy, why *are* you here?"

James flushed, wishing he could fade into the night and become unnoticeable. But he knew that even if Charles didn't notice him, Ling—and perhaps Bellacroix—would.

"I… I…" James stammered. "I needed to make sure you were ok. Listen, I need to go away for a little while. But I'll be back, I promise. Just wait a little while longer." His cheeks burning, James dashed from the holding area, his steps just a hair softer than completely careless.

He dashed across the camp, traveling in the other direction from where the shadow-beast lay sleeping (or dead, hopefully dead.) James did not encounter a single living soul, and yet the embarrassment of being seen by Ling when he was trying *not* to be seen consumed his thoughts. James ran past the camp's perimeter, into the evergreen woods, and ascended a snowy bank until he found a small rocky overhang, forming an impromptu shelter. Only when he was tucked away, did James allow himself to stop. His heavy breathing took several minutes to finally calm.

She's the one, James thought. *Ling has got to be the one. She's the key to all of this. I have to get close, but not (Rule Four) not too close.*

But at the same time, James knew that the Frozen World was just one world of many. And even if this world *was* dying, unless James could figure out how to survive in his own world, and his own life, the plight of countless other worlds wouldn't matter.

James reached into his coat and removed the tattered copy of *An Alternative History of Universal Dynamics*. As before, the pages were blank until James opened himself to the *Essence* of the world. At first, he was seized by the nausea of feeling the world's sickness, but he pushed the feeling aside. If he was to survive both this world and recollect the remnants of his own tattered life, he needed to learn.

James opened to the first page, and began to read.

"First off, a word of congratulations for not being dead…"

* * *

Time passed in the Frozen World. The sun rose, then set, then rose again. Time also passed on James's homeworld, though in ways he didn't yet understand. Time passed on the strange ocean world with the multi-colored sky. Time passed in a world of metallic lakes and toppled stones. Time passed on a world faceless except for windswept sand. Time passed on a city crumbling, lashing out in the throes of death. Time passed in all worlds and all places, each of a thousand destinies were born, some fulfilled, and others passing from existence to fade once more to nothingness.

Through it all, James read. And then—

He fell.

Of worlds, there are many.
Of gods and men, countless.
Of chances, infinite.
But of your life, there is only one.

PART TWO

22. Practicing

The floor of the gymnasium shone with the reflective gloss of having been newly polished and swept. The lines forming the half-court line, the three-point arc, and the paint were of white and sky blue—Carolina blue to James. From the hue of the floor to the spacing of the bleachers, to the slight musk of sweat and aroma of courtside vendors, the replica was perfect.

James grabbed one of the basketballs from the sideline and drove up the center before doing an easy lay-up. He allowed the ball to bounce to a stop after dropping through the net. When the ball came to a rest, the stadium felt again eerily quiet. He assumed that this must be how the stadium was at night after all the players and janitors have left. Then again, the court, the stadium, the basketballs, even the smells—none of this was real. At least, it hadn't been real five minutes ago. That was one of the advantages of Grand Central. The doors lining its endless corridor could open onto anything in any world, or even something existing only in the mind.

The first place James had conjured was the ocean shore on Greeson's Island. He had then imagined Myrtle Beach and Washington DC before considering that if someone had been watching, they might be able to figure out what world he was from. Rule One and all that. The Tar Heel basketball court had been just to see if he could do it. Still, it showed too much about him. James allowed the replica stadium to linger for only a moment before replacing it with what he hoped was a suitably generic environment. He closed his eyes, formed the thought in his mind, then opened them to a forest populated by the giant sequoias he had seen on a trip to California last spring. But unlike Sequoia National Park, James's version was blanketed with manicured grass that would have looked more appropriate on a golf course putting green.

James sat on the soft ground and opened *An Alternative History of Universal Dynamics* back to the marked chapter. Grand Central, the book claimed, should always be used as the venue for any sort of training or experimentation. To do so around people would inevitably raise suspicions. The *History* claimed that no matter how careful you were, there was always a risk of someone learning you were from a different world. And while that would be problematic if the discoverer was a native of that world, it would be disastrous if the person was one of the Styx. Even the *History* didn't know why the Styx crusaded to end worlds, but the "why" was secondary. The only way to stop the Styx was to save the world first.

According to the *History* a Traveler had two tools at his disposal: Fate and Existence. James had heard Huckabee and the vagrant talk about the Fate bit already. "Fate" was the will of the world, manifested in the suspension of coincidence. Every world wanted to save itself from disaster, which is why it called Travelers to help. And because the world wanted help, it would work hard to put the Traveler in a position where he could help.

Fate could take many forms: It allowed a Traveler to speak the local language. It encouraged the natives to be accepting of the Traveler. It made the things one said more believable. And it worked in subtle ways to put the Traveler at the heart of the problem, in a position to do the most good. But once accepted by the natives and in a position to help, Fate could do no more. That was when the Traveler's other great tool came into play—Existence.

According to the *History*, Travelers did not *really* exist in the worlds they visited. They could interact with the natives, they could speak, they could observe, and they could influence. But a Traveler wasn't completely there. And because a Traveler only *kind of* existed, they could manipulate that existence. James had seen this already. When he tried to make himself unnoticeable, he was simply drawing himself away from the reality of the world to where he was nothing to the natives but a whim, a daydream, a passing fancy. But being ignored was simply the beginning.

An expert Traveler had complete control over their existence. They could be invisible, or change shape, or walk through walls, or be in two places at once, or nowhere at all. The expert Traveler had no limits within their own existence… except two. If a Traveler broke Rule Three, and killed something, or Rule Four, and fell in love, the partial existence would become actual existence. And not only would the Traveler lose control over himself, he would be unable to leave the world forever. To a Traveler, "existing" was a little like death.

The tools of the Traveler—Fate and Existence—could give him an advantage in his mission. *But* (and there is always a "but") the tools didn't always work. Travelers weren't the only ones with special abilities. Often those at the center of a world's disaster were also gifted. These "VIPs" were immune to trickery and the efforts of Fate, just as other Travelers were. So the closer he came to the central problem, the more he wouldn't be able to rely on his abilities.

And so James had an idea.

If he could somehow figure out who these VIPs were, then he could figure out the heart of the world's problem. All he needed to do, was to keep trying tricks until he found someone it didn't work on. And orange was the key.

Fluorescent orange is a color rarely found in nature. According to the *History*, a Traveler could change their shape, size, their whole appearance. Such things were, of course, extremely difficult. Not only were they difficult, but they were generally unnecessary. Most worlds tended to ignore if a Traveler looked out of place—Fate at work. A Traveler with white skin could be amongst an all-black village and no one would think twice about it. If that same Traveler had Asian features, or Hispanic, or was three feet tall—or eight—most of the time no one would notice. For a world, it wasn't what someone looked like, it only mattered what they did.

James didn't think he had it in him to change his shape, but he was fairly certain that maybe he could change his color. If he could make his hands fluorescent orange—and he wasn't mistaken—then the only people who would notice anything strange would be the VIPs. Anyone else wouldn't pay attention.

And while the change seemed like a small one, James didn't want to do anything strange with people watching. That was why he had come to Grand Central.

James placed his hands palm-up in front of himself. He wiggled his fingers, opened and closed his hands; then clapped them together.

"Orange!"

James concentrated on his hands, willing their normal sun-darkened tan to brighten into orange. But nothing happened. He tried holding his breath, gritting his teeth, shouting a few choice magic words—and a few less couth swear ones—but his hands remained their earth-toned selves.

Snorting in frustration, he flipped open the *History* again. But while the book explained what he should be able to do, it didn't tell him how.

And so in this case, the *History* was useless. Or was it? What the book lacked in "how," it made up for in expectation. Maybe all that James needed to do to make his hands orange was to believe, truly and completely, that his hands *were* orange.

"I can do this," James muttered. He closed his eyes and imagined the fingers on his hands. He wiggled the fingers and as he did so, imagined that he could see the movement of each one. He clapped, and imagined the clap. He cracked his knuckles, and imagined the soft click of his joints. Then, he imagined them orange.

James opened his eyes. No orange.

"Seriously, I can do this. I just have to believe. I need to know these hands are orange, just like I… Grand Central."

Knowing his hands were orange was like knowing that Grand Central was supposed to be Greeson's Island, or the UNC basketball court, or a redwood forest with a carpet of grass. James hadn't once doubted that he could make Grand Central look like he wanted it to look, because both the *History* and Dr. Huckabee said it *would* look how he wanted it to look. And while the book didn't necessarily say that his hands would be orange, there was no reason that they couldn't be. If a basketball court could exist from nothing, then James's hands could be orange.

James looked down, not expecting to see his hands glowing a healthy fluorescent orange, but instead *knowing* they would. He didn't hesitate, he believed completely and utterly. He turned his hands over and opened his fingers to reveal an orange as bright as a construction worker's coat. It wasn't close to what James had imagined, it was exactly, 100% what he expected. And there was another thing he was certain of, you would have to be crazy, blind, or both to miss that his hands were orange. And if everyone in the Frozen World noticed, nothing was lost. But if only Ling noticed, and maybe one or two other people, then the experiment would be a success.

With a smile on his face, he thrust his bright-orange hands into his pockets. Now was the time to put it to the test, to get to the Frozen World, to find the problem, find a solution, and save the world. He closed his eyes, concentrated, and then—

James fell.

23. Gate

"Ow, dangit ow!"

James snapped alert to sharp pain on his forearm. Unlike the lazy return to his body when last he entered the Frozen World, his consciousness slapped him in the face. Needles. He was being stuck with needles. And they hurt.

"Ow, what are you doing? That hurts, stop it!"

Brine looked up, the needle and ink in his hand. There was a look of genuine puzzlement on his face. "I told you before, laddie. The skin is a mite more sensitive here, aye? So it'll hurt a wee more. You're embarrassing yourself, really. And us. Sailors aren't for squirming."

James looked down at his arms in horror. Brine was tattooing him—tattooing *runes* on him. He already had one on his left arm, one on his thigh, and another on his right shoulder. The runes were dark black, spiraling like the henna tattoos once popular among the girls at school. No, they weren't like those at all. They were just like the ones worn by the Scrim.

"Runes!" James squeaked. "Why are you putting runes on me? What if they kill me? What will they do to me? I didn't say you could do this."

Brine shook his head. "I wonder about you, laddie. I really do. We've been over this time and again. These aren't real runes, they're just tattoos. So they won't kill you, they don't do anything, and you *did* ask me to do this. As a favor, I might add. Why on the last two you

were admiring 'em. So unbunch your small clothes and grit your teeth."
Brine paused for a second. "Or did you have one of your wee spells?"

James winced. His "spells" were what his parents called it when he
fell. But how could he fall in another world? Wasn't that all behind
him?

"What spells?"

"Bloody winds and bloody tides and… Look, Jay, we all know you
forget things. It's ok, really. But you need to pay attention, or we're
going to get in trouble when we get there. The Kai'ja aren't ones to be
fooling around with, lad. So hold still."

As Brine bent back over his design, James gritted his teeth and
allowed the sailor to complete his task. After all, despite the initial pain,
James *did* have to admire the man's handiwork. He showed incredible
talent for a person so massive. The coexistence of size and skill seemed
to James oddly improbable, as though the benefits of size meant that
talent and intelligence were necessarily bereft. James shrugged off the
thought as a little judgmental, then took to examining the tattoos.

Each tattoo was of dark ink, which spiraled and looped around
itself. The markings were large, refined, intricate… and *extremely* cool.
James chuckled to himself at the horror his mom would experience if
she saw her innocent baby boy getting covered in body art. He smiled
in spite of himself, then winced at the thought the tattoos might follow
him back to his homeworld. But he didn't think that would be the case.
After all, his body back home was probably on its way to school or
something.

Brine snickered. "Oh, so now you're back to liking them again?
Grinnin' like a jester filched the crown off the king's own head you are.
You're flighty, Jay. I'll give you that. Now, I think that will round out
the final touches, and… There we go. A masterpiece, if I do be saying
so myself."

James hopped to his feet and took one last admiring look at the
tattoos. Then he took a good long look at his hands. They were

certainly not the same fluorescent orange they had been moments ago in Grand Central. James imagined the color being washed away in the winds of the Cosmos. Or maybe Grand Central James still had orange hands, just like Frozen World James had tattoos, and Home World James had bruises from the fight at school. Were there different versions of him running around in all the worlds? What happened to the him in the Ocean World with the multi-colored sky? Did it get tired and drown? James shuddered at the thought of his body floating lifelessly on the seas of some foreign plane.

Or, perhaps James had just expected to see his hands their normal tan and so that's what he got. He decided against trying to turn his hands orange with Brine watching. If there was a chance that the large man was a "VIP" and Brine *did* see the color change, it might raise questions James couldn't answer.

"What are you staring at?" Brine asked. "I hope you don't want tattoos on your palms. I hear that's quite the painful operation, and we don't want you to be tender there. How else are you going to help haul the gear?"

James shrugged. He folded his arms across his chest. "So, how much farther to, uh, wherever we're going." James smiled. "I'm sure you just told me. But, you know, I am a forgetful one."

"Fair enough, laddie. Won't argue you that one. The place is Kai'nau, and we're almost there. We stopped just to get the wagons ready and for everyone to get changed and presentable-like. That's a big thing for the Kai'ja. Appearances: pomp and ceremony and the such. And that's exactly why you are going to keep your mouth shut and stay out the way. Try not to be noticed."

James smiled involuntarily. "Then what am I supposed to do?"

"You're not supposed to do anything. Stay by my side. If anyone asks, you're a deckhand. And under my orders. You'll carry Sylph's bags and that's that. She'll have other things to worry about, ere we get there."

"Ok, uh, and who are the Kai'ja?"

The groan from Brine put his previous wails of frustration to shame. For all James knew, Brine had explained who the Kai'ja were fifty times already. But—and now James was taking things on faith—if the *History* was correct, and Fate was on his side, then Brine would tell him once more.

"This is it, laddie. This is the last time I explain this, and the last time you're allowed to ask. So all you get is the wee version, 'cause that's all I'm telling." Brine sighed once more. "The Kai'ja are runics, like the Scrim. But while the Scrim have their talent in designing runes, the Kai'ja are the best in the world when it comes to etching them. They're a strange lot, too, James. Not mercenaries and merchants like Slagish and the Scrim. They're more on the mystic side. I suppose that's why they live at Kai'nau versus a more respectable place. So, watch yourself, and keep your eyes open. You'll see for yourself soon enough."

James felt a lurch as the snowcat began to move again. It was the first time he realized that he was even in a wagon as opposed to being out in the cold and snow. He stuck his head out the door to see that he was once again in a snowcat train, just like the one he had been in when he first fell into the Frozen World. The most noticeable thing about the wagons was that they bore remarkable similarity to the wagons belonging to the bandits that had captured him. James shuddered at the thought of the shadow-beast. He pulled his head back inside.

"Brine, I know I probably asked this before too, but were those other kids ok? Ling, Charles, and"—James hesitated for a second to remember the third Blank's name—"and Bellacroix?"

"Yes, you asked me before. And yes, they're fine, just fine. The Scrim mixed up a good spell to take out all the bandits but not harm them Blanks. But then again, I suppose that's what they do best." Brine winked. "And before you ask—again—we've got the Killdevil III back in one of those gods-forsaken shrinking runes too." Brine clapped

James on the shoulder and set down his needles. "All done. Now clean yourself up and let's step outside. I hear that the approach to Kai'nau is not something you want to be missing."

James hopped out of the wagon with Brine following behind. The forest behind had emptied into a narrow crevasse, no more than one hundred feet wide. The walls of the canyon were nearly vertical and looked to have been hewn out of ice. Turrets hung from the cliffs in regular intervals fixed to the ice by immense spikes. The pitons incited a spiderweb of cracks which formed a splintered halo around the turrets. Huddled inside each structure were archers bristling with red-feathered arrows. The men all wore oversized headpieces reminiscent of African tribal masks. James couldn't imagine how the archers had gotten in place as he didn't see ladders along the walls.

"Are those Kai'ja?"

"Yes and no. Mostaways no." Brine shrugged. "Some are, probably. But I ken the rest were failed runics or just prisoners. Taking a turn as a sentry isn't exactly volunteer work, aye? From what I understand, criminals and slaves get sentenced to the turrets iffin they won't behave."

"But how do they get up there? I don't see any tunnels or anything behind them. And if they can't get down, then what do they eat?"

Brine shrugged. "The Kai'ja are runics, Jay. They don't play by the same set of rules. I imagine they *don't* eat. At least not until their sentence is served. And I imagine someone *put* them there."

James watched the turrets as the wagons passed beneath. The faces of the sentries were expressionless behind the masks. He opened himself to the world's *Essence* to see if he could glimpse the prisoners' faces. But even with heightened senses, he could see nothing except the whites of the prisoners' eyes.

James surveyed the narrow canyon. There was an opening ahead, less than a quarter of a mile away. Whatever was beyond that opening was large and dark, a shadowed mass in perfect contrast to the white of the surrounding walls. As the wagons drew closer, the black structure fully emerged. The snow covering the walls and everything in the Frozen World stopped abruptly. The black mass was a mountain of obsidian nestled like a dark egg in a nest of ice and snow. The rock walls reflected both the setting sun and the pale white of their surroundings. He couldn't tell how much of the rock was a fortress, and how much was the mountain.

Then James realized why the snow was absent. Even from a quarter-mile away, he could feel the heat radiating from the mountain. A glance up completed the story. A plume of smoke circled skyward, and with a distinctly different appearance than the cook fires and camp fires of homes or industry. The mountain itself was smoking. James swallowed hard. Why *wouldn't* the Kai'ja have built their home here? Why *wouldn't* Kai'nau be the tunneled hulk of an active volcano? Where *else* would a runic cult choose as the center of their world?

The wagon train stopped at the border between ice and obsidian. The melting ice formed a moat of ashen sludge circling the mountain. James couldn't tell if the wagon train had stopped because the water was deep, or whether the Scrim were reluctant to cross into the realm of the Kai'ja. James flinched as a horn sounded from the leading Scrim wagon. One by one, the doors of the wagons opened and the Scrim filed out. The travelers trudged to the sludge border, heads held high and chests thrust out with pride. James followed Brine to the front of the wagon train to join the Scrim. But in James's eyes, seeping from through the bravado of the Scrim was an air of nervousness.

The booming voice of Lord Slagish cut through the murmurs of his compatriots. While the man had always been the sole authority amongst his crew, he now looked the part as well. Slagish wore an array of silver jewelry, which stood out against his pale features and jet-black hair. James looked to see that the rest of the Scrim were similarly adorned in earrings, nose rings, bracelets, and necklaces. Only Teak, Brine, James, and the three Blanks wore their normal clothes. Even

Sylph was now wearing a supple leather coat fringed with shined brass. Her shirt was starched, her pants creaseless, her hair gathered behind her head by three intersecting pins. Only Sylph's gun belt retained its ordinary weathered look. The contrast made her seem at once earthy and ethereal.

Lord Slagish called to the mountain in a voice as melodious as his dialect was sometimes harsh. James assumed that he was now speaking in the language of the Kai'ja. And just as the *History* predicted, the language, which James had never heard until that second, was as clear and understandable to his ears as any other. Polynesian. Definitely Polynesian—or at least close to it. The language had the same gentle crescendo of vowels and ease of diction that wove each word into a tapestry of song. Even the Russian-sounding accent of Slagish deferred to the beauty of the language.

"I am Slagish of the Ebon Delta. Son of the many sons of my father of fathers, and lord over all the Scrim. I demand to be recognized."

The silence of the Scrim was punctuated by the crunching of nervous feet on cracking snow. James looked to the mountain in expectation. There was no reply, not the slightest hint of movement except the waft of smoke coming from the obsidian peak.

Again the Scrim leader called to the mountain, repeating his same mantra of introduction, and again there was silence. Then again. And again. By the time James started counting the man's hails, the Scrim leader had yelled a dozen times. By the twentieth hail (by James's count) the Islanders shifted where they stood. By the fiftieth hail, James was certain they were calling to an empty hold. Perhaps this place had suffered a similar fate to that of the bandits. Perhaps the Kai'ja had become victims to one of their creations.

James's thoughts were interrupted by a peal of thunder echoing around the icy crater. In the wake of the boom, he saw the first hint of movement from the fortress. A single door, some twenty feet tall but no more than two feet wide, opened outward as though the rock was splitting in two. A thin figure emerged from the crack and walked toward them. James corrected himself. To say the person was walking was not entirely accurate. The figure, distinctly feminine, slithered toward them. Each step seemed an unceasing glide of movement, incapable of being distinguished from the last.

The woman's appearance caused James to blush in embarrassment. She was slender, muscular, and adorned only with a chain of gold linked with teeth. The chain coiled around her legs and torso, around her left shoulder, and descended around the woman's right arm, wrapping tighter and tighter until ending in a metal cuff housing a single blood-red ruby. The chain was the only adornment the woman wore, and the only shred of clothing as well. The glimmer of gold shone against skin as equally bronzed. Only the recognition that the woman was unblemished by runes made James relax.

"Hail, Slagish of the Ebon Delta," the woman spoke in the smooth cadence of the Polynesian language, tinged with elements of the archaic. She turned to the waiting Scrim. "And hail, tribesmen," she spoke in the Russian dialect. "And hail, Captain," she spoke in the Islander's language to Sylph. The woman resumed speaking in the language of the Kai'ja, pausing only long enough for Slagish to translate her words. "I bid you welcome to my home. Welcome to the mother Kai'nau from whom all life is sprung. You may cross this threshold by freedom of your will. You may not leave but by my leave. Do you understand?"

Slagish assented in the language of the Kai'ja, then translated.

"And do you understand?" the Kai'ja woman asked in Scrim. "And you?" she continued in the Islander speech.

Each group muttered their understanding of the rules. James himself was careful to reply only to the one spoken in the island language, so as not to betray his understanding of the other tongues. Brine had made it clear that James was to keep a low profile. After all, a limited knowledge of the language would probably prevent James from easily moving around. And he had no intention of limiting his mobility. He still had to figure out why he was here in the first place.

This last thought caused James to smirk. The nervousness of being a stranger in a strange place was somehow assuaged by no one knowing who he was or where he came from. *This must be the power of anonymity,* James thought. *It's a strange world. But to them, I'd be the strangest of all—if, of course, they noticed me.* At this, James looked down at his hands—once again with the utmost certainty—and found them a vibrant fluorescent orange. James glanced around the crowd of Scrim, but none seemed to notice the foreign boy with the day-glow hands. Perhaps the Kai'ja queen was more entrancing. Or perhaps they couldn't tell the difference.

James snapped back to attention as the Scrim returned to their wagons, just as the Kai'ja queen started back to the door in the mountainside. What surprised James at first was that there was no move to drive the wagons forward. Instead, both Scrim and Islanders grabbed their bags and slogged across the ash-filled moat to the opening in the rock. He wondered if the wagons weren't allowed inside, or if they simply wouldn't fit through the entrance. Sylph motioned James her way and shoved a large duffle at him to carry. He glanced over his shoulder to see that both Brine and Teak had equally large burdens on their backs. But what was most interesting was what they carried between them. Suspended from two poles like a litter was Sylph's ebony chest. James saw the Scrim eyeing the chest jealously.

"Let's get going, lads," Sylph ordered, her voice stern but even. "And cut your gawking. There are enough lookers around."

James turned to reply, only to notice that Sylph was not carrying anything. He was about to comment how heavy her bags were when he remembered that not only was she the captain and his boss. But she was also armed. Maybe her role was to keep the Scrim at bay. The thought of Sylph as a guardian angel caused James to hasten to her side.

The ashy moat was just deep enough to soak James to his knees in black sludge. The water was quite warm to the point of being almost uncomfortable, like a bath tolerable to the skin, but only if eased into properly. James sloshed across the moat and stepped in line with the Scrim. Together, they entered the mountain.

24. Into Kai'nau

When James first entered the tunnel, his eyes struggled to adjust to the dark. For almost a minute James squinted until the small torches on the walls became sufficient light for him to see. He wasn't alone. Sylph's crew and Scrim alike fumbled in the darkness. James wondered if the Kai'ja watched from the shadows.

The first hundred feet of the tunnel were coarse and unrefined. The obsidian walls chipped, but unpolished. But as they continued, two things began to happen, each subtly overpowering the other. The first and most noticeable was the heat. The outside temperature leading to Kai'nau had been well below freezing. The area right outside had been much warmer. And now the heat was growing steadily more impressive. James had felt this temperature only once before, in a sauna.

Brine and Sylph had begun to sweat profusely, though the Scrim, whom James had always thought underdressed, seemed as unaffected by the heat as they had been by the cold. Teak took the temperature change in stride as well. Then again, little seemed to rattle him.

The second change was that the rough-hewn mine shaft was becoming gradually more reinforced, and more refined. The rough stone took on a more regular arch, and the dirt floors had been swept to reveal polished obsidian tile. The irregular pieces were carved and joined so closely that James could barely make out the mortar between them. Also, to break the monotony of darkness, the sporadic torches assumed a greater and greater regularity until the tunnel pulsed with orange light.

James edged closer to Sylph as she stepped with easy purpose. "Where are we going?"

Sylph glanced over her shoulder without slowing her pace. "We've been allowed into Kai'nau, lad. But that just be the first step. Next, we will be received—officially—in the main hall. Trade won't begin 'til tomorrow. I wager we'll banquet tonight, but not as honored guests. Slagish will receive that honor. The Kai'ja will treat *us* as his servants. With luck, the Scrim will ignore us, at least for a while."

James shrugged. "Well, I imagine they'll ignore us until it's time to go back. Our job is just to sail the boat, right?"

Brine interrupted in a stern voice lessened in severity by a slight chuckle. "Well, laddie, we've got a bit more of a part to play than just manning the sails. Or did you lose your curiosity about what's in the box?"

Teak barked, "Oy. That's enough, Brine. That ragger don't need to know a lick more than he already does. Which is too much by far, I'll wager."

"Well, I think that's the Cap'n's decision, don't you?" Brine replied.

Sylph darted her head around. "Settle down, lads. We'll discuss this later. Too many ears what can hear."

James shut his mouth. In a way, he wasn't convinced the chest was so important. At least not yet. But he certainly wasn't drawn to it as he was to Sylph or Ling.

Thinking of the Blanks caused James to twist his head around to search for them. They were following about ten people back in the procession, armed guards both leading and trailing them. The three Blanks wore chains and yet carried them with acceptance. James had never seen or considered anyone to have the acquiescence to captivity that the Blanks did. Certainly not him. He had been in a near panic when he was put in a cage. Then again, it took no more than a thought for him to break out of it.

James glanced down at his hands. The palms all but glowed with their fluorescent orange hue, and yet no one had mentioned the color, not even Sylph, and James had been convinced she was one of the world's VIPs. *Someone will notice*, James thought with certainty. *Even if it's just Ling. Someone will notice, and then I'll know what to do.*

But would he? James was relying on what the *History* called Fate to be led to the world's problem. But what if the book had been wrong?

Sylph gasped in astonishment, an emotion that James found ill-suiting. "Sweet winds and waves of Mistress Luck—I don't believe it."

James had been so preoccupied that he didn't notice the tunnel until it had reached its end. The path transformed from being carved from the rock to being suspended from it. Apart from the obsidian floor, the sides dropped away into the darkness below. The tunnel became a stone bridge which arched through the darkness and over a pit of nothingness. The walkway then connected with nine other arches ending in a platform, perfectly circular and three hundred feet in diameter.

The dais had been carved from obsidian and inlaid with gold reminiscent of the Scrim's runes. But not quite. The pattern of these runes was subtly different. Flourishes ended to the right versus the left; connecting lines were ever-so-thinner, and the strokes somewhat more refined. James knew that while these were still runes, they were the runes of the Kai'ja—not the Scrim.

James found his theory to be true as he saw the first inhabitants. The dais swarmed with them. Their copper bodies were draped in deep brown cloaks of almost the same color. Some of the Kai'ja wore their robes so that almost none of their features could be seen, hoods covering their faces. Others wore their robes open, or draped to the waist, to reveal bodies covered in runes. With every rune James saw, he received a flash of inspiration as to their meaning: "Nightshade," "Lilac Breeze," "Winter's Aura," "Bison's Dance."

In the center of the dais, a platform was raised with a small circle of red velvet cushions forming a sunken nest. The woman that had greeted them at the gates was lounged on one side of the cushioned circle, with two other women sitting across from her. Just outside the ring was a host of guards carrying thick-bladed swords and covered with runes, each of which conjured thoughts of pain and death.

James felt a mounting nervousness as they crossed the land bridge and stepped onto the dais. This was too open. He was too exposed. His mind screamed that somewhere nearby was the reason he was here. The slightest opening of his awareness to the *Essence* of the world confirmed it. In the center of that platform was the source of the event. Some tragedy that would soon occur. Feeling exposed, James glanced at his fluorescent hands and willed them to return to their natural color. If whoever or whatever was responsible discovered who he was, James was finished. No need to make himself seen when obscurity had worked thus far.

The procession of Scrim, Islanders, and Blanks paused at the edge of the pedestal before dividing to form a ring around it. The Kai'ja closed in behind them, their voices dropping to murmurs.

At first, there was no movement from the queen, as if she was feigning annoyance at the same visitors she had spoken to so recently. She then rose to her feet. With a nod of dismissal, the other women on the pedestal drifted into the crowd to leave her standing alone.

The queen declared loudly in Scrim, "Lord Slagish of the Black Hand. Why have you crossed into the heart of Kai'nau? What business have you in this most sacred of places?"

The Scrim leader stepped to the front. "We wish to negotiate an etching."

"Upon whom will you etch?"

The Scrim parted to allow the Blanks to be led to the front of the circle. The High Priestess glided down from her perch to place a hand on the forehead of each in turn. James couldn't see her face as she examined the Blanks, but when she turned back to face them, there was a wild exhilaration in her eyes.

"And your rune?"

James was surprised to see all eyes turn in his direction. Well, not his direction precisely, but to Sylph. The captain motioned to Brine who re-gripped the chest so that he carried it without Teak's assistance. Brine followed Sylph to the pedestal and set the chest on the ground. He took a step back and then turned to face the onlookers. Brine cradled his shotgun as he fixed his eyes upon the crowd.

Sylph hunched over the chest to twist the knobs and pull the levers. Her hands moved in an intricate ballet as she worked the mechanisms. After two minutes of arranging, the lid of the chest opened and the Kai'ja queen peered inside. At first, her face was the mask of boredom, then puzzlement, and finally an excitement bordering on elation—or perhaps rage. She reached her hand toward the chest, but Sylph snapped the lid shut. The queen glared with vehemence, murder in her eyes.

Sylph said, "The Scrim insist, quite clearly, no more than a glance for ye. No more 'til the deal's finished." She spoke the words, to James's surprise, in the language of the Kai'ja.

The High Priestess's face was twisted in fury, but she quickly gained her composure. "Not *all* your Blanks are fit for such a rune."

Sylph spoke again, her voice a stony calm. "The other two are but payment. Slagish said 'tis all agreed."

"You overstep your place, courier," the High Priestess hissed. "Now be gone. There is much to consider, and my eyes grow weary of your presence."

Sylph motioned to Teak and Brine to grab the chest. But as they made to lift it, two large rune-covered Kai'ja stepped between them.

Though the two men were heavily muscled, Brine still stood head and shoulders above them. Teak, on the other hand, simply bristled. He dropped his hand to the sword at his side.

Sylph said, "That's mine to protect."

"Perhaps, yet I trust you not. Nevertheless, the secret to open may remain yours. I will keep this under my protection." She paused. "Or do you wish I act on other judgment?" The last of these words were directed not at Sylph, but Slagish. James could tell this was a test of trust. If Slagish was to refuse, he would have to confront the queen himself. And yet if he acquiesced, he had the advantage of showing his position over Sylph.

Slagish smiled, the corners of his tapered mustache rising in harmony. He shrugged and flicked his hand toward the Kai'ja. The deal was settled.

Sylph's eyes smoldered, but she did not reply. She also nodded, but at her companions. Brine took the lead, followed by Sylph, and Teak trailing. James hopped to keep up as they wove through the throng of Kai'ja and then through the Scrim as well. As they passed the Blanks, James darted to the side where they were held.

"I'll come to see you later," James whispered to Ling. He gave a quick nod to Charles, and a cursory smile to Bellacroix before being pushed aside by one of the Scrim guards. Without waiting to be told, James hurried to catch up to Sylph, Teak, and Brine, leaving the mass of Kai'ja behind.

"What was that…?" James began. He was silenced by a hiss from Brine. Chastised, James stepped silently in line. Sylph's bags weighed heavily against his back, and his confusion weighed heavily on his mind.

The three Islanders and James passed across the suspended bridge, and through a series of twisting tunnels, some rough-hewn and others works of delicate mosaic. They eventually wound to a bronze-plated door which their guide opened before waving them inside. When the door slammed shut, Teak sprang from his feet and placed his ear against it. He listened for a few moments, turned, and nodded to Sylph.

Captain Sylph visibly relaxed, dropping the tension in the room. She flung herself onto one of the lounging sofas and exhaled sharply. She emitted an uncharacteristic giggle.

"Whew. Tell you, lads, that was a close one. Right to the edge, we were."

"I thought we were all but one last tilt to turtle. Thank the gods we at least got rid of that bleedin' chest. We owe Slagish for that one," Brine chimed in. He took the bag from James and fished around inside until producing a decanter. Brine located some glasses on the mantel and poured four cups, handing one to each of them. "To Lady Luck and fortune plenty. We made it."

James toasted along with the three Islanders and lifted the brown liquid to his lips. He reacted with a violent cough as the whisky burned his throat.

"Just a little sting, Jay." Brine smacked his hand down on James's back. Even Teak snorted once in mirth.

James recovered quickly. "Ok, so *now* will you tell me what's going on?"

Teak sipped his drink, then fixed his stony gaze at James. "Quite simple, innit? The stakes are big, so ain't nobody to be trusted. Slagish needed us to cross the Alpinsea, but the captain needed assurance that we weren't going to be turned on as soon as we did. And he wouldn't let her hire enough crew as an escort. So she locked their rune away in her chest. We don't open it until the deal is done and we get our cut." Teak continued. "Of course, Slagish had to make sure that we didn't run off with his Blanks, either. So he keeps it a secret which one is the real Blank to be etched, and not just a decoy. We guard the rune, he guards the Blanks and we're all kept on the level."

James frowned. "But Slagish had more men. He could've just made the captain tell him how to open it."

"Not a chance. She'd never break, and the Scrim knew better'n to try. Us Islanders have a bit of a reputation for being stubborn."

"Then we could've stolen all the Blanks…"

"We could never have smuggled out all three. Not and kept our boat too. Like I said, only one is probably worth anything." Teak squinted at Sylph. "You figured that out yet, Captain?"

Sylph shook her head. "Not yet. The Blanks don't know themselves. I spent quite a bit of time with the one called Ling, too. This brings me to another point, lads. If something happens to me, I've given her the combination to open the box."

James wrinkled his forehead. Now he was confused. "Why tell Ling? Why not Brine or Teak?"

"Cause I gave my word I wouldn't tell me crew, of course." Sylph smiled. "But that doesn't mean I want the secret to die with me—in case I have an accident. And I certainly wasn't going to tell the Scrim."

James nodded in dull understanding. "Ling is the one, anyway. You were right to pick her. She's special, I can tell."

Teak replied with surprising intensity. "What do you mean you can tell? Tell what? Special how? You think she's the one to get the rune? Spill it, boy. What *do* you *know?*"

"I don't *know* know. It's just a hunch," James stammered. "She just has this way about her that I…"

"He's lying again," Teak snapped. "Speakin' of rats, that kid ain't told us the truth since we found him. You still pretending you got no memories?"

James, feeling threatened, tried to make himself less noticeable, less *in* the world. The effects happened almost immediately. James could see Brine's and Sylph's gaze sliding to one side of him, and their conversation diverted to the whisky. Teak, however, was not dissuaded. He stomped toward James and crouched until the two saw eye to eye. "Look, Jay, or whoever you are. Your little stunt isn't going to work on me. I can do it meself, eh? I'm watching you, and I don't trust you for a second. One way or another, I'm going to figure out what you're up to. And you best hope yer up to nothing. You got that?" Teak poked James once hard in the chest, causing James to stagger back.

"Look, I don't…"

"And quit your lyin'."

James slunk away from Teak. His hand fumbled for the door as he grabbed the pull and slid outside. He took a few steps down the torch-lit corridor before sliding to the base of the wall. He wrapped his arms around his knees.

Is it Teak? Is he the one that is going to bring the world down? Or is he the one to save it? He and maybe Ling. But which one? They can both see me, but who is the one helping, and who is hurting?

Runes. The thought came clearly to James. This whole world seemed to revolve around runes. And if his hunch was right, then whatever rune was written inside that chest—presumably to be etched on Ling—was the important piece. It didn't seem important before, but that was because until it's etched, it's just a drawing. *I have to find out what it means,* James thought. But where had the Kai'ja taken it? And how could he convince Sylph to open it? She was too duty-bound for such a thing.

James stewed for a second, then realized that he had the answer. Ling could also open the chest. Sylph had just said as much. He didn't need to break open anything. And no one needed to know he'd even looked… except for Ling, of course. But James felt like he could trust her. After all, if he could fall through a cage, then he should at least be able to get one person to tell him a secret. Was persuasion one of his fated abilities? Well, if the answer to *that* question was anywhere, it was in *An Alternative History of Universal Dynamics.*

"Grand Central, here I come," James chuckled—

Then he fell.

25. Backward

The billion stars of the Cosmos rushed past James like a torrent of ocean foam. He felt the wash of worlds rattling against his soul and felt both elated and detached at the same time. Feeling at ease in the Cosmos for the first time, he directed his attention on the axis of light he had come to understand as Grand Central.

But as James tried to reach through the black and grasp the axis, he was jerked violently back. The cascade of stars first paused, then rushed him in the opposite direction as he fell, plummeting, spiraling, and flailing toward a familiar world. James barely squeaked in surprise (even though he had no body or voice) as he hurled into the white light of a world.

His world.

26. Kovek

James did not open his eyes lazily to his surroundings. Instead, he was hurled as if thrown from a moving car. The spiritual reunion of his mind with his body hit not from above, but rather from down and to the side, hurling him up and to the right, where he collided (a pure physical collision) with a stainless-steel cabinet bolted against the hospital wall. The impact echoed loudly through the wall and knocked over a side table scattering the floor with an array of helpful pamphlets on prescription drugs.

He was in a hospital. James had been in enough hospitals to know what one looked like, and this was a *real* hospital, not just the fake one he had first thought of in Grand Central. James pulled himself to his feet and made his way to the medical chart at the foot of his bed. He felt fine, so he probably didn't break anything, unless they had given him some kind of pain killer. And he didn't feel the least bit groggy.

The door flung open and in walked James's father. The usually jovial man had a stern look on his face and a stack of books and papers held close under one arm. James panted in surprise and disbelief, half expecting to be looking into the eyes of the ice-faced woman.

"What day is it?" James blurted, only to realized how tactless the question had been. "I mean *time*. What time is it?"

His father shook his head. "Nice try, son. But don't bother. I know what's going on."

James stumbled to the hospital bed and sat down in disbelief. "You do? How can you know?" He paused, hopeful. "Is this thing hereditary? Did the same thing happen to you when you were young? Does it still?"

His father took a seat in the fake leather chair in the corner. "I don't mean that, James. I've told you before that there's no history of fainting in my family. What I meant was, I know you've been having some gaps in your memory. But I've got good news. They found something in your school. It's going to be ok. You're going to get better."

James's mind spun. What could they have found? What possible explanation would be offered next?

His father continued, "Your school has a gas leak—had a gas leak rather. Radon. It's poisonous and affects all kinds of people in all different ways. For some people, like you, the gas can cause fainting, seizures, and *especially* memory loss. Dr. Kovek explained everything in detail."

"Dr. Kovek?"

"Don't you get it, James? It's over. No more fainting. No more forgetting where you've been or what you've done!" His father's eyes welled in tears. "You can live a normal life again. It's going to be all right!"

James allowed the possibilities to race through his mind. What if his father was correct? What if his fainting, the gaps in memory, and his visions of strange worlds and strange people were nothing but dreams brought on by something as mundane as a gas leak. Maybe his mind just reacted violently to the gas when other people hadn't even been affected. But how could it be possible? The other worlds were so real. They were more real in a way than his own. And what about Dr. Huckabee, or the *History*, or the Cosmos, or Grand Central? Was it possible none of that was real?

His head pounded with the possibility. As James thought more and more about Grand Central, the Frozen World, and even the world with the colorful sky, they seemed more distant and less real. Had he really thought his way through an iron cage? Could he really speak every language there was? Could he really read a book that no one else could see? Was he really cured?

James answered tentatively, "How long until I'm better, Dad? How long until the radon won't bother me anymore."

"It could take a little while. There is a medicine the doctor prescribed, a way to counteract the gas. But it may take a little while to work out of your system." His dad cracked a smile. "But at least you don't have to go right back to school. They've canceled classes for a week while they fix the problem. I guess the leak got strong enough recently that it started affecting more people—not just you."

James nodded slowly. An increase in a gas leak may explain why he had shifted from just short falls to the bizarre dreams of bizarre worlds. It all fit together. A little. But the whole thing still stank.

"And just so you know, James. I'm not blaming you for anything you might not remember. It's all behind us now. You've been through enough."

"What did I do?"

"You don't remember anything? Nothing about the library?"

A chill went down James's spine. In his memory, he had been chased by agents of the ice-faced woman. That must have been a hallucination too. But what had he done? More importantly, what did his father think he had done. James shrugged in reply.

"It seemed like a big to-do to me. After all, I hardly think that someone forgetting to check out one book could be such a big deal. I mean, with all the crime in the city, a library book shouldn't be that big of a deal. Why wouldn't they think it was a mistake?"

"Dad, what are you talking about?"

His dad sighed. James thought the sigh eerily similar to that of Brine when the large man explained the Kai'ja. "About a week ago, we started hearing it all over the news. Some rare book had been stolen from the library. We asked you about it, of course. But you said you didn't know anything. Then we started hearing about the radon at your school, and Dr. Kovek came around and talked to all the parents. She told us to watch for strange behavior, anything out of the ordinary, especially memory loss."

"Wait. You said she?" James felt his heart quicken.

"Yes, Dr. Kovek is a woman. Women can be doctors, too, James. But that's not the point. She explained the symptoms, and we started to think that maybe it fit in with you. We thought maybe the radon was causing you to faint, and then we started to ask you questions about your day. We wanted to see if maybe you had any of the other symptoms Dr. Kovek spoke of. And we found them. In a big way."

"You did?"

"Yes, we did. James, do you remember what you did yesterday."

"I think so." James went out on a limb, hoping he was right. "Yesterday was Sunday."

"No. Today is Sunday. That's what I mean, James. You've got holes in your memory. That's why I forgive you about the book."

James shook his head. "I don't understand. What are you talking about? What book?"

"This one." James's father reached into his computer bag and removed the all too familiar book. "*An Alternative History of Universal*

Dynamics. I found it under your bed. Strange title. But why would you steal it? Why didn't you just check it out? Did you just forget?" His father shrugged. "You probably don't remember, so I won't tell anyone it was you. I'll return it tomorrow."

"Dad, did you read any of that book?"

"Of course not. It's not written in English. I think it's in Arabic or something."

"But you just read the title."

"Of course, but… that's weird." His father's brow furrowed. "Huh, I guess maybe I heard it on the radio or something. Or maybe it's inside the cover. But I guess this ratty thing doesn't even have a cover."

James stared in disbelief. The book *clearly* had a cover. And the cover *clearly* said the title. Then another thought crept into his mind. There was no radon leak. More likely, the ice-faced woman had made up the radon story to get parents to test their kids. And now she'd found him. Or perhaps not. If his dad didn't tell anyone about the book, maybe he was still safe. Rule Number One.

Or maybe you're still crazy. Ever think of that? This is all still pretty crazy.

James weighed his options. He could either be careful or crazy. He could be nuts. Or… he could be an inter-dimensional traveler tracked and hunted by a mysterious woman and her cronies bent on undoing his life and destroying his world. Oddly, both sounded plausible. But if the second option *was* true, he *had* to be careful. If he was just crazy, he had nothing to fear.

Better to be careful, James thought.

"Alright, Dad. You're right, and I don't remember that book. If you give it to me, I'll take it back to the library right now. I don't know why I'd take that, or if I really did."

James's father smiled. "That's what I wanted to hear. Now let's get out of here. And now don't tell your mom I said this, but hospitals give me the willies. Dr. Kovek can wait."

Another chill. "Is she coming here?"

James's father shrugged. "She stops by once a day or so, asks you a lot of questions to see what you say. Weird questions, too. She says they are supposed to see if you are going to have more delusions. Always Probability this, or Possibility that. And she's always taking notes. I've never seen a woman take so many notes."

"Right. Let's just go." James fought to control the nervousness in his voice.

"You don't have to ask me twice."

His father fished into one of the cabinets and pulled out a gym bag which he tossed at his son. James opened up the bag and wasted no time changing out of the hospital gown and into the far more familiar shorts and T-shirt. After buckling his belt and slipping on his sandals, he heard someone open the door and walk in. Actually, that wasn't quite right either. James *felt* someone open the door and walk in. He didn't have to turn around to know.

"Dr. Kovek, how nice of you to drop by," James's father spoke cheerily. Despite the tone, he sensed unease in his father's voice.

"Mr. Winters. And James, it appears you're back. Welcome home."

James felt his cheeks flush, then struggled to get a hold of himself. He forced himself to be calm and turned to face her. With no emotion more than slight puzzlement, he replied.

"Back? I've been here since Wednesday."

The ice-faced woman's self-assured smile melted from her face, replaced with a hint of uncertainty. "Is that so, James? I'm glad to hear you're feeling better." She turned to his father. "Do you mind if I take a moment alone with the boy? I just have a few more questions. Sometimes children are more, *honest*, when their parents aren't around."

James's father shrugged. "Sure, but we're on our way home as you can see. And I don't want to be late for dinner. And..." His voice trailed off. "I mean, sure. Take all the time you need." James's father shuffled out the door and closed it quietly behind him. No sooner had the door shut, the ice-faced woman strode up to him and squinted at him with a discerning eye.

"Are you there, James? Are you back? Don't bother lying to me. I can tell if you lie. I can tell if you're here or gone."

His heart began to beat faster. "I don't know what you're talking about. Why do you always ask me these questions? Are you trying to trick me? A lot of the other shrinks would say one thing but mean something else. Why do you always ask me the same things?"

"And what things are those, James?" Her voice dripped with sugar.

"Probability this, Potential that. Positively this…"

"Possibility. It's Possibility." The ice-faced woman's expression went sour. James could sense that her accusing nature had been replaced with uncertainty. If she was so concerned that James *was* there (and not, he assumed in some foreign world with his body walking around without him) she was no longer sure. The ice-faced woman smoothed her skirt. "Listen, puppet. When James gets back, tell him that I *know* who he is. And his father won't always be standing there ready to snatch him up. You tell him we have business, and it will conclude whether or not he is willing."

James could feel his temperature rising, though fought to shove it deep inside. "Why do you say I'm not here? I'm right here, talking to you. Who do you think I am if I'm not James? Read that chart on the table, it's got a picture of me and…"

"Puppets," she muttered. "No respect from puppets." The ice-faced woman whisked away. She threw open the door and strode past James's father without so much as a nod in his direction. And from what James could tell, his father didn't even notice she had passed him. Maybe the ice-faced woman was just as unnoticeable as he sometimes was. But more importantly… what had just happened?

"Are you done in there? And…" James's father peered around the room. "Did she already leave? Are you finished? Well, let's get going."

Trying not to wear his confusion around his shoulders, James grabbed his gym bag and hopped over to his father. "Let's go, Dad. Let's get out of here. You're right. Hospitals give me the willies too."

27. Bus

"And then she started calling me a puppet and told me to tell the 'real' James that she was waiting for him. I don't get it, Seth. I honestly don't get it."

Seth propped himself on his elbows. He twirled a magnolia leaf by its stem and allowed it to drop to the ground. "You're topping yourself, Jimbo. I mean you're really going over the top on this one. Are you sure you didn't suck down a little too much radon? You were in the hospital for like a week from that stuff. And I saw how weird it made you act."

James gritted his teeth. The 'radon story' may have been contrived by Dr. Kovek to draw James out, but it had also conveniently helped James and Seth patch up their friendship. Seth had become much more forgiving of James's behavior once he'd been "poisoned." And now, James was trying to get his friend to help him think of a way out of the predicament—but without telling him outright about being a Traveler.

"Look, Seth. All I'm saying is I think something bigger is going on. I think she's trying to trap me."

"What do you mean 'trying to trap you?' She had you in a hospital room by yourself. That's trapped, James. You don't get more trapped than hanging out in a room with a locking door wearing nothing but a nightgown with your butt hanging out. If she wanted to catch you, man, you're caught."

"But what if she *is* after me, Seth? What do I do?"

"She isn't. Listen to me. If someone is after you, and they catch you, they're no longer after you. That's how being chased works."

"You're no help at all," James muttered.

"And you're—no offense—not just crazy anymore. You're crazy *and* paranoid. I'm only hanging out with you cause it's fun to watch you come down from whatever little binge you've been on. Because while you've definitely gone paranoid, at least you aren't just spouting lies like you have been. So do me a favor, Jimbo. Let's not talk about this boogeyman doctor-lady anymore. Ok?"

James didn't reply as Seth wasn't helping. The only thing James had learned from talking to Seth was that whether insane or not, he couldn't convince anyone otherwise. The other point, and less of a real point, than something that he had made James see, was that the ice-faced woman *had* caught him. Kind of. Maybe she wasn't 100% convinced that James was a Traveler, but she talked about Probability and Possibility and talked about James leaving and returning to his body.

So if she knew what James was, why did she need to talk to the real him and not the "puppet" him? If she was going to kill him, she could have just as easily killed the puppet. And then, for all James knew, skipped off to whatever world she came from. If she could escape as easily as he could, then having his dad waiting outside really didn't make a difference. Unless, he supposed, she wasn't from some foreign realm. Maybe she just happened to know about people that could Travel. If that was the case, then a dead little boy in a hospital was still a pretty big deal.

James shuddered. *Or maybe she just wants to kill me good and dead. All of me. Maybe she doesn't want some otherworld me running around unleashed. And the only way that she can make sure is to kill the part of me that can Travel. Which means she'll wait until I'm in my body. She probably doesn't care two nits for the "puppet" me. She wants the real deal.*

"But I care," James called out loud, sending Seth into a flail.

"Don't do that!" Seth shouted. "Jesus, Jim. You can't just do that when someone is trying to relax. I've got a bad heart you know."

James snickered. "No, you don't."

"Well, I'll have a heart attack if you keep doing that."

James shook his head, momentarily distracted from his thoughts of the ice-faced woman. He knew that Seth didn't have the answers. And the only thing that had answers, *An Alternative History of Universal Dynamics,* had been returned to the library. James wasn't about to spring that trap again. No, he was alone for now.

James stood up and brushed the leaves from his pants. "You're no help, Seth."

"And you're beyond help, Jimbo. So, where are you off to now?"

"My bus is here."

"Oh right. Have fun at the beach."

James didn't reply. He waited for the long silver metro transport bus to pull to a stop and hopped inside. It was only five miles from his house to the beach, and he thought that a little salt air would help him to think. Seth had refused at first saying that he had to be at home, only later to leak the truth that his mom was getting more and more uncomfortable about the boys hanging out together. When James had suffered from fainting spells, Seth's mother had felt bad for him and encouraged the friendship. But she had soured on him lately—it was the lies, according to Seth. Now she took steps to make sure that the two boys didn't spend too much time together.

He walked halfway into the bus and then sloughed into a vacant seat on the bus's left side. The bus's hydraulic doors hissed as they pulled shut, then reopened again to allow a disheveled, clearly homeless man to enter. The man wore a collection of motley coats and pants, all ragged. His face was grimy to the point that his complexion was obscured. The man nodded to the driver then lumbered toward the end of the bus, his rags rustling like an antebellum petticoat. When the homeless man reached James's seat, he turned stiffly and sat beside him. Without a glance in his direction, he leaned his head back and closed his eyes.

James looked with confusion at the man who elected to sit next to him, despite the bus being no more than a quarter occupied. James grabbed his book bag and started to stand.

"Don't try to run," the homeless man whispered without opening his eyes.

James's heart leaped in his chest. He prepared to open his mind to the *Essence*, to fall from this world to the safety of another where this man, obviously sent by the ice-faced woman to test him, could not find him.

"Running or Traveling. Either is obvious. So stay put."

James struggled to calm himself, trying to decide if it would be better to look for a chance to escape or begin screaming and yelling. No one on the bus would mistake this man for James's father, and he'd at least have a chance. He paused; there was something oddly familiar about the man. It wasn't the face, or even the voice, as someone as ugly, filthy, and heavily accented would certainly have been memorable. It was the man's... *presence.*

"Dr. Huckabee?" James ventured.

"Yes, but don't use that name. I'm in disguise. And they're definitely following me. I had to warn you, so you didn't do anything stupid. I'm pretty sure she's found you, too. In this world, she calls herself Dr. Kovek."

James dropped his voice to a whisper. "She has found me, but..."

"No time for that now," Dr. Huckabee interrupted. "Just be still a second and listen. I came here for one reason and one reason alone. This may be the last and most important advice I can ever give." The doctor sighed. "If she catches you... *If* she catches you, don't try to Travel. No matter what she or her lackeys threaten or how much they scream, don't Travel. I know it sounds like a good idea, but if you Travel, she can follow you. And in whatever world you land in, she won't have to be so polite. She may not even be a 'she' for that matter.

And then not only will she kill you, but then she'll have her claws on that world too."

"But who is she?" James stammered.

"She's someone out to stop us. Probably Styx, but not necessarily. Doesn't matter per se. One is likened to the other and they're both dangerous." Dr. Huckabee gathered his coat and stood. "Listen, James. Remember that what we do is important. There aren't just lives at stake, we're talking *worlds* here. So keep a low profile, watch your back, and for goodness sake: Rule One!"

"But what do I do if…" James had barely started his sentence before Dr. Huckabee was gone. Not disappeared, simply not there anymore. Almost as though he'd never been there in the first place.

James leaned back, trying to integrate one more nonsensical piece of information into this ridiculous puzzle. Dr. Huckabee wasn't exactly assuring. He said that James shouldn't Travel if he was caught as he might be followed. So what *was* he supposed to do if caught? He was as good as caught already!

"The Frozen World," James muttered to himself. All these risks, everything Dr. Huckabee had said, was all so James could do this insane task he didn't even understand. How was he to save a world? And if he didn't? Well, Dr. Huckabee seemed to think that millions of lives and the world itself were at stake. Somehow, that seemed worse to James than anything that could happen to him.

James exhaled loudly, drawing a stray look from one of the other passengers. His thoughts returned to the Frozen World. He knew that he had to help it. The world was dying as surely any other piece of this mad puzzle. But it was too much. James was torn between trying to race to the Frozen World to save it or trying to patch up the pieces of his life here. But if he Traveled, time would slip away here. And if he didn't, time would slip away there. Either way, clocks were ticking. The clocks were always ticking.

James's eyes widened in realization. *But they weren't.* The clocks weren't always ticking. When he had fled from the shadow beast, he felt time grind to a halt. And when he returned, the shadow beast was still suspended mid-pounce—barely any time had passed at all. James squinted his eyes, trying to recall something the ice-faced woman had said. Or maybe it was Teak or Huckabee. One of them had talked about time waiting for him. So maybe all James had to do was slow time down right before he jumped. Then, even if *some* time passed, he wouldn't lose weeks.

"Time to give it a try."

James took a deep breath and opened himself to the *Essence*. His vision snapped into crystal clarity. Then James reached into his mind. Without expecting and hoping, only *knowing*, he dropped the world into slow motion. Slower, slower, slower—

James fell.

28. Sneak

James tumbled through the Cosmos; the lights from a million words raced so furiously that he felt as though he was free-falling through a luminous fog. Within an instant in this timeless realm, he saw the cold point of light that he knew to be the Frozen World. Faster and faster he coursed until what once was a pinprick occupied his entire field of vision. The dazzling light sharpened and focused as it crashed toward him like a relativistic bullet. James felt himself gain weight and momentum as he collided with his body in the Frozen World. But though he had rejoined himself, he didn't stop, he still hurtled forward. James realized he no longer traveled spiritually, but physically. He was sprinting down a dimly lit tunnel of the Kai'ja stronghold, his lungs burning and his muscles aching.

And he didn't know why.

With a quick stutter, James skidded to a halt. He placed his hands on knees as he panted to catch his breath, only to watch Ling, the mysterious Blank, dart past him. She, too, was running as fast as she could.

"Hasten, Jay! Come now! They are making ground. They are making ground!"

James lurched forward to resume his run to catch up to the fleeing Ling. At a whim, he opened himself to the *Essence* of the world, and the fatigue drained from his legs. James thought that perhaps he could slow time down, to try to see who was chasing him, but he hadn't quite recovered from the jump to the Frozen World. He wasn't sure if he should try anything particularly dangerous. He focused on catching Ling, still difficult despite his weightless legs. He had almost reached her when she darted behind a stone pillar, jerking James to the side when he passed.

Ling dropped to her belly and started worming into a small recess in the wall that James could see was where the wall parted slightly from the floor. If he had been back in his own world, James would have thought it looked like an air duct. But that didn't make sense here. Without hesitation, he lay down and slid in after Ling, receiving an inadvertent kick from her blackened foot for being too close. For several yards, they shimmied until the duct opened into another tunnel. When both Ling and James had made it to the other side, they collapsed against the wall. Ling was panting heavily, sweat dripping from her forehead. In an effort not to look suspicious, James released the *Essence*. His exhaustion came back in a torrent. He sweated and panted just as heavily as her.

"That… was… too… close," Ling gasped.

James nodded fervently, hoping she'd offer more explanation.

Ling continued, "It isn't worth it to try and do this. You are full of persuasion, strange boy. But I should not have minded your urging. If they find me outside my cage, they shall certainly punish me."

"They would do that?" James's eyes widened. "I thought you were like, the most valuable Blank there's ever been."

"You say such things. But I do not understand your certainty. There is a two-thirds chance I am worth nothing. I find it easier to believe that I am just a servant, and Charles and Bella are the Blanks. Certainly, I'm some kind of Blank, since they transported me this distance. But I might not be the one they're looking for. I am not special."

"Well, *I* think it is you. You're special, I can feel it." James shot her his best smile. "No matter what you say."

Ling shrugged. "I know you believe this, Jay. But pardon my distrust. Three weeks ago, you had to be schooled as to what a Blank was."

"Right… I. Wait, three weeks? Is that how long we've been here?" James stumbled to recover, to make it seem like he hadn't lost the time. "I mean, it seems like shorter than that."

"I disagree. I believe the time has passed far too slowly. The deliberations are of too great a length. I confess my timidity and my fear. That is why I agreed to lead you here. For no other reason would I risk this."

James nodded. Memory loss, forgetfulness, or not, he needed to know where he was trying to go and what he was trying to do. And the overly formal Blank didn't seem to be helping. "All right. So what's the plan again?"

Ling wrinkled her nose in distaste. "You are not one prone to listen, Jay. Perhaps this time you shall?" Ling closed her eyes, her face assuming a level of serenity even greater than normal. "According to the runics, your friends' coffer is in the Kai'ja's slave quarters. No one but the queen and the slaves is permitted in such a place. I believe that is why they think it safe. The slaves are ordered to defend their home upon peril of death—even against the other Kai'ja. Only the queen is allowed free rein."

"The queen and us, right?"

"As a Blank, I am excepted. I am like as a slave to them. You are not. But you did say you could get by somehow? Is that not your talent?"

"Yeah, I'm…" James groped for the words, "I can be forgettable if I want." He waited for a few moments before continuing. "Ok, so we find the chest. And then what?"

Ling raised a slender dark eyebrow. "I'm beginning to think this wasn't your plan. Must I repeat all to you that you have once explained to me?"

"Humor me."

"Very well. Once I open the chest, you check the plans for the rune, and we make haste to leave."

The memories crept back. Sylph had said she taught Ling to open the chest as a backup plan in case anything happened to her. "Ok, I remember."

Ling jerked to her feet. "Are you quite prepared and rested? Shall we continue?"

"Yeah, I suppose. But if we see another Kai'ja patrol, I don't know if I've got enough left in me to get away again."

Ling rose into a low crouch and scuttled down the passageway, careful to stay in the shadowed areas where light from the flickering torches didn't quite reach. James followed close behind, his eyes open not only to the far end of the hall, but to the *Essence* of the Frozen World. Every groove and crack on the wall stood out in James's mind with sharp relief. And yet, the world's screams of pain and desperation were nearly overwhelming in this place. James held on to the *Essence* for a few moments more before he was forced to let go out of fear that he might vomit on the floor.

"Down here," Ling whispered, dropping to her belly as she spoke. She inched forward and disappeared in yet another of the narrow vents. James followed suit and after a few short feet, Ling came to a stop.

"This is the place. We must wait until it's clear. And… *now.*" Ling shot forward, with James hurrying behind her.

When he stood, he was in an open chamber with a domed ceiling pooled alternately in light and darkness. The dome was supported by a forest of columns that felt far more numerous than could possibly be practical. Only by further inspection did he determine that the columns weren't columns at all, but instead the carved remnants of where stalactites and stalagmites had grown together.

James looked to his right to see Ling shimmying into the plain white dress marking her as a Blank. And James, hearing the first whisper of voices and thud of footsteps, pulled himself away from the world in hopes the runic slaves did not see him.

"If you are endeavoring your magic, know that you are still visible."

"You're the only one who'll notice me. So don't stare. Now lead on."

Just as James focused to keep himself unnoticeable, Ling put on her own guise of unnoticeability. Only for her, the effect was through body language. She tucked her shoulders low, bowed her head, held her hands close to her sides, and kept her steps shuffled and tiny. She looked to him like a sedate chickadee, or a bashful pup. In turn, he kept close to her back, trying to mimic her movements, but even more so, to keep himself unnoticeable.

James and Ling wove through the columns until the ceiling had disappeared into the darkness above. Though they made an effort to stay away, he could see that the room was clustered by benches and sofas where the runic slaves reclined. Like the Kai'ja, the runics were bared to the waist, clothing hardly necessary beyond maintaining decency in the inferno of the mountain. But what James also noticed was that the slaves were not ethnically Kai'ja. They were every size, shape, race, and color. The one thing they had in common was their runes—all different, but all bearing the distinct characteristic of the

Kai'ja's style. And by the flashes of intuition that James got with the sight of each rune, he became aware of yet another fact. This chamber wasn't a living area for runics, it was a warehouse for them. The Kai'ja were holding these people until they could be sold.

"I can't believe they're all slaves," James whispered, though received only a stern glance from Ling.

They continued to weave through the columns and crowds until he noticed a subtle change in the appearance of the room. Just as the lighting shifted from a soft orange to an ethereal blue, James noticed that the light was no longer emitting from torches, but from the columns themselves. The light was coming from a luminescent rock that carried a glow both attracting James and putting him ill at ease. The other significant difference was that none of the runic slaves were this close to the center. James wondered if that was due to the lighting, or some unspoken fear of the contents within.

"This is our destination. In here." Ling quickened her pace as she came to one last enormous column, so large its walls disappeared into the darkness. To one side of the column was an arched doorway that opened into what must be the hollow interior. James followed Ling inside, only to almost choke on his breath. As they passed the threshold, the temperature of the room dropped to the point where the sweat dripping from their bodies turned to frost.

"What happened?" James stammered.

"The cold keeps everything preserved, but also acts as a barrier. Only the Kai'ja's queen can remove an object from this room."

"Look"—James pointed to the far corner—"there it is."

Carefully set against the wall, and bearing a brightly colored blaze that James assumed was the Kai'ja version of a luggage tag, was Sylph's ebony chest. The box gave James the same chill it had on the two other occasions he had seen it. And it made him a little nervous to think of what may be inside. An etching, according to Sylph, but of what?

Ling dropped to her knees in front of the chest and began whirling the knobs furiously, though not quite with the same level of precision as Sylph had done when first presenting the contents to the Kai'ja queen. James struggled to follow the ballet of turns but was lost within moments. Before he could return his focus, the clasp snapped open. Ling lifted the lid.

James crept forward, his skin tingling with anticipation as the lid lifted to reveal a single piece of parchment, unadorned in any way except for a rune which crept across the page like a cancerous rash of exquisite beauty And yet this wasn't the center of it all. The rune was *not* what James was looking for.

"What do you see?" Ling whispered nervously.

"This isn't it."

"It's not what?"

"This isn't the problem; this isn't what I'm looking for."

"But what does it say? What does it mean?"

"It means," a feminine voice hissed behind them, "that the unknown will always be the greatest lure." They darted around to see the queen of the Kai'ja, dressed in dark robes and flanked on either side by muscled runics.

James lowered his voice, the picture finally becoming clear. The epiphany rattled through his head with the subtlety of a car crash. The realization was certain as it was terrifying. The words barely crept past his lips. "The rune isn't what will destroy us. She is. It's her."

Before Ling could protest, a runic guard had grabbed her and toppled Ling into a sack. James, still reeling from the newfound knowledge, gave not the slightest protest as he, too, was seized and bagged. He was at first stunned by the bruise, gave a momentary struggle, then relaxed as he was thrown over the massive runic's shoulder. Ling, on the other hand, squealed loudly, the sounds of her struggle uncharacteristic to her normally demure demeanor. James, however, simply acquiesced, hoping that the Kai'ja queen may say something that would give her motives away.

I could just Travel away, James thought. *But what would I gain? It's time to find out what's happening here. It's time to start doing what I was meant to do.*

29. Caught

James wasn't sure how long he and Ling were carried within the sacks; his mind was too preoccupied with the newfound knowledge that the queen of the Kai'ja was the reason the Frozen World stood at the brink of death. But was it something she was going to do that would destroy this world? Or was she the only thing remaining between the world and its destruction? In a way, James knew, but not by logic, that the queen of the Kai'ja must be stopped from doing… *something.* But what?

Without forewarning, James felt the sack upended and he was toppled onto the damp floor of a small, tunneled chamber carved into the rock. The room reminded James of the basement beneath his friend Seth's house. The floor dipped down in the center to where a small hole, a hand's width wide, opened into the floor. James guessed that it was either for drainage or simply a latrine.

James rubbed his arms and shoulders, inspecting himself for bruises. He found his skin unmarked and dismissed the oddity as another aspect he couldn't explain. Ling, however, looked a little worse for wear. James wondered if she had received a harsher treatment for putting up a fight. He felt a little bad about not struggling more, but he knew better than to try and wrestle those guards. And who knows? Maybe this was for the best. There was no other way to get an audience with the Kai'ja queen.

A clang and a snap as the door to their cell swung shut, only to open moments later as the Kai'ja queen walked in. The slender priestess stopped at the door, as though not deigning to enter the damp cell. As before, she wore a dark cloak that cinched loosely around her waist. When her skin peeked through, the silver chains wrapped around her appeared in glimpses. She nodded to her guards who brushed past her and closed the door behind them as they left.

"I must say," the queen began, her voice poured honey, "that my guesses as to who had invaded my vault were quite wrong. The Scrim, I assumed, or a curious slave, or one of my cousins. But I did not expect a Blank." The queen's glance stopped and lingered on James. She remained silent as though trying to decipher what she saw. "And you, boy. You came with the Islanders. But I see you are *not* one of them. The eyes, the hair." The queen ran a finger alongside James's cheek. "From what land do you hail? I have seen, owned, and etched upon every peoples, and yet you look… peculiar."

James shifted uncomfortably. Whatever made him unnoticeable and accepted didn't work on the queen, just as it didn't seem to work on Ling.

"I didn't know my parents," James squeaked, hoping that his ability to lie had not also gone away. "I've traveled the ports. Never thought much about it."

The Kai'ja queen's gaze lingered on James for a moment longer before finally shifting away. James allowed himself to relax slightly but braced for the next question.

"And what is your business within my vault? For what reason should I release you?"

Ling began, her demure personality returned. "Your highness, we just…"

James broke in. "Ling's my friend. I… I couldn't bear the thought of her being etched without knowing what the rune would be. We just wanted to see, that's all. I just wanted to make sure she would be ok." He knew he was babbling, and yet gained momentum and confidence that the queen might accept his story. "Some of the Scrim's runes, well, they're just hurtful. The wearer… they *do* things to them and I wanted to see if that's what this one was."

The queen smiled. "Perhaps you forgot, there are three Blanks brought by the Scrim. Why do you think she is to be etched?"

James set his jaw. "Because Ling is different. I can feel it. I know that you can tell who's who, and maybe I can't do it like you can. But I know she's special."

The Kai'ja queen studied Ling carefully, then looked over to James, and back to Ling again. Her eyes narrowed and her lips pursed, then cracked, then smiled. The Kai'ja queen laughed spitefully. "Ah, perchance to love as a child once more. To see things where they are not. To know with certainty, absolute certainty of what they will be. On another day, I might see your acts as a fancy. But on this day"—the queen's face darkened—"I am not amused."

The Kai'ja queen darted forward, her hand seizing Ling's throat. She lifted the girl into the air, as though she had no weight at all. The queen whipped a thin blade from her belt and touched it to Ling's cheek. Without turning toward James, she spoke sharply, her voice unwavering. "How did you open my chest, prisoner?"

"I watched the captain do it. She doesn't know," James blurted, yet another lie passing easily from his lips.

"And how did you know where the chest was kept?"

"I heard one of your slaves talking about it."

"And the name of my betrayer?"

"I don't know the name. They didn't say." The queen pressed the blade ever so closer to Ling's cheek, a rivulet of blood traced down her cheek. James shouted, "I don't know their name, I swear!"

The Kai'ja queen turned from Ling, the arm holding the knife drifting to her side. She released Ling who collapsed onto the dank floor. Ling's hands jumped to rub where the blade had cut her. "And what did you see?"

"A rune. It was just a rune."

"You speak in lies. You came here not to glimpse a rune you couldn't read. Tell me what your eyes did see." The queen cast her arm to the right, the blade pointing to Ling. "I shall not ask again."

"It said… it said 'Gateway'! It said 'Gateway'." James spat the words. "I don't know what it *does* or what that means. I just know it scares me. You scare me. This whole place scares me." He dropped to his knees. It was all too much. He looked up at the queen, terrified of her next move, and yet even more terrified of what would happen if he tried to return to his own world. What would happen to his body here? What would happen to Ling?

The queen pursed her lips. "Correct. Most interesting." She knocked on the cell door, which immediately opened, and the two guards hurried in. The queen pointed to a dark rune on the first guard's shoulder. "Now read me this."

James wrinkled his brow. He opened himself to the *Essence* and examined the rune. He was hit with a flash of inspiration. "Um, it says 'Raven-Swift.'"

"And this?" The queen pointed to another rune, this one on the man's forehead."

"'Lion-eye-far-see'… I don't understand what you want."

"And this." The queen walked forward, dragging the other guard forward by the wrist; she pointed to a rune on the palm of his hand.

"'Obedience of Poison Clock.'"

"And now"—the queen's voice stayed cold—"tell me not their words, but their meaning."

James concentrated, the meaning slowly bubbling to the surface of his mind, then crested with certainty. "The first makes him faster, but only at night, but it makes him more sensitive to fire. And the second allows him to see better in the dark and at a distance, but blinds him in daylight and makes it so he can't focus up close."

"And the third?"

James winced. "That one, I think, makes him have to tell the truth when you ask him a question. And if you die, then he will die as well."

"Remarkable." The queen pursed her lips. "But all you can tell me of the other is 'Gateway'?"

"I can't really read them," James mumbled. "I just kind of all of the sudden know what they mean. But it's different when they're not on a person. It's as if they aren't all there."

The queen smiled. "Away with this girl," she ordered the guards. "I need her not." The guards flung Ling over their shoulder and exited the cell. The queen dropped to one knee. "What is your name, child?"

"Jay."

"You have a gift, Jay. And you speak correctly that a written rune differs from one un-drawn. But you are only right in part. It says… "Gateway to.'"

"Gateway to what?"

"That, you will not know until the etching is complete. It takes the full soul of the inscribed to make a rune known. And when I do complete my etching, only then will we know if the Scrim spoke truth."

"No!" James blurted. "Don't do it. It'll kill us all. Trust me." The panic rose in James's voice. "You have to trust me, *don't do it.*"

"Another intuition, child?"

"Something like that."

The queen smiled again. James was beginning to dislike the queen's smiles. "I think you may yet be of use." And with that, the queen turned on her heels and strode from the room. James jumped as the cell door slammed shut. He crossed his legs and dropped his head into his hands.

"Well, so much for keeping a low profile," he muttered. James pulled himself to his feet and walked to the cell door. There was a small opening at the top crossed by bars which James could see out of if he stood on his tip toes. Outside the cell, a corridor with an even sequence of cell doors stretched silent in the torchlight. Just beyond his field of vision, only noticeable from the sound of rustling armor, a guard stood vigilant. James pressed his face to the bars.

"Ling? Ling are you out there? Are you ok?"

"Quiet," the guard barked.

"Ling? Where are you?"

James lurched back as the guard swung at the bars with his club. But there was not an answer from Ling. James briefly opened his mind to the *Essence* but didn't sense her in the air either.

Ok, just need to get through these bars, and…

James paused. What *did* he need to do? Sure, he knew that the Kai'ja queen was somehow tied to the world ending. He guessed it had to do with etching the runes. But what was he supposed to do about it? And even if he knew, wasn't he forgetting about his problems back in his homeworld with the ice-faced woman? No, it was time to check back into Grand Central and see if he could find Dr. Huckabee. Maybe the doctor could tell him what he should be doing. Or at least give him enough info to not mess things up.

But first things first. James leaned over and plucked a pebble from the ground. He opened himself to the *Essence* of the world, the walls cutting themselves into sharp relief from the meager torchlight coming through the door. James tossed the pebble into the air, then concentrated on slowing time down, slower… slower… until the seconds passed so slowly that the pebble seemed to hang suspended. And then—

James fell.

30. Trials

When James became aware, he was standing in the dead center of the Grand Central Hallway, the corridor extending to infinity in front of him. The domed ceiling and unbroken pattern of doors lining the eaves were the same, but that was all. The varieties of peoples did not meander, each with their own purpose. Instead, they poured at him, racing one step short of a stampede. Bewildered, James grabbed the shoulder of a man in leaf-green tights and waistcoat.

"What's happening? What's going on?" James asked.

"They *got* him. They finally caught him!" the Robin Hood stunt double chirped.

"Got who?"

"Just come on. Follow me, this is huge!"

Bewilderment enveloped James as he turned to run with the tide, becoming one more body in the mass. As he ran, he could see that for as many people as the corridor held, just as many kept winking into existence to follow the herd. Inexplicably, the corridor of Grand Central, once so uniform, had expanded to allow for the volume. And then James saw the door. It was shaped just like the others but hundreds of feet high and wide, complete with a doorknob the size of a small house. James followed the tide through the door, his vision flooded with white as he passed the plane.

When his sight returned, James was seated in a stadium that stretched in all directions, housing an incomprehensible multitude. Millions of people filled the stands, their collective voices sounding anxiously in as many different languages, accents, and pitches as there were people. Even "people" was a stretch, as the collection seemed more akin to patrons of the Mos Eisley Cantina. At that moment, something flickered at the center of the stadium. A man in a white robe walked out into the light.

James pondered for only a moment why he could see the man in the center of the stadium with perfect detail, and even hear the man's footsteps on the slate-colored tile. Then, he realized that this was merely one more trick of Grand Central's warped perception.

"Fellow Travelers," the man spoke, surprisingly in a voice that sounded like James's own. And not the voice James would hear when listening to a recording, but instead the same tone of the voice of his thoughts. "We bring you today joyous news. The most wanted criminal in all the worlds has been found. Today, he is to be brought to justice." The crowds exploded into applause, and James, caught by the tide of millions, cheered beside them. "I give you the man responsible for breaking the laws of the countless worlds more times than could be counted. I give you: Dr. Thomas Huckabee!"

Cheers ripped through the masses as a hunched man in a red waistcoat and brown trousers was led to the center of the stage, his hands in shackles. The man didn't *look* like the Dr. Huckabee James had known. His skin tone, features, hair, and stance were all different. But just as clearly, James knew that this *was* the same person. A chill ran up his spine. But if Dr. Huckabee was the enemy…

James's thoughts were interrupted by the boom of the announcer. "Dr. Huckabee, you are charged with the unforgivable crime of meddling in the events of worlds not your own. In doing so you have altered the fate of those worlds. You have violated the first and greatest rule of the Countless Worlds and the League of Travelers. What have you to say for yourself?"

James shook his head in disbelief. *But Rule One is to not tell anyone who you are… What rule is this guy talking about?*

Dr. Huckabee spoke, the crowd hushed as he opened his mouth. "I only allowed the worlds to live—to continue on. It is our responsibility to keep them from the doom brought by the Styx." Huckabee hissed the last word, and on cue, the crowd released a roar of fury.

"Order, Order!" the judge barked. "You will not utter such a slur before this court. There has been no Styx in millennia. And remember that the crimes of that fictional society are no greater or less than your own. You have violated Rule One: you have changed the fate of a world. And for that, you will be punished. Your verdict stands as the obliteration of your spirit from this and the countless worlds. Have you a final statement?"

Dr. Huckabee looked into the crowd, and though from an unfathomable distance (though such a thing didn't seem valid in Grand Central) James could swear that the doctor was looking at him. "What I do, what *we* do, is right."

A protest roared from the crowd; the judge banged his gavel, "Order, order."

"And the Styx are real, whether you'll admit it or—"

With these last words, Dr. Huckabee was engulfed in a light that filled his entire body… then vanished, leaving behind but an afterimage. James knew—with certainty—that Dr. Huckabee was gone forever.

As the horror sank in, he was gripped by fear. These people, these millions of people, were not on Dr. Huckabee's side. They were Dr. Huckabee's enemy. And that meant they were his enemy. They were against "meddling" in a world. And yet, for the Frozen World, James knew that if he didn't help, that that world would be destroyed, and Sylph, Teak, Brine, Ling—*everyone*—with it. Nevertheless, Grand Central wasn't safe for him. Safe places, it seems, were in short supply.

And with that—

James fell.

31. Vagabond

The hiss of the hydraulic door shook James into alertness. The realization that he had returned home made him jump to glance at his watch. He had last jumped to the Frozen World on a Sunday, and according to his watch—James smiled—it was still Sunday. Furthermore, from what he could see out the window, only a few minutes had passed. The grin spread sloppily over James's face. He'd done it. He'd figured out how to solve the problem of skipping time. But the smile fell just as quickly when James thought of what he'd seen in Grand Central. Dr. Huckabee had been tried and executed. James had lost the only person who had ever tried to help him understand what was happening. He felt terribly alone.

A gravelly voice spoke, "Ok, friend, so it wasn't all true. I guess you can know that now." James looked to his right to see that the bus seat, empty only moments ago, was occupied by the same homeless man that had warned James not to run from the ice-faced woman. Only he wasn't the same. This wasn't Dr. Huckabee. It looked like him—or at least the 'him' James had seen on the bus—but it was most certainly a different person. But James recognized this person as well. This was Huckabee's friend, the one he'd met in the world with the metallic lake.

James whispered, "The doctor's gone. You know that, don't you?"

"Yes. I too was there. It would have been, how do you say, a bit suspicious had I not been."

James didn't reply.

"Things have changed for us, my friend," the man continued. "We all have to risk a little bit more, and we all have to be a lot more careful. If those bastards caught Huckabee, there's no telling what they found out. I should not be so near to you." The man scratched his shoulder and coughed loudly. If he *was* acting, James thought him perfect. "Of course, I'm not about to let the last wish of my friend go unfulfilled. The doctor, he didn't like things left unfinished. And right now that means you. Huckabee saw something in you. And I have to trust that. Because once, he saw something in me, too."

"But what if…" James had barely uttered the word before he was cut off again.

"Listen. It is not safe to speak here. They could be watching. Now I'm going to get off at the next stop and start walking. You follow after me, ok? Once it's safe, I'll wave you over. But not a moment before. Nod your head."

James nodded.

"Then here we go."

The bus pulled to a stop and the vagrant rose from his seat and shuffled to the front of the bus. James waited for only a moment before rising to follow him. He uttered a quick word of thanks to the driver and then stepped into the sunlight.

The day was grey and humid, hot and threatening of an afternoon thunderstorm that might or might not occur. James recognized that he was in the strip of land separating the main town from the beach, a haven of construction and new development, as though every business in the world was set on erecting strip malls and fenced communities at the same time. And as none of the buildings around him were complete, he could only assume that the bus stop existed as a dropping point for construction workers and tradesmen.

The vagrant—though James knew that was just a disguise—was ambling with a sort of shuffled gait toward a vacant lot where an unfinished wooden frame was half-erected. James ambled behind, though not quite so close that he was immediately noticeable. The man walked past a jumbled lumber pile, across a discarded stack of piping, and to the incomplete building. He traced the man's footsteps to where they ended in the shadows.

James felt a soft tap on his shoulders and turned to the vagrant who nodded and then gestured for him to have a seat on the cross beam of one of the frames.

"You look different than last time," James said. He set his book bag down and then sat down beside it.

"We always look different. Or at least we should. And while it may seem that we're way past Rule One here, I don't break that for nothing."

"I thought Rule One was not to meddle in a world's fate… or something like that."

The vagrant shook his head. "That's *their* Rule One, friend. Not ours. But then, that's what I came to talk to you about. Huckabee told you about the Styx, of course. But he didn't tell you about everyone else. He didn't tell you the whole truth about Grand Central. Or did he?"

"How would I know if he told me everything? Or if what he did tell me was true? Seems like everyone is trying to out-lie each other."

The vagrant shrugged off the commend. He crouched and drew in the sand with his fingertip. "When I first met you, I asked if you wanted to help, or just be a tourist."

"Look, I'm *trying* to help, it's just that…"

"Let me finish. What you have to realize is that most Travelers *are* just tourists. The people in Grand Central, the people in that audience, almost everyone is just a tourist. They believe that you shouldn't interfere with a world. It's their greatest Rule. That's the reason we can't say we're trying to save worlds. The Styx, well the Styx are still very real, and very dangerous. But it's not just them that are against us. It's everyone."

James tightened his jaw. "Why didn't you just tell me. Why did you have to say it was the Styx that was after me? Why couldn't you tell me the truth?"

"Because Dr. Huckabee wanted you to see things for yourself. He wanted you to decide if you were going to help or not by yourself. We didn't make you want to help, we just presented it as an option. But we didn't tell you *not* to help either. And that's what those in Grand Central would have done. They would have picked you up, and brainwashed you, and you'd just be another tourist."

James scratched his head. "But are they right? *Should* we just stay out of it? Let the world live out its destiny."

"Perhaps we should. But if that's what you think, you are forgetting one major piece. The Styx *are* real. And they *do* exist. And they *will* see a world to its death. So even if most Travelers should leave worlds alone, people like me are needed just to counter-balance the Styx."

For a moment, James sat silently, trying to digest the words of the vagrant. When he looked up once more, the man was staring at him intensely.

"So, the question, my brother, is did he get to you? Are you going to pick a side in this fight, or are you going to just stand by?"

"I…" James paused. Though he wondered if he'd be damning himself, he chose. "I'm with you. I've got friends out there now. I don't want them to die when their world comes down."

The vagrant smiled. "Good. Good man. And good choice." He coughed into his hand. "In that case, I'm here to help you with your little problem."

"Which problem?" He paused. "The ice-faced woman?"

"Who? Oh. I guess that's a good name for her. She goes by Dr. Kovek here, if you didn't know. And she knows who you are."

"Yeah. She told me as much… only she thought I was a 'puppet'—if that makes sense. I think she meant my body when I'm *out* of it, you know."

"A good a word as any. We think she tracked Huckabee here when he was, er, *recruiting*. But if they haven't moved on you here, then it's unlikely they've traced you to any other worlds. That's good. It means that if you can get rid of them here, you're safe out there. For now."

James squinted in confusion. "But… why? Why would you come here if you knew that *they* were here? Why risk it? I don't even know what I'm doing out there. Not that anyone told me what I was *supposed* to be doing. But why do you even care about me?"

The vagrant snapped his head in James's direction so quickly that James recoiled. "Look, friend. So, what if I don't care about you? That doesn't mean that Huckabee didn't. You think he was trying to confuse you? That he thought it was funny? He saw potential in you, I said that before. And don't forget that it's not you that matters. What matters is what you can do, what I can do, and what Huckabee could do. We save worlds. Clear? And the more of us out there, the better chance we have. This is a war. And me and Huckabee's other friends don't give ground easily. I don't care if you've been to one world, or a billion. I won't give the Styx that victory. And *that* is why I'm here. And *that* is why we have to set things in order."

For a moment James remained silent, feeling the full impact of the tongue lashing, and a little embarrassed at not appreciating what Dr. Huckabee had done for him. He took a deep breath, released, and then looked back over at the vagrant with far more appreciation. "Ok. I understand. But I thought you said you didn't know if they were the Styx. And… how are we supposed to 'set things in order'?"

The vagrant reached into his coat and pulled out a small, bundled package. He unwrapped it as he spoke. "It's a good question. If Dr. Kovek was just an agent from the countless worlds, she'd be gone by now. But since she's stuck around, and since she's taken an interest in you, she's most certainly one of the Styx." The man finished unwrapping the bundle to reveal two dull grey pistols. He began opening and checking each one individually, then slid a clip into each handle. James looked on in horror. "The Styx work in teams of three. Three people per world. It gives them more muscle than us who work alone. But it makes them more vulnerable too. They can't hide as well. Since there are more of them, they are easier to find. Now, have you seen any of Dr. Kovek's accomplices?"

"Yeah. I got chased by these two guys at the library one day and… Wait a minute! I thought you weren't allowed to kill anyone. Isn't that Rule Three?"

The vagrant snapped the clip shut and examined the weapon. "Can't kill a native, can't kill a local. But another Traveler is free game for the killing. A Traveler isn't part of the world and so won't tie you to it if you kill one. That's what Rule Three is for. It's not about morality. And the Styx feel the same. But that's not why you're still here. Dr.

Kovek knows that if she traps you, she can trace you to the other worlds you've visited. She wins one, she wins them all."

"So, you're going to hunt the Styx?" James could feel the cold sweat running down his back.

"We probably don't need to kill them all. Cut off the head, and the body will die. If we take out Dr. Kovek, we should be clear. And…" The vagrant lurched forward. He held a pistol in each hand. "Quiet. Did you hear that?"

James got ready to seize the *Essence* when the vagrant smacked him with the barrel of his gun. "Are you crazy, don't even try it. You're native here. We can't give you away. But it's happening now. Get down and stay down." The vagrant gestured to a gap in a pile of boards. "Hide until I get back." The man sprang forward, no trace of the lumbering shuffle remaining. Instead, he seemed as spry as an Olympic athlete.

James wedged himself down below the boards, pulling his book bag in beside him and grabbing a loose piece of discarded plastic to cover his entry. He peeked over the piece of plastic and looked out into the vacant lot where the vagrant crept low to the ground, one gun held alert near his forehead, and the other dropped behind him.

A sound like thunder cracked and a puff of dust erupted from just to the side of the vagrant. The man whirled, both guns blazing then… *shifted.* James couldn't think of another world to describe it, except that he slid to one side, a blur of motion counter to his normal movement. There was another blur, this one atop a pile of lumber, and James saw another man come into focus. He immediately recognized him as being one of the people who had chased him from the library. And like the vagrant, he held a gun in each hand, though this man held onto a pair of what James guessed must be Uzis.

There was another hail of gunfire, and the Styx agent on the frame leaped into the air, his body moving impossibly fast. The woodpile where he once stood exploded in splinters. James winced, reflexively closing his eyes, only to reopen them a moment later, with no sign of either the vagrant or the Styx agent. Then they were back again, both moving at incredible speeds and both unleashing torrents of gunfire at the other.

James felt his stomach knot in anticipation as the two men blurred around the construction site, the bullets soaring and pieces of wood and metal fragmenting in all directions. And then, as though through some twist of fate, both men had somehow collided. They were together, grappling desperately. James heard two gunshots sounding so close together he thought they were one… and then they were gone. The vagrant and the Styx agent popped out of existence like an exploding balloon, their forms twisting and writhing, leaving only nothingness behind.

He waited for fifteen minutes, paralyzed with fear before he finally crept from his hiding place. He inched to the center of the yard where the vagrant and the agent had once stood. In the middle, amidst a network of footprints and a low settling cloud of dust, lay four guns: two pistols, and two Uzis. But of the men, there was nothing.

"They killed each other," James spoke aloud. "But… but they're just *gone*." The unreality of the escapade washed over him, and he began to wonder if this had been yet another dream. He bent down and picked one of the pistols from the ground. The metal was warm and heavy. It felt real enough, and the bullet holes riddling the yard looked real enough. But it couldn't be.

"This *is* real," James said with resolve. "This is real. And it's here. And I'm a part of it." He walked back to his hiding place, the cooling pistol still in his hand. He wrapped the gun in the vagrant's discarded coat and then slipped the bundle into his book bag. Seized with sudden fear, he began to run.

James didn't run with the even pace of the marathon runner, and not with the effortless glide of a person riding the *Essence*. Instead, he ran like a boy, alone and afraid amid things far larger than himself. He didn't know where to go, and he didn't know who he could turn to, in any world.

Dr. Huckabee was gone. The vagrant was gone. Dr. Kovek knew his name and where he lived. His father thought he was a thief; his mother thought he was a liar; his best friend thought he was insane. And those people out there weren't figments of his imagination. If James needed proof, the unmarked gun, wrapped in the clothes of a man who no longer existed was all the proof he needed. But there was no one where left to turn. Even the *Alternative History* was locked away and guarded and Grand Central full of enemies. To top it all off, James knew that on a far-off world in a different plane of reality, another James—Jay there—was trapped in a prison cell.

He wanted it all to be over, to just be a normal kid again. But he knew that ship had sailed. And if the vagrant had been right, it was more than a single world that rested on James's shoulders. It was all worlds. Not just the one today, but every world he visited until the end of his days.

"Arrrghggg," James cried in frustration. He quit running and aimed a kick at a nearby can. The aluminum can skid into the bushes. "I don't even know what I'm supposed to be doing! It isn't fair!"

James stopped and panted. He toyed with the idea that some wise old man would step from the bushes and explain exactly why it was fair, and exactly what he should do. But though he waited, no one arrived. His sides ached and his head pounded, but James knew he had to refocus.

"Think dammit, think." He walked the edge of the path where a small spillway created a miniature waterfall where the drainage from the creek spilled out over the rocks to pool below. At the base of the pond, a skinny orangish cat with a hint of black tiger-striping on his side was staring intently at the minnows below. The cat raised a paw and kept motioning as if to strike but did not quite act.

"I'm not allowed to talk to anyone, you know," James said to the cat. The feline paused from his watch to regard him with wide green eyes. "I can't get advice because I can't talk about it. And I can't tell anyone what's going on, or I'll get caught. Do you know what that's like?" James sighed. "Feel free to go Cheshire Cat on me if you want. At least it would be nice to have someone to talk to."

The cat cocked his head, but neither smiled as a Cheshire should smile, nor taunted as one would taunt.

"They're all chasing me. They know I'm here because they know Dr. Huckabee was here. And Dr. Huckabee was here because he thinks the Frozen World is important. And since I'm the only one who's been to the Frozen World, I guess that makes me important. And the Styx— or whoever—wanted Huckabee dead, so I guess that makes them want me dead too. Probably, so I can't do whatever it is I don't know how to do in the Frozen World because…"

James paused. The answer shone apparent, reflected in the cat's eyes.

"They're only chasing me because of the Frozen World. If I can fix things there, then I don't matter anymore. I'm just a kid. Huckabee may have cared about me, but maybe these guys don't. What if the Styx don't care about me at all? What if it *is* all about that other world? If I can fix that… I'm saved!"

James reached down to pet the stray cat rubbing against his leg. He lifted the cat in one hand and smiled. "Hate to do this to you, kitty." In a smooth motion, he gave the cat a slow underhand toss. At the peak of the arc, the cat began to twist, his muscles moved to realign himself, and though he moved, James saw the motion slowing, slowing, until every ripple of hair in the wind and the cat's mouth yawned in surprise as the meow stretched to infinity. And then—

James fell.

32. Oak

The waters of the purple sea lapped gently across James's arms. The sunset, changing from blue, to green to red, and then to a pulsing fuchsia, added a psychedelic feel to the seascape. James didn't know if this place was a haven. He was certain it wasn't. After all, according to Dr. Huckabee, he could only Travel to worlds that were dying. And in James's mind, that meant every world he visited was perilous. But this world with its bizarre ocean and radical sky didn't scream with the same urgency of the Frozen World. Instead, it gave a slow whine like a needy puppy. James vowed to return to soothe that pain. But for now, he had work to do.

Grand Central wasn't safe; Dr. Huckabee's capture proved that. So James went to the only other place that was even a little known. The alien sea, the first world to which James had accidentally Traveled. Finding the sea had been just as easy as returning to the Frozen World, even though it was but one pinpoint of light in the entire Cosmos. It felt easy, familiar, even though he had only been there once before.

James looked skyward, the sun which had shown so many shades of color on his last excursion was beaming from overhead, a warm pink that gave the ocean the feel of sunrise despite its noon-like position. And just like the last time James had visited, there was no shoreline in sight, no birds, no evidence of anything alive except himself.

"Perfect," James said with pride. He knew that in both the Frozen World and in his home world, time had been slowed to almost a stop. That meant James could concentrate on what he came to do. And what he needed to do, was to learn how to escape a prison.

He knew it could be done. He'd done it once by accident when he had been in the cages with Ling, Charles, and Bellacroix at the bandits' camp. And James was convinced that he could do it again. Just like he'd been able to turn his hands orange, just like he'd been able to make himself unnoticeable. The only problem was that there were no walls here.

James allowed himself to drift back, enjoying his weightlessness in the waters for a moment before opening himself to the *Essence*. Again, he felt the slightest twinge of something *wrong* with this world. James allowed his mind to drift beyond the world's sickness and further from his body. In his mind's eye, he caught the tiniest hint of an island, and only a few miles away. James reopened his eyes and began to swim.

An hour later, James was exhausted. Yet he did not grasp for the *Essence* to rejuvenate him. There was going to be enough of that in a moment. And there it was, a small island—correction—it was a flyspeck, a fifteen-foot by fifteen-foot patch of land with a single tree growing from it. James would have sworn it was an enormous North Carolinian live oak, just the kind that would bring a tear to the eye of a mint-julep sipping southern gentleman. The branches extended wide and low along the water; the leaves fluttered in the wind.

James swam up to the island only to find that this wasn't an island at all, but rather a wide mess of roots that was keeping the oak tree afloat as a single buoyant fortress. He climbed atop the roots and found them remarkably stable, and pleasantly tranquil.

But James knew that he wasn't here to relax. He was here to learn to walk through walls. Or at the very least, a tree.

"All right, here we go," James muttered. He swung his arms back and forth to stretch them out a little. "And, now!" He launched himself at the trunk of the tree, a vision in his mind of passing cleanly through to the other side, only to rebound backward. He fell painfully on the raft of roots.

James rubbed the base of his skull. Then he bounded to his feet. "I see how it's gonna be. And… now!" Again, he launched himself at the tree, and again the force of the blow ricocheted him onto the ground, this time spinning him so that he received a hefty scrape across each knee. He leaped up and threw himself again at the tree, then again, then again, all with the same result.

"Remember, it's not about trying, it's about knowing." James looked up at the massive oak. He decided that maybe he should try to 'know' something a little smaller first. He first performed his orange hands trick, this time with ease. Next, he picked up a dead branch that had fallen from the oak onto the rooty base. He held the branch upright with one hand and then stared at the orange palm of his other hand.

"Here we go." With the same certainty James assumed when knowing his hands would be orange, or that Grand Central would resemble a basketball court, James closed his eyes tight and swung his right hand from left to right. Without surprise, only the smug satisfaction of realizing a certainty, his hand met with no resistance. James opened his eyes and stared at the branch, repeating the action with the same image locked in his mind. This time, he watched his arm pass through the branch. "Alright. Now let's try two branches."

* * *

By the time James was ready to tackle the oak again, the pale blue sun had shifted six times through the spectrum of color, risen four times, though (inexplicably) set only twice. James poised himself in front of the oak, the remnants of the branches he'd been passing arms, legs, hands, and head through strewn around him. He did not close his eyes, he stared straight ahead. He did not look at the tree, but beyond it. Capturing the image of himself as nothingness, the mere whim of the world's imagination, James leaped at the oak. He felt a wisp of chill as the oak passed through his inconsequential body. With a soft thud, he landed on the other side.

He allowed himself one last breath of the warm salt air, and one last feel of the saltwater splashing around his toes. He looked up to the sky, opened his mind to the *Essence* of the world, and then—

James fell.

33. Warnings

James entered the Cosmos and allowed himself to drift, not race, to the light containing the Frozen World. As he floated, he allowed his mind to brush against the other stars. He could feel a variety of senses flood back. Not all of the stars were sick, some were quite healthy, and in being so, did not feel *accessible*. The door to entry was inexplicably closed. Other worlds seemed like they should be open, but the hue of light left a foreign taste in James's mouth. It was as though the worlds were either too simple or too frighteningly complicated for him to understand. What he found himself left with was not the billions upon billions of worlds that he saw, but a dusty collection of realities both accessible due to some unnamed sickness, and like the Baby Bear's porridge, just right in fit.

His bodiless awareness flitted across the Cosmos for a moment more, before James set his eyes on the distant light of the Frozen World. With the smallest hint of will, he felt himself flung. Light rushed at him until filling his field of vision until—

* * *

"Jay! But… when did you get in here? You startled me."

James lurched with uncertainty to find Ling looking at him with no small degree of surprise. Not surprise exactly, more like puzzlement. He doubted the demure girl could show surprise.

Ling's cell was similar to his own, smooth clay floor with rounded stone walls. The cell was like James's in all ways except that it *wasn't* his cell. In his time away from the Frozen World, his puppet-self must have walked through the wall without his help. But now James was just stuck in a new location, and in a position where he needed to do some explaining.

"Are you ok? How did you get in here? I would have sworn you weren't there a moment ago, and…"

"Shhh." James put a finger to his lips. "We've got to get out of here."

"No, we don't," Ling retorted.

"What?"

"They put us here for our disobedience. We shall stay here until released. It was foolish for us to overstep our bounds, and unlucky we were caught. We deserve this, Jay. *I* deserve this. You forget that they *own* me. I shall not displease them again."

He shook his head in disbelief. "How can you say that? We need to get back. We have to warn Sylph and the others."

"And what shall you tell them? That the rune we saw is of great power? They knew such already."

James shook his head. "We have to warn them that if the Kai'ja queen isn't stopped, she'll destroy the world! It's the rune in that chest, it's her, it's… well *you*. You're a part of this too, Ling. You're a VIP. We have to stop it."

Ling raised a curious eyebrow. "Now you are being foolish. Bella was right, you *are* troubled in the head. But perhaps, you will listen to reason. If they find that you've escaped, and then catch you again, you won't just be thrown back into jail. They'll do something much worse. I will not be party to such."

James gritted his teeth. Ling's passivity was infuriating. "Fine, I'll take care of it myself." He rose from the cool clay ground and stepped to the cell door. He pressed his face against the bars, relieved to see that no one was watching. Then James grasped the *Essence* of the world, making himself first unnoticeable, and then insubstantial. Like a ghost, he stepped through the cell door.

Once through, James wanted to hold on to his intangibility, to race through the halls, unseen and untouched like a specter. But the concentration and effort were too much. Unlike in the Ocean World, things here seemed far more reluctant to allow him to play his tricks. He felt his head begin to pound; he was barely able to release the

Essence before he passed out. James sank to his knees, his temples throbbing, cold sweat running across his brow. He'd escaped. But he didn't know how long until he was rested enough to try something like that again.

The thud of footsteps snapped James to attention. He scuttled toward a patch of shadow and tried to make himself unnoticeable, only to find that he was too mentally exhausted from walking through the door. From the sound of the steps, there were at least two people, perhaps more. James hunkered low. He pulled his shirt above his head and turned toward the wall, in hopes that even if someone looked his way, he might be mistaken for an errant stone.

The approaching group got closer, and to James's dismay, paused in front of the cells. He heard the tinkering of the door latch and a cell door—*his* cell door—swing open.

"Criminy, wrong cell. He's not here. Bleedin' Kai'ja must have told us the wrong one." The voice was laced with Teak's characteristic disdain. At the sound, James peeked from his hiding place to see Sylph and Teak looking into James's empty cell. He leaped to his feet.

"I'm right here."

The two Islanders spun around, both drawing their weapons so that James had one of Sylph's pistols and Teak's sword pointed his way. As recognition set in, Sylph and Teak returned their weapons to their holsters. Sylph was the first to speak.

"Jay? How did you get out of your cell, lad?"

"That's not important. We've got a problem. A big problem. But let's get Ling out of here first."

Teak shook his head. "I'm not likely to take orders from you, boy. The Blank stays. The deal we made was just for you."

"No," James spoke nervously. "You don't understand. I know what's happening now. I know what the problem is. We don't have a lot of time."

Sylph lowered a stern look at James. "The problem, lad, is that you took our cargo and broke into an off-limits area during negotiations. If they'd asked for your head, I'd have given it to 'em. But I guess that's *not* what they wanted. Leastways not at the moment. And now you've put me in a right tricky situation."

"What situation?"

Teak snorted. "Tell him, Captain."

Sylph replied, "We didn't come to rescue you, lad." She looked at the vacant cell and James standing on the other side of the door. "Not that we needed to. We came because the Kai'ja ordered it from us. Unless we do exactly what they say, they'll tell the Scrim that we tried to steal that Blank lass. And for the Scrim, that's as good as breaking our deal."

"And then what?"

Teak spat on the dusty floor. "And then, we ain't got ourselves no payday, no way out, and you can kiss the Killdevil goodbye while yer at it. We're a long way from the ocean, Jay. And unless everything here goes according to plan, we're in a bit of a sticky widget."

"So, what do they want?"

Sylph tilted her head. "Not here, lad. We're already late. Follow me and I'll explain."

Teak jerked James by the shoulder, and he hopped to keep pace with them. The three walked down the torch-lit hallway, the doors of the prison cells becoming more and more sporadic until they dropped away entirely. James could feel the palpable chill emanating from both Teak and Sylph. And while Sylph kept her eyes forward, Teak kept glancing back at James, as though trying to puzzle something out about him. The glances made James more and more uncomfortable. After an unbearable minute, he broke the silence.

"So, what's this…?"

Sylph interrupted, "The Kai'ja found out you're a Reader, Jay. Which is funny, 'cause you never mentioned such to us."

"What's a Reader?" James asked, inspiring a smack in the back of the head from Teak.

"A Reader is someone who can tell what a person's runes can do."

"But the Kai'ja are all runics. Can't they read the runes themselves?"

Sylph shook her head. "The written part of a rune is only half the rune. Or so I'm told. The other half is supplied by the person it's inscribed on. So even if you see part of a rune, you don't know the limits. A Reader, on the other hand, can tell what a rune means not just by reading the character, but by seeing it on the person. Such abilities are rare." Sylph quit walking and turned to look at James. "But I'll bet you'll say you didn't know that."

James squeaked in protest. "I didn't even know what a rune was until I met you guys."

Teak snorted. His voice was heavy with sarcasm. "Right, right. I forgot all about *that* little piece of nonsense."

"I'm serious. I didn't know."

"Enough." Sylph stamped her foot. "Do the Scrim know you're a Reader, or not?"

"I didn't even…"

"Let me try this again. Do the Scrim know that you can read their runes?"

"No," James mumbled.

"Alright, then we still have ourselves a go at this." Sylph resumed her pace down the hallway. James hopped to catch up. "The Kai'ja have thrown a feast to celebrate the negotiations' end. What they want us to do, and what you *will* do, is to study the Scrim and then tell the Kai'ja their runes do."

"And then?"

"And then nothing. We wait and see if that's enough," Sylph replied.

James bit his lip. "But why do they even care?"

"If the Kai'ja know what the Scrim can do, it gives them an advantage. In negotiations, in arguments, and if it comes right down to it, a fight." Sylph gave James another long look. "Do you think you can handle that wee task?"

"Yes… I mean. Wait! None of that's important. We've got bigger problems."

Teak scoffed, "Being able to get home isn't important, eh? Maybe not to you, boy. But I've a mind to not stay here forever."

"No, that's not what I mean. It's the Kai'ja queen. If she's not stopped, she's going to destroy the world. The whole *world*, I'm telling you."

Sylph said, "Jay, you're being ridiculous. But she can certainly destroy us. And in my mind, that's the same thing. But the whole *world*, James. I don't even know what that means."

"But…"

"Hold on a second, Captain. I think this may be important." Teak paused. "Jay, what makes you so sure about all this?"

James hesitated for only a moment. If he was going to stop this catastrophe, he needed allies. And Sylph's crew were the only ones he trusted. But something itched at the back of James's mind, telling him he was giving away too much. So, James decided to tell the truth, just not the *entire* truth.

"It's like the runes. I can look at a rune and I know what it means. No one taught me, but I just know. And you know how I can speak your language and Scrim and Kai'ja…"

"You can speak Kai'ja?" Teak asked. "Do you speak every language?"

"I-I think so. But that's not important. What I'm saying is that I don't know how I can do that either. I just know. And when I saw the rune, and then when I saw the Kai'ja queen, I knew—I *knew*—that we have to stop her. You've got to believe me."

For a moment, neither Sylph nor Teak replied. After a few seconds, Teak spoke, his voice low and uncertain. "What did that rune say, Jay? What does it mean that makes it so bleedin' dangerous?"

James sighed. "It means 'Gateway to', but that's all I know. I don't know *where* the gateway would go, or even what kind of gateway."

Teak said, "I thought you could read any rune? That you knew exactly what they meant."

"Only once they're on people. Until then it's just a feeling."

"Bloody winds and bloody tides." Sylph grimaced. "I get it now."

"Get what?" Teak and James said together.

"We're not the Scrim's way home. We're just their backup plan."

Teak said, "I don't follow you."

"I've heard about gateway runes before. The Scrim were talking about them on the Killdevil, but that wasn't the first time. A gateway rune opens a portal that allows a small group of people to instantly cover vast distances. For a fighter, it's nothing short of brilliant. But the technique… it's too advanced a rune for a Scrim to draw. Too dangerous to risk. So, they had to come here, to Kai'nau. That's what this's all been about."

Teak scowled. "And if it works, they just hang us out to dry? Doesn't make sense. We've still got a good ship and a crew for her."

"But they won't need a ship anymore." Sylph shook her head. "And we'd be a liability anyhow. Such a rune is better kept secret."

James wrinkled his brow in frustration. Comprehension trickled through his mind. "Captain, you said something I didn't quite get. You said that the Scrim weren't skilled enough to make the rune themselves. What would happen if they tried?"

Sylph replied, "There's a chance they could get it right. More likely the rune would be useless, and either ruin the Blank or kill him altogether. There's a chance, of course, of something failing in a big way. And the bigger the rune, the worse it could go."

"What about a world? Could a mis-drawn rune destroy everything?" James asked, panic in his voice.

"That seems extreme. I would think that a bad gateway rune would just open a portal to the wrong place. Though that could be dangerous too."

Teak broke in. "Yeah, like let's say they opened a gateway to the western isles—but was fifty feet too far down and opened into the ocean. Then we'd all be a couple of done drowned rats. Or let's not forget this here's a volcano. Be a little off target and we'd be dropped in a lake of fire. There a million ways in a million days for a rune like that to go bad. I wouldn't say world-killers, Jay, but it could sure snuff our candles."

James gritted his teeth. "Ok, well we'd still be dead. Is that enough reason to help me stop it?"

Teak swore under his breath. "No. But I still think you're a bit mad. And if we don't cooperate, we're either stuck here or dead. We've come this far. We're committed. What's your take, Captain?"

Sylph pursed her lips, she eyed James warily. "For now, we play the Kai'ja's game. But we watch both them and the Scrim. I'm not getting stranded, but I'm not going to risk our lives over a job, either. Look, I'm going to go get Brine. Meet me back here in fifteen minutes. We'll go to the Kai'ja's banquet, and we'll keep our eyes open. For now, that's all we can do." Sylph stormed off, ducking down a passageway to the right. Teak simply waited and watched James with a wary eye.

"You better hope you're a prophet, Jay. Cause I've got my doubts."

James gritted his teeth. "You need to trust me on this, Teak. Just trust me."

For an uncomfortably long moment, Teak studied James up and down. The man seemed to be ticking off certain points of information on his fingers, his mouth moving noiselessly. Finally, he looked up at James, an odd glint in his eyes.

"Maybe I will, Jay. Just one question."

"What's that?"

"Did you think we wouldn't find you out?"

"Huh?"

"Come on, Jay, the Styx see everything. And this world is ours. Mine."

And then, seized with panic—

James fell.

And Teak followed.

34. Fleeing

James hurled himself through the Cosmos. Though the number of worlds was countless, and the space was as infinite as it was incomprehensible, James could feel Teak's presence bearing down on him like a dream of being chased where you have no time to turn around. Desperate to escape, to somehow hide, James flung himself at the closest accessible world. The aura of the world, just like all the others he'd visited, was just a little weak, slightly ailing. And yet the world did not seem too complex—or too simple—for him. The yellow-hot world consumed his vision, and its reality snapped around him.

This time, James braced himself for the fall, hoping that he wouldn't be dropped from as high as when he'd landed in the ocean, or as unpredictably when he dropped onto the mountainside of the Frozen World. James was both relieved, surprised, and oddly accepting to find himself a mere six feet off the ground and upside down. And as soon as James winked into existence, gravity took hold. He fell, landing and skidding down the face of a sand dune.

James let out a momentary yelp before skidding to a stop. He spat the sand out of his mouth and, even before he had absorbed his surroundings, started to run. He took off as fast as his legs could move.

But he did not try and grab the world's *Essence* out of fear that whenever Teak arrived—assuming Teak had followed him—that to do so would make him a target. So, he ran on, his lungs quickly burning from the effort.

From the top of the dune, a sound like a hollow gunshot issued. James snapped his head around to look, only to see Teak wink into existence in the same location where James had fallen. Teak twisted his body, rotating deftly to land neatly on his feet. The Islander whipped his sword from its scabbard and leaped into the air, an impossibly high vault that covered half the distance between the two of them. Teak released a roar of triumph and leaped again.

At the height of Teak's arc, James opened himself to the *Essence* of the world and simultaneously tried to slow the passage of time. When he did so, two things happened James had not anticipated. The first was that the body of Teak seemed to radiate a malevolent greenish glow, as though tendrils of energy were both carrying him and feeding through him. James knew that this energy was not part of this new world, but rather something Teak had carried inside him.

The second thing that James hadn't expected, and was now facing with horror, was that his attempt to slow the passage of time was only of varying success. James could see a whirling dervish from the corner of his eye that rotated like a lazy top; he could see strange gargantuan birds moving with deliberate flaps. But one thing that didn't slow down, was Teak. The Islander—correction, the agent of the Styx— moved as though James had done nothing at all. With a surge of alarm, James dove to the right. He narrowly avoided Teak's blade as it plunged into the sand where James had rested moments before.

"Teak! What are you doing? Let's talk about this!" James scrambled to his feet and looked at his attacker, now coiling for another assault.

"Ain't a thing to discuss, Jay. No more dabbling for you. The Runic's World—it's mine. Ain't no one else goin' to touch it. I'll see to that." Teak lunged forward again, and this time James dodged to the side, at the same time forcing his body into intangibility. But though James was certain he'd acted exactly as he had practiced with the floating oak, Teak's sword sliced into James's shoulder. Pain flooded his body; his skin flared with white-hot anguish.

"It's yours, take it!" James yelped, his hand darting to hold his wound.

Teak laughed. Though he still crouched in readiness, he did not advance. "Grovel all you want, precious. We both know that's impossible. I won't let you go, and you wouldn't let *it* go. I know how your friends operate. Dr. Huckabee wouldn't have left it be, and neither would you."

James's eyes went wide. "You knew the doctor?"

"I helped bring him in. Ah, he was a worthy adversary. A million worlds must have been turned on his watch. A true master of his craft. I'll give him that, however despicable he was. And to think he sent a nobody to the Runic's World. Ain't an easy one to save, is it, love? But I think that was just a mistake. I'll bet that world was your first."

James eyed Teak. The Styx agent was no longer moving in for the kill. Instead, he paused, enthralled by cornered prey. And James realized something else, his own strength was regaining. Soon he would have the energy to Travel again. He just needed to keep Teak talking.

"My second, actually. I'm still learning."

"Of course, you are, munchkin. And that probably saved your skin. If you weren't so… so *ignorant*, I'd have caught you sooner. You made it quite some way. If it's any consolation, you were right about the rune. It is the key, but I have to thank you for telling me what it does."

"You couldn't read it?"

"We all have different talents, Jay. Allow me to show you one of mine." Teak lunged forward again, the blade tracking towards James's heart with deathly precision—

And James fell.

* * *

James returned to the Cosmos. He desperately sought another world, one where maybe he'd have some chance to escape. In hopes that maybe by jumping quickly he could lose Teak, he raced at the first star he saw. This world shone so palely that James could hardly believe that it existed at all. The world wasn't in danger of dying; rather, it was in its last throes. He flung himself at the world, sensing that Teak was close behind.

* * *

James gained awareness in pitch blackness, surrounded by a stench pressing in from all sides. Lashing out with both arms and legs, he inadvertently kicked open the top of the container. He pushed upward and the top came cleanly off.

He was in a city consumed by thick fog which roiled between colossal buildings which towered overhead, the tops lost in the city's industrial miasma. Looking down, James realized that his pungent prison was nothing more than a city dumpster, and one filled with all manners of rotting organic matter. For a moment James's disgust overrode his fear, and he scrambled to escape the container.

A crack of thunder sounded, and James at first thought that Teak had followed him once again. Instead, lightning snaked through the canopy of buildings, to crash against one of the walls. The building erupted in flame; debris cascaded from the side, showering James in a rain of sediment. *Good Lord,* James thought. *This place is crumbling.*

The terror of the dying world was replaced by static in the air. This was the sound of another Traveler entering the world. James knew he had precious moments before Teak arrived. He dashed down the nearest alleyway, hoping to lose Teak in the snaking fog and chaos of the dying world.

"Crack!" The muffled gunshot of Teak entering the dying world sounded. James knew that Teak had arrived in the same dumpster he had. James knew that the fog wouldn't hide him. If Teak opened his eyes to the *Essence*, the fog would be laid bare. But perhaps the rubble surrounding the streets would provide some camouflage. He darted toward a collapsed building and wriggled beneath the wreckage.

The sound of the dumpster opening, and then the double pad of booted feet on pavement sounded eerily distant from James's hiding spot. Another crack of lightning and another cascade of rubble echoed through the buildings. James listened for the screams of the inhabitants, but the streets remained silent.

"You cheeky monkey… where are you? Can't hide forever," Teak screamed, his voice vibrating with rage. "An' you can't run forever. You must be getting a little *tired*." With the last word, James heard the distinct sound of a sword being plunged through metal. Teak was lashing out, and yet James remained hidden.

"Jay, look around you. This is a dying world, one at its end. Do you think you can stop this? An end to all things in their own time."

James remained silent.

"Such dyin' is just natural. We'll die one day too… in time. What the *Styx* do, it's not for spite. We serve a higher purpose. And that is something you will never understand."

James fought to keep his breaths even. With every word, Teak was ambling closer, as though he smelled James's presence on the wind. Another flash of lightning ensued, chained by seven more, as each bolt sparked another, and yet another. A red glow flooded the sky, and he felt heat roll over him. The flash was followed by a sharp drop in temperature, and within moments, James could see his breath puffing from his nostrils.

"Listen, boy. If you won't respond to reason, maybe I'll take a different kind a go. Take the stick, not the carrot, eh? So let me say this." Teak paused for a long moment before continuing. "We know where Dr. Huckabee traveled. I assume one of those worlds was yours."

James remained silent.

Teak continued, "We can make sure those worlds are dying worlds, even if not quite their time. Even yours. It takes more work of course. But worth it, I think. As an example, like."

James felt a rush to his head. His family, his friends, his schoolmates, everyone he'd ever known could be in jeopardy—assuming Teak was telling the truth. And then he thought of something else. Even if Teak didn't know which world was James's, it wouldn't stop him from trying to destroy other worlds, each filled with people whose lives were just as real as his own. No, he couldn't let this go further. James wriggled from his hiding place and stood tall in the street. A chain of lightning curled overhead.

"Leave my friends out of this, Teak. They're not the ones you want." James tried to sound defiant, but his words felt hollow. He had no defenses left.

Teak laughed, "Shoulda figured that would get you talkin'. Then again, that's how we caught Huckabee. You're all so righteous. But guess what? Once you're gone, I'm going after your home, anyway. I promise you that."

James steeled his voice. "No, Teak. I won't let you." James reached for the *Essence*; he could feel the tearing fabric of reality all around him. And though he knew it would take the last shred of his strength, James prepared for one last leap into the Cosmos, this time going to the most familiar place of all. He readied himself for the trip home. And then—

James fell.

35. Teak

When James entered the Cosmos, he no longer needed to search for a world to land in, he knew exactly where he was going, and he hoped that his gamble was correct. If not, he would be bringing destruction to the place he wanted it least of all. The flood of worlds streaked past James as he angled toward the familiar world, shining with a clear blue light. His vision was filled and then—

* * *

The striped cat was still frozen mid-twist in the air when James arrived back in his body. The feline's claws flexed imperceptibly, and from his mouth, a slow meow crept forth. James, knowing that no trick of time could save him from Teak, snapped his awareness back to normal. The cat, too, snapped into full motion, his body completing the half twist to land neatly on his feet. The tabby darted away, disappearing in the bushes.

Thanks for the idea.

James darted forward, diving headfirst underneath an overhanging holly bush. The gap between the foliage and the ground provided just enough room for him to hide—barely. Teak would notice him within moments, but James hoped that would be enough time.

Despite the fear coursing through his veins, he still hesitated. Then, with fear overcoming a fading morality, he ripped open his backpack to grab the heavy object wrapped in the vagrant's shirt. James removed the pistol, checked the safety, and then pointed it, gripping with both hands, in the location where he had appeared only moments ago. He held his breath, praying luck would finally favor him.

James felt the wave of energy before he even saw it, as though the air became pregnant with unearthly potential, one bursting to be realized. Teak winked into existence with a muffled crack like thunder. The agent of the Styx had his sword drawn, and a grim expression set upon his face. But before Teak's feet had even hit the ground, James jerked his finger against the trigger, and a belch of flame spurted from the end. The bullet caught Teak in his side, spinning him as he fell. He uttered a half scream of otherworldly rage, and then *folded*. Teak's body twisted much like the vagrant's had into a skewing of shred and flesh, like a popping balloon.

And then there was nothing.

For a moment, James didn't move. His hands gripped the pistol so tightly that his knuckles were turning white. The thunder of the gunshot had left a high-pitch ringing in James's ears, which faded so slowly that he couldn't tell when the sound had actually stopped. James remained frozen as a drop of sweat trickled down his brow to slide across his nose and drop from the tip.

James released his breath. He took a moment to flip the gun's safety and then wriggled from beneath the bush, the sharp tips of the holly scraping against his skin. He rose to his feet, one hand still gripped on the gun's handle. He stepped forward to examine where the Styx agent had landed, but of Teak, there was nothing. The only trace remaining were a few errant drops of blood that had splattered from the bullet's impact. James leaned down to examine the drop, only to cover it up with a thin layer of silt.

"He's gone," James whispered, the words barely forming against his breath. "I killed him."

A wave of nausea hit James, pulsing over his body in waves. He dropped to his knees and emptied his stomach onto the mossy North Carolina ground. Moments later, James was assaulted by an emotional wave, this one not of remorse but of the full realization of just how close he had come to death. Teak had intended to kill him. And not only him, but his very world. James knew he had made the only possible choice, and yet it didn't pain him less.

Worlds were at stake. James knew that now. And if the Styx succeeded and the Frozen World fell, would his be next on the list?

"I've got to get back," James muttered. "They have to be stopped." And then—

James fell.

36. Banquet

When James regained his awareness, he was sitting at a banquet table. An array of meats, fruit, bread, and pies were spread out in front of him. Goblets of wine and ceramic mugs frothing with dark liquid flanked the platters. The table was low to the ground, raised just enough so that the diners could kneel or sit cross-legged on the cushions lining the floor. James glanced down the table's length to see that it spread sixty feet in both directions. The Scrim sat at the end to his left, and the Kai'ja spread down the table to his right, with the queen at the head. Directly across from James knelt Captain Sylph and Brine, and to his right, an empty cushion.

James looked warily across the low table, the words of the vagrant echoing in his ears. When the Styx came to a world, they moved in groups of three. Were Sylph and Brine also members of the Styx? Was it Ling? Was it Slagish? The queen? One of the Blanks? James knew that he probably wouldn't wind up on top if he had another confrontation like the one with Teak. Although, James mused, maybe it would be useful to have a trap or two set in one of those other worlds. He shook his head. There was no time for that now.

"What's eating you?" Brine boomed, not pausing to swallow the bite he'd ripped from his drumstick.

"Oh, just, uh, you know." James tilted his head at the empty cushion.

"Don't worry about it, lad," Sylph replied. "You don't know Teak like we do. He disappears sometimes. And sometimes for quite a long while. Doesn't matter where we are or what we're doing. When Teak goes, it's not worth trying to find him."

Brine snickered. "I still think he's a lycan."

"A what?" James asked.

"A lycan—lycanthrope. Like a werewolf or somethin'. Maybe he turns into an albatross when we're not looking. There are all kinds of interesting curses out there. I wouldn't put it past Teak to have picked up one or two."

James nodded. He didn't want to raise suspicion on himself by asking too many questions. But if Sylph and Brine were part of the Styx, James had no way to tell. So much for allies.

A gong sounded, the metallic reverberation tapering all conversations to silence. James looked past the far end of the table where a procession of Kai'ja was filing onto a large stage. At the head of the procession were two scarred men covered in runes. They flanked to either side of the stage, drawing oversized swords which they held at attention. Following the guards, four Kai'ja carried in an ivory altar. The sides were carved and inlaid with silver, while the top was smooth and unblemished. The bearers set down the altar, proceeded to the rear of the stage, and then knelt.

The gong sounded again, and this time three Scrim entered. Each held a chain looping around the necks of the three Blanks: Ling, Charles, and Bellacroix. James gasped in the realization of what was about to occur, only to receive a sharp kick beneath the table from Sylph. "Time for your part of the deal, lad. Start with those three and work down."

James winced. He'd completely forgotten after the run-in with Teak that he was supposed to be interpreting the Scrim's runes. James gritted his teeth. He may not have any intention of letting the Kai'ja etch the rune on one of those Blanks, but he knew better than to anger the queen again. He opened his mind to the *Essence* and studied the runes on the Scrim. James had seen most of the runes before, but never tried to fully interpret them. Unlike the Kai'ja, these seemed less complex but more powerful. It was as though the Scrim had strength where the Kai'ja had art. James made a mental note of each runic's abilities. He then drifted his gaze down the table, beginning with the Scrim leader, and his "Nothingness" ability, and ending with some kind of a healer.

Another gong, this time from the other side of the table. All heads turned to look at the Kai'ja queen. With a thin smile across her lips, she pushed back her cushion and rose to her feet. To James's surprise, no one at the table rose to greet her. The Kai'ja queen spread her arms and the black robes swathing her body fell to the floor, leaving the queen dressed only in the entwining chain she had worn when they had first arrived at Kai'nau. She stepped easily on top of the low banquet table and began to slink down the length. Her feet deftly wove around the trays of food and goblets of wine. She passed directly in front of James but did not glance in his direction. The queen's eyes remained locked with Lord Slagish on the far side of the table.

When the queen reached the end, she stepped from the table up to the stage using the Scrim leader's shoulder as a step, eliciting a small grunt from the mustached man. The queen walked to the altar, her back to the banquet table, and extended a single finger to point in the direction of the Blanks. James winced in surprise that she pointed not to Ling, but to Charles.

Charles's eyes were wide, but he gave no hint of resistance as the Scrim holding his chain walked him to the ivory altar and laid him down on the alabaster surface. The gong sounded again, and another pair of Kai'ja entered, these carrying the ebony chest containing the rune. Sylph rose from her seat, but before she had taken a step, the bearers had popped open the chest and handed the parchment containing the rune to the Kai'ja queen.

Sylph emitted a squeak of surprise that the chest had been opened without her and then returned to her seat, red-faced and furious. However, she did not make any further sound or disturbance. James's mouth parted in disbelief. Sylph hadn't expected this, but she probably wasn't alone. But knowing that he wasn't the only one surprised did not make him less nervous. And yet, he could think of no way to stop the ceremony without being struck down by the Kai'ja guards. Even if he tried to stop time, he would only be drawing the attention of the other two Styx still hiding somewhere in the ranks.

The Kai'ja queen held her arms above her head. The horrid memory of the last etching flashed in James's memory. The queen spread her fingers wide. In a sharp convulsion, the chain wrapping the queen's body exploded in white light, the glow so intense that James had to shield his eyes. The light pulsed through the chain, and then surged again as the queen's hands flared in response. The light spread from her hands across her entire body until she appeared to be a being of light itself.

And then she struck.

The Kai'ja queen swiped at Charles. The Blank winced with every strike. His face was wrenched in pain. The blows became faster, frantic, and more furious until it seemed that there was no body of the Kai'ja queen at all. Charles radiated intense white light. The glow became brighter, and still brighter still, until James could no longer look, even through the filter of his hands. And then, with a sharp pop, the light was gone.

James raised his eyes to the stage, the afterimage burned into his vision. The Kai'ja queen no longer glowed, though her body glistened with sweat. Her once-immaculate hair was now frayed and unkempt. Her exhausted heaves and the satisfaction shining from her eyes made her appear like a savage after a kill. The queen looked down at her work and then lifted Charles effortlessly from the altar. She turned to face the banquet table and presented him as though he was a sacrifice.

Charles lay limp in the queen's arms. An intricate and elaborate rune crawled across his skin from top of his head to the soles of his feet. The design was so dark and so complicated that the boy appeared to be dripping with ink.

The banquet table, so long wreathed in silence, murmured with awe. With the spell broken, Brine leaned forward to look at James.

"Alright, Jay," he whispered, "how about that one? What does that one say?"

James allowed his mind to brush the *Essence*. He shuddered and released it immediately. "It says 'Gateway,'" he murmured. "It says 'Gateway to the Living Worlds.'"

"Ok, got it. But what's it mean?"

Fear surged in James's belly. "It means nothing's safe anymore. Living or dying, no world will be safe from them." James shuddered, knowing now exactly why the Frozen World was so important. The rune on Charles gave the boy the same power James had, the power to cross worlds. But the rune could do more than that. There were no limits to the portals Charles could create. Unlike James, who could only journey to a world calling for help, the portals that Charles could make could open to *any* world, sick or healthy. And so if the Styx controlled that rune, they too would be unbound. They probably meant to use the rune to destroy this world, and then move on to the next. And to the next.

James felt a hand on his and jumped involuntarily, only to see Sylph looking at him with concern in her eyes. She switched to the language of the Islanders. "Jay, this is important. Where will that gateway lead?"

"Anywhere." James's eyes begin to water. "Anywhere at all, and if the Styx get it, nothing is safe."

"If the *who* get it…? Safe from *what*?"

James parted his lips to respond, but the simultaneous ringing of both gongs aborted his reply. The table's nervous conversations quieted once again. One of the Kai'ja, who had been seated directly to the right of the queen stood and addressed the table.

"The etching has been completed. But the sun will rise ere the rune takes root. At sunrise on the morrow, on temple's top, our handiwork must be tested. So too, will your welcome in Kai'nau end. If you have business of other sort, you must conclude before dawn." The gong sounded again, and the people of the banquet hall rose from their seats. James remained seated and looked nervously at Sylph.

"So, I have until morning?" he asked.

Sylph replied, "We've all got until morning. And you've got a lot of explaining to do before then."

37. Packing

James followed Sylph and Brine back to their quarters, holding his tongue until they were behind safe walls. Or at least what he hoped were safe walls. He'd done a lot of thinking about whether Sylph and Brine could be trusted, and he'd landed on a very important point. James had witnessed both of them take the life of another. And while he knew that not every Traveler paid attention to the rules that Dr. Huckabee had taught him, he was fairly certain that the Styx weren't immune to Rule Three. For a Traveler, taking a life would risk being stuck in a world forever. James had seen Sylph shoot a bandit. He had seen Brine run someone through on the Killdevil III. And if they weren't Travelers, then they couldn't be part of the Styx. And (hopefully) they weren't trying to get him.

Brine swung open the door to their chambers. At the far corner of the room was a person wrapped in a dark-black cloak. Brine called out in his ordinary jovial voice, "Well, Teak, you missed all the fun, and a heck of a dinner to boot. And…"

The cloaked figure turned, and to James's great relief, it was not Teak who looked back at them. Instead, James found himself staring into the eyes of the Kai'ja queen. She flipped the hood from her head and locked eyes with James.

"Tell me, boy, of my enemies the Scrim."

James launched into his report without hesitation. He told of the Scrim leader and his ability to conjure nothingness, the combat medics and their ability to heal, the fire-hurlers, those with strength, and those who could see in the dimmest of lights. When he had come to the end of his litany, he asked the question that had been building inside.

"If… if the Scrim are your enemies, why did you draw their runes?"

The queen chuckled. "I still serve my interests. Slagish and I have a bargain beyond simple treasure. And when the time comes, I intend to know far more about them than they do of me. Their rune worries me not. It can do no harm."

"Yes, it can," James burst. "It'll hurt us all, it…" He clapped his hands over his mouth. He'd seen when looking at the *Essence* of the world that the queen would be the world's destruction. He shouldn't tell her a thing.

The Kai'ja queen regarded him with a sidelong glance. "The rune opens a gateway, as I'm sure a Reader would know. I too have use for such and have bargained my needs. But still…"

Sylph broke in. "You think they'll invade. That they'll open a gateway to ambush you. And if not tomorrow, then someday. That's why you need to know their abilities. You need to prepare for a battle. And right you should. But Jay is right, why risk it? Why etch the rune at all?"

The queen laughed again. "Two readers, are you. A reader of runes, and a reader of minds. I want those skills on my side. And yes, I must be prepared for battle. But I do not fear the Scrim." She lowered her voice. "And I have my strengths as well. If the Scrim betray our trust, then I will retake the rune so freely given."

Brine shifted uneasily. "Captain, I know it's not my place, but…"

Sylph silenced Brine with a gesture. "If you are looking to make a deal with us, you best speak with reasons. We're pledged to the Scrim, not to mention they have our ship."

"No, Captain, I have your ship. I bargained to hold until the rune was tested. So, if Lord Slagish breaks his deal, with whom will you stand? Will you do what is needed to earn *my* favor?"

"And what's that?" Sylph asked.

"If Lord Slagish turns traitor, end his life." The Kai'ja queen let her words hang in the air before continuing. "You will be near enough, and armed. I've heard of your skill and you can do what I cannot. Your *weapons…*"—the Kai'ja queen looked with disdain at the guns on Sylph's belt—"have their advantages. They are quick. And they cannot be blocked by a runic's skill."

"Oh? And what about *your* other strengths?"

The Kai'ja queen pulled the dark hood back over her head. "The time will come for my strength as well." She walked to the door, running her finger along Brine's cheek as she passed. "But I ask not for charity. If the time comes, and you choose to aid me, I will grant not just your ship, but any rune you desire." The queen passed into the hallway, her black robe quickly fading into torch-lit shadows.

Brine raised his hand to touch where the queen had brushed his cheek. He shook his head and then turned his eyes to Sylph. "Cap'n? Your call here. Are we on point for this or not?"

"Not yet. I do think Slagish merits a visit, but I'm no mutineer. If that gateway opens, and a fight does start. I say we cross through and leave them both on the far side. That could be our only way home."

"And what of the 'Devil? Or Teak?" Brine asked.

"If Teak doesn't show by tomorrow, he's on his own. I've warned him before. As for the Killdevil III, well I'd rather get to work on the Killdevil IV than lose my life."

"No!" James jumped between the two. "If the gateway opens, it won't matter what side you're on. It'll be over."

Sylph narrowed her eyes. "Alright, lad. You're so convinced that it'll kill us all. You say you have some kind of divine intuition of sort. Well, if you're so certain, then why don't you do something about it?"

James blinked. "What do you mean?"

Sylph nodded to her right. "Brine?"

Brine, his face grim, reached into his coat and removed a short dagger. He offered it handle-first to James.

Sylph continued, "I know you say you're some kind of monk. I know you say you'll never touch a weapon. I know you say you made an oath… or some nonsense. But if the gateway will end the world. I'd say your choice is still pretty easy. Well?"

James looked with horror at the knife. He thought of Teak folding to nothingness in front of him. Then he thought of the difference between that and a cold knife, and the blood. Killing Teak had been self-defense, James did not doubt that. But killing Charles—an innocent—would be murder. And even if James succeeded, he would be trapped in the Frozen World forever.

Despite his horror, James reached forward and grabbed the handle. "I might not come back, you know."

Brine frowned deep. "I don't expect you would, laddie. But if that's the side you choose. That's the side on which you need to stand."

James turned to the door. He paused and looked over his shoulder. "You know, Teak wasn't who you thought he was. I just thought you should know."

Brine regarded James with a cold glare. "We knew he wasn't, Jay. But neither are you."

* * *

James wrapped himself in unnoticeability and took off down the corridor. Charles may be the Scrim's property, but James doubted that the Kai'ja would release their creation until the rune was tested. But even if Charles was not with the Scrim, Ling would be. And James had an idea that Ling would know where Charles had been taken, even if no one else did.

In the time James had spent in Kai'nau, he had never been to the Scrim's quarters—at least not that he could remember. He assumed that he had been there at least once before when he had snuck Ling out so they could go look at the rune. But that had been the "puppet" James. The real him didn't know what to expect.

The Scrim had taken residence not far from where Sylph and the Islanders stayed. But while the Islanders were housed in a room much like one found in a temple, the Scrim were placed much further away, three hundred feet of darkened corridor between the entrance to their wing and the rest of Kai'nau. James padded softly down the corridor, noting that in the darkest part of the shadows, Scrim guards stood sentry. A brush with the *Essence* showed James that the guards all had runes allowing them to see in the dark. Yet none of the guards noticed James any more than they noticed the occasional hot wind drifting through the halls of Kai'nau.

James passed between the final set of guards and then brushed open a set of hanging purple curtains, which oddly complemented the volcanic glow of the surrounding rock. He did not draw the slightest nod of attention from the Scrim runics standing guard, or those milling around the anteroom. But as soon as James passed through the doors, he allowed his perception to return to normal. After all, there were still two of the Styx out there somewhere. And James didn't want to draw attention to his abilities. *On the other hand*, James thought, *everyone here has abilities… would the Styx even notice the difference?*

The chamber beyond the doorway was so immense that the ceiling disappeared into the darkness overhead. Much like the cavern that held the Kai'ja's slave quarters, a collection of stalactites melding with stalagmites formed colossal geologic columns. Unlike the slave quarters, the Scrim had transformed the dwelling into their own with a collection of dark-purple tapestries, each covered with a repeated emblem that James assumed must be that of their tribe. The decorations, however, were being busily packed and removed, much like the rest of the Scrim's camp. Everything was being bundled together to prepare for tomorrow's journey. According to Sylph, the group would not return to

Kai'nau after the testing of the rune. One way or another, their time in the volcanic caverns was drawing to a close.

James made his way to where several heavily runed Scrim were rolling their sleeping mats. The men regarded him with the dull acceptance that he attributed to his association with the Islanders. If anyone was neutral in this affair, Sylph and her crew were.

"You looking for Slagish, boy? He's not here," one of the Scrim muttered.

James replied in the man's language, "I'm here to see the Blanks. The ones left, that is."

The guard grunted in reply, hastily pointing at the back end of the cavern. James offered his thanks and then skipped away.

He wove through the Scrim soldiers. The group, though relatively small when compared to the number of Kai'ja, was heavily armed, both with weapons and runic abilities. The sight of the Scrim's runes made James shiver with the thought of the one now wrapping Charles from head to toe, and what would happen if it were unleashed.

At the far wall of the cavern, James saw the familiar faces of Ling and Bellacroix. Their expressions, however, were difficult to read. While Ling wore a mask of disappointment, Bellacroix looked positively bitter. James forced a smile, trying not to consider the peril of the moment. Or the cold dagger concealed in his pocket.

"Hiya Ling. Hey Bella. What's up?"

James received equally pained and scornful looks from the two Blanks, and James thought he knew why. The lightest pattern on Ling's shoulder and Bella's hand betrayed that these two were Blanks no more. Though while James could sense a faint whisper of Ling's abilities, he sensed nothing at all from Bella.

"Did they… did they etch runes on you two?"

Ling's demure nature crumbled in an outbreak of tears filling her serene eyes. "Jay, it was so painful… You cannot imagine the pain we've endured. And for what? For this?" Ling pulled up her sleeve to reveal her shoulder. Three small runes, each no larger than a silver dollar, had been inscribed there. James read each rune, the same idea repeated in three separate ways: Luck, Fortune, and Fate.

Bellacroix interrupted, "We weren't done nothin' to dem. No potential in da either of us. Just a distraction. Now we just be slaves, not even runic slaves at that. A few runes of luck for her, and nothing but a still tattoo for me." Bellacroix bared her teeth. "Dassum long way for nothing."

"Don't say that," James replied. His voice was small. "You don't even know what Charles's rune will do to him. You're the lucky ones."

"Hah," Bellacroix spat on the ground. "Lucky to not done be a god? Ling's de one with all de luck now."

Ling sighed. "Such is not fortune. I didn't have the strength for a real rune. All these do, if they do anything at all, will mayhaps help me find my fate."

James swallowed hard. His fate had found him in a big way. And now these two were no longer part of it. He'd been so convinced that Ling had been the one, too. Then what had he seen in her? She still shone with brilliance. But why? James shook his head unconsciously. "What did they do with Charles anyway? Is he not with you?"

Bellacroix shook her head. "What, and leave him to de mortals? De Kai'ja keep him through de night, to make sure nothing bad done happen. Not all runes are stable."

"But you're here," James replied, forcing naivety into his voice.

"Dey's teeny runes, boy. Teeny runes, teeny risk. But Charles," Bellacroix paused to give James an appraising look. He squirmed uncomfortably. "Big runes, das'um big risk. He'll spend de night on de mountain, at de peak of Kai'nau. And dere he will be until de time has come."

James closed his eyes, receiving a flash of inspiration. The image of the volcano's smoky top streaked across his vision. "Oh, ok." James turned to leave.

"Where you going, boy? What did you be wanting with us?" Bellacroix looked at James again, her eyes seeming to peer into his heart.

"I… I'm going to check on Charles. I want to make sure he's ok." He hastened his step, not looking back at the two slaves. James kept walking, his eyes low, trying not to draw the attention of the Scrim, and yet restraining himself from assuming his unnoticeability. In the back of his mind, he realized how bizarre his behavior would seem to Bellacroix and Ling, but he didn't care. He had work to do.

The exit to the Scrim's quarters was now only a few feet away. And while James didn't want to risk being seen by the Styx, he didn't want to have any problems with the guards either. James paused. He prepared to open himself to the *Essence* of the world. And at that moment, felt a hand on his shoulder.

James froze, a surge of adrenaline shot through his body with the realization that he'd been caught once again.

"Jay?"

He turned in surprise to see Ling's soft eyes and delicate features.

"Jay? But why are you so quick to leave? Are we so unpleasant to you now? Are we so changed now bearing runes? Won't you stay and speak?"

"About what?" The words sounded clumsy in his ears.

"The future. Tomorrow we all go to the testing. But where will you go afterward?"

James tried to return to character, to think of himself not as a trans-dimensional traveler, but just a deckhand. "Well, we're all going back together, aren't we? Or are you staying here?" A strange thought assaulted James. "The Scrim didn't sell you, did they? Are they leaving you here?" He paused. "I guess it's not all that bad here. At least it's warm."

"I know… but. But I was thinking, that perhaps…well…" Ling bit her lip before continuing. "These runes, they are truly nothings. Naught but decorations. So, I was thinking that maybe… well maybe Captain Sylph could use me on the boat, like you. I'm not afraid of the water, and I can cook. And I'm obedient."

James laughed, and instantly regretted it. "I'm sorry, Ling. I'm sorry. I just don't take you for the pirate type. Or whatever the Islanders are." He paused. He wasn't a pirate either. If anything, Ling was more a part of this world than he would ever be.

She hung her head.

James looked up, then shook his head. "I didn't mean that. It's just…" He thought of the knife in his belt and Charles at the mouth of the volcano. If he didn't stop that rune from going off tomorrow, there wouldn't be a Ling, a Sylph, Kai'nau, or even the Alpinsea. The whole world would be destroyed if he didn't do something. And right now, he only had one solution. Then another thought came over him. Would it really be that bad to be stuck here? He could learn how to sail the seas with Captain Sylph, and maybe Brine could even teach him a thing or two. And if Ling came along? Well, that wouldn't be bad at all. A warm feeling came over James and he realized his cheeks must be turning bright red. He tried to look at Ling but had trouble meeting her eyes. "Um, yeah… I, I'll talk to the captain, if you'd like. I mean, she'd have to work out something with the Scrim of course, but we'll have plenty of time to talk on the way back."

This time, Ling was the one that blushed. "Look, Jay, this may seem peculiar to you… but I don't think the Scrim plan to return by ship." She dropped her voice to less than a whisper. "It has something to do with…"

James gave a slow nod. "I know."

"You know?"

"Yes. But just wait until tomorrow." He felt the warm feeling inside of him turn suddenly cold. "Anything can happen in a night. And I don't think the captain plans on being stranded."

Ling opened her mouth to reply, then shut it again.

"Look, Ling, there's something I have to do. I can't talk about it right now, but I promise it'll make sense tomorrow. Can you wait until tomorrow?"

She looked at him with unblinking eyes.

"All right, then I'll see you then. Now go back and see if you can't cheer up Bella. She's scary when she's mad." James forced his biggest grin. "I'll see you later."

Ling hesitated for a moment before heading back toward the far corner of the cavern. When she had taken several steps away, James opened himself to the *Essence* and wrapped himself in unnoticeability. Without pausing to be more discreet, he ran for the exit and did not stop even after passing the last of the Scrim guards. He ran on and on, driven by an inexplicable sense of direction as he began to wind higher and higher into the reaches of Kai'nau. When his lungs burned and his head ached, he slowed to a stop.

James fought back a surge of emotions. He believed that what he was going to do was the right thing to do, that it was necessary for this world to survive. But he wasn't ready yet. He was physically ready for it; he was emotionally ready to perform the task. But he couldn't do it without first saying goodbye. James knew that it would be risky to return to his homeworld. Yet he needed to say goodbye to his family.

Pausing for only the slightest moment to slow the time of the Frozen World—

James fell.

38. Goodbye to Home

James dropped to his knees in the North Carolina dust, his head swimming and his vision flooded with white before focus finally returned. His muscles surged with energy as adrenaline still raced in his veins from when he was last here. With it came the flooded memories of his confrontation with Teak, and the gun still warm in his right hand. James let the pistol fall to the ground with a dull thud.

Sitting on his heels, he looked around. There was no sound of any commotion or reaction to the gunshot. In this world, the gun had been fired only moments ago. And though Teak had evaporated, James was aware of what would happen if anyone found him with a weapon. He laughed mirthlessly at the thought of being "in trouble." Such a thing felt insignificant versus all he'd seen. Somewhere, far across the Cosmos of a billion nameless worlds, the Frozen World was on the brink of collapse. And the only way he knew to save it would trap him there forever. *That* was important. These other things, these little bits of life paled in comparison.

But still, James knew that he owed it to his family to say goodbye. He didn't think he would ever get another chance.

He stood up, pausing to brush the dark soil from his knees. He reached down to retrieve the gun, scraping the grime from it before returning it to his backpack, tucking it away beneath his gym clothes. He slung the pack over his shoulder and then scurried away, his feet one step shy of a run.

The roads were unsafe; nowhere was safe. And standing at a bus stop was asking to be seen. The Styx might not know about Teak, but they certainly knew James's face. Dr. Kovek was still out there, he didn't doubt that. The only consolation was that he knew her face as well, and he was pretty sure he'd recognize the man who chased him from the library, and Huckabee's friend had destroyed the other. Compared to the Frozen World, where there were likely at least two of the Styx still lurking, this almost felt like a fair fight. Still, he had to be careful.

James pushed through the brush, paying no mind to the briars leaving small red scratches along his legs. He focused on the highway ahead. He'd just have to hitchhike, that was his best chance not to be noticed. If he tried to walk, the Styx may notice him. And as long as they didn't pick him up, he'd be safer with a stranger than out in the open. James hurried to the street, dashed across to the far side, and then stuck out his thumb.

Whether through luck or fate, after only the fifth car had passed, a dusty blue pickup truck hit the brakes. The truck came to a stop and then backed up to where he stood. James first looked in the bed of the truck when he noticed it was so full of broken bits of wooden furniture, that he had nowhere to sit. He walked up to the cab, opened the door, and slid in.

"How far you going, man?" the driver asked. James pegged him to be in his mid-twenties. His head was shaved clean, and his arms and neck were covered in an array of tattoos. Unlike the runic's tattoos, these were a multi-colored mural of roses, angels, waves, and crowded caricatures. The man grinned as he motioned for James to take a seat.

"Down toward Dogwood Street. Anywhere near there is fine."

"Right on, brother." The driver brought the truck up to speed and was soon barreling down the highway. The man's concentration was on the road, and James allowed the miles to pass in comfortable silence. After several minutes, the man spoke again. "Look, kid. Let me give you some advice. You're too young to be thumbing it. Lot of weirdoes out there these days. That's why I stopped. Didn't want you catching the wrong kind of ride."

James felt a flush of heat in his cheeks and sweat forming on his brow. He knew it had been too good to be true. It was a trap. Another trap. He began maneuvering his backpack, his thoughts on the gun hidden within. The driver must have sensed James's nervousness. He shook his head.

"Whoa, whoa. I'm just saying be careful out there, kid. No need to get jumpy. You said Dogwood, right? Well, here we are." The driver pulled to the side and slowed to a stop. He rested his elbow on the wheel as he looked over toward him. "Now be good, kid. And be careful. Don't forget that."

James looked back at him, unsure if he was expected to do or say anything in return. Instead, he grabbed his bag, unlatched the door, and prepared to get out. He turned back to the driver. "Are you one of them, too?" He forced a smile. "One of the Doctor's friends?"

The driver smiled and shook his head. "Look, kid, not a whole lot of my friends are doctors. I'm just a guy." He nodded to the door. "But I have to get moving, so…"

James muttered his thanks and hopped down from the cab. He swung the door shut, and then stepped aside as the truck pulled away.

He was just a guy, James thought. Not everyone was part of the mad theatrics of world jumping, Travelers, Styx, runics, and Cosmos. There were some normal people out there too. He paused, then smiled. That's why he needed to do the right thing. It wasn't just about him. It wasn't about his friends, or his family, or his life. This was about *everyone's* friends, and *everyone's* family, and *everyone's* life. So as soon as he said goodbye, he would go and do it. James would do what he had to in order to save the Frozen World. He just hoped that if his own world was in the same kind of trouble, that someone would be looking out for it, too.

James quickened his pace. The emotion he felt wasn't happiness or contentment, it was a satisfaction of purpose. He had a reason for things now in an otherwise senseless world. He walked up to his house's front door, took a deep breath, and then turned the handle to enter.

As he opened the door, his heart lurched. The house looked like a hurricane had hit. The tables were overturned, books pulled from the shelves. The pictures on the walls were crooked, the glass fractured. Debris covered the floors as though every drawer in the house had been emptied and scattered. And there in the center, his parents. Both were lying on their sides, duct tape binding their hands behind their backs and strapping their ankles together. Another strip of tape covered their mouths. At seeing him, both lurched and cried out from behind their gags.

James sprang forward; his veins spiked with adrenaline. "Mom! Dad!" But in that same moment, he froze. He wasn't alone in the room. Just to one side, seated in his father's favorite recliner, was the ice-faced woman, Dr. Kovek. She wore a dark business suit with her legs crossed and held a cup of tea in her right hand.

Dr. Kovek looked at him, a humorless smile spreading her thin lips. "That's him," she said. James heard movement on both sides of him as two large men, pockmarked with scars and smelling strongly of bourbon, lunged at him. He tried to dive out of the way, only to trip on a toppled lamp and crash to the ground. The men were on him in an instant, unyielding hands wrapped around his wrists and shoulders as they jerked him from the floor.

"Get off me!" he screamed. Some remnants of an after-school program reminded him to be as loud as possible in case someone was walking nearby. "Get off me! They're in here! Help! Help!"

Dr. Kovek said, "Shut him up."

One of the thugs released James's wrist just long enough to punch him in the side of his head. Once, twice. His vision blurred and went dark for a moment, his limbs turning to jelly. And then in a moment he was back kicking and screaming once more as them men shifted to put him in a headlock, one arm wrapped around his throat, while the other across his mouth.

"Mom!" he tried again, but the sound came out muffled, and then dropped to nothing. Dr. Kovek was perched just above his mother, a thin knife in her hand pointed at her eye. The look of fear on his mother's face was immediate and terrible. Dr. Kovek didn't need to speak the threat. James let his muscles give way, the fight draining from his body. And then the other thug drove his knuckles into James's stomach once more.

Dr. Kovek said, "Good. We now understand each other." She nodded to the side. "Take him into the next room."

The men carried him into the kitchen. His body felt limp from both injuries and the evaporation of his will. They produced a roll of duct tape and mechanically worked to secure his hands behind his back and then bound his ankles. They rudely propped James on one of the kitchen chairs and then ran a few more binds of tape around his waist to secure him further. As they finished, Dr. Kovek walked in, her tea still held in one hand, and the knife hanging loosely in the other. She slid one of the kitchen chairs out with her foot and sat primly down. She took a sip from her tea and studied her captive.

Dr. Kovek turned to the two men. "You can leave us. Keep a close eye on the others." She flipped her hand dismissively. "And take whatever you want." The thugs shuffled into the next room, glancing back once at the ice-faced woman before shutting the door behind them.

James looked at Dr. Kovek with hatred. His neck and side throbbed in pain. His heart pounded from the struggle. "Those men don't know, do they? They're not like you."

She laughed. "Them? Of course not. Those two are natives. Easy enough to find. Men are so willing to perform services—for the right price of course. That is the same in any world." Her face turned grim. "And my other men… they seem to be missing, hmmm? Huckabee's assassin is skilled, but he isn't here to help you now. And Huckabee? Well, I think you saw what happened to him."

Dr. Kovek darted forward, moving so quickly she nearly blurred. James felt the cold edge of her knife against his throat. "Now before we had the good doctor removed, he said a great many things. He didn't want to, of course, but after time, anyone starts to chatter. I *know* you have been meddling in worlds, but I still don't know which ones. So, you're going to show me. That, or we'll have consequences. And then we'll just start over again. Do you understand?"

James looked up in confusion, "No, I don't understand. What are you trying to do here? And why did you destroy my house? I mean… what's even the point of that?" He wanted to ask about his parents but thought it was better to keep her focus on him.

Dr. Kovek eased off on the knife and took a step back. She glanced around at the broken shelves. "Well, I was… looking for something. Something you may have brought back, a souvenir, perhaps. Many Travelers collect things—keepsakes, mementos, knick-knacks, sometimes tools. All with a little trace of where they came from. If I had that, I'd know exactly where you've been."

He thought about the strange coin. What would happen if she found it in his pocket? Would she follow it back to wherever Dr. Huckabee had gotten it in the first place? Would that distract her? At least for a moment?

He shook his head, trying to clear the fog. There was something else she said, something that just now clicked. Dr. Kovek said she was alone. Not just one, but *both* of her henchmen must be gone if she was turning to natives for help. That meant she was the last Styx in his world. And that gave him a chance. If he could figure out a way to deal with her, then he'd be free. The Frozen World would still be in peril, but at least his own world would be safe.

Dr. Kovek's lips pulled back across her too-white teeth. "You didn't answer my question. Do you understand your position?"

James replied, trying his best to sound brave, "You can't kill me, I know that much. In this world, I'm—what did you call it? Native. You'd be stuck here forever."

Dr. Kovek leaned forward, her nose nearly touching his, her breath hot on his face. "Well, not by myself. Not directly. But I can still do quite a lot of damage if that were my intent. Perhaps you are too noble to care about yourself. But I doubt your indifference when it comes to your parents. After all, they were *so* happy to know you'd been cured.

That their poor baby wouldn't have any more of his falling spells. I guess they should have been less trusting."

James could take no more. The only way to save his parents, his life, and maybe his whole world, was to get rid of the ice-faced woman. But here, bound and restrained, he didn't have a chance. He *knew* she was goading him for a reason. He *knew* he was running into her trap. But that didn't matter anymore, he had to risk it. And so—

James fell.

39. Kovek and Kai'ja

James raced through the Cosmos, as he had hoped—but also as he had feared—he felt the ice-faced woman pop into existence behind him. She followed close on his tail, moving as he did. James knew that unlike his confrontation with Teak, he wasn't trying to lose Dr. Kovek. It was crucial that he didn't. As long as she was following him, then it meant that his parents, frozen in time in his homeworld, would be safe in that suspended instant. As James raced through the Cosmos, he realized that he didn't have a plan, not even a tentative one. He also knew that if the ice-faced woman sensed he was being untruthful, she might take that anger out on his parents. So, James did both the best and worst thing he could think of. He focused his attention on the Frozen World.

We all have different abilities, Teak had said. James had been surprised when the Styx agent arrived in different worlds with his weapons. What would the ice-faced woman's abilities be? James didn't have time to fully grasp the thought before colliding with his body, still stuck mid-stride walking from the Scrim's lair. And before the next step was taken, James launched into a dead sprint.

Unfortunately for James, he had been running when last he left his body. His legs were already tired, and his heart already pounding.

Without breaking stride, James opened himself to the *Essence*, and the pain dissolved away. But just as he had collected his strength, he sensed the ice-faced woman pop into existence behind him. He didn't have to turn to see if she was still armed. The gunshot ringing from behind him was indication enough.

She knows she's in the right place. Good, James thought as he turned sharply into the next corridor. *She must be able to feel the sickness in the world. Wait… that's it!*

James's mind exploded in excitement. He had a chance. One chance, but it might work. He looked through the *Essence* until he found the bright, twisted point that he knew was to be the source of the world's demise. And he knew that that point was the Kai'ja queen. Her spirit burned low and offensive, almost directly below him, in the center of Kai'nau, at the volcano's heart.

One shot at this, got to make it count.

James leaped in the air and drew his arms and legs tightly together to form a ball. As the ice-faced woman's pistol echoed again, James pulled himself further from the reality of the world. Just as he had practiced when walking through the tree, and just as he had done when he escaped his cell, James removed his tangibility from the Frozen Word. And when he came down, he fell, passing cleanly through the floor. But he didn't stop there. Further and further, he dropped, gaining speed as corridors and tunnels of Kai'nau passed by like the frames of a movie. And when he had almost reached the bright burning point of *Essence* of the Kai'ja queen, he released. James returned to full existence and collided like a rocket onto the gilded floor.

He felt his limbs buckle from the impact, but though he had fallen what must have been thirty stories, he seemed uninjured. While physically intact, his mind was in a state of complete and utter exhaustion. James could barely keep his eyes open, and yet he did not let go of the *Essence*. Instead, with his last ounce of strength, he pulled himself back once more. And though James could neither move, nor rise, nor cry out in pain, he managed to make himself unnoticeable.

A strange gusting sound whistled overhead. James saw the ice-faced woman streak through the ceiling, the rock rippling like a mirage as she passed through, only to resume its solidity once she passed. The ice-faced woman landed in front of James in a half-crouch, one knee dropped, the gun held behind her in her right hand, and a dagger clenched and before her face.

"Clever, boy. But such games are for children. And once I end your life, I will take this world for my own."

James tried to open his mouth to respond, but he was too weak to move, and certainly too weak to try and jump to another world. He simply concentrated on being unnoticeable, hoping his gamble would pay off.

"Intruder!" The shout echoed through the room, and James, out of the corner of his eye, for the first time took in the rest of the room. The chamber was gilded from floor to ceiling, the only interruption being obsidian inlay mirroring the runes drawn upon the Kai'ja's slaves. At the far end of the room, lounging upon a bed of crimson silks, the Kai'ja queen bolted upright. The scream, however, had not come from her, but instead one of the sixty guards lining the walls.

The screaming guard drew a scimitar and charged at the ice-faced woman. Dr. Kovek, momentarily distracted from James, made a flicking motion with her hand and the guard was hurled head over heels to fall at the base of the wall. But even as he crumbled, the other guards were beginning their attack. Roars of fury in the melodic language of the Kai'ja erupted through the corridor.

In a matter of moments, the soldiers had descended on the ice-faced woman. But if she was concerned, it did not show on her chiseled face. She seemed to brush off the attacks like a colossus waving away flies. The blades that touched her skin either passed through her or were simply deflected. Then, as though she had grown weary of the ineffectual display, the ice-faced woman rose into the air. Her body radiated a purple darkness which shed the attacks like a force field. She turned her attention away from the Kai'ja warriors, as though they didn't even exist, and returned her gaze to James.

With a flick of her wrist, the ice-faced woman's gun whipped back into her hand. She leveled the barrel at him. "So long, James. You couldn't run forever. And now this world is…"

But the ice-faced woman did not finish her thought. For even as the swords and arrows of the Kai'ja were being repelled, each and every guard had been preparing their second attack. This attack, however, was not physical, but the dread force of runic energies. A wave of power struck from all sides, from flames to electricity, to unnamed power and pulsing energy. The attack hit the ice-faced woman. She was hurled across the room to collide with the gilded wall.

Dr. Kovek leaped to her feet, crouched like a cornered tiger, and flung the full might of her energy back at the Kai'ja runics. Unlike before, where she had brushed them off, reversing their attacks and disabling, this time she struck. The air was again filled with energy. This time it was the black radiance of the ice-faced woman as her power cut through the soldiers, dissolving them into oblivion. In a single sweep, half of the guards had been eradicated. But as she raised her arms to strike again, she became stark still. In a cry of twisted fury, the ice-faced woman *folded*. Like Teak before her, her death was a twist of reality and a dissolving into nothingness, like a card thrown into the air, only to rotate into nothing when the small edge turned.

Even as the ice-faced woman blinked from reality, James could see the source of her demise. Standing behind her was the Kai'ja queen. A golden dagger, slick with the blood of the Styx, was grasped in her hand.

"A Traveler's tricks don't work on everyone," James whispered. The phrase from *An Alternative History* rang through his ears. He remembered the tiniest statement saying that VIPs could not easily be brushed off by the magic from a world walker. The Kai'ja queen was still destined to destroy this world. But she had inadvertently saved James's own.

He propped himself on his elbow. His mind still swam, but his strength had regained to the point that he could begin to move. James, though still wrapped in unnoticeability, looked in horror as the Kai'ja queen approached.

"Wonders surround you, boy. And now you have brought death to my guards." She pointed the tip of the bloody sword at James. "Speak now as to why your life should be spared."

James tried to swallow but found his throat dry. From the eaves, he could see the runic guards approaching. There was puzzlement on their faces, and so he dropped his guise, making himself noticeable again. The runics blinked in surprise, as though they had always known James had been lying there, only just now starting to think it peculiar.

James looked at the Kai'ja queen. "She's not the only one. There are others. And if they succeed, your world will die." He tried to speak the words with vehemence, but he found himself so weak that the sounds drifted away.

The Kai'ja queen lowered her blade slightly. "You are no Islander."

"No. I'm from somewhere else."

* * *

James leaned back on the bed. The sea of cushions cradled his exhausted body, still weak from his feat of mind. The seconds passed in blissful silence, until the velvet curtains forming the entrance to the chamber parted and four Kai'ja runics entered, followed lastly by the Kai'ja queen. She still carried her sword, though it now rested in a scabbard against her bare thigh.

"You will speak. Or you will die." The queen rested herself on a couch across from James, propping herself on her right elbow, while stroking the hilt of her sword with her left.

"They're called the Styx," James blurted. "They come to dying worlds and seek to destroy them."

"And your role in this?"

"I'm here to stop them."

The Kai'ja queen's eyes narrowed. "But perhaps not to warn me. Or we would have spoken when last we met."

"I couldn't give myself away, or they'd have come after me first. You saw that earlier. I… I can't fight them myself."

"How did you plan to stop what you could not fight?"

He bit his lip. "I don't know—I still don't know. I have to do it however I can."

The Kai'ja queen stood and faced the far wall. "More importantly is how, child, did you learn our world is to perish."

She knew! The thought blazed through his mind. *She knows even though I don't.* James coughed his reply, eager to learn the source of the world's problem. "I can feel it, sense it. It's like how I can read those runes. Or speak your languages."

The Kai'ja queen shifted her tone and accent. She spat out a string of words that, while James knew he had never heard spoken before, understood the meaning of clearly: "Many wear those runes."

"But I don't have any runes," James replied. "Not real ones anyway." He gestured to the tattoos Brine had given him. "I just know things."

"So, you know our world ends upon the morrow. Who else knows?"

James swallowed. "It's *tomorrow?*"

The queen turned to face him. "Of course. Our seers have long seen the end of this land. The Scrim have seen it also. That is why Slagish came to this place. That is why we reached an accord. After all, only the dark minds of the Scrim could ever design that rune. But none but a Kai'ja could etch it. And now I have my gateway, child. Now I have my escape. The sun that rises will not set again upon the Kai'ja.

We will have crossed into other worlds. This world may perish, and our beloved Kai'nau fall. But the Kai'ja will live on."

"But the gateway *is* what destroys the world."

"Nonsense, our death will come by a falling star. We have known such for millennia."

James's head swam. They *knew* the world was ending. How could they have known all along? "But you don't know for sure! What if that's like, a metaphor or something?"

The queen frowned. "I know not of this 'metaphor.' But a star *does* fall. You can see it wax nightly."

"Ok, so even if you're right—which you're not—then why did you want Captain Sylph to shoot Slagish? If you lose him, then you won't even have your gateway."

The queen signed in exasperation. James had heard that sound made before. It was the sound of someone who knew everything being forced to explain it to someone who didn't know anything whatsoever. "When the Scrim open the gate, they will open it to this other world. One in which we all are to seek haven. But if they try and betray me, and try to call their army to my temple, we will fight. I trust not in the Scrim's generosity. So, if deals be broken, we will be ready. *Then* I reclaim mine gateway."

James brimmed with frustration. "But you're wrong! It's the Styx you need to worry about. If you stop them, you don't have to go anywhere. You saw what they can do to you. They want Charles for themselves. And once they have him, they won't save you, they'll drag you under. You'll never touch your gateway."

The Kai'ja queen ignored his words. She began strolling around the chamber. "And from what world do *you* hail? Tell me of *your* home."

"No! You can't go *there*. We don't even have magic. That's crazy. I just got it made safe. And... no, you're getting it all wrong. You need to worry about the Styx, because you can't..."

"I care not for your world, only my own, now and future. And I will keep my own counsel in such times. What you will do is tell me what you know. How might I find these Styx? And speak no lies, lest your friends suffer."

"Sylph and Brine don't even know who I am."

"Not your Islander friends, I speak of another closer to you." The Kai'ja queen snapped her fingers. Led in on an iron chain, and appearing rather disheveled, was Ling. "Now speak. And *this* time speak all."

40. Luciferous

The arctic wind whipped against James's cheeks in the frosty pre-dawn. At his side, Ling was wrapped in an immense fur coat, every scrap of skin was covered except where her wrists showed, bound by an iron manacle. A chain connected to the center linked to a matching manacle on James's hands. Both Ling and he had been up all night as James answered the same questions again and again from the Kai'ja queen. And when the queen grew tired, she was replaced by another interrogator, who in turn was replaced by a third. But despite the questions they asked, and despite their anger at him, there was little James could tell them. The Kai'ja now knew what he was, a traveler between worlds. It was only a matter of time before the Styx discovered him as well.

"Tell me of your home, Jay," Ling whispered. She hadn't spoken to him in several hours.

James sighed. He tried to form his words in a way she would understand. "It's busier. Lots of machines everywhere, lots of engines. There aren't any runes or runics. I mean, some people have tattoos, but they don't do anything. And there aren't slaves, and nobody walks around with guns and swords—at least not where I'm from. You'd probably think it's boring. At least compared to all this."

"No, it sounds very pleasant." For a minute neither spoke, each occupied in their thoughts. "Is it as cold as Kai'nau?"

"Well, parts are, sure. Up in the mountains or way up north. I mean, it's a whole world, you know. There are deserts and forests and jungles and cities and suburbia and caves and plains. It's got everything. It's not like in Star Wars where you only have one climate."

"Star Wars? Climate? I'm afraid I don't understand."

"It's this movie where every planet just had… Uh, never mind. It's nice, ok."

The night shone brilliant and cold. The volume of alien stars staggered James. Even after witnessing the Cosmos, the beauty of the night sky still had a majesty to it. He tried to enjoy this moment with Ling, even though they were here against their will. He tried to think of the day ahead, and how he would weather it. What he tried not to think of, was his family, bound in duct tape and held captive in another world. James had vowed that he would not return until he was positive that no Styx could see him or would follow him. Though hard to believe, he felt they were safer now without him.

Ling made an exasperated sound and then let out the smallest of sobs. "Earlier tonight, when you came to visit … you didn't go to check on Charles, did you? You were going to kill him to stop the gateway. Please, tell me the truth."

James felt his head become heavy. The weight of that decision seemed heavier now than when he had made it. And now he wasn't so sure it had been the right decision at all. What if the Kai'ja queen was right? What if it was really a falling star and not the gateway that would destroy this world? Then James would be a murderer and trapped in a world about to die. Where would he be then?

"Yes, I was. I… I thought it would save the world."

"But you would be trapped here as well. Is that not one of your Rules?"

"Yeah, but. I decided it would be worth it. There are a lot of people in this world. And I may not like all of 'em, heck I barely know any of them, but it still seems like a fair price to pay."

"Even if you would never again see your mother or your father?"

James shut his eyes tight, the emotion welling inside of him. "It doesn't matter anymore. There's nothing I can do now."

"But certainly, you could escape again? I know these chains hold you only so long as you wish."

James paused. He was trapped here, not bound by the chains, but by obligation. On the one hand, he didn't dare risk going home until the task was complete. There were still two agents of the Styx out there, and if they followed him home, then the cycle would begin again. And on the other side, there was Ling. The Kai'ja queen had made it very clear that if James tried to escape that it would mean death for his friend. Both forces led to the same conclusion. He would remain in the Frozen World until this world's fate had been set.

"Jay, why must you evade my questions?" Ling's voice interrupted his ponderings. "Tell me. Why don't you just escape?"

"I can't. Not now. I need to see this through to the end."

Ling gasped in amazement. It took James a minute to realize it was not his words that caused such shock. "Look! Look at the moon!"

James jerked his eyes skyward. The moon, brilliant and round, appeared to be tearing. The right hemisphere was bulging to one side. Then the bulge separated, forming an offshoot of the moon which gleamed pale and blue in the night sky. James's mouth opened. He realized that it wasn't a splitting moon he saw. It was the falling star of the Kai'ja queen. And it was enormous.

James heard the crunch of footsteps on the snow behind him. "Ahhh, she has come to grace us. Come hither, my lovely." The Kai'ja queen walked to stand at James's side. She turned her eyes to the heavens and then closed them, allowing the moonlight, and the light of the falling star, to bathe her face. "Behold Luciferous, star of the fourteenth heaven, first seen one thousand years past, by one with a rune of long sight." The queen turned to face James. "One child every generation is given the same rune. And we watch the star draw ever closer. At one time we feared the arrival. But it is not the way of the Kai'ja to shirk our fate. But the Scrim, our brothers to the east, had other plans."

The Kai'ja queen walked around to James's front and produced a key. She unlocked the chain connecting his wrist to Ling and handed the still-connected chain to one of her attendants. She nodded to the large, tattooed man holding the chain and then, taking James's hand in her own, led him to the edge of the cliff. From their perch, he could see the entirety of Kai'nau blotting out the pristinely star-filled sky. At the base of the volcano, the first stirrings began. Guards were forming lines, and the large doors were being cranked open.

The queen continued, "The Scrim sent their envoy, the same prophet who told them of Luciferous's fall. And while we had known for millennia of our destruction, we had given no thought to escape. But the Scrim offered a plan. They devised a rune, powerful beyond measure, that could open a gateway to a place beyond our stars. They called the world 'Haven.' But while they could draw the rune upon parchment, they hadn't the skill to etch it upon flesh. We agreed to the etching, but only if we, too, could pass through.

"And so we waited, until our eyes and ears in the port in the Western Isles told us that the Scrim, guided by an Islander, were headed for the Alpinsea."

James broke in, "Sylph knew about all this? Am I the only one that didn't know?"

"Only Lord Slagish and his prophet knew the true nature of their mission. All others knew only the value of their cargo. To say more would invite peril. The prophet warned of that as well."

James narrowed his eyes. "So, this prophet was the one that told the Scrim about the Haven?"

"Yes."

"And he was the same one that told the Scrim to keep quiet?"

"Again, yes. Explain yourself, boy."

"And I'll bet he introduced the Scrim to Teak as well."

"Excuse me?"

James shook his head. "Sorry, I was thinking aloud."

The Kai'ja queen curled her lips. "You think you are clever, boy. But I know your mind. You think our prophet is your Styx."

James shifted uncomfortably.

"And perhaps he is—but I think such is not. Your Styx wants worlds to end. Why would he give aid?"

"Because maybe he thought that if you tried to save your own, that maybe it would end up destroying even more." James tried to sound defiant, and yet he found by the end of his sentence that he wasn't sure himself.

"To trick a world into saving itself… but only to kill it? You are unskilled at persuasion."

James narrowed his eyes. The Kai'ja queen didn't sound sorry. And maybe she was right. It did seem like a lot of unnecessary work. James thought he'd have to look elsewhere for the Styx. But one question remained unanswered.

"Why am I still here? I've told you everything I know. I don't understand what you want with me."

The Kai'ja queen looked scornfully at James. "You are a child that can walk between worlds. You think you are of no use? I would be a fool to waste such skill."

"But what about right now? What do you want with me *now*? Why are we outside in the cold, freezing our butts off?"

The Kai'ja queen snapped her eyes to James. "Because, first, I needed you to witness the peril of Luciferous. I will not tolerate more foolishness. Especially to my newest runic, and especially as you offer no other solutions."

James frowned. She had him there. He thought he could save the world from the Styx. But how could he stop a falling star? He tried to think of a movie he'd seen where an asteroid was going to hit Earth. The solution had been nuclear weapons and a spaceship. James didn't even have his knife anymore. But then again… wait a minute.

James struggled to grasp an idea. There was something he read in the *History*, something about the power of a world always being similar to the world of a Traveler. The Frozen World may not have cars and airplanes and nuclear warheads, but they did have runics. And from what he had seen, they could do things even more amazing than he'd seen with technology. After all, they had managed to figure out how to open a gateway to another world. Untested, true, but they had still done it. So, was there something strong enough to stop the star?

James said, "But there's still something else. Isn't there?"

"Perhaps. But you must be patient. For now."

The questions running through James's head were interrupted by the crunch of approaching footsteps. He turned to see a collection of runic guards approach the Kai'ja queen. The guards framed a box around Captain Sylph and Brine. Both of the Islanders were now dressed in their snow gear, and both looked equally sour about bailing James out of another bad situation with the Kai'ja.

The queen barked a quick order for James to stay put and then walked up the slope to intercept Sylph and Brine. James opened himself to the *Essence* to sharpen his hearing, but the words were the same. Sylph refused to aid the Kai'ja queen until her contract with the Scrim had ended. And she no longer seemed to care what happened to James at all. What he did notice, was that the Kai'ja queen made no reference to him being from another world. At most, she tested the waters to see if Sylph knew. The smug look on the Kai'ja queen's face when she returned indicated to James that that was really the only thing that she had intended to find out in the first place.

James looked back out over the hillside. The gates of Kai'nau had been opened fully, and hordes of people, Kai'ja and Scrim alike, were spilling onto the soot-dirtied snow. The character of the two groups, however, was entirely different. For while the Scrim were heavily laden with the luggage they would load onto their wagons, and each holding a torch, the Kai'ja held only their weapons. The Kai'ja seemed to have no need for torchlight, the clear sky and the combined light from the moon and Luciferous providing ample glow on the frozen land.

He felt a strong hand on his shoulder and turned to see Brine's stern face. "Oy, come on, laddie. This is the last time we bail you out. We've got to get moving too."

James pointed to the masses below. "Brine, that's everyone. You know that, right? Even the children are there."

The large man nodded.

"So, you know what the Kai'ja and Scrim plan to do with the gateway?"

"As like as not. The captain found out from the queen. But I don't think the Kai'ja even know. They're prepared for a fight, I'll wager, but not a journey. And if they do know, they're playing it off pretty well."

"Maybe they don't need to know. Maybe we can still stop it."

Brine cast a sidelong glance at James. "Stop the gateway or stop the star?"

"I think, I think the only way to stop the gateway, *is* to stop the star. I still have a bad feeling about what that gateway can do in the wrong hands. But if we don't stop the star, then the world still dies."

"Well, laddie, we're kind of running out o' time here."

"Sorry, I just found out—no thanks to you. I don't have a plan yet."

Brine reached forward and tousled James's hair. He hated it when people did that, but he understood that the large man was just being friendly. "Well, you've got about two miles and two hours to come up with something. Otherwise, we'll just have to see where that gateway goes together."

"Can we take Ling with us? Or does she have to go back with the Scrim?"

Brine turned around to look, but the strange girl had already been absorbed into the mass of Kai'ja guards. "Don't sweat it, laddie. We're all heading to the demonstration. She'll be there, too."

"Right. You're probably right. I just… well it seemed weird that they'd keep us together only just to split us apart now."

Brine frowned. "I'd say it's a coincidence, but the Kai'ja aren't big on leaving things to chance. Now come on, we need to get moving." He paused. "And I wouldn't give Sylph too hard a time. She's pretty upset that we're bailing you out again. She hates the Kai'ja getting the upper hand."

James pulled the fur coat that the Kai'ja had wrapped around his shoulders tighter. He knew he could ignore the cold if he wanted, but at the same time didn't want to pull himself away from the moment any more than he needed. He had precious time to figure out a way to survive this. And now he had the added issue of wondering what the Kai'ja queen had in store for him, not to mention the presence of two more of the Styx out there, a falling star… James shook his head. How was he going to worm his way out of this?

Brine took a quick stutter-step to catch up with Captain Sylph, and James skipped to follow. He received a glare from the captain when he smiled up at her, and then promptly looked away to avoid her eyes. "I'm just trying to help," he muttered under his breath, though his words didn't even inspire a backward glance.

The small procession of the Kai'ja queen and her bodyguards, the Islanders, and finally James and Ling did not set off down the mountain to regroup with the masses. Instead, they hiked along the ridgeline. Their smaller numbers soon outpaced the travelers on the valley floor, until the only evidence was a small orange glow as the torches from the Scrim spilled into the night air. Even the sound of the migrating group, the voices carrying easily across the snow, faded into nothing.

With the masses behind them, the march took a decidedly more solemn tone. The Kai'ja were even quieter than usual, and neither Sylph nor Brine seemed interested in a conversation. Ling, the only other person James felt comfortable speaking with, was at the far end of the procession, not to mention surrounded by guards. In a way, he was glad. How much more was there to be said?

"There she is." Brine's voice shattered the silence. James looked up to see where the large man was pointing. A hundred yards ahead, the ridgeline transformed from packed snow to what looked like the top level of a Mayan temple. Stone steps, dusted with a thin layer of snowfall, climbed upward to a large plateau. James rubbed his eyes, confirming that the edifice really was a ziggurat, and not carved into the mountain. He soon decided that whether constructed or carved, this would be the location of the final act.

James felt a hand on his shoulder, far lighter than Brine's normal steady grip. He turned to face the Kai'ja queen.

"Boy, come with me." The queen motioned for the rest of the group to continue, while she led James to the foot of the ziggurat, where a hooded Kai'ja stood waiting. James hadn't seen the man with the rest of the group, and so assumed he had been stationed there for quite some time.

The Kai'ja queen nodded to the hooded figure but exchanged no words. She waited patiently until the rest of the group had disappeared from view up the steps of the temple. When they were completely alone, the queen turned to James.

"And now, child, the time has come to prove your worth."

The Kai'ja queen turned to the hooded figure and gestured with a flip of her finger. The black-robed man nodded. He slowly raised his hands to his hood and flipped it back, to reveal a pale white, shaven head. The man was a runic, a tattoo spiraling from his right eye to spiderweb around his head and then disappear beneath the folds of his cloak. James had but to glance at the rune, and he knew its meaning. This man could see things. This man could see everything.

A chill ran down James's spine as the man turned an eye, as pale and white as the surrounding snow, to look at him. The other eye appeared to be missing but not missing from the socket. Instead, smooth skin covered where the eye should have been. James couldn't be sure if the eye had been removed to make way for the rune which passed over the missing socket, or if it was because the man was missing his eye that the rune could be drawn in the first place. Either way, James felt the man's gaze boring through him.

"This is my seer, boy. He can show us the Scrim's Haven." The Kai'ja queen turned to the man. "What do you see?"

The man did not meet the queen's gaze, his one seeing-eye fixed on James. "What is this spirit you have brought before me? This is but a shadow of a creature. No… *substance*. He is not real."

James's heart jumped in his chest. He'd already been caught, and so that fear was gone. His misgiving was replaced by hope. This man could see him for what he was. Just like James could see the difference between worlds, so could he. And if this man could see through him, then perhaps he could see through others.

"He, he can tell what I am… He knows I'm not from your world. That means… that means he can see through the Styx too! He can pick them out and you can take care of them. Excuse me, sir, have you seen anyone else like me? Anyone else who wasn't the *whole* way there?"

The runic watcher did not answer James, did not acknowledge him at all. He merely turned to the queen. "What would you like to see, my queen?"

"Our new world. Show us Haven. Show me what lies beyond my gateway."

The runic hissed. "The Scrim's gateway can lead wherever the heart desires. But I can show you Haven if you wish." The runic waited for a moment, and seeing no response from the queen, took her silence as assent. The man drew his robe up and kneeled in the snow. He placed his hands on his knees and closed his one seeing eye. And then—though James didn't understand how—the other eye, the missing eye, opened. The eye was not, however, a regular eye, but instead a window of nothingness. James peered inside and found that the eye was like a gateway itself. As he looked, his vision seemed to grow, until he found that he was seeing what the runic saw. And what he saw—was another world.

The image of the world was like existing within a painting. The grass underfoot was a mossy green swaying in an unseen wind. But James could not feel the blades. The sky had the rosy tint of a setting sun, yet he could not feel the warmth of the sun on his back. The clouds overhead swirled at impossible heights, almost to the point where they looked not like clouds at all, but celestial wisps—but James could not feel the breezes which incited their dance. While the ground was dotted in pale blue monoliths—perhaps immense, perhaps tiny— James was powerless to walk further to investigate. Looking into the eye of the runic seer was not so much as looking through a window, as being outside the window. And yet, James knew that he was still in the Frozen World, and this was only a picture. Through the smallest breath of will, James forced himself to turn around. As he did so, the Frozen World snapped into focus. James stood again on a snowy tundra on the icy plane, the ziggurat looming overhead, and the Kai'ja queen eyeing him critically.

"Could you see?" the queen asked.

"Yes, that… that was weird. Amazing. I mean it was amazing." James paused. "But I still don't understand. What do you want from me?"

The queen pursed her lips. "What the Seer can show is only a shadow of the world, only a small glimpse. We need to go to the other side to truly know. But even once the gateway is open, those who cross may not return. The rune will only open in one direction. But you, boy, can do just that. I don't want to run blindly. I want you to go now. You must tell us if it is a trap."

James nodded. "Ok, so now you need something. But what's in it for me? It's not a matter of where the gateway leads, it's the gateway itself that will break the world. Falling Star or not, there has to be another way."

The queen's face filled with scorn. "The star *will* fall. And I intend to save myself and my people before that happens. Will you destroy a people as their world fails? Perhaps this is what you came to do. But if you need a reason, then I offer two. If you complete this task, I will have my Seer turn eyes upon your Styx." The Kai'ja queen's face turned cold. "And if not, I will see to it your Ling does not live until sunrise, whether in this world or the next. Have we a deal?"

James thought for only a moment, then nodded. He turned to the Seer. "Ok, I need to see inside again. I think I know how to do this."

The Seer nodded. Again, he closed his good eye, and again he opened the void eye into nothingness. James peered inside. Soon, the image of the strange world filled his vision. He allowed himself to become immersed. And with the smallest effort of will, he allowed himself to *be* within the image. He allowed the last vestiges of the Frozen World to slip from his fingertips. And then—

James fell.

41. Haven

James's drift into the World of Haven did not end as gently as it had begun. For the moment that he released his hold on the Frozen

World, he was jerked with the subtlety of a train wreck. James wasn't guided so much as seized into stark reality.

And the burning began.

His skin was first. The pain snapped in an instant, like being caught in a shower when the cold water drops to nothing, an encompassing burn that no twisting or shaking can evade. Next came his lungs: each breath of air was a blaze of acrid smoke, stinging to breathe and acidic in taste. Lastly was the sound: James's ears were assailed by a screeching, complete and total, as though a million cars were squealing a million brakes all at once. The pain was overwhelming, and James's mind seemed ready to shut down to escape. With his last shred of awareness, he pulled himself away—just slightly—from the world's harsh reality.

As though a switch had been flipped, the burning ceased, the sound died, and his breaths became normal. James realized that he had in a way returned to the peaceful view of Haven that he had seen through the eye of the runic. When not immersed in the world, the flowing landscapes and pale sky seemed appealing. But the differences remained.

The earth beneath James's feet pulsed. The pale of the swaying grass no longer seemed grass-like at all. Instead, the earth seemed covered by a fine fur influenced not by the wind, but rather writhed and searched like probing tentacles. The cilia tried to grasp James's feet, yet whether they found him unpalatable, or his being removed from the world acted as some manner of protection, they did not seize him. But they didn't need to. The earth shifted and moved, the landscape undulating and twisting. The ground was alive. But though it crawled, James couldn't tell in what direction, or to what purpose.

The undulation of the ground became more noticeable. The steady thrum of its interior heartbeat changed to a rhythmic heave as the landscape rolled like a wave, small at first and then rippling like a sheet in the wind. James lost his footing. He was being skidded like a miniature surfboard across the land's heaving surface. At first, James was filled with fear. But terror became exhilaration as he rode the furry swell. Then terror returned when he saw where he was being carried. The wave was taking him to a wide opening in the furry hills—a gaping maw.

James's initial reaction was to leave the world entirely, to jump back out, drift through the Cosmos, and return to the Frozen World. But the leaping from reality to reality that had become a familiarity was suddenly an act of extreme exertion. He tried three times to Travel, but though he concentrated, he could not pull himself any further from the world's existence.

He snapped his head around. He was speeding closer to the open mouth, and his options of simply jumping away seemed less and less viable. He turned to scramble, fighting an uphill battle, but his boots slid on the strange surface.

Then, just as his mind passed from panic, he saw the answer. James flung himself face down and seized the waving cilia in both hands. Fortunately, the hairs did not break free. The wave which had rolled James swelled, and he was carried to the top. Then, with the crest passing, he released his grip. He slid down the backside of the geologic wave, coming to rest in the valley below. He turned to look at the wave of skin, but the disruption had settled, dissipating to nothing.

James took a deep breath and then leaped to his feet as the cilia probed at him once more. The panic of the flesh-wave was replaced by something far more common. He believed the technical term was "the willies."

"Yeeaa-yuck! Woohoohoh!" James hopped and danced, scraping the imagined offenders from his body. He shook his head in disbelief. "Ok, so the ground just tried to eat me. That is not ok." He cast his eyes around. "But what now?"

James looked across the alien landscape. He certainly couldn't go in the direction of the open mouth, not unless he wanted to risk becoming dinner. But where could he go? The only other things here were the stone monoliths dotting the landscape, though they now looked decidedly more like teeth than anything else. But even if the monoliths offered no shelter, they must at least be more stable than the living ground. And maybe they'd give James the vantage he needed to assess this strange world.

After turning around once, James picked the monolith that looked the closest and took off across the field at a trot. Even though the ground no longer moved with the swell of the ocean, it was still spongy and did not lend itself to quick travel. As though his footsteps had reawakened the beast, the ground began to undulate again. But this time, James knew what to do. Crouching low, he grabbed two handfuls of cilia and held on tight. The swell became pronounced, nearly violent, and then subsided again. Once the flap was over, James resumed his gait. In less time than he expected, he was within range of the monolith.

The monolith loomed before him, rising sixty feet in the air. The surface, appearing smooth from the distance, was gnarled like a stump, the surface swirling and porous. James crept closer, each step on the ciliated ground more tentative than the last. The pores on the monolith were becoming more defined. He saw that the edifice was so riddled with holes, that it was likely to be as hollow and insubstantial as a honeycomb.

I could climb that, James thought. *It's big, sure, but that thing's nothing but handholds. I could climb it in no time.* James shook his head. Why should he even try? For that matter, why should he take another step?

Without shifting his feet, he cast his eyes across the swelling moss-green plane, and then back at the porous monolith. He could sense danger in the air. Peril surrounded him.

"What am I even doing here?" James spoke. Hadn't he seen enough of this world to know that the people could never live here? The air was unbreathable, the temperature far too hot. And if the grass itself was hostile, then how could the Kai'ja and the Scrim possibly expect to make this their home?

"Or maybe I'm jumping to conclusions. Maybe this is just a bad spot. Maybe I could get used to the air, and the heat. Maybe I just needed to adjust myself."

Slowly, tentatively, James allowed himself to return to the reality of the World of Haven. He thought he'd give it one last chance to show itself livable.

James breathed in tentatively; the air no longer was filled with sulfur. The temperature no longer seared his skin. Even the din of screeches sounded no fiercer than a windy day. Was it not all that bad, or was he just getting accustomed because he was a Traveler? Could the Kai'ja and the Scrim survive as well?

He tentatively sniffed the air. The sulfuric burn had dissipated to a low musk, like the air in a sauna. Not pleasant, but not decidedly foul.

"This isn't so bad." James grinned. He opened his mouth and shouted at the top of his lungs, "I said you aren't so *bad*!"

This time, Haven answered. The monolith emitted a low groan, a pained bleat as though the song of a whale was recorded and played back at quarter speed. The wail was both painful and deafening. The sound called out so loudly, and for so long, that when it faded to silence, James couldn't be certain if the cry had ended, or persisted in his ringing ears. The next sound was not a wail at all, but rather a pervasive scratching rasp. As the rustle grew loud, James's eyes grew wide.

From the pores of the monolith, bright-orange, football-sized insects poured out, flowing down the sides and headed at James, their obvious disturber. The creatures were striped like bees and had four limbs that jutted at obtuse angles. Their eyes shone like polished mirrors, each surface reflecting the fear in James's own. They didn't look evil, so much as alien. So completely unworldly that James could barely assess their intent. And he didn't need to. The decision was made.

He had to get out.

In one jerked motion, he dropped to his knees. He clutched his hands together and shut his eyes. James reached into the foreign *Essence* of Haven, and then back to the *Essence* of himself. But something was missing, some stepping-stone kept him from leaping into the Cosmos, some piece missing from the puzzle. And James knew what it was. He had crossed here from the Frozen World. Somehow, he must ignore Haven and the Cosmos and return the way he came. James's mind searched for the Runic World. He seemed to find a tiny trickle of a path. As the bee-creatures swarmed closer, James grabbed the thread with his mind and hurled himself at it. And then—

James fell.

42. The Gateway

James erupted into the Frozen World from the near-improbable location of the runic seer's eye. He was spit like a watermelon seed, flung even as he was contorted and returned to his original shape. James skidded along the surface of the snow. He dragged a path into the tundra and collided into a snowbank.

The cold was immensely painful. James had managed to become accustomed to Haven and now had to readjust. His lungs burned once again, but this time each breath made him cough from the cold. His skin was both shocked and numb. James squinted his eyes and gritted his teeth. He fought the pain until his body adjusted. And in less than a minute, he felt he had returned to normal—though that was a term he no longer believed applied to him.

The Kai'ja queen regarded James with a wary eye. When she finally spoke, no emotion echoed from her voice. "And what did you think of our Haven?"

"A haven?" James shook his head fiercely. "No. Absolutely not. I was there for ten minutes, and I almost got eaten twice, burned a hundred times over, and still can't believe I made it out alive. And that was with me pulling every trick I knew. I doubt your best would last ten seconds."

"And should you be trusted?" The queen regarded him with a sidelong glance, then cast her eyes to the Seer and then back to James again. "You who have spoken so strongly against the gateway?"

"Listen. There are *things* on the other side. And it's hot, too hot. I don't think you could breathe the air even if the living ground and the bee-creatures left you alone. Look, I would explain more, but do we even have time?"

The Kai'ja queen remained unshaken. "But you're still alive."

James met her gaze. "Only because I ran. Ten seconds longer and I'd have never come back. And don't forget," James puffed with false confidence, "changing worlds is what I *do*."

The Kai'ja queen nodded slowly. "It's settled then. We follow the Scrim through the gateway."

"*What?*" James jerked in surprise. "But I just said…"

"Unless you find another solution, another way… Otherwise, Haven remains our only chance. But now we must go." The Kai'ja queen walked with slow even steps to the base of the ziggurat. Even as she took her first step, he could hear the rush of the Kai'ja cresting the hillside. James brushed the snow from his arms and legs and hopped to the temple base, skirting just behind the Kai'ja queen, the Seer, and a steadily growing number of guards.

Slowly, each step measured and elegant, the queen ascended the temple. She was the leader of a procession that flooded the steps of the temple and disappeared beyond the hillside. The volume of people was made more amazing by their silence. James had been in crowds before, the noise of thousands of voices settling to a muted hum. But the procession of Kai'ja was quiet but for the crunch of snow and the whoosh of clothing.

James kept step with the ascending masses, his eyes straining to pick out Sylph, Brine, and Ling from the crowd. Their appearance, so different from either Kai'ja or Scrim, was unmistakable. James's eyes met Sylph's and she gave him a quick nod. Her eyes were cold and calculating, and James knew that his own must shine with terror. He turned again to face the steps.

Higher and higher they climbed, a herd of wraiths processing in unanimity. As James rose, the landscape was laid before him. Frozen, twisted, and hostile. The snow, once lit by the moon, glistened with the growing light of pre-dawn. The hint of sunrise caused James to jerk his eyes skyward. Luciferous, the falling star, was growing brighter as well, though James found it impossible to know how far away the meteor was, much less determine its size. He tried to walk faster, but the tide of pilgrims would move at the pace of the Kai'ja queen, and no more.

When at last they reached the temple's top, the queen continued forward. Yet the guards flanking her on either side came to a halt. The runic guards barked orders, and James knew that not everyone was allowed on the hallowed peak. The guards pointed in turn to individuals in the masses, and one by one, people were let through to join the queen. James felt a surge of fear as the guards extended a finger at him. He ascended the last step to the temple heights.

The top of the ziggurat was square, thirty feet wide on each symmetric side. Carved into the center of the temple, twenty feet in diameter, was a stone dais, perfectly round and set with polished black stone. On the far side of the temple, the Scrim had begun to arrive, their path taking them up the steps on the opposite side. The tattooed warriors stepped forward. They lined along the edge of the dais with Slagish at the exact center. Unlike the Kai'ja, whose thousands spilled down the side of the temple and stretched to the valley below, the Scrim were small enough to cover little more than their half of the temple top. Yet James did not sense that these warriors, no matter what befell them, expected anything less than victory.

He followed the direction of the Kai'ja guards and lined the edge of the dais. He was soon joined by Brine on his left and Sylph on his right, both of their faces etched in concentration. Looking around the circle on the Kai'ja side, he saw a variety of runic guards on the outskirts. The Kai'ja queen was flanked by her seer on one side, and, surprisingly, Ling on the other. On the opposite side of the circle, Slagish stood with his friends and accomplices. Two non-Scrim stood at his immediate left and right. On one side, Bellacroix—another source of puzzlement to James. And on Slagish's right was a man dressed in a sky-blue robe embroidered with silver fleck. James snapped his eyes downward. That must be the prophet, the one who started this whole mess. James didn't dare drawing the man's attention, on the chance he was one of the Styx.

A crescendo of drums lurched James to attention. The steady thrum cut through the silence, and then stopped as suddenly as it had begun. All eyes flitted between the Kai'ja queen and Slagish of the Scrim. Each of the two leaders walked to the center of the dais, with their attendants beside them. The queen, the Seer, Ling, Slagish, Bellacroix, the prophet, and lastly Charles. They stood in opposition, regarding the other warily.

Ling reached into the mess of furs she had been wearing since she and James had spoken on the mountainside. She pulled something from the folds, polished silver, and yet as gnarled and twisted as swampwood. One end was pointed like a spear, and the other, etched and curved like an enormous key. It was a scepter, industrial and organic all at once.

James snapped his head around to Sylph. The question was at his lips, but the stern look he received indicated that this was not the time to ask. Bellacroix pulled something from her robe as well. A broad object wrapped in a cloth of black silk. She held the object outstretched.

The Kai'ja queen extended her right hand and Ling placed the scepter in her palm. Then, the queen nodded to Bellacroix, who reached into the black cloth bag and removed a polished silver object, flat and oval like the head of the mirror. Bellacroix offered the object first to one of Slagish's men, who in turn presented it to the queen. She took the key-like end of the scepter and inserted it in an opening of the mirror piece. They snapped into place with a satisfying click.

The queen held the mirror to the sky, rotated it once, then offered the completed scepter to Slagish. The Scrim lord grasped the scepter, but the queen did not release. She regarded Slagish with suspicion, then relaxed her fingers.

"Excellent." Slagish chuckled, clearly pleased. "Now, how does it work?"

The Kai'ja queen whispered in response. And though her words were as soft as the wind, they resounded across the ziggurat top. "Envision your destination. As long as you hold the scepter, your new runic can see through your eyes, and can open the gateway. The power is within him, of course. The scepter is but the key."

Slagish smiled. "Ah, but such a wonderful key it is. Now, may I be so kind as to borrow your seer?"

The queen nodded. "Show him his Haven."

The Seer dropped to his knees, just as he had done at the temple steps. He placed his hands flat across his lap. The Seer closed his eye tightly, and the other eye—the nonexistent eye—opened. The Seer lifted his face to Slagish who peered within the abyssal socket. For nearly a minute, Slagish stared, his face expressionless, his eyes unblinking. When he looked away, he looked at the scepter with bewilderment, and then his features hardened once again.

Slagish grasped the scepter in his hands; he closed his eyes and furrowed his brow. For a moment there was nothing, and then Charles's body stiffened, convulsed once, and then exploded in light. His skin radiated a glow, at first deep purple, but soon becoming white-hot with energy. The glow was so bright that soon Charles's arms and legs were no longer distinguishable. And for a moment, James felt that he was watching a star being born even as one fell overhead.

The ball of energy that once was Charles, stretched and parted, so that it was no longer a single flare, but shifting into a ring of white-hot fire. The ring steadily widened in diameter, precipitating both Kai'ja and Scrim to back away. Only Slagish, sweat forming on his brow, and the Kai'ja queen, her face as serene as ever, did not budge from their places.

The ring grew wider, and wider still, until it was thirty feet high, and again as far across. Then, with a strange shimmer, the vacant center of the ring simultaneously blurred, and then snapped into focus. The crowd of onlookers, eerily quiet until that moment, released a gasp of amazement at what they saw within. James's eyes narrowed. He had seen such an image before. The gateway showed the way to the World of Haven.

Slagish sank to his knees, the scepter still gripped in his hand, though he allowed his eyes to open. There was disbelief on his face that the gateway had opened. And unlike before, such disbelief was not replaced with the snide arrogance that he wore so well. The Kai'ja queen, too, seemed astonished. Though whether her amazement was that the gateway functioned, or simply that Slagish had opened to Haven and not to somewhere an army lay in wait, James could not be sure.

A soft hand rested on James's shoulder. He turned and was surprised to see, not Ling or Sylph, but the queen's seer. The man looked at James with his one penetrating eye. His lips spread in a thin smile.

"We keep our bargains, shadow. Even with ones such as you."

"Huh?" A chill ran along James's neck.

"You asked if there were others, others not *completely* here. And you were correct. There are two." The Seer extended a long bony finger. James was unsurprised to see that he pointed at the Scrim's prophet.

"But who is the other?"

As if spurred by James's words, lonely Bellacroix, the third of the three Blanks brought from the western isles, sprang into action. In a single motion, she whipped the robe from her back and flung herself at Slagish's bodyguard. With the rapidity of a striking cobra, she plucked the sword from the guard's scabbard and twisted to strike him on the knee. Kicking with one foot against the guard's chest, she bowled him over while executing a backflip, landing directly in front of Slagish. Again, Bellacroix spun, and again the blade of the guard whipped through the air, this time severing Slagish's arm. The Scrim leader cried in surprise as the gateway scepter was plucked from his hand. And as it was taken, the ring of fire that opened to Haven, blurred. The other world disappeared, and the white-hot fire was replaced with a dark-purple flame. James had seen such flame before. It was exactly what had spewed from the hands of the ice-faced woman.

Bellacroix's face, a momentary expression of triumph, turned to horror as she too was flung back with a crack of thunder. James saw that Sylph had acted on instinct. The captain held a smoking gun in each hand, her sights fixed on the fallen target. For the briefest of moments, James wondered if Bellacroix had indeed been one of the Styx, but as her body folded and disappeared into nothingness, so did his doubt. The gateway scepter clattered to the ground, as there were no fingers left to hold it.

And hell broke loose.

While Sylph had been the first to react, she had only beaten Kai'ja and Scrim by tenths of a second. The furious response was no surprise to James. Each side, Scrim and Kai'ja alike, believed they had been betrayed by the other. Weapons were drawn, readied, and striking before the gateway scepter had clattered to a rest.

The Kai'ja with their superior numbers flooded the temple. But the Scrim had all been chosen for their powerful runic abilities. The warriors did not yield so easily. The Scrim's blue-robed prophet, the last remaining Styx, had abandoned all pretense of disguise. He unleashed terrible energies against the Kai'ja. James could tell that the man wasn't as powerful as the ice-faced woman, yet the destruction was incredible. Then James realized that the prophet's actions were not as haphazard as they seemed. The man was moving steadily toward the fallen scepter.

Spurred to action, James lunged for the scepter. But even as he dived, a roar beyond any sound he had ever heard seemed to collide from all angles. The cacophony caused everyone on the temple, Kai'ja, Scrim, Islander, and Styx, to cast their eyes to the heavens. There was one last guest at this party. Luciferous, the falling star, had begun to drop through the atmosphere. The meteor howled as it burned. The roar of its fire drowned all screams and the sounds of battle in its immensity. James knew that impact was nigh.

The distraction of the star gave James the edge he needed. He dove, and the scepter was within his hands. As James touched the mirrored surface, he could feel Charles emanating from somewhere within. The boy lived within the ring of fire. The purple blaze had been replaced by viridescent green as James's fingers gripped it tightly. And at that moment, he realized what he must do—even if it meant a world must die for his decision. If he didn't act now, far more worlds would be lost. James closed his eyes, and with the Frozen World's *Essence* surrounding him, he dropped the flow of time.

The chaos of Armageddon slowed—but it did not stop. Time passed, moving at a quarter speed. James could see axes and bullets flying in slow motion. He could see the ricochet of lightning and the blaze of fireballs. He could also see the leaping body of the Styx agent. The last veneer of "prophet" had been stripped clean. The man's face pulsed with rage, his hands wreathed in deadly purple flame. James winced in anticipation, knowing he had moved too slowly. But the prophet did not hit him. Just as he fell, the man jerked sharply to the side. The man's side turned crimson, the bullets from Sylph's gun striking true. The man, like his comrades before him, collapsed into nothingness.

Without pausing for thought, James clenched the gateway scepter. He opened his mind, linking it with Charles. At James's command, the ring of fire spun, twisting from perpendicular to the ground to hovering above it. As the ring twisted, it exploded outward, its size multiplying by a hundred, a thousand, a million, until the edges were barely a hint of light on the horizon.

James looked skyward. He could feel the heat from Luciferous as it prepared for its sudden and terrible collision. But just before the star hit, the gateway flickered, first blurring, then focusing. The gateway snapped open, but not to Haven. The gateway opened to a nothingness so dark it seemed to suck the daylight from the rising sun, and yet it was a place James had been before. The gateway howled as air rushed through the hole between worlds. And into the darkness that was neither Haven nor the Frozen World—

The Star fell.

As did James.

43. The Fallen

James Winters awoke in pain. His head ached with the force of a train wreck. His skin felt as though it had been seared from tip to tail. The individual joints of his fingers, wrists, elbows, knees, hips, toes, and even his teeth cried with a long wail of anguish. He wasn't sure if he was dead, or if he merely wished he was.

"Here's another one!" a deep voice called. James heard footsteps racing in his direction. He was surprised to see a tall, helmeted man wearing a long black coat with reflective yellow striping on the shoulders. As battered as he was, James recognized the emblem across the helmet instantly. New Hanover County Fire Department. James had come home, but what had happened to his home was something else entirely.

To the firefighter's protests, James sat painfully upright. As he did so, he felt a plastic oxygen mask placed in front of his face, and a blanket cast around his shoulders. He glanced around with his watering eyes. If this was his home, it looked like it had been hit by an atom bomb. *Or,* James thought, *a falling star.*

"What happened?" James managed. And only seconds later, "Are my parents ok? What happened here?"

"Everyone's going to be fine, kid. Not those hoods, though. Whatever hit here, hit them first. They're saying gas leak, but I think those two must have had some dynamite or something. No other reason for this kind of damage. Your parents are fine. Just some scratches like you. The blast must have missed them. They got out in time." The firefighter shook his head. "Quite a mess though. Your folks have insurance?"

James shrugged. His head was too fuzzy to process much. But his parents were ok. And even if his house was gone, perhaps his world, the Frozen World, and maybe all worlds were just a little bit safer.

He leaned forward and clamored to his feet. The firefighter again protested, but he paid him no attention. He needed to see for himself. James wandered to where a collection of ambulances and trucks were assembled in the street. He stumbled through the rubble, only vaguely aware of the fireman's hand steadying him. Then he saw them. Huddled on a row of folding chairs, wrapped in blankets and holding each other, were his parents.

"Mom, Dad?" James called excitedly, his throat crying in protest at his shouts. "You're all right!" He broke from the fireman's steadying grip and rushed to embrace his parents.

His mother's eyes brightened. "James, oh James, thank god you're ok. We were worried you didn't get out. But we weren't sure because… because…"

James's dad finished, hugging him tighter. "We're all a little foggy about what happened. I remember the break-in. And those punks and their guns. But not much after you showed up. I think we all got knocked around pretty good. Do you remember what happened?"

James smiled. "I remember a little. But I… I don't really know what happened in there." He closed his eyes. That much was the truth. He *didn't* know what had happened to the house. But at least the Styx were gone—not just here but in the Frozen World as well. There was no one left who could betray James's secret.

The firefighter called from the rubble. "Looks like we've got another one. This one's not moving. I need a stretcher and oxygen. Go!" The paramedics swarmed where the firefighter picked through the debris. James, like his parents and the onlookers, all migrated with curiosity.

"Look at those burns. He's covered in them." The firefighter glanced behind him. "Get those people back. This kid is torn up, but he's alive. Get them back. Let the paramedics through."

James tried to focus, but the pounding in his head made it difficult. Something was tickling the back of his mind. Something was reawakening within him. Something wasn't quite right.

"I said get those people back." The firefighter nodded as two men in drab blue scrubs shuffled beside him with a stretcher. "Watch him. I don't see any bleeding, but he isn't conscious. Take a look at those burns."

One of the paramedics pulled a flashlight from his chest pocket and shined it into the victim's eyes. "Yeah, he's out all right. Ok, let's get him to the hospital. One, two, three." The paramedics lifted the victim onto the stretcher, immediately covering him with a brown woolen blanket. James's heart skipped a beat when he saw the face within. It wasn't one of the punks that had held them hostage. It wasn't the ice-faced woman or one of her lackeys. And it wasn't one of the neighbor's kids. Despite the soot covering his face, the platinum-blonde hair was telling. And the rune unmistakable.

"Charles!" James cried. He lunged for the stretcher. "Charles, are you ok?"

The paramedic glanced over his shoulder at James, though didn't break his stride to the ambulance. "You know this kid?"

"Yeah, um. He's, uh, he goes to my school." The lie slipped easily from James's lips. He promised himself it would be one of the last. "Is it ok if I ride with him?"

The paramedic looked at James, covered in soot and wrapped in the emergency blanket. "Sorry, kid. Only if you're in the stretcher. Be thankful you're not." He paused, and then glanced at James's parents, and then looked again at him. "Unless that's what you folks want?"

His mother looked at her husband. "No, we can't let James go by himself. Not now."

"But I need to see if he's ok," he pleaded.

James's father looked pained, rested a hand on his wife's shoulder, then nodded. "It's alright, you can go. Someone needs to stay with that boy." His father nodded to the paramedic, then turned back to James. "Son, we have to stay here and talk to the police. We'll be along as soon as we can. You tell the doctors everything, ok?"

James nodded and crawled up in the ambulance. He smiled and waved to his parents as the paramedic shut the back doors, then skipped around the side and hopped in the driver's seat.

"You two ok back there? We're traveling light."

"Fine. Just go," James replied.

The paramedic nodded and the sirens roared to life. They began to accelerate, first slowly, then quicker as they hit the highway. James looked down at Charles. The rune covering the boy's body was half-covered by the soot and debris. Hopefully, the confusion would keep away the questions. He took his hand and lightly patted Charles's face.

"Charles? Charles, you ok?"

The boy, comatose a few seconds earlier, flinched at James's touch. He opened his sky-blue eyes and looked at him groggily. There was both terror and relief in his eyes. "Jay, is that you? Did we stop it? I didn't know what you were doing at first, but I think I got it. Did we stop it? I know you wanted to, but I couldn't make the gateway any bigger, I couldn't quite… and then something happened to you, and I'm not sure what happened. Something pulled me along. It was that silver thing, and… Did we stop it?"

James leaned back against the rumbling ambulance wall. He clutched harder on the handhold. "I think so. I think we got it. I can't be sure." He gritted his teeth. That wasn't true. He needed to be sure. And even if he didn't, Charles didn't belong here. Despite his reasons, James knew he needed to cover his tracks.

"Alright, Charles, I'm going to try something. And I've never done this before, so I'm not sure how it's going to work out. Now I want you to hold tight to my hand and concentrate on me. Whatever happens, don't lose your focus. Can you do that?"

Charles nodded. He grasped James's hand, his grip both determined and feeble all at once. "I'm ready."

James opened his mind to the *Essence*. He felt the rhythm of the world slow. The furious pulse of the siren diminished to a single slow wail. And then—

They fell.

* * *

The Cosmos whooshed by. The lights of the countless worlds raced with relativistic speed. Though James didn't have a body in this ethereal world, he could still feel Charles's hand gripped tightly in his own. They were Traveling, but it wasn't James who guided their path. He and Charles raced, pulled with unmistakable fury through the Cosmos. James couldn't slow down or redirect. But he realized he didn't need to. Their destination was obvious. And so, James relaxed. He allowed the Cosmos to blur until the familiar blue light of the Frozen World appeared in the distance. The incandescent ball grew larger, and then larger still, until the light flooded James's vision. But as the otherworld's reality crashed in, James felt Charles's fingers slip from his grasp.

* * *

James entered the reality of the Frozen World three feet above the ship's deck. When gravity realized it had a new customer, he was dropped hard. He landed with an unceremonious thud onto stained wood. He felt pain shoot through his backside, only to realize his other pains, the ones encompassing his entire body, were now absent.

Shortly after his rude landing, James was engulfed in sweltering heat. And to no surprise, he was dressed in the thick furs of the Kai'ja, yet the climate was not arctic but tropic. He hurried to rid himself of the bulky furs, stripping to the waist in a matter of moments. Only when he was down to the loose canvas shorts did he hear the voice behind him.

"Alright, runic, hands up or you're going overboard."

James turned to see the familiar face. It was Brine, though he too was no longer dressed in furs, wearing instead knee-length leather pants. Brine's face looked remarkably different as well. His cheek now bore a slender scar, which stood out stark white on skin darkly tanned.

"Well, I'll be… Jay! You're back. Dropped out of nowheres once again. And… Cap'n, get up here. We got another one."

"Another…?"

James was cut off by the crashing of footsteps as heads began to emerge from the ship's belowdecks. Sylph came out first, looking as deeply tanned as Brine if not less battle-scarred. But it was the next faces that gave James the most surprise. For the next two people to emerge were Ling—also tanned—and Charles, who appeared to be fighting off an absurd sunburn but otherwise none the worse for wear.

"Jay? Jay, it's you. You, you came back!" The chorus of cries and familiar faces surrounded him.

Captain Sylph, reserved as ever, held up the palm of her hand. Her crewmen's voices fell to silence. "So, you did come back, after all, lad. We all thought you two had been killed at the temple. They never found your bodies, but there were a lot of people not found. Too many runics to ever be sure." Sylph shook her head. "And from what the Kai'ja queen told us, we wondered if you'd maybe just gone back to your own world."

James looked at his feet. He felt the shame of lying to Sylph about who he was all over again. But when he looked up, she was smiling.

"Of course, when Charles here dropped on our deck a few weeks ago, we didn't know what to make of it. He told us he'd seen you, but we thought it was just a dream. We'd given you up for gone."

"Charles, are you ok?"

"Sure thing, mate. Right as rain. The sun's bloody hot down here, but I'm getting used to it."

James nodded dully. "What happened at the temple? Did we stop the star from falling?"

Sylph shrugged. "Well, you stopped it from hitting, lad, but I don't know where you sent it. That's for you to tell. As for afterward, the Kai'ja and Scrim didn't last too much longer. Nothing to fight over, I guess. And without Charles, they barely missed this." Sylph pointed to the top of the ship's mast. A silver object glistened in the tropical sun. James knew it instantly for the gateway scepter.

"Did you try to use it? After Charles came back, of course."

Brine replied. "No, we tossed the headpiece overboard once we hit deep water. We figured it was kind of a gesture or something."

James put his hands on his hips and glanced around him. It had all worked out. His family was safe, his homeworld was safe, and Sylph had replaced her crew. There was only one thing left to check.

He opened himself to the *Essence* of the Frozen World—not quite so frozen in these parts, but he would never think of it differently. The world snapped into crystalline precision. James could see the individual crests of waves, he could hear the long-off calls of birds, and smell the different types of salts riding the winds. But the screams of agony, the desperate pleas for help, were gone. The world seemed whole. And while James felt satisfaction in the job well done, a twinge of pain touched his heart. This world no longer needed him. Just as Charles, a runic boy, did not belong in the back of an ambulance, James knew he didn't belong here. Not anymore.

"What's the matter?" James felt a soft hand on his arm. He released the *Essence* and opened his eyes to see Ling standing in front of him. "Your eyes are watering."

James wiped the tears from where they had spilled onto his cheeks. "It's just, well, I've done what I came to do. At least I think so. And, well, I won't be able to come back."

Brine's booming voice interrupted him. "What are you talking about, boy. We're always here for a visit. And you've always got a mop with your name on it, at least so long as we keep running through Killdevils. What do you think of the 'IV', anyway?"

James glanced around, realizing that this was not the same vessel that had crossed the Alpinsea. "It's a great boat, but, no, you don't understand. I have to go. It's…"

Sylph broke in. "James, you don't need to teach us duty."

He flinched. "You know my name?"

"Everyone knows your name. Well, they all know what you did, anyway. And it's turning into a hell of a tale. But you do what you have to do. And if you do come our way again… Well, Brine is right, you've got a place on my crew."

James smiled. He wanted to stay and enjoy the sun, the waves, and the company of his otherworld friends. But he had to get home. There was going to be a very confused paramedic back there, and so James may have one story left to tell.

"Be good, ya'll. And stay out of trouble." He gave one last smile. He closed his eyes tight and took a deep breath of the salty air. The last thing he felt before he left the Frozen World forever, was the soft touch of Ling kissing his cheek. And then—

James fell.

44. CODA

The branches of the dogwood tree tapped rhythmically on the windowpane. The sun shone brightly outside, and James wished he was outside enjoying the autumn day instead of sunk into a dank leather couch, the oily texture cool and slick against his skin. He watched the pendulum of the ubiquitous grandfather clock that seemed present in all psychiatrists' offices. He wondered what the next doctor would bring.

James didn't blame his parents for continuing his therapy. Even though he hadn't had a fall in several weeks, and his behavior had been normal since the house exploded. The arson forensics had given up trying to figure out what went wrong, and the insurance company didn't have any reason to contest a claim that took two criminals in the blaze. Nevertheless, such events should be traumatic for a boy James's age. Thus the psychiatrist. And so James was back in a chair not unlike that in Dr. Huckabee's office.

A man pushed his way into the room. He greeted James even as he sat. "James Winters, I presume. My name is... ah, well. You don't care to know my name, anyway. Probably helps if I don't have one."

James looked up to see the stereotypical professor, complete with a shaped grey beard, spectacles perched on the end of his nose, and the tweed suit that someone must have decided was comforting.

"Now, James, you know why you're here, don't you?"

"Post-traumatic stress syndrome?" he ventured. He'd done his research.

"Well, yes. I guess that dropping a falling star uninvited into a world could be stressful. But regardless, it's highly unordinary, and altogether impolite. Just because a world is dying, doesn't mean you get to use it to take out your trash."

James leaped forward in his chair. "Dr. Huckabee? Is that you?"

The man nodded, then shook his head. "Only after a fashion. The doctor you once knew met his fate. But there will always be others, more of us to take on his cause. I only came to clean up a little, remove a few last traces. Once I'm gone, you don't ever have to worry about one of us visiting you here again. But you can't keep souvenirs. That's a strict Rule. Not one of the big ones, but a rule nonetheless. Now hand it over." The doctor held out his hand, palm up, and fixed a stern look on James.

At first, James was puzzled, until he finally understood. He reached into his pocket and pulled out the thing that was only there because he knew that it would be. He took one last sentimental look, and then dropped the peculiar coin into the man's hand.

"All's well, I suppose," the doctor hummed. "And now to your business."

"My business?"

"Your work has just begun, my friend. And you'll get better with time. But there's been a change—in management, so to speak."

James raised an eyebrow. "What kind of change?"

"Well, my brother, the old way was just a little too dangerous. Good for secrecy, to be sure, but not always the safest. So, we're taking a page from the book of our enemies. And hopefully, be stronger for it."

James rolled his eyes. If this was Huckabee's successor, then the man had taken his lessons in obscurity to heart. "Listen, sir. And please, just come right out and say it. I've had enough dancing around and half-truths to last all year. What are you talking about?"

"Oh, the change in rules of course. We're no longer Traveling solo, anymore. Three Styx versus one of us is just not sporting. You'll be given a partner. You two will work together, and I hope you'll be the better off for it."

Finally! James's mind rushed with elation. A partner. Someone who could cut through the half-truths and lies. Someone he could talk to.

"You can come in now."

The door behind James creaked and he twisted in his chair to look. James's mouth parted in disbelief when he saw who walked through the door. Wearing a pair of faded blue jeans, and a beige turtleneck, her long dark hair pulled back into a braid, was Ling. She stepped past his chair to stand by Huckabee's replacement.

James's mouth had not yet closed. "So *that's* it? *That's* why you could see me when no one else could? You weren't a VIP at all. You're a Traveler! But why didn't you tell me?"

"Because," Ling replied, her voice as calm and serene as ever, "I didn't know yet. I only just learned." She looked down at the floor. "But don't be angry, I am here to learn."

The psychiatrist clapped his hands together. "Excellent! Then you two can get started. But remember… don't ever let down your guard. Remember the Rules and keep up the fight. So, are you ready?"

James stood from his chair and walked beside Ling. He placed a steady hand on her shoulder. "I'm ready, are you?"

She nodded.

James smiled at Ling, and even as he did so, the doctor winked from existence into a realm that he knew well. James also knew that as much as he'd wanted to take a break from Traveling, he had a job to do. They both did. But they'd need to go somewhere if they were going to talk. And what better place than under a floating oak on a purple sea?

James closed his eyes, concentrated. And then—

Acknowledgements

Books aren't grown in isolation. They may spend a long, long time in the dark, but to fully emerge in the light of day takes a lot of support. I'd like to thank Sarah for her insight and encouragement from the earliest drafts until today. Thanks to members of both "Write or Die" and "Third Thursdays" writers' groups who provided feedback throughout different stages, and to Celestian and Cherie who helped with the finishing touches. Lastly, thanks to Amanda for her sage advice into the world of publishing which helped put me on the path.

Also by Phil Coleman

For middle grade readers:
The Quickwild Odyssey: Magic in Antarctica
The Quickborn Odyssey

For young adult and adult readers:
When James Fell
Riddled Worlds
Lockspell

About the Author

After college, Phil left North Carolina for the west and then never managed to go home again. When not living and breathing books, he likes to hike, mountain bike, ski, and appreciate being where the air is thin, and the cows outnumber the people.

His books and stories are all about taking an idea and then pushing it far beyond the bounds of our own reality. After all, we have more than enough real life in our real life.

Phil currently lives in the mountains of Colorado with his wife and two daughters.

Web: https://www.philcolemanbooks.com
Facebook: https://www.facebook.com/philcolemanbooks/
Instagram: https://www.instagram.com/philgoodbooks/
TikTok: https://www.tiktok.com/@philgoodbooks

www.ingramcontent.com/pod-product-compliance
Lightning Source LLC
Chambersburg PA
CBHW070849160726
48004CB00003B/992